The Captain of the Janizaries

A story of the times of Scanderberg and the fall of Constantinople

James M. Ludlow

Alpha Editions

This edition published in 2021

ISBN : 9789354754579

Design and Setting By
Alpha Editions
www.alphaedis.com
Email – info@alphaedis.com

As per information held with us this book is in Public Domain. This book is a reproduction of an important historical work. Alpha Editions uses the best technology to reproduce historical work in the same manner it was first published to preserve its original nature. Any marks or number seen are left intentionally to preserve its true form.

PREFACE

The story of the Captain of the Janizaries originated, not in the author's desire to write a book, but in the fascinating interest of the times and characters he has attempted to depict. It seems strange that the world should have so generally forgotten George Castriot, or Scanderbeg, as the Turks named him, whose career was as romantic as it was significant in the history of the Eastern Mediterranean. Gibbon assigns to him but a few brief pages, just enough to make us wonder that he did not write more of the man who, he confessed, "with unequal arms resisted twenty-three years the powers of the Ottoman Empire." Creasy, in his history of the Turks, devotes less than a page to the exploits of one who "possessed strength and activity such as rarely fall to the lot of man," "humbled the pride of Amurath and baffled the skill and power of his successor Mahomet." History, as we make it in events, is an ever-widening river, but, as remembered, it is like a stream bursting eastward from the Lebanons, growing less as it flows until it is drained away in the desert.

Though our story is in the form of romance, it is more than "founded upon fact." The details are drawn from historical records, such as the chronicles of the vi monk Barletius—a contemporary, though perhaps a prejudiced admirer, of Scanderbeg—the later Byzantine annals, the customs of the Albanian people, and scenes observed while travelling in the East.

The author takes the occasion of the publication of a new edition to gratefully acknowledge many letters from scholars, as well as notices from the press, which have expressed appreciation of this attempt to revive popular interest in lands and peoples that are to reappear in the drama of the Ottoman expulsion from Europe, upon which the curtain is now rising.

CHAPTER I

From the centre of the old town of Brousa, in Asia Minor—old even at the time of our story, about the middle of the fifteenth century—rises an immense plateau of rock, crowned with the fortress whose battlements and towers cut their clear outlines high against the sky. An officer of noble rank in the Ottoman service stood leaning upon the parapet, apparently regaling himself with the marvellous panorama of natural beauty and historic interest which lay before him. The vast plain, undulating down to the distant sea of Marmora, was mottled with fields of grain, gardens enclosed in hedges of cactus, orchards in which the light green of the fig-trees blended with the duskier hues of the olive, and dense forests of oak plumed with the light yellow blooms of the chestnut. Here and there writhed the heavy vapors of the hot sulphurous streams springing out of the base of the Phrygian Olympus, which reared its snow-clad peak seven thousand feet above. The lower stones of the fortress of Brousa were the mementoes of twenty centuries which had drifted by them since they were laid by the old Phrygian kings. The flags of many empires had floated from those walls, not the least significant of which was that of the Ottoman, who, a hundred years before, had consecrated Brousa as his capital by burying in yonder mausoleum the body of Othman, the founder of the Ottoman dynasty of the Sultans.

But the Turkish officer was thinking of neither the beauty of the scene nor the historic impressiveness of the place. His face, shaded by the folds of his enormous turban, wore deeper shadows which were flung upon it from within. He was talking to himself.

"The Padishah[1] has a nobler capital now than this,—across the sea there in Christian Europe. But by whose hands was it conquered? By Christian hands! by Janizaries! renegades! Ay, this hand!"—he stripped his arm bare to the shoulder and looked upon its gnarled muscles as he hissed the words through his teeth—"this hand has cut a wider swathe through the enemies of the Ottoman than any other man's; a swathe down which the Padishah can walk without tripping his feet. And this was a Christian's hand once! Well may I believe the story my old nurse so often told me,— that, when the priest was dropping the water of baptism upon my baby brow, this hand seized the sacred vessel, and it fell shattered upon the pavement. Ah, well have I fulfilled that omen!"

The man walked to and fro on the platform with quick and jarring step, as if to shake off the grip of unwelcome thoughts. There was a majesty in his mien which did not need the play of his partially suppressed fury to fascinate the attention of any who might have beheld him at the moment. He was tall of stature, immensely broad at the shoulders, deep lunged, comparatively light and trim in the loins, as the close drawn sash beneath the embroidered jacket revealed: arms long; hands large. He looked as if he might wrestle with a bear without a weapon. His features were not less notable than his form. His forehead was high and square, with such fulness at the corners as to leave two cross valleys in the middle. Deep-set eyes gleamed from beneath broad and heavy brows. The lips were firm, as if they had grown rigid from the habit of concealing, rather than expressing, thought, except in the briefest words of authority,—Cæsar-lips to summarize a campaign in a sentence. The chin was heavy, and would have unduly protruded were it not that there were needed bulk and strength to stand as the base of such prominent upper features. Altogether his face would have been pronounced hard and forbidding, had it not been relieved as remarkably by that strange radiance with which strong intelligence and greatness of soul sometimes transfigure the coarsest features.

These peculiarities of the man were observed and commented upon by two officers who were sitting in the embrasure of the parapet at the farther end of the battlement. The elder of the two, who had grown gray in the service, addressed his comrade, a young man, though wearing the insignia of rank equal to that of the other.

"Yes, Bashaw,[2] he is not only the right hand of the Padishah, but the army has not seen an abler soldier since the Ottoman entered Europe. You know his history?"

"Only as every one knows it, for in recent years he has written it with his cimeter flashing through battle dust as the lightning through clouds," replied the young officer.

The veteran warmed with enthusiasm as he narrated, "I well remember him as a lad when he was brought from the Arnaout's[3] country. He was not over nine years of age when Sultan Mahomet conquered the lands of Epirus, where our general's father, John Castriot, was duke. As a hostage young George Castriot was brought with his three brothers to Adrianople."

"Are his brothers of the same metal?" asked the listener.

"Allah only knows what they would have been had not state necessity——" The narrator completed the sentence by a significant gesture, imitating the swirl of the executioner's sword as he takes off the head of an offender.

"But George Castriot was a favorite of the Sultan, who fondled him as the Roman Hadrian did his beautiful page, Antinous. And well he might, for a lad more lithe of limb and of wit never walked the ground since Allah bade the angels worship the goodly form of Adam.[4] Once when a prize was offered for the best display of armor, and the provinces were represented by their different champions in novel helmets and corselets and shields, none of which pleased the imperial taste, it was the whim of the Padishah to have young Castriot parade before the judges panoplied only in his naked muscle, and to order that the prize should be given to him, together with the title Iscanderbeg.[5] And well he won it. In the after wrestling matches he put upon his hip the best of them, Turcomans from Asia, and Moors from Africa, and Giaours[6] from the West. And he was as skilful on a horse's legs as he was on his own. His namesake, Alexander, could not have managed Bucephalus better than he. I well remember his game with the two Scythians. They came from far to have a joust with the best of the Padishah's court. They were to fight singly: if one were overthrown, the other, after the victor had breathed himself, was to redeem the honor of his comrade. Scanderbeg sent his spear-head into the throat of his antagonist at the first encounter, when the second barbarian villain treacherously set upon him from the rear. The young champion wheeled his horse as quickly as a Dervish twists his body, and with one blow of his sword, clove him in twain from skull to saddle."

"Bravo!" cried the listener, "I believe it, for look at the arm that he has uncovered now."

"It is a custom he has," continued the narrator. "He always fights with his sword-arm bared to the shoulder. When he was scarce nineteen years old he was at the siege of Constantinople, in 800 of the Hegira,[7] with Sultan Amurath. His skill there won him a Sanjak.[8] Since that time you know his career."

"Ay! his squadrons have shaken the world."

"He has changed of late, however; grown heavy at the brows. But he comes this way."

As the general approached, the two bashaws bowed low to the ground, and then stood in the attitude of profound obeisance until he addressed them. His face gleamed with frank and genial familiarity as he exchanged with them a few words; but it was again masked in sombre thoughtfulness as he passed on.

Near the gate by which the fortress was entered from the lower town was gathered a group of soldiers who were bantering a strange looking creature with hands tied behind him—evidently some captive.

"What have you here?" said Scanderbeg, approaching them.

"That we cannot tell. It is a secret," replied the subaltern officer in charge of the squad, making a low salâm, and with a twinkle in his eyes which took from his reply all semblance of disrespect.

"But I must have your secret," said the general good-naturedly.

"It is not our secret, Sire," replied the man, "but his. He will not tell us who he is."

"Where does he belong? What tongue has he, Aladdin? You who were once interpreter to the Bey of Anatolia should know any man by his tongue."

"He has no tongue, Sire. He is dumb as a toad. His beard has gone untrimmed so long that it has sewed fast his jaws. He has not performed his ablutions since the last shower washed him, and his ears are so filled with dirt plugs that he could not hear a thunder clap."

The face of the captive seemed to strangely interest the general, who said as he turned away, "Send him to our quarters. The Padishah has taken a fancy to deaf mutes of late. They overhear no secrets and tell no tales. We will scrape him deep enough to find if he has a soul. If he knows his foot from his buttocks he will be as valued a present to His Majesty as a fifth wife.[9] Send him to our quarters."

The general soon returned to the fortress. A room dimly lighted through two narrow windows that opened into a small inner court, and contained a divan or couch, a table, and a motley collection of arms, was the residence of the commandant. A soldier stood by the entrance guarding the unfortunate captive.

"You may leave him with me," said Scanderbeg approaching.

The man was thrust into the apartment, and stood with head bowed until the guard withdrew. The general turned quickly upon him as soon as they were alone.

"If I mistake not, man, though your tongue be tied, your eye spake to me by the gate."

"It was heaven's blessing upon my errand reflected there," replied the man in the Albanian language. "I bear thee a message from Moses Goleme, of Lower Dibria, and from all the provinces of Albania, from every valley and every heart."

"Let me hear it, for I love the very flints on the mountains and every pebble on the shore of old Albania," replied Scanderbeg eagerly.

"Heaven be praised! Were my ears dull as the stones they would open to hear such words," said the man with suppressed emotion. "For since the death of thy noble father—"

"My father's death! I had not heard it. When?" exclaimed the general.

"It is four moons since we buried him beneath the holy stones of the church at Croia, and the Sultan sent us General Sebaly to govern in his stead."

"Do you speak true?" cried Scanderbeg, laying his hand upon the man's shoulder and glaring into his face. "My father dead? and a stranger appointed in his stead? and Sultan Amurath has not even told me! Beware, man, lest you mistake."

"I cannot mistake, Sire, for these hands closed the eyes of John Castriot after he had breathed a prayer for his land and for his son—one prayer for both. Moses Goleme was with us, for you know he was thy father's dearest friend and wisest counsellor, and to him thy father gave charge that word should be sent thee that to thee he bequeathed his lands."

"Stop! Stop!" said Scanderbeg, pacing the little room like a caged lion. "Let me think. But go on. He did not curse me, then? Swear to me,"—and he turned facing the man—"swear to me that my father did not curse me with his dying breath! Swear it!"

"I swear it," said the man, "and that all Albania prays to-day for George Castriot. These are the tidings which the noble Moses bade me bring thee, though I found thee at the Indus or under the throne of the Sultan himself. I have no other message. That I might tell thee this in the free speech of Albania I have kept dumb to all others. If it be treason to the Sultan for thee to hear it, let my head pay the penalty. But know, Sire, that our land will rest under no other rule than that of a Castriot."

"A Castriot!" soliloquized the general. "Well, it is a better name than Scanderbeg. Ho, guard! Take this fellow! Let him share your mess!"

When alone the general threw himself upon the divan for a moment, then paced again the apartment, and muttered to himself——

"And for what has a Castriot given himself to the Turk! Yet I did not betray my land and myself. They stole me. They seduced my judgment as a child. They flattered my conceit as a man. Like a leopard I have fought in the Padishah's arena, and for a leopard's pay—the meat that makes him strong, and the gilded cage that sets off his spots. I have led his armies, for what? For glory. But whose glory? The Padishah cries in every emergency, 'Where is *my* Scanderbeg? Scanderbeg to the rescue!' But it means, 'Slave, do my bidding!' And I, the tinselled slave, bow my head to the neck of my steed, and the empire rings with the tramp of my squadrons, and the praise of Scanderbeg's loyalty! Pshaw! He calls me his lightning, but he is honored as the invisible Jove who hurls it. And I am a Castriot! A Christian! Ay, a Christian dog,[10] indeed, to fawn and lick the hands of one who would despise me were he not afraid of my teeth. He takes my father's lands and gives them to another; and I—I am of too little account to be even told 'Thy father is dead.'"

Scanderbeg paused in the light that streamed through the western window. It was near sunset, and a ruddy gleam shot across the room.

"This light comes from the direction of Albania, and so there comes a red gleam—blood red—from Albania into my soul."

He drew the sleeve of the left arm and gazed at a small round spot tattooed just above the elbow—the indelible mark of the Janizary.

"They that put it there said that by it I should remember my vow to the Padishah. And, since I cannot get thee out, my little talisman, I swear by thee that I shall never forget my vow; no, nor them that made my child-lips take it, and taught me to abjure my father's name, my country's faith, and broke my will to the bit and rein of their caprice. It may be that some day I shall wash thee out in damned Moslem blood. But hold! that would be treason. Scanderbeg a traitor? How they will hiss it from Brousa to Adrianople; from the lips of Vizier and pot-carrier! But is it treason to betray treason? But patience! Bide thy time, Castriot!"

A slight commotion in the court drew the attention of Scanderbeg. In a moment the sentry announced:

"A courier from His Majesty!"

The message told that the Ottoman forces had been defeated in Europe—the noted bashaw, Schehadeddin, having been utterly routed by Hunyades. The missive called the Sultan's "always liege and invincible servant, Scanderbeg, to the rescue!" Within an hour a splendid suite of officers, mounted on swift and gaily caparisoned steeds, gathered about the great general, and at the raising of the horse-tail upon the spear-head, dashed along the road to the coast of Marmora where vessels were in waiting to convey them across to the European side. Scanderbeg had but a moment's interview with the dumb captive, sufficient to whisper,

"Return our salutation to the noble Moses Goleme; and say that George Castriot will honor his confidence better in deeds than he could in words. I know not the future, my brave fellow, and might not tell it if I did, even to ears as deaf as yours. But say to Goleme that Castriot swears by his beard—

by the beard of Moses—that brighter days shall come for Albania even if they must be flashed from our swords. Farewell!"

The man fell at the general's feet and embraced them. Then rising he raised his hand, "By the beard of Moses! Let that be the watchword between our people and our rightful prince. Brave men scattered from Adria to Hæmus will listen for that watchword. Farewell, Sire. By the beard of Moses!"

Scanderbeg summoned a soldier and said sternly, "Take this fellow away. He is daft as well as dumb and deaf. Yet treat him well. Such creatures are the special care of Allah. Take him to the Bosphorus that he may cross over to his kin, the Greeks, at Constantinople."

CHAPTER II

A little hamlet lay, like an eagle's nest, high on the southern slope of the Balkan mountains. The half dozen huts of which it consisted were made of rough stones, daubed within and without thick with clay. The roofs were of logs, overlaid with mats of brushwood woven together by flexible withes, and plastered heavily. The inhabitants were goatherds. Their lives were simple. If they were denied indulgence in luxuries, they were also removed from that contact with them which excites desire, and so were contented. They seldom saw the faces of any from the great world, upon so large a portion of which they looked down. Their absorbing occupation was in summer to watch the flocks which strolled far away among the cliffs, and in winter to keep them close to the hamlet, for then terrific storms swept the mountains and filled the ravines with impassable snow.

Milosch and his good wife, Helena—Maika Helena, good Mother Helena, all the hamlet called her—were blessed with two boys. Their faces were as bright as the sky in which, from their lofty lodgings, they might be said to have made their morning ablutions for the eleven and twelve years of their respective lives. Yet they were not children of the cherubic type; rather tough little knots of humanity, with big bullet-heads thatched over with heavy growths of hair, which would have been red, had it not been bleached to a light yellow by sunshine and cloud-mists. Instead of the toys and indolent pastimes of the nursery they had only the steep rocks, the thick copse, the gnarled trees, and the wild game of the mountains for their play-things. They thus developed compactly knit muscles, depth of lung and thickness of frame, which gave agility and endurance. At the same time, the associations of their daily lives, the precipitous cliff, the trembling edge of the avalanche, the caves of strange beasts, the wild roaring of the winds, the awful grandeur of the storms, the impressive solitude which filled the intervals of their play like untranslatable but mighty whispers from the unknown world taking the place of the prattle of this,—these fostered intrepidity, self-reliance, and balance of disposition, if not of character. For religious discipline they had the occasional ministrations of a Greek priest or missionary monk from the Rilo Monastir, many leagues to the west of them. They knew the Creed of Nicæa, the names of some of the saints; but of truly divine things they had only such impressions as they caught from the great vault of the universal temple above them, and from the suggestions of living nature at their feet.

By the side of Milosch's house ran—or rather climbed and tumbled, so steep was it—that road over the Balkans, through the Pass of Slatiza, by which Alexander the Great, nearly two thousand years before, had burst upon the Moesians. Again, within their father's memory, Bajazet, the "Turkish Lightning" as he was called because of the celerity of his movements, had flashed his arms through this Pass, and sent the bolts of death down upon Wallachia, and poured terror even to the distant gates of Vienna. Often had Milosch rehearsed the story of the terrible days when he himself had been a soldier in the army of the Wallachian Prince Myrtche; and showed the scar of the cut he had received from the cimeter of a Turkish Janizary, whom he slew not far from the site of their home.

Their neighbor, Kabilovitsch, a man well weighted with years, not only listened to these tales, but added marvellous ones of his own; sometimes relating to the wars of King Sigismund of Hungary, who, after Prince Myrtche, had tried to regain this country from the cruel rule of the Moslems; more frequently, however, his stories were of exploits of anonymous heroes. These were told with so much enthusiasm as to create the belief that the narrator had himself been the actor in most of them. For Kabilovitsch was a strange character in the little settlement; though not the less confided in because of the mystery of his previous life. He had come to this out-of-the-way place, as he said, to escape with his little daughter the incessant raids and counter-raids of Turks and Christians, which kept the adjacent country in alarm.

Good Uncle Kabilovitsch—as all the children of the hamlet called him—named his daughter, a lass of ten summers, Morsinia, after the famous peasant beauty, Elizabeth Morsiney, who had so fascinated King Sigismund.

Morsinia often braided her hair, and sat beneath her canopy of blossoming laurel, while Constantine, the younger of Milosch's boys, dismounted from the back of his trained goat at the mimic threshold, and wooed her on bended knee, as the good king wooed the beautiful peasant. Michael, the elder boy, was not less ardent, though less poetic, in the display of his passion for Morsinia. A necklace of bear's claws cut with his own hand from a monster beast his father had killed; a crown made of porcupine quills which he had picked up among the rocks; anklets of striped snake skin—these were the pledges of his love, which he declared he would one day redeem with those made of gems and gold—that is, when he should have become a princely warrior.

To Constantine, however, the little maiden was most gracious. It was a custom in the Balkan villages for the young people, on the Monday after Easter, to twist together bunches of evergreens, and for each young swain to kiss through the loops the maid he loved the best. With adults this was regarded as a probationary agreement to marry. If the affection were mutually as full flamed the following Easter, the kiss through the loop was the formal betrothal. Constantine's impatience wreathed the evergreens almost daily, and, as every kiss stood for a year, there was awaiting them—if the good fairies would only make it true—some centuries of nuptial bliss.

The little lover had built for himself a booth against the steep rocks. Into this Morsinia would enter with bread and water, and placing them upon the stone which answered for a table, say, in imitation of older maidens assuming the care of husbands, "So will I always and faithfully provide for thee." Then she would touch the sides of the miniature house with a twig, which she called her distaff, saying, "I will weave for thee, my lord, goodly garments and gay." She would also sit down and undress and redress her doll, which Constantine had carved from wood, and which they said would do for the real baby that the bride was expected to array, in the ceremony by which she acknowledged the obligations of wifehood.[11]

But Michael was not at all disconsolate at this preference shown his brother; for he knew that Morsinia would prefer him to all the world when she heard what a great soldier he had become. Indeed, on some days Michael was lord of the little booth; and more than once the fair enchantress put the evergreen loop around both the boys in as sincere indecision as has sometimes vexed older hearts than hers.

CHAPTER III

In the winter of 1443—a few months subsequent to the events with which our story begins—the Pass of Slatiza echoed other sounds than the cry of the eagle, the bleating of the flocks, and the songs and halloos of the mountaineers. Distant bugle calls floated between the cliffs. At night a fire would flash from a peak, and be suddenly extinguished, as another gleamed from a peak beyond. Strange men had gone up and down the road. With one of these Uncle Kabilovitsch had wandered off, and been absent several days. Great was the excitement of the little folks when Milosch told them that a real army was not far off, coming from the Christian country to the north of them, and that its general was no other than the great Hunyades, the White Knight of Wallachia—called so because he wore white armor—the son of that same King Sigismund and the fair Elizabeth Morsiney. How little Morsinia's cheeks paled, while those of the boys burned, and their eyes flashed, as their father told them, by the fire-light in the centre of their cabin, that the White Knight had already conquered the Turks at Hermanstadt and at Vasag and on the banks of the Morava, and was—if the story which Milosch had heard from some scouts were true—preparing to burst through the Balkan mountains, and descend upon the homes of the Turk on the southern plains. Little did they sleep at night, in the excitement of the belief that, at any day, they might see the soldiers—real soldiers, just like those of Alexander, and those of Bajazet—tramping through the Pass. The tremor of the earth, occasioned by some distant landslide, in their excited imagination was thought to be due to the tramp of a myriad feet. The hoot of the owl became the trumpet call for the onset: and the sharp whistle of the wind, between leafless trees and along the ice-covered rocks, seemed like the whizzing flight of the souls of the slain.

Once, just as the gray dawn appeared, Kabilovitsch, who had been absent for several days, came hurriedly with the alarming news that the Turks, steadily retiring before the Christians, would soon occupy the Pass. They were already coming up the defiles, as the mists rise along the sides of the mountains, in dense masses, hoping to gain such vantage ground that they could hurl the troops of Hunyades down the almost perpendicular slopes before they could effect a secure lodgment on the summit. The children and women must leave herds and homes, and fly instantly. The only safe retreat was the great cave, which the mountaineers knew of, lying off towards the other Pass, that of Soulourderbend.

The fugitives were scarcely gone when the mountain swarmed with Moslems. The mighty mass of humanity crowded the cliffs like bees preparing to swarm. They fringed the breastworks of native rock with abattis made of huge trunks of trees. During the day the Turks had diverted a mountain stream, so that, leaving its bed, it poured a thin sheet of water over the steepest part of the road the Christians were to ascend. This, freezing during the night, made a wall of ice. The Christians were thus forced to leave the highway and attempt to scale the crags far and near; a movement which the Turks met by spreading themselves everywhere above them. Upon ledges and into crevices which had never before felt the pressure of human feet clambered the contestants. Every rock was empurpled with gore. Turkish turban and Hungarian helmet were caught upon the same thorny bush; while the heads which had worn them rolled together in the same gully, and stared their deathless hatred from their dead eyes.

The Turks in falling back discovered the mouth of the cave in which the peasants had taken refuge. As the Moslem bugles sounded the retreat, lest they should be cut off by the Christians who had scaled the heights on their flanks, they seized the women and children, who soon were lost to each other's sight in the skurry of the retiring host. The hands of Constantine were tied about the neck, and his legs about the loins, of a huge Moslem, to whose keeping he had been committed. An arrow pierced the soldier to the heart.

It seemed as if more than keenness of eye—some inspiration of his fatherly instinct—led Kabilovitsch on through the vast confusion, far down the slope, outrunning the fugitives and their pursuers, avoiding contact with any one by leaping from rock to rock and darting like a serpent through secret by-paths, until he reached the horsemen of the Turks, who had not been able to follow the foot-soldiers up the steep ascent. He knew that his little girl would be given in charge to some one of these. He, therefore, concealed himself in the growing darkness behind a clump of evergreen trees, close to which one must pass in order to reach the horses. A moment later, with the stealth and the strength of a panther, he leaped upon a Turk. The man let go the tiny form of the girl he was carrying; but, before he could assume an attitude of defence, the iron grip of Kabilovitsch was upon his throat, and the steel of the infuriated old man in his heart. Under the sheltering darkness, carrying his rescued child, Kabilovitsch threaded his way along ledges and balconies of rock projecting so slightly from the precipitous mountain that they would have been discerned, even in daylight, by no eye less expert than his own. At one place his way was blocked by a dead body which had fallen from the ledge above, and been caught by the tangled limbs of `the mountain laurel. Without relinquishing his load, he pushed with his foot the lifeless mass down through the entanglement, and listened to the snapping of the bushes and the crashing of loosened stones, until the heavy thud announced that it had found a resting place.

"So God rest his soul, be he Christian or Paynim!" muttered the old man. "And now, my child, are you frighted?"

"No, father, not when you are with me," said Morsinia.

"Could you stand close to the rock, and hold very tight to the bush, if I leave you a moment?"

"Yes, father, I will hold to the bush as tight as it holds to the rock."

Kabilovitsch grasped a root of laurel, and, testing it with main strength, swung clear of the ledge, until his foot rested upon another ledge nearly the length of his body below. Bracing himself so that he spanned the interval with the strength of a granite pillar, he bade the child crawl cautiously in the direction of his voice. As she touched his hands, he lifted her with perfect poise, and placed her feet beside his own on a broad table rock.

"Now, blessed be Jesu, we are safe! Did I not tell you I would some day take you to a cavern which no one but Milosch and I had ever seen? Here it is. Unless Sultan Amurath hires the eagles to be his spies—as they say he does—no eye but God's will see us here even when the sun rises. You did not know, my little princess, what a coward your old father had become, to run away from a battle. Did you, my darling?" said he kissing her. "Never did I dream that Ar———, that Kabilovitsch would fly like a frightened partridge through the bushes. But my girl's heart has taken the place of my own to-night."

As he spoke he slipped from his shoulders the rough cape, or armless jacket, of bear-skin, and wrapped the girl closely in it. He then carried her beneath the roof of a little cave, where he enfolded her in his arms, making his own back a barrier against the cutting night wind and the whirling snow. The cold was intense. Thinking only of the danger to the already half-benumbed and wearied body of the child, he took off his conical cap, and unwound the many folds of coarse woollen cloth of which it was made, and with it wrapped her limbs and feet.

Thus the night was passed. With the first streak of the dawn Kabilovitsch crept cautiously from the ledge, and soon returned with the news that the Turks had vanished, swept away by the tide of Christian soldiers which was still pouring over and down the mountain in pursuit.

Horrible was the scene which everywhere greeted them as they clambered back toward the road. The dead were piled upon the dying in every ravine. Red streaks seamed the white snow—channels in which the current of many a life had drained away. The road was choked with the hurrying victors. But the old man's familiarity with the ground found paths which the nimble feet of the maid could climb; so that the day was not far advanced when they stood on the site of their home. Scarcely a trace of the little hamlet remained. Whatever could be burned had fed the camp-fires of the preceding night. The houses had been thrown down by the soldiers in rifling the grain bins which were built between their outer and inner walls.

The old man sat down upon the door-stone of what had been his home. His head dropped upon his bosom. Morsinia stood by his side, her arm about his neck, and her cheek pressed close to his, so that her bright golden hair mingled with his gray beard—as in certain mediæval pictures the artist expresses a pleasing fancy in hammered work of silver and gold. They scarcely noticed that a group of horsemen, more gaily uniformed than the ordinary soldiers, had halted and were looking at them.

"By the eleven thousand virgins of Coln! I never saw a more unique picture than that," said one who wore a skull cap of scarlet, while an attendant carried his heavy helmet. "If Masaccio were with us I would have him paint that scene for our new cathedral at Milano, as an allegory of the captivity in Babylon."

"Rather of the captivity in Avignon. It would be a capital representation of the Holy Father and his daughter the Church," replied a companion laughing. "Only I would have the painter insert the portrait of your eminence, Cardinal Julian, as delivering them both."

"That would not be altogether unhistoric; for the deliverance was not wholly wrought until our time," replied the cardinal, evidently gratified with the flattering addition which his comrade, King Vladislaus, had made to his pleasing conceit. "But if to-day's victory be as thorough as it now looks, and we drive the Turks out of Europe, it would serve as a picture of the captivity in which the haughty, half-infidel emperor of the Greeks and his daughter, Byzantium, will soon be to Rome."

"But, by my crown," said Vladislaus, "and with due reverence for the great cardinal under whose cap is all the brain that Rome can now boast of—I think the Greeks will find as much spiritual desolation in Mother Church as these worthy people have about them here."

"I can pardon that speech to the newly baptized king of half-barbarian Hungary, when I would not shrive another for it," replied Julian petulantly. "The son of a pagan may be allowed much ignorance regarding the mystery of the Holy See. But a truce to our badgering! Let us speak to this old fellow. Good man, is this your house? By Saint Catherine! the girl is beautiful, your highness."

"It was my home, Sire, yesterday, but now it is his that wants it," replied Kabilovitsch.

"And where do you go now?" asked the cardinal.

"Towards God's gate, Sire; and I wish I might see it soon, but for this little one," said the old man, rising.

"Holy Peter let you in when you get there," rejoined His Eminence, turning his horse away.

"Hold! Cardinal," replied the king. "I am surprised at that speech from you. You have tried to teach me by lectures for a fortnight past that Rome has temporal as well as spiritual authority, all power on earth as well as in heaven. Now, by Our Lady! you ought to help this good man over his earthly way towards God's gate, as well as wish him luck when he gets there. But the priest preaches, and leaves the laity to do the duties of religion. Credit me with a good Christian deed to balance the many bad ones you remember against me, Cardinal, and I will help the man. The golden hair of the child against the old man's head were as good an aureole as ever a saint wore. And that Holy Peter knows, if the Cardinal does not. Ho, Olgard! Take the lass on the saddle with you. And, old man, if you will keep close with your daughter, you will find as good provision behind the gate of Philippopolis as that in heaven, if report be true. And, by Saint Michael! if we go dashing down the mountain at this rate we will vault the walls of that rich Moslem town as easily as the devil jumped the gate of Paradise."

Kabilovitsch trudged by the side of Olgard, who held Morsinia before him. It was hard for the old man to keep from under the hoofs of the horses as the attendant knights crowded together down the narrow and tortuous descent. Suddenly the girl uttered a cry, and, clapping her hands, called,

"Constantine, Constantine!"

The missing lad, emerging from a copse, stood for an instant in amazement at the apparition of his little playmate; then dashed among the crowd toward her.

"Drat the witch!" said a knight—between the legs of whose horse the boy had gone—aiming at him a blow with his iron mace. Constantine would have been trampled by the crowding cavalcade, had not the strong hand of a trooper seized him by his ragged jacket and lifted him to the horse's crupper. "So may somebody save my own lad in the mountains of Carpathia!" said the rough, but kindly soldier.

"Ay, the angels will bear him up in their hands, lest he even dash his foot against a stone, for thy good deed," exclaimed a monk, who, with hood thrown back, and almost breathless with the effort to rescue the lad himself, had reached him at the same moment.

"Good Father, pray for me!" said the trooper, crossing himself.

"Ay, with grace," replied the monk, extricating himself from the crowd, and hasting back to the side of a wounded man, whom his comrades were carrying on a stretcher which had been extemporized with an old cloak tied securely between two stout saplings.

As night darkened down, the plain at the base of the mountain burst into weird magnificence with a thousand campfires. The Turks were in full retreat toward Adrianople, and joy reigned among the Christians. It was the eve of Christmas. The stars shone with rare brilliancy through the cold clear atmosphere.

"The very heavens return the salutation of our beacons," said King Vladislaus.

A trumpet sounded its shrill and jubilant note, which was caught up by others, until the woods and fields and the mountain sides were flooded with the inarticulate song, as quickly as the first note of a bird awakens the whole matin chorus of the summer time. Cardinal Julian, reining his horse at the entrance to the camp, listened as he gazed—

"'And with the angel there was a multitude of the heavenly host praising God!' Let us accept the joy of this eve of the birth of our Lord as an omen of the birth of Christian power to these lands, which have so long lain in the shadow of Moslem infidelity and Greek heresy. Our camps yonder flash as the sparks which flew from the apron of the Infant Jesu and terrified the devil.[12] Sultan Amurath has been scorched this day, though the infernal fiend lodge in his skin, as I verily believe he does."

"Amurath was not in personal command to-day. At least so I am told," replied Vladislaus. "He is occupied with a rebellion of the Caramanians in Asia. Carambey, the Sultan's sister's husband, led the forces at the beginning of the fight. He was captured in the bog, and is now in safe custody with the Servian Despot, George Brankovich. Hunyades and the Despot have been bargaining for his possession. But the real commandant, as I have learned from prisoners—at least he was present at the beginning of the fight—was Scanderbeg."

"Scanderbeg?" exclaimed Julian with great alarm. "What! the Albanian traitor, Castriot?—Iscariot, rather, should be his name—This then, Your Majesty, is no night for revelry; but for watching. The flight of the enemy, if Scanderbeg leads them, is only to draw us into a net. What if before morning, with the Balkans behind us, we should be assaulted with fresh corps of Turks on the front? There is no fathoming the devices of Scanderbeg's wily brain. And never yet has he been defeated, except to wrest the better victory out of seeming disaster. Does General Hunyades know the antagonist he is dealing with? that it is not some bey or pasha, nor even the Sultan himself, but Scanderbeg? I have heard Hunyades say that since the days of Saladin, the Moslems have not had a leader so skilful as that Albanian renegade: that a glance of his eye has more sagacity in it than the deliberations of a Divan:[13] and that not a score of knights could stand against his bare arm. We must see Hunyades."

"I confess," replied King Vladislaus, "that I liked not the easy victory we have had. I would have sworn to prevent a myriad foes climbing the ice road we travelled yesterday, if I had but a company of pikemen; yet ten thousand Turkish veterans kept us not back; and they were led by Scanderbeg! There is mystery here. Jesu prevent it should be the mystery of death to us all! Let's to Hunyades! If only your wisdom or prayers, Cardinal, could reclaim Scanderbeg to his Christian allegiance, I would not fear Sultan Amurath, though he were the devil's pope, with the keys of death and hell in his girdle."

Hunyades was found with the advance corps of the Christians. But for his white armor he could scarcely be distinguished from some subaltern officer, as he moved among the men, inspecting the details of their encampment. The contrast of the commander-in-chief with the kingly and the ecclesiastical soldier was striking. He listened quietly to their surmises and fears, and replied with as little of their excitement as if he spoke of a new armor-cleaner:

"Yes! we shall probably have a raid from Scanderbeg before morning. But we are ready for him. Do you look well to the rear, King Vladislaus! And do you, Cardinal, marshal a host of fresh Latin prayers for the dying; for, if Scanderbeg gets among your Italians, their saffron skins will bleach into ghosts for fright of him."

The cardinal's face grew as red as his cap, as he replied:

"But for loyalty to our common Christian cause, and the example of subordination to our chief, I would answer that taunt as it deserves."

CHAPTER IV

The company which Kabilovitsch and the children had joined was halted at the edge of the great camp. Other peasants and non-combatants crowded in from their desolated homes; but neither Milosch's face, nor Helena's, nor yet little Michael's, were among those they anxiously scanned. The command of King Vladislaus secured for the three favored refugees every comfort which the rude soldiers could furnish. The boy and girl were soon asleep by a fire, while the old man lay close beside them, that no one could approach without arousing him. He, however, could not sleep. On the one side was the noisy revelry of the victors; on the other, the darkness of the plain. Here and there were groups of soldiers, and beyond them an occasional gleam of the spear-head of some sentinel, who, saluting his comrade, turned at the end of his beat.

The dusky form of a huge man attracted Kabilovitsch's eye. As the stranger drew near, his long bear-skin cape terminating above in a rough and ungraceful hood, and his long pointed shoes with blocks of wood for their soles, indicated that he was some peasant. He seemed to be wandering about with no other aim than to keep himself warm. Yet Kabilovitsch noted that he lingered as he passed by the various groups, as if to scan the faces of his fellow-sufferers.

"Heaven grant that all his kids be safe to-night!" muttered the old man.

As the walking figure passed across the line of a fagot fire, he revealed a splendid form; too straight for one accustomed to bend at his daily toil.

"A mountaineer? a hunter?" thought Kabilovitsch, "for the field-tillers are all round of shoulder, and bow-backed. But no! His tread is too firm and heavy for that sort of life. One's limbs are springy, agile, who climbs the crags. A hunter will use the toes more in stepping."

Kabilovitsch's curiosity could not keep his eyes from growing heavy with the cold and the flicker of the fire light, when they were forced wide open again by the approach of the stranger. The old man felt, rather than saw, that he was being closely studied from behind the folds of the hood which the wanderer drew close over his face, to keep out the cutting wind which swept in gusts down from the mountains. He passed very near, and was talking to himself, as is apt to be the custom of men who lead lonely lives.

"It is bitter cold," he said, with chattering teeth, "bitter cold, by the beard of Moses!"

The last words startled Kabilovitsch so that he gave a sudden motion. The stranger noticed it and paused. Gazing intently upon the old man, who had now assumed a sitting posture, he addressed him—

"By the beard of Moses! it's an awful night, neighbor."

"Ay, by the beard of Moses! it is; and one could wear the beard of Aaron, too, with comfort—Aaron's beard was longer than Moses' beard; is not that what the priest says?" said Kabilovitsch, veiling his excitement under forced indifference of manner, at the same time making room for the visitor, who, without ceremony stretched himself by his side, bringing his face close to that of the old man, and glaring into it. Kabilovitsch returned his gaze with equal sharpness.

"What know you of the beard of Moses?" said the stranger. "Was it gray or black?"

"Black," said Kabilovitsch, studying the other's face with suspicion and surprise. "Black as an Albanian thunder cloud, and his eye was as undimmed by age as that of the eagle that flies over the lake of Ochrida."[14]

"You speak well," replied the stranger, pushing back his hood.

His face was massive and strong. No peasant was he, but one born to command and accustomed to it.

"You are——Drakul?" asked the man.

"No."

"Harion?"

"No."

"Kabilovitsch?"

"Ay, and you?"

"Castriot."

Kabilovitsch sprang to his feet.

"Lie down! Lie down! Let me share your blanket," said the visitor. "This air is too crisp and resonant for us to speak aloud in it; and waking ears at night-time are over quick to hear what does not concern them. We can muffle our speech beneath the blanket."

Kabilovitsch felt the hesitation of reverence in assuming a proximity of such intimacy with his guest; but also felt the authority of the command and the wisdom of the precaution. He obeyed.

"I feared that I should find no one who recognized our password. I must see General Hunyades to-night; yet must not approach his quarters. Can you get to his tent?"

"Readily," said Kabilovitsch. "During the day my little lass yonder won the attention of King Vladislaus, and he gave me the password of the camp to-night for her safety. '*Christus natus est*.'"

"You must go to him at once, and say that I would see him here. You will trust me to keep guard over these two kids while you are away? I will not wolf them." "Heaven grant that you may shepherd all Albania,"—and the old man was off.

"I knew that the prodigal Prince George would come back some day," said he to himself. "Many a year have I kept my watch in the Pass, and among the mountains of Albania. And many a service have I rendered as a simple goatherd which I could not have done had I worn my country's colors anywhere except in my heart. And, 'by the beard of Moses!' During some weeks now I have carried many a message, had some fighting and hard scratching which I did not understand, except that it was 'by the beard of Moses!' And now Moses has come; refused at last to be called the son of Pharaoh's daughter, and will free his people. God will it! And George Castriot has lain under my blanket! I will hang that blanket in the church at Croia as an offering to the Holy Virgin.—But no, it belongs to the trooper. Heaven keep me discreet, or, for the joy of it, I cannot do my errand safely. I'll draw my hood close, lest the moon yonder should guess my secret."

Kabilovitsch was challenged at every turn as he wound between the hundreds of camp-fires and tents; but the magic words, "Christus natus est," opened the way.

A circle of splendid tents told him he drew near to headquarters. In the midst of them blazed an immense fire. Camp-tables, gleaming with tankards and goblets of silver, were ranged beneath gorgeous canopies of flaxen canvas, which were lined with blue and purple tapestries. A multitude of gaily dressed servitors thronged into and out of them. Here was the royal splendor of Hungary and Poland; there the pavilion of the Despot of Servia; there the glittering cross of Rome; and, at the extreme end of this extemporized array of palatial and courtly pride, the more modest, but still rich, banner of the White Knight.

Kabilovitsch approached the latter.

"Your errand, man?" said the guard, holding his spear across the flapping doorway of the tent.

"Christus natus est!" was the response.

"That will do elsewhere, but not here," rejoined the guard.

"My business is solely with General Hunyades," said Kabilovitsch.

"It cannot be," said the spearman. "He has no business with any one but himself. If you are a shepherd of Bethlehem come to adore the Infant Jesu—as you look to be—you must wait until the morning."

"My message is as important to him as that of the angels on that blessed night," said the goatherd, making a deep obeisance and looking up to heaven as if in prayer, as he spoke.

"Then proclaim your message, old crook-staff! we have had glad tidings to-day, but can endure to hear more," said the guard, pushing him away.

"No ear on earth shall hear mine but the general's," cried the old man, raising his voice: "No! by the beard of Moses! it shall not."

"A strange swear that, old leather-skin! Did you keep your sheep in Midian, where Moses did, that you know he had a beard. Your cloak is ragged enough to have belonged to father Jethro; and I warrant it is as full of vermin as were those of the Egyptians after the plague that Moses sent on them. But the ten plagues take you! Get away!"

"No, by the beard of Moses!" shouted Kabilovitsch.

"Let him pass!" said a voice from deep within the tent.

"Let him pass!" said another nearer.

"Let him pass!" repeated one just inside the outer curtain.

The goatherd passed between a line of sentinels, closely watched by each. The tent was a double one, composing a room or pavilion, enclosed by the great tent; so that there was a large space around the private apartment of the general, allowing the sentinels to patrol entirely about it without passing into the outer air.

At the entrance of the inner tent Hunyades appeared. He was of light build but compactly knit, with ample forehead and generous, but scarred face; which, however, was more significantly seamed with the lines that denote thought and courage. He was wrapped in a loose robe of costly furs. He waved his hand for Kabilovitsch to enter, and bade the guards retire. Throwing himself on a plain soldier's couch, he drew close to it a camp seat, and motioned his visitor to sit.

"You have news from the Albanians, by the beard of Moses?" said Hunyades inquiringly.

A moment or two sufficed for the delivery of Kabilovitsch's message.

"Ho, guard! when this old man goes, let no one enter until he comes back; then admit him without the pass, instantly," said Hunyades, springing from the couch. "Now, old man, give me your bear skin—now your shoes—your cap. Here, wrap yourself in mine. You need not shrink from occupying Hunyades' skin for a while, since you have had to-night a more princely soldier under your blanket. Did you say to the north? On the edge of the camp? A boy and a girl by the fire; and he?"

The disguised general passed out.

CHAPTER V

"By the beard of Moses! I'll break your head with my stick if you come stumbling over me in that way," growled Scanderbeg from beneath his blanket, as a peasant-clad man tripped against his huge form extended by the camp fire.

"Then let the cold shrink your hulk to its proper size," replied the stranger. "But you should thank me, instead of cursing me, for waking you up; for your fire is dying out, and you would perish, sleeping in the blanket that exposes your feet that it may cover your nose. But I'll stir your fire and put some sticks on it, if I may sit by it and melt the frost from my beard and the aches from my toes. But whom have you here?"

The man stooped down and eagerly removed the blanket from the partially covered faces of the children. "Constantine!" he exclaimed, "God be praised! and Kabilovitsch's girl,—or the starlight mocks me!"

"Father!" cried the boy, waking and throwing his arms about the neck of the man who stooped to embrace him.

"And Michael? is he here, too?" asked Milosch.

"No, father," said the child. "We were parted at the cave, and I have not seen him except in my dream."

"In your dream, my child? In your dream? Jesu grant he be not killed, that his angel spirit came to you in your dream! Did he seem bright and beautiful—more beautiful than you ever saw him before—as if he had come to you from Paradise? No? Then he is living yet on the earth; and by all the devils in hell and Adrianople! I shall find him, though I tear him from the dead arms of the traitor Castriot himself, as I was near to taking you, my boy, from the grip of the Turk whose heart I pierced with an arrow the day of the fight;—but I was set upon and nigh killed myself by a score of the Infidels."

"And our mother dear?" asked Constantine. "She is safe?"

"Ay! ay! safe in heaven, I fear, but we will not give up hope until we have searched our camps to-morrow; nor then, until we have burned every seraglio of the Turks from the mountains to the sea. But who brought you and the lass here?" asked Milosch, eyeing the form of the surly man beside him.

"Why, good Uncle Kabilovitsch did," said the boy, staring in amazement at the spot now usurped by the strange figure of Scanderbeg. "Kabilovitsch went to fetch some fire-peat from the gully I told him of," muttered Scanderbeg.

"Yes, he is coming yonder," said Milosch, as Kabilovitsch's well-known hood and cape were outlined against the white background of a snow-covered fir tree a short distance off. "But he has found no fuel. Wrap close, my hearties: you will have no more blaze to-night. Ha! Kabilovitsch!" said he, raising his voice, as the familiar form seemed about to pass by. "Has the fire in your eye been put out by the cold, that you cannot find your own place, neighbor? I would have sworn that, if Kabilovitsch were blind, he could find a lost kid on the mountains; and now he hardly knows his own nest."

The assumed Kabilovitsch came near, and gave an awkward salute, which, while intended to be familiar, was not sufficiently unlimbered of the habit of authority to avoid giving the impression that its familiarity was only assumed.

"By the beard of Moses! I had almost mistook my own camp, now the fires are smouldering," said he, approaching.

"He is not Kabilovitsch," said Milosch, half to himself and half aloud.

"No," replied Scanderbeg. "But I'll go and find Kabilovitsch. Perhaps he has more peat than he can carry. And, stranger, I'll help you find what you are seeking—for you seem daft with the cold—if you will help me find him I am to look for. By the beard of Moses! that's a fair agreement; is it not?"

"A strange swear, that!" said Milosch, looking after the two forms vanishing among the fir trees. "It is some watchword, and I like it not among these camp prowlers. I fear for Kabilovitsch. The newcomer wore his clothes, which I would know if I saw them on the back of the cardinal; for good Helena cut the hood for our neighbor as she cut the skirt for his motherless child, little Morsinia there. Some mischief is brewing. I shall watch and not sleep a wink."

Had one been lurking in the copse of evergreens to which the men withdrew, he would have overheard conversation of which these sentences are parts.

"Yes, General Hunyades, the time has come. I can endure the service of the Sultan no longer. But for what I am about to do I alone am responsible, and must decline to share that responsibility with any other, either Moslem or Christian. I believe, Sire, that I am in this directed by some higher power than my own caprice. I am compelled to it by invisible forces, as really as the stars are dragged by them through the sky yonder."

"No star," replied Hunyades, "has purer lustre than that of your noble purpose, and none are led by the invisible forces to a brighter destiny than is Scanderbeg."

"Let not your Christian lips call me Scanderbeg, but Castriot," said his companion. "Yes, I believe that my new purpose comes from the inbreathing of some celestial spirit, from some mysterious hearing the soul has of the inarticulate voice of God. Else why should the thought of it so strangely satisfy me? I cast myself down from the highest pinnacle of honor and power and riches with which the Moslem service can reward one;—for I am at the head of the army, and even the Vizier has not more respect at Adrianople than have I wherever the soldiers of the Sultan spread themselves throughout the world. To leave the Padishah will be to leave every thing for an uncertain future. Yet I am more than content to do it."

"Not for an uncertain future, noble Castriot," replied Hunyades warmly, grasping his hand. "The highest position in the armies of Christian Europe is yours. My own chieftaincy I could demit without regret, knowing that it would fall into your hands. The army of Italy you can take command of tomorrow if you will; for that scarlet-knobbed coxcomb of an ecclesiastic, Julian, is not fitted for it. Or Brankovitch, the Servian Despot, will hail you as chief voivode.[15] You have but to choose from our armies, and put yourself at the head of whatever nation you will: for the legions will follow the pointing of your invincible sword as bravely as if it were the sword of Michael, the Archangel."

"No! No! These things tempt me not," said Scanderbeg. "I must live only for Albania. That strange spirit which counsels me comes into my soul like a pure blast from off my Albanian hills. The voices that call me are like the dying voice of my father, the sainted Duke John, who prayed then for his land and for his son—for both in the one breath that floated his soul to God. Let me look again upon the rocky fastnesses of the Vitzi, the waters of little Ochrida and Skidar, and call them mine; I shall then not envy even the plume on your helmet, generous Hunyades; nor regret what I forsake among the Moslems, though my estate were that of the entire empire which the Padishah sees in his dreams, when, not the city of Adrian, but the city of Constantine shall have become his capital."

"Christendom will hardly forgive the slight you put upon it, noble Castriot, by declining some general command, and will soon grow jealous of your exclusive devotion to little Albania," said Hunyades, with evident candor.

"Christendom will not lose, but gain, thereby," replied Scanderbeg. "For is not Albania, after all, a key point in the mighty battle which is still to be waged with the Turk over these Eastern countries of Europe, from Adria to the Euxine?"

"How so?" asked Hunyades. "Have we not this day broken the power of the Turk in Europe? and is he not now in headlong haste to the sea of Marmora?"

Scanderbeg replied with slow, but ominous, words:

"General Hunyades, the Moslem power was not this day broken. Trust not the semblance. My arm could have hurled your soldiers down the northern declivities of yonder mountains with as much ease as yours shattered the Turkish ranks at Vasag and Hermannstadt. The armies still in front of you wait but the word to assail your camp with dire vengeance for their mysterious defeat—ay, mysterious to them. And the Padishah is hasting with the hordes released by his victories over the Caramanians, to join them. No, Sire, the battle for empire on these plains, and in Macedonia, and along the Danube, has not ended: it has but just begun. And Albania will be the key spot for a generation to come. No Ottoman wave can strike central Europe but over the Albanian hills. A Christian power entrenched there will be a counter menace to every invasion from the side of the Moslem, and a tremendous auxiliary in any movement from the side of Christendom. My military judgment concurs with the voice of that spirit which speaks within me, and bids me as a Christian to live for Albania."

"I see in your plan," replied Hunyades, "a gleam of that far wisdom that won for you the title of 'The eye of the Ottoman,' as your valor made you the 'right hand of the Sultan.' While my view of the relative power of the two civilizations now fronting each other on our battle-lines might be different from yours, and I should place the key point in the great field rather on the lower Danube than so far to the west, I yet submit my judgment to yours. Assign to me my part in the affair you would execute, and, my word as a soldier and a Christian, you shall have my help."

"Nay," replied Scanderbeg. "As I said, I can share the responsibility of my action with no one. Grave charges will ring against my name. My old comrades will scorn my deed as treacherous. Even history will fail to understand me. Let me act alone; obeying that strange voice which will justify me, if not before men, at least at the last day of the world's judgment. The Moslem has wronged me; outraged my humanity; slit the tongue of my conscience that it should not speak to me of my duty; and tried to put out the eyes of my faith. The Divinity bids me avenge myself. But the vengeance is only mine, and God's. No other hand must be stained with the blood of it, least of all thine, noble Hunyades. My plan must be all my own. I only ask that, when I have extricated myself from Moslem ties, I may have the friendship of Hunyades. Especially that the way may be left open for my passing through the places now held by your troops, without challenge and delay. All else has been arranged by a handful of faithful Albanian patriots."

"It shall be as you desire, General Castriot. Choose your password, and it shall open the way for you though it were through the back door of the Vatican."

"Let then the 'beard of Moses' be respected. My trusty Albanians are accustomed to it."

"Good!" replied Hunyades. "And I will seal our compact by taking Adrianople in honor of the departure of its only defender."

"Nay," said Scanderbeg. "It will not be wise to press upon the capital. Every approach is guarded more securely than were those at Vienna by the Christians. The Padishah's engineers are more skilful than any in the land of the Frank or German. The new compound of saltpetre and sulphur, of which you hardly know the use, is buried beneath every gate; and a spark will burst it as Ætna or Vesuvius.[16] Even the valor of the White Knight cannot conquer the soulless element. The black grains never blanch with fear. No panic can divert a stone ball hurled from cannon so that it shall not find the heart of the bravest. I advise that your armies pause awhile with the prestige of having scaled the Balkans. In a few months opportunities may have ripened. Once I am in Albania, Sultan Amurath shall know that the name of Scanderbeg—the Lord Alexander—was not his, but Fate's entitling; for, unless my destiny is misread, the Macedonian legions of the Great Alexander were not swifter than my new Macedonian braves shall be. This will encourage the Venetians and Genoese; and with their navies on the Hellespont, the timid Palælogus pressing out from his covert of Constantinople, and insurrection everywhere from the Crimea to Peloponnesus, there will not, a generation hence, be left a turban in Europe. Believe me, General, the Turk's grip of nearly a century, since he pinched the continent at Gallipoli, cannot be loosened in a day."

"To no other than Castriot would I yield my judgment; and not to him, but that his words are as convincing as his sword. Then so let it be," was the reply of the Christian leader.

The Albanian disappeared.

CHAPTER VI

Hunyades, closely muffled in his bear-skin disguise, returned to the camp.

"A desperate adventure that of Castriot," thought he. "It is well that he permits no voice but his own to speak his plans, and no ear but mine to hear them.

"Hist!

"No; it is but the ice crackling from the balsams. Yet who knows what interlopers there may have been? and if the brave Scanderbeg may not be hamstrung before he reaches his own camp? The ride will be long and rattling after he enters the Turkish lines. Will it excite no suspicion? Nor his absence? Heaven guard the brave heart, for the very mole holes in the ground are the Sultan's ears, into which he drinks the secrets of his soldiers. By the way, I must lift the dirty cap from the fellow who called me Kabilovitsch at the herdsman's fire; for the messenger who brought me word surely said that only Castriot and the two children were there. Who may this other one be? I must discover; and if he knows aught he should not, he shall know no more this side of hell-gate, or my dagger's point has grown so honest that it has forgotten the way to a knave's heart."

Approaching the little group, Hunyades went behind them, that, if possible, he might overhear some words before any persons there knew of his presence.

Milosch had been ill at ease through the continued absence of his friend Kabilovitsch, the peculiar action of the strange man who had taken his place beneath the blanket, and the apparition of the one who wore the cap and cape which he thought he could not mistake. There had always been a mystery about Kabilovitsch's early life, which their long and close neighborly relations upon the mountain had not enabled him to solve. The girl, he often thought, was of too light a build and too fair featured to be the child of the mountaineer. The story Kabilovitsch often told about the early death of the child's mother, Milosch's wife never heard without impatience and a shrug of the shoulders. Who was the child? Could there be any plot to carry her away among persons who knew the secret of her birth? Milosch could reach one definite conclusion about the matter, and that was that he ought to guard the child just now. So, with senses made alert by suspicion, he heard the soft footfall of Hunyades through the crust-broken snow; and though with head averted, noted his stealthy approach.

The caution observed by the stranger made Milosch feel certain of the intended treachery. Loosening the short sheath-knife, which hung by the ring in its bone handle from his girdle, he grasped it tightly, and with a sudden bound faced the intruder.

"Your business, man?" said he, eyeing him as a hunter eyes a wolf to anticipate the spring of the brute, that the knife may enter his throat before the fangs strike.

"A rude greeting to a neighbor, that," was the quiet reply.

"A fair enough greeting to one who wears a neighbor's fleece, and prowls by night about his flock. Stop! not a step nearer! or, by the soul of Kabilovitsch, whom, for aught I know, you have murdered, I will send you to meet him!"

A motion of the stranger toward his weapon was anticipated by the mountaineer, who gripped the intruder with the strength of a bear, pinioning his arms by his sides, and falling with him to the ground. In an instant more, however, the dagger point of his antagonist began to penetrate Milosch's thigh. Clenching tighter to prevent a more deadly thrust, he felt beneath his opponent's rough outer robe the hard corselet woven with links of iron—not the coarse fabric such as was worn by common soldiers, but the lighter steel-tempered underwear of knights and nobles.

"You have murdered another better than yourself, damned villain, and have stolen his shirt. But it shall not save you this time."

As he let out these words one by one and breath by breath, Milosch worked the knife into such a hold that he could press it into the back of his antagonist. Slowly but surely the stout point made its way between the hard links until the man's flesh quivered with the pain. Then Milosch hissed through his clenched teeth:—

"Who are you? If you speak not, you die. If you lie, let the devil shrive your black soul! for I'll send you to him on the knife point. Speak!"

"I am General Hunyades," replied the almost breathless man.

The words relieved him from the pressure of the knife, but not from the crunching hug of his captor.

"Prove it!" hissed Milosch. "I have heard that Hunyades has a scar on the left side of the neck. Uncover your neck!"

Milosch released Hunyades' left hand sufficiently to allow him to reach upward. In an instant the leathern string which bound the bear-skin cape about his neck was broken, the lacings of a velvet jacket loosened, and the fingers of Milosch led over the roughened surface of the scarred skin.

The herdsman rose to his knees, and kissed the hand of the general. "Strike thy dagger into me! for I have raised my hand against the Lord's anointed," cried he in shame and fear.

"Nay, friend," said the chief; "the fault was mine, and yours shall be the reward of the only man who ever conquered Hunyades. Your name, my good fellow?"

"Milosch!"

"Milosch, the goatherd of the Pass? I have heard tell of your strength; how you could out-crunch a bear; I believe it. You have been faithful to your absent friend, as you have been severe with me."

"But what of my friend Kabilovitsch? You surely wear his gear," said Milosch.

"Yes, I borrowed these of a passing stranger—I know not that he be Kabilovitsch—with which I might pass disguised among the guards. The owner of this cape and hood is keeping warm in a tent hard by until I return. But whom have you here?"

"The lad is mine. The lass is my neighbor's. He calls her Morsinia, in honor of your fair mother," replied Milosch.

"Then I must see her face. She should be fair with such a name."

As he raised the coarse-knit hood which closely wrapped her, a flicker of the dying fire-light illumined for an instant the features of the child. The uncombed mass of golden hair made a natural pillow in which lay a face unsurpassed in balance of proportion and delicacy of detail by any sculptor's art. Her forehead was high and full, but apparently diminished by the wealth of curling locks that nestled upon brow and temples; her nose straight and thin, typically Greek; her lips firm, but arched, as with some abiding and happy dream; her skin, purest white, tinged with the glow of youthful health, as the snow on the Balkans under the first roseate gleam of the morning sun.

"A peasant's child?" asked the general. But without waiting for reply, continued, "No, by the cheek of Venus! It took more than one generation of noble culture, high thoughts and purest blood, to mould such a face as that. She was not born in your neighbor's cot on the mountains? Will you swear that she was? No? Then I will swear that she was not. And the boy? Ah!" said he, scanning Constantine's face. "I know his stock. He is a sprig of the same rough thorn-tree that came near to tearing me to pieces just now. But his face is gentler than yours. Yet, it is a strong one; very bold; broad-thoughted; deep-souled; a sprig that may bear even better fruit than the old one."

"Heaven grant it may!" said Milosch, fervently.

"Yes, if you will let me transplant it from these barren mountains to the gardens of Buda and the banks of the Drave, it will get better shelter than you can give it. The boy shall be my protégé for to-night's adventure, if his father will enter my personal service. You see, you gave me so warm a welcome that I am loath to part company with you, my good fellow."

"Heaven bless you, Sire!" replied Milosch; "but my heart will cling to these cliffs until I know that my faithful wife and other boy are no longer among them."

"I shall give orders that the camp be searched," promised Hunyades. "If they live, and have not been carried away by the Turks, they must have sought refuge somewhere in the host. Farewell! When you will, Hunyades shall stand the friend of Milosch."

The apparent old herdsman returned through the heart of the camp to headquarters.

"Methinks, comrade, that you bandied words with a greater than you knew, when you teased the old goatherd awhile ago," said a sentinel, thrusting his thumb into the side of the spearman at the entrance to the general's hut. "Do you note his mien as he comes yonder? That crumpled old bear skin cannot hide his straight back; nor those shoes, as big as Spanish galleons, break the firmness of his tread. If the gust of wind should lift his cape you would see at least a golden cross on his shoulders. You cannot hide a true soldier."

The bear-skin passed between the fluttering canvas without challenge. Hunyades made a playful salute to Kabilovitsch, who rose to meet him.

"I found your camp. I have looked into the face of your little daughter."

"Mary save her!" said the old man with gratified look.

"I say I saw your daughter, your *daughter*, you know," said the general again, quizzing Kabilovitsch with his eyes.

"Ay, my daughter! and the Virgin Mother never sent a fairer child, save Jesu himself, to prince or peasant."

"Come, now," said the general, "tell me, did the Holy Virgin send this child to prince *or* peasant?" "Why?" said Kabilovitsch, "these horny hands should tell thee, Sire, that I was not royal born."

"But the girl may be, if you were not. Is she your child?"

"Yes, my child, if heaven ever sent one to man."

"But, tell me," probed the general, "how did heaven send you the maiden? Did the mother bring her, or did the angels drop her at your door? For, if that girl be your child, heaven did not know you even by sight; since it put not a freckle of your dark skin upon her fair face, nor one of your bristles into her hair. The stars are not begotten of storm-clouds; nor do I think she is your daughter."

To this the old man replied, more to himself than to his interrogator, "If she is not mine by gift of nature, she is mine by gift of Him who is above nature."

"I will not steal your secret," said Hunyades. "Her name has excited my interest in her and her heaven-given or heaven-lent father. She needs better protection than you can give her in the camp. I will send her to headquarters."

"I would gratefully put her under your protection for a few days," said Kabilovitsch. "My duty takes me away from her for a while; dangerous duty, Sire, and if I should fall—"

"If Kabilovitsch falls, Hunyades will be as true father to the lass. Have you any special desire regarding her or yourself, my brave man? You have but to name it."

"But one, Sire," replied Kabilovitsch. "That I may see her safely conditioned at once. For it may be that before the day dawns I shall be summoned. I serve a cause as mysterious as the Providence which watches over it."

"An Albanian mystery? They are generally as inscrutable as a thunder cloud; but are revealed when its lightning strikes!" replied Hunyades, dismissing the old man, accompanied by two guards, who were commissioned to obey implicitly any orders the herdsman might give regarding the party of refugees by his camp-fire.

CHAPTER VII

The Christian host prolonged the festival of the Nativity from day to day, until the mustering forces of the Ottomans summoned them from dangerous inactivity again to the march and the battle. The latter they found at Mount Cunobizza, where the enemy had massed an enormous force. The Christian army, with its splendid corps of Hungary, Poland, Bosnia, Servia, Wallachia, Italy and Germany, was not a more magnificent array than that of their Moslem opponents. For the most part of the day the field was equally held, but in the afternoon the Turkish left seemed to have become inspired with a strange fury. The Janizaries, at the time renowned as the best disciplined and most desperate foot-soldiers in the world, were rivalled in celerity and intrepidity, in skilful manœuvring and the tremendous momentum with which they struck the foe, by other Moslem corps; such as the squadrons of cavalry collected from distant military provinces, each under its Spahi or fief-holder; and the irregular Bashi-Bazouks, who seemed to have sprung from the ground in orderly array. Their diverse accoutrements, complexions, and movements suggested the hundred arms of some martial Briareus, all animated by a single brain. The war cry of "The Prophet!" was mingled with that of "Iscanderbeg!" In the thickest of the fight appeared the gigantic form of the circumcised Albanian, his gaudy armor flashing with jewels,[17] his right arm bared to the shoulder, his cimeter glancing as the lightning. The Italian legions opposite him, upon the Christian left, were hurled back again and again from their onslaught, and were pressed mile after mile from the original battle site. Hunyades inflicted a compensatory punishment upon the Moslem left, shattering its depleted ranks as a battering ram crashes through the tottering walls of a citadel. The chief of the Christians saw clearly Scanderbeg's plan[18] to leave the victory in his hands, and at the opportune moment he wheeled his squadrons to the assistance of King Vladislaus, thus combining in overwhelming odds against the enemy's centre, which Scanderbeg had effectually drained of its proper strength. As soon, however, as it was evident that the Christians were the victors, Scanderbeg, by superb generalship, interposed the Janizaries between the enemy and the turbaned heads that, but for this, were being whirled in full flight from the field. The rout was changed into orderly retreat. Hunyades found it impossible to press the pursuit, and muttered,

"Scanderbeg commands both our armies to-day. We can only take what he is minded to give."

At length night looked down upon the camps. Few tents were erected. Hunyades sat for hours beneath a tree, waiting for he knew not what developments. On the Turkish side even the Beyler Beys, the highest commanders, were content to stretch their limbs with no other canopy than the three horse-tails at the spear-head, the symbol of their rank and authority. Far in the rear were the few pavilions of the suite of the Grand Vizier, who represented the absent Sultan Amurath. Late into the night the Vizier sat in counsel with the Sultan's Reis Effendi or chief secretary, to whom was entrusted the seal of the empire. He was enstamping the many despatches which fleetest horsemen carried to distant Spahis, summoning them with their reserves to rally for the defence of Adrianople.

Just before the dawn the secretary was left alone. Even he, and, in his person, the empire, must catch an hour's sleep before the exciting and exacting duties of the new day. He reclined among his papers. But a summons awakened him: the messenger announcing Scanderbeg. The guards withdrew to a respectful distance from the outside of the tent.

"Do not rise," said the general, gently pressing the secretary back to his reclining posture. "I only need the imperial seal to this order." The secretary scanned the paper with incredulous eyes. It was a firman, or decree of the Sultan, passing the government of Albania from General Sebaly to Scanderbeg, with absolute powers, and ordering the commandant of the strong fortress of Croia to place all its armament and that of adjacent strongholds in Scanderbeg's hand as the viceroy of the Sultan. As the secretary lifted his face to utter an inquiry for the relief of his amazement, knowing that the Sultan, then absent in Asia, could not have ordered such a document, the strong hand of Scanderbeg gripped his throat, and his poniard threatened his heart.

"The mark!" whispered the assailant.

The terrified man tremblingly reached the seal, and pressed it against the wax. The weapon then did its work, and so suddenly that the secretary had no time for even an outcry. Then silently, so that the guards, who were but a few paces distant, heard no commotion, he laid the lifeless form on the divan, and covered it with the embroidered cloak it had worn when living.[19]

Passing out, Scanderbeg gave orders that the tent should not be entered by the guards until morning, that the secretary might rest. He gave the password, "The Kaaba," as sharply as if his lips would take vengeance on the once sacred, but now hated sound. His military staff joined him at a little distance. Vaulting into the saddle he led the way toward the north. At the edge of the camp by a rude bridge he halted, and said to his attendants, "I meet at this point the Beyler Bey of Anatolia, whose staff will be my escort to his camp. The Padishah's cause needs closest conference of all the commanders; for treason is abroad. Ah! I hear the escort. Return to quarters, gentlemen!"

Riding forward alone in the direction of the noise, he cried, "Who comes?"

"The Kaaba at Mecca," was the response.

"Well, if the Kaaba takes the trouble to come to me it is a good omen, by the beard of Moses!"

"By the beard of Moses!" murmured a group of horsemen, bowing their turbaned heads in the first gray light of the approaching day. The cavalcade closed around the fugitive chieftain, and moved along in silence, except to respond to the sentinels. As they passed the extreme picket of the Turks they halted. A wardrobe had been secreted in a cave beyond a copse near the road. Dismounting, the men exchanged their turbans for caps of wolf or beaver skin. Their gaily trimmed jackets, such as were worn by the Turkish foot-soldiers, gave place to short fur sacks. Their flowing, bag-bottomed trousers were kicked off, leaving abbreviated breeches of leather. In a few moments the splendidly uniformed suite of a Moslem bey was transformed into a rough, but exceedingly unique-looking, band of Albanian guerillas. Scanderbeg assumed a helmet, the summit of which carried as a device the head and shoulders of a goat—since the times of Alexander the Great the symbol of the powers in, or bordering upon, Macedonia. The Turkish uniforms were bundled upon the cruppers for future use. The men stood for a moment, each by the side of his horse. At a motion of the officer in charge they gave the salute; touching their bared foreheads, and bowing to the ground. The officer then approached Scanderbeg, and, presenting his sword, said:

"Sire! to thee, as the son of our Duke John, we give our swords together with our hearts and our lives." Instantly every sword was laid upon the ground; and the crisp air rattled with the cry, "Long live Duke George! A Castriot forever!"

Scanderbeg gazed silently for a moment upon the faithful group. There was no doubt of their loyalty: for they had proved it by an adventure of rare daring in penetrating the Turkish camp. The face of the great general, usually masking so completely his strongest feelings, lost now its rigidity. His eyes were moist; his lips trembled; every lineament was eloquent with the emotion he could neither conceal nor tell in words. After a few moments' impressive silence, he returned the sword to the officer, and, pointing westward, cried,

"Forward to Albania!"

CHAPTER VIII

"Thank Heaven! the plan did not fail," said the chief officer, riding by the side of the fugitive general.

"In no particular has it failed, Colonel," replied Scanderbeg. "And for this every praise is due your wise precautions. I have never known better work of brain or nerve. With such grand soldiers as you and your men, I fear nothing for Albania. But your name, Colonel?"

"Moses Goleme," replied the officer courteously.

Scanderbeg reined his horse, and gave him his hand heartily. "A man as grand as he is brave! And do I really look into the face of him whom I was to have sought out in Dibria, that I might tell him his words had been to me like a voice from heaven? Heaven reward you, good Moses! But you must vow to stand by me yet as patiently as you have done hitherto— during my apostasy. I shall need your charity still; for I am but a returning prodigal; a half-Christian; a man of strange ways; of a temper which I understand not myself, and which will disappoint you. Pledge me that you will be my good angel. Counsel me frankly, fearlessly, as a man should always counsel a man. Rebuke me freely: but bear with me in your heart, as you would with a child."

"I may not advise the most capable general in the world," replied Moses Goleme. "I vow to obey. Let that be my part. As I have already imperilled my estates by open opposition to the Turkish rule, and given my life to the liberty of my country, so I offer all to thee, Sire, the sovereign of my heart, until you shall be acknowledged the sovereign of Albania, and a new empire be founded on the east of the Adriatic which shall take the place of the decaying powers of Italy on the west." "The task your patriotism proposes is vast," replied Scanderbeg; "too vast for one man and one lifetime."

"Too great for any but the great Castriot!" was the answer, evidently as honest as it was reverent. "But you do me too much honor, General, in praising my plan of meeting you. I was ably seconded by my men, and especially by two of them. One of them was wounded."

"I trust you speak not of a brave fellow who brought me the time and place of the rendezvous: for I never saw such strength and daring in my life."

"The same, I fear," said Moses. "A Servian, whom I had not known before yesterday. But he was boiling over with rage for the slaughter of his family, and commended to me by our most trusted scout."

"Did he tell you how he found me out, and communicated your plan to me?"

"No, for he was too severely hurt to speak much."

"I will tell that part for him, then," said Scanderbeg. "It was in the hottest of the fight. My own body-guard was thrown into confusion. A fellow, clad like one of my own staff, crowded close to my side. His horse actually rested against my own, and I would have severed his head from his shoulders for his impudent valor, had not his oath at his beast been 'by the beard of Moses!' Seeing that I observed it he grunted, 'At the brook to the north!' as he dodged the circles of the cimeters; and 'Near the Roman road!' he hissed as he pared the cap from a Christian's head with his sword; and 'At the ninth hour to-night!' he shouted as he parried a thrust. Before I had breathing space—for I was closely beset at the time—he had gone; borne back by a Spahi,[20] who envied him his place and emulated his valor. But he was not skilful in using his weapon or managing his horse. I am grieved, but not surprised, at his receiving hurt. I thought he must have fallen. But who was the other?"

"Yonder old fellow with a huge green turban on the saddle before him. If his brain were as big as his head-piece, he could not have planned better. He has dwelt about here lately."

"I must thank him in person," said Scanderbeg, riding back toward him.

"What!" he exclaimed as the full daylight fell upon the man's features, "Kabilovitsch?"

The old man diverted Scanderbeg's compliments by an expression of solicitude for Milosch, whom he had permitted to undertake the desperate venture already narrated, although until a few days before he, being a Servian, had no knowledge of the project of the Albanians.

"We must haste, Sire," said Moses. "It is advised that you cross to the north of the pass in the Balkans, and take thence the valley way between Caratova and the Egrisu. A message from General Hunyades informs me that relays can be provided along the road, and that every facility shall be given us."

"Kabilovitsch will accompany us?" asked Scanderbeg.

"On one condition, Sire," replied the old man. "My little daughter must go with me: a lass of ten spring tides—"

"Impossible! for our ride must be night and day."

"Then I may follow, but cannot accompany you," said Kabilovitsch.

"I need such men as you with me. No true Albanian will delay for a child. Country must be child and mother to us all," said the general.

The cheeks of Kabilovitsch whitened; his eyes flashed. Looking Scanderbeg squarely in the face, he said quietly, but putting intention into every word,

"George Castriot may lead, but may not rebuke the patriots who have watched for Albania with sacrifices he knows not of, while he has been among our country's enemies. An old man, thy father's friend before thou wast born, may say that, Sire."

Scanderbeg grew pale in turn. He had been unaccustomed to brook insubordination, however righteous. Who had dared to question him? Who to fling the taunt into his face? The hot words were upon his lips. But he paused, at first from the mere habit of self-restraint. Then, because he was a wise man, and realized that he was no longer the tyrant, with power of life and death over his soldiers—men who had been hired, stolen, impressed into the service, and transformed into mere machinery of flesh and blood—but was to be the public liberator of a people every man of whom was already as free as he. Then, he had become a just man. Strange and sanguinary as had been the events accompanying his desertion of the Turks, he had taken this step only after a deep moral struggle. He had revolted from his own past life; and felt an inward disgrace for what had been his outward glory—the service of the Moslem; he despised himself more than any other person could. It was this sense of the justice of Kabilovitsch's rebuke that checked the rage which had blanched his face, and sent the flush to his temples, as he slowly, replied, "I bow to the merited chastisement of your words. Your years and your better life give you license to utter them. My future shall atone for the past. But cannot your child be left safely where she is?"

"She is safe where she is; but I may not leave her without providing for her future. Milosch is lying in a cottage but a little before us. If his wounds are not fatal—as I believe they are not, though the leech thought otherwise—I may bring the girl to him, and still overtake you before you come in sight of the Black Mountains. I can cross this country by paths through which I could not direct you. During many years, for justice's sake and our country's, I have wandered over these mountains where only the eagle's shadow has fallen."

"I will stop with you at the cottage," said Scanderbeg, "for, though the moments are precious, I would bless the brave fellow for his work yesterday."

There were several wounded Christian soldiers at the little hovel. A Greek monk was administering both spiritual and physical comfort; for Rilo Monastir had sent its inmates along the track of the Christian army in spite of the insults of the Latin soldiers, who, though in sight of the common enemy of their faith, could not repress the meanness of their sectarian jealousy and hatred. Milosch was doing well. His wounds were, one in the fleshy part of the shoulder, the other a contusion on the head, from a blow which had stunned him. A few weeks would put him again upon his feet, though perhaps his fighting days were over; for the flesh wound lay across an important muscle, and would permanently destroy the strength of the right arm.

Milosch fell in with the proposition of Kabilovitsch regarding Morsinia. Though a Servian, he had lost interest in his own country because of the vacillating course of the Despot, George Brankovitch, who was half Christian and half Moslem, according to the policy of the moment. Milosch would identify himself with the cause of Albania, for which he had already done and suffered so much.

The two men entered into what is known among the Servians and Albanians as "Brotherhood in God," covenanting in the name of God and St. John to devote their lives, each to the other, and both to their common cause. The compact was sealed by each putting the left hand upon the other's heart, and holding up the right hand in invocation of the Divine witness. Kabilovitsch said:

"My brother, I commit to thy keeping our daughter, Morsinia, thine and mine, from henceforth. She is all I have but life to share with thee, which also I freely give."

To this Milosch replied: "My brother, I commit to thy keeping our boy, Constantine, thine and mine from henceforth. He is all I have that I wot of to share with thee, but my life which—God spare it—I freely give."

"Bismallah!"[21] said Scanderbeg. "And if the girl and the boy were the ones I saw asleep in each other's arms by the fire the other night, the compact is good for two generations at least."

It was agreed that, upon his sufficient recovery, Milosch should bring the children from the camp of Hunyades to Albania.

The ride by the Vitosh and Rilo Mountains where the mighty ranges of the Balkans, the Upper Mœsian, and the Rhodope are thrown close together, was sufficiently grand to engross the eye and mind of the dashing riders. Thus most of the day was passed in silence, broken only by the clatter of the horses' hoofs against the rocks; the roar of cascades making their awful plunge hundreds of feet from the precipices; the complaint of rivers far down at the bottom of ravines, fretting beneath the prison roof of ice and snow; and glorious pines, pluming the brow of crag and ledge, through which the everlasting winds breathed the dirge over fallen empires of men.

As they forced their way up a long and tedious ascent, Scanderbeg joined Kabilovitsch and said:

"To relieve the tedium of this slow part of the journey you must tell me about that lass you would not leave for the love of Albania. A sweet face as I saw it. I could have run off with it myself, had I not other business on hand. And I can pardon a father's heart for clinging very closely to such a child. You will forget my rude speech a while ago. I played with a little lass like that when I was a boy. The face of your child, that night I watched for you, carried me back to those happy days. I could see my little sweet-heart in her; though thirty years have thrown their shadows of dark events across my memory."

Kabilovitsch turned familiarly to Scanderbeg with the query,

"May I read your thoughts, Sire?"

"Yes, he is welcome to do so who can find my soul beneath this battered face."

"That child was the fair Mara, the daughter of the noble George Cernoviche, whose castle ruins lie now by the shore of Ochrida. Am I not right?"

"Right! but I knew not of the fall of her father's house. Can you tell me aught of the history of my little maiden. If she lives, she must be a goodly matron now."

"Yes, I can tell her story and more. She married the noble Musache de Streeses, whose castle once stood near the Skadar."[22]

"Ah! I have heard of his sad fate," replied the general. "Oh, for vengeance on these villains who have despoiled the land! Musache de Streeses was the richest of all the land-owners on the coast of Adria, the soul of honor, a genuine patriot, with whom my father held confidential intercourse. His purse and sword were freely offered for service against the Turk. It was a favorite scheme of my father to some day unite our families. I hear that my nephew, Amesa, has become possessed of those estates, being also nephew to De Streeses, who was slain by the Turks. But my fairy, Mara, you said was married to De Streeses. It was she, then, who, with her infant child, was killed by the Turks during the raid?"

"Noble Castriot! De Streeses and the Lady Mara were murdered, foully, treacherously," said the old man, reining his horse, and speaking with terrible passion.

"Oh, to take vengeance!" exclaimed Scanderbeg. "By the fair face of Mara! this, with the thousand other murders of these years, shall be washed out, if my sword drains a myriad veins of Turkish blood to make sure of his who struck so brutal a blow!"

"Your sword need not search so wide as that," said Kabilovitsch. "The family of De Streeses were murdered by hands we both know but too well."

"How know you, Kabilovitsch?"

The man removed his cap as if inviting the inspection of his face, and, lowering his voice, replied,

"I am not Kabilovitsch, I am Arnaud."

"Arnaud, the forester of De Streeses? Arnaud, whose shoulders I bestrode before I ever mounted a steed?" exclaimed Scanderbeg, turning his horse and stopping, but at his companion's motion indicating caution, lowering his tone, and moving close beside him.

"The same, Sire. And the Turks who murdered the nobleman and his beautiful wife were not such Turks as you have been accustomed to command. Too white of skin and too black of heart were they. I would not say this, but that I give you also my reasons for so grave an accusation. Turks in raiding do not discriminate in their depredations; but these harmed not a leaf beyond the castle of De Streeses. Nor do Turks swear by St. John, as I heard one of them do as he cursed a fellow villain for some slip in the plan. Nor again would Turks, seeking only for plunder, have shown as much eagerness to kill the little babe as they did to slay its father; and this they did, searching even among the ashes for evidence that the tiny bones had been sufficiently charred to prevent their recognition. But the child was not in the castle at the time. My good wife was suckling it—the Lady Mara being of delicate condition—and that night the babe was at the lodge. As soon as the commotion was heard at the castle the child was hidden in the copse."

"But where is this child now?" asked Scanderbeg eagerly.

"You have gazed upon her by my camp-fire, sire; and your soul saw in her face that of the sainted Mara, though your eyes detected her not."

"And you know the perpetrator of this damnable deed?" asked Scanderbeg.

"I may not say I know, since your noble father refused to believe that any other than Turkish hands did it. But he who possesses the estate now knows too much of this affair to thank God in his prayers for his inheritance. I saved the child; yet Lord Amesa has sworn that once a Turk who fell beneath his sword in a private brawl confessed to him that his hands had strangled the infant on the night of the raid. Some one interested had suspicion of where the truth lay, for my own cot was raided, and my wife slain one night during my absence. But the child was safe elsewhere. Since then, knowing that her life was secure only through her being secreted, I have been a wanderer. A price was secretly set upon my head by Amesa. In the mountains of Macedonia, in the pass of the Balkans, have I kept watch over my sacred charge. I want not to see Albania, but as I can see justice done in Albania. Therefore I said I would go only if the lass might go with me, and under the strong protection of a Castriot who knows the truth, whose very soul recognized the child of Mara."

"The child's life shall be as sacred to me as if Mara had become my wife as she vowed in her play, and the child were my own," said Scanderbeg. "But this perplexes our cause. Amesa is one of our bravest, wiliest voivodes. To antagonize him with this old charge would imperil my reception with the people and the liberty of our land. But I pledge you, my good Arnaud, that though vengeance waits, it shall not sleep. In the time when it shall be most severe upon the offender, and most honorable to the name of Albanian justice, the bolt shall fall."

It was readily foreseen by both that only at the peril of her life could Morsinia be allowed to accompany her foster father, Arnaud or Kabilovitsch, to the camp of Castriot. The former forester would be recognized and suspicion at once excited as to the person of his ward. It was, therefore, determined that she should be domiciled safely in a little hamlet on the borders of Albania, where her history was unknown; and that, to elude suspicion, Milosch and the boy, Constantine, should accompany her, as her father and brother, neither of whom knew her true history. The "Brotherhood in God" between Kabilovitsch and his old neighbor gave sufficient warrant for Milosch's claim to paternity.

CHAPTER IX

But while these refugees from the little hamlet on the mountains were so favored of good Providence, what of the others? Our story must return to the day of the battle in the Pass of Slatiza. Mother Helena fell beneath the sword of a Turk while defending herself from his insults. The boy, Michael, with arms bound above the elbows and drawn back so that, while retaining the use of his hands, he could not free himself, was driven along with others under guard of several soldiers. As they descended the mountains the band of captives was steadily increased by contributions from the cottages and hiding places along the way. They were mostly boys and girls, the old men and women having been slain or left to perish in the utter desolation which marked the track of the army. Some of the captives were children too young to endure the tramp, and were carried upon the horses of the mounted soldiers. No one was treated unkindly. After the first day their bands were untied so that they moved without weariness. They shared the best of the soldiers' rations—sometimes feasting while their captors fasted—and were snugly wrapped in the blankets by the camp-fires at night. The daily march, after the Christian army had abandoned the pursuit, was of but a few miles, with long intervals for rest. Indeed, Michael thought that the troopers were more anxious about his being kept in good condition, even in fresh and comely appearance, than Mother Helena would have been. As they approached Philippopolis they were all made to wash at a stream. Their matted locks were combed:—a hard job with the mass of rebellious red bristles which stood about Michael's head, like a nimbus on the wooden image of some Romish saint. In some instances the captors went into the city and returned with pretty skirts of bright colored wool or silk, and caps made of shells and beads for the girls. Fantastic enough were the costumes and toilets which the rough old troopers forced upon the little maidens; but if they were pleasing to the captors they would prove, perhaps, as pleasing to the rough slave buyers in the market square of Philippopolis, who purchased the girls for disposal again at the harems of the capital. An officer of excise presided over these sales, and, before the property was delivered to the purchaser, retained one-fifth the price as the share of the Sultan. If any of the girls were, in the judgment of the officer, of peculiar beauty or promise, they were reserved for the royal harem; the value of them being paid to their captors out of the tax levied upon the others. This gave occasion for the extravagant and often ludicrous costumes in which the diverse tastes of the soldiers arrayed their captives for the contest of beauty.

The boys, however, were not sold. They were the special property of the Sultan, to be trained as Janizaries for military service, or employed in menial positions about the royal seraglio. The captors received rewards according to the number and goodly condition of the lads they brought in.

The band of boys to which Michael was attached was marched at once to Adrianople. Several hundreds were gathered in a great square court, which was surrounded by barracks on three sides, and on the fourth faced the river Marissa. A great soup kettle, the emblem of the Janizary corps, was mounted upon a pole in the centre of the square, and seemed to challenge the honors of the gilt star and crescent, the emblem of royalty, that gleamed from the tall staff in an adjacent court of the seraglio. There were scattered about utensils for domestic use; the tools of carpenters, blacksmiths, armorers, harness-makers and horse-shoers; old swords, battered helmets, broken wagons, bow-guns, the figure heads of veteran battering rams; indeed all the used and disused evidences that within these walls lived a self-sustaining community, able to provide for themselves in war or in peace.

For several days the new boys were fed with delicious milk and meats, prepared by skilful hands of old soldiers, who knew the art of nursing the sick almost as well as they knew that of making wounds. For a few nights the lads slept upon soft divans, until every trace of weariness from the journey had disappeared. They were then stripped naked and examined carefully by the surgeons. If one were deformed, or ill-proportioned, or failed to give promise of a strong constitution, he was taken away to be trained as a woinak or drudge of the camps. Perhaps three-fourths of the entire number in Michael's company were thus branded for life with an adverse destiny.

The more favored lads were graded into ojaks, or messes; and among them were daily contests in running and wrestling, according to the results of which the ojaks were constantly changing their members; the strongest and most agile living together in honorary distinction from their fellows.

The officers in charge of these Janizary schools were old or crippled men, whom years or wounds had rendered unfit for service in the field, and who were assigned to the easier task in compensation for past fidelity. The spirit of the veterans was thus infused into the young recruits by constant contact and familiarity with them; and the rigid habits of the after service were acquired almost insensibly through the daily drill and discipline.

Michael's rugged health and mountain training enabled him to advance rapidly through the various grades. Though almost the youngest in his company, he was the first in the race, and no one could take him from his feet in the wrestling match.

"A sturdy little Giaour," said old Selim, a fat and gouty Janizary, the creases of whose double chin were good companions to the sabre-scar across his cheek.

"Ay, tough and handy!" responded Mustapha, an old captain of the corps, ogling Michael with his widowed eye, and stroking his beard with his equally bereaved hand, as he watched the boy wriggling from beneath to the top of a companion nearly double his size. "If the little fellow is as agile in wit as he is in limb he will not long be among the Agiamoglans.[23] A splendid build! broad in the shoulders; deep-chested, but not flat; narrow loins; compact hips—just the make of a lion. As lithe a lad as you were once, my now elephantine Selim, when Bajazet stole you from your Hungarian home. Ah! you have changed somewhat since the old Padishah had you for his page. I remember when your waist was as trim as a squirrel's—but now—from the look of your paunch I would think you were the soldier who drank up the poor woman's supper of goat's milk, and had his belly ripped open by the Padishah to discover his guilt.[24] Only goat's milk swells like that. Let us see if some of the butter sticks not yet to your ribs," said the old soldier, making a pass at his comrade's middle.

"That's not a true soldier's pass, to strike so low," said Selim, laughing. "But you, Mustapha, were once a better runner than yon lad will ever be."

"I was as good with my legs as with my arms," replied the veteran, pleased with the compliment, and fondling his bare calves with his hand. "But at what match did you see me run?"

"I only saw you run once," said Selim, "and that was at Angora, when Timour the Lame[25] was after you to get your ugly head for the pyramid of skulls he left there as a monument. But see the lad! He tosses the big one as a panther topples an ox. We have not had his match in the school since Scanderbeg was a boy."

"Poor Scanderbeg!" said Mustapha.

"How now!" inquired Selim, "is there any news from him?"

"Yes. He has met his first defeat. He was in command at the last battle under the Balkans. Carambey got fast in a bog, in the first battle, and Scanderbeg was unable to redeem the defeat in the second. But he lived not to know it. He sent a host of gibbering Giaour ghosts to hell while on his way to heaven. 'In the crossing of the cimeters there is the gate of paradise,' says the Koran; and, though his body could not be found, he went through the gate, beyond a doubt."

"That is a loss, comrade, the Padishah can never make good with any man in the service. But have you not noted, Mustapha, that Scanderbeg never fought so well against Christians as against the Caramanians, the Kermians and rebellious Turks. In Anatolia I have seen his lips burst with blood,[26] through sheer rage of fight; but in Servia he seemed listless and without heart for the fray. The Grand Vizier has noted it, and twitted him with remembering too well that he was Christian born."

"And how did he take that?"

"Why, the color came to his face; his lips swelled; his whole body shook;—just as I have seen him when compelled to restrain himself from heading a charge, because the best moment for it had not arrived."

"Did the Vizier take note of his manner?"

"Yes, and spoke of it to the Padishah. Amurath looked troubled, and I overheard him say, 'I must not believe it, for I need him. No other general can match Hunyades.' And the Padishah said well; and he had done well if he had taken the Vizier's head from his shoulders for such an insinuation. For Scanderbeg only half loyal were better than all the rest of the generals licking the Padishah's feet. But, Mustapha, we must train the little devil yonder to forget that he ever heard the name of Jesu, Son of Mary, except from the Koran."

"Let us see if he has as much courage as he has cartilage," said Mustapha. "The day is one fit for the water test. Let us have the squad on the river's bank. If you will bring them, I will go and arrange the test."

"It is too cold, and besides I do not like it," said Selim. "I have known some of the best and hottest blood that ever boiled in a child's veins to be chilled forever by it. It is too severe, except for trout."

"But it is commanded. And to-day is as mild as we shall have for a whole moon yet," was the reply, as Mustapha moved toward the water.

The river Marissa was covered with thin ice, not strong enough to bear the weight of a person. A young woinak had attached a small red flag to a block of wood, and whirled it out over the slippery surface some three rods from the shore. The boys gathered naked and shivering at the barrack doors, and, at a signal were to dash after the flag. All hesitated at the strange and cruel command, until a whip, snapping close to their bare backs, started them. Some slipped and fell upon the rough and icy stones of the paving in the court. Others halted at the river's edge. Only a few ventured upon the brittle ice; and they, as it broke beneath them, scrambled back to the shore. One or two fainted in the shock of the cold plunge, and were drawn in by the woinaks. But three pressed on, breaking the ice before them with their arms, or with the whole weight of their bodies, as they climbed upon its brittle edge. Soon they were beyond their depth; one dared to go no further, and, blue and bleeding, gave up the chase. The prize lay between Michael and his companion. This boy was larger and older than he; and finding that the ice would sustain his weight, stretched himself on it, and crawled forward until he grasped the flag. But the momentary pause, as he detached it from the wooden block and put it between his teeth, was sufficient to allow the crackling bridge to break beneath him; and he sunk out of sight. At the same instant Michael disappeared. Though several yards from his companion, he plunged beneath the ice, and reappeared carrying the flag in his teeth and holding his comrade's head above the water until the woinaks could reach and rescue them both.

"Bravo!" shouted the attendants. The boys were hurried into the barracks, and given a hot drink made from a decoction of strong mints; while the woinaks smeared their bodies with the same, and rubbed them until the shock of their exposure was counteracted by the generous return of the natural heat.

"I thought," said old Mustapha, "that we would have drowned some today. It is a cruel custom; but it is worth months of other practices to find out a lad's clear grit and power of endurance. The two boys who got the flag will some day become as valiant as ourselves, eh, Selim?" and the living eye of the veteran nodded to the empty socket across his nose—the nearest approach to a wink he was capable of.

"As the boys were floundering in the water," said Selim, "I thought of a scene which I saw about at the same spot—now three score years have gone since it—for it was just after I was brought into the Janizary's school. Our Padishah's great grandfather, the first Amurath, had erected a high seat or throne on the river's bank yonder. You know that Saoudji, the Padishah's son, had joined the Greeks; but the young traitor was captured. Well! old Amurath bade the executioner pass the red hot iron before his son's eyes until the sight was dried up in them. Then, while the blind prince was groping about and begging for mercy, the Padishah, his father, commanded a circle of swordsmen to be formed about him, swinging their cimeters, so that his head would fall by the hand of him whom he chanced to approach. Thus it might be said, that since he was a king's son, he had used the princely privilege of selecting his own executioner. And having thus set them an example of paternal duty, Amurath commanded the fathers of the Greek youths, whom he had captured, to cut off the heads each of his own son. Those whose fathers were not known or could not be found, were tied together in groups and thrown into the stream; the Padishah betting heavily with the Grand Vizier upon those who should float the longest. So, cruel though our customs are, you see, Mustapha, we are not so barbaric as our ancestors."

"Nor so abominably vicious as the Greeks," said Mustapha. "With them the loving mothers put out the eyes of their children.[27] No, we are quite gentle nurses of the lads committed to our charge, though sometimes our tiger claws will prick through the velvet."

"Come, help me up! good Mustapha," said Selim, trying to rise from a bench in the sunshine of the court where they were sitting. "The cold stiffens my bones."

"Bah! comrade, you have no bones, only flesh and belly. How will you balance your fat hulk on the bridge that is finer than a hair and sharper than the edge of a sword that takes you over hell into paradise? I fear me, Selim, that I shall have to content myself with the company of the Prophet and the houris in heaven, for you will never get there, unless I give you a lift across Al Sirat,"[28] said Mustapha, giving his comrade a jerk which sent him far out into the court, where with difficulty he kept his feet upon the slippery stones.

The old fellow took the rough play good-naturedly, and replied,

"You will never see paradise, Mustapha. The houris will have nought to do with so ugly a face as yours. It will turn them all squint-eyed to look at you."

"Do you think I know not the art of love-making?" said Mustapha, striking the attitude of a fashionable young man of the day.

Selim roared with laughter. "Mustapha making love? The thing is impossible; since, if the houri be in the sunshine of your good eye, you have no arm on that side to embrace her; and if you embrace her with the arm you have got, you have no eye on that side to look upon her beauty. Trust me, you old moulted peacock, that I shall get over Al Sirat before Mustapha has found a houri———"

"Hist!" said Mustapha, pointing to the entrance of the square from the seraglio court adjoining, and assuming an attitude of the gravest dignity. In a moment more the two officers knelt, and resting their foreheads on the ground, remained in that position until a lad of some twelve years approached them and touched the head of each with his foot, bidding them rise.

"I have come, good Selim, to see what new hounds you have for me," said the young Prince Mahomet.[29]

"Ah! my little Hoonkeawr![30] the Prophet, your namesake, has sent you a fine one; as lithe as a greyhound and as strong as a mastiff; and, if I mistake not, already trained for the game; for he came from the Balkans, where foxes run wild when and where they will."

"That is capital. I shall like him," cried the prince, with delight. "I must see him."

"Not to-day, your highness; for the boys are under the leech's charge. They have been put to the water-test, and are all packed snugly in their beds."

"The water-test, Selim, and you called me not?" said the boy, looking furious in his rage. "You knew I wanted to see it; and you told me not for spite. You will pay for this one day, you fat villain! And I want the hunt now. I came for it; did I not, Yusef?" addressing a eunuch, an old man with ashen face and decrepit body, but gorgeously arrayed, who accompanied the prince as his constant attendant.

"We must wait, I suppose," said the man, with a supercilious tone and toss of his head, as if to even speak in the presence of the soldiers were a degradation to his dignity.

"To-morrow we will have the hunt in better style than we could arrange it now were the boys able," said Selim, endeavoring to appease the young tyrant.

The prince and his escort moved away without deigning a reply

"It is best not to insist," said the eunuch. "A wise maxim I will give thee, my prince:—Beware of demanding the impossible—check back even the desire of it. The rule of the Janizary school is that the boys have rest after the water-test, and the Padishah would not allow even his own son to break it. I would train thee to self-command; for the time may come when thou shalt command the empire. Your brother, Aladdin, is mortal."

"So you always interfere with me. You hate me, Yusef; I know you do. I wish the boys had all been drowned in the river, and old Selim, and you too," cried the royal lad, giving way to an outburst of childish rage.

"Wait until thou canst get the bit between thy teeth before attempting to run thine own gait," coolly replied the old eunuch.

CHAPTER X

Beyond the walls of the seraglio lay the royal hunting grounds. Many acres of the city were enclosed within high walls of clayey earth, packed into huge square blocks and dried in the sun; on the top and outside of which bristled a miniature abattis of prickly vines. Some parts of this park were adorned with every elegance that the art of landscape gardening could devise. In the summer season these portions were covered with floral beauties, interspersed with water-jets, which tossed the light silver balls like fairy jugglers; broad basins sparkling with gold fish; and walks leading to little kiosks and arbors. Even its winter shroud could not conceal from the imagination what must have been its living beauty in summer.

The greater part of this reserve was, however, left in its natural state. Gnarled old olive trees twisted themselves like huge serpents above the dense copses of elder and hazel bushes. Dusky balsams rose in pyramids, overtopped by the pines, which spread their branches like umbrellas. Here and there were open fields, encumbered with stinted underbrush, and either broken with out-cropping rocks, or smooth with strips of meadow land now white and glistening under the snow.

This section of the park presented a fascinating appearance on the day of the fox-hunt. Scores of lads from the Janizary school were there, dressed in all shades of bright-colored jackets, and short trousers bagged at the knees; the lower part of the limbs being protected with close-fitting stockings of leather, terminating in light, but strong, sandals. Each wore a skull cap or fez of red flannel, from the top of which and down the back hung a tassel, that, by its length and richness, indicated some prize won by its wearer in previous games. Old soldiers gathered here and there in groups; some, the Janizaries, wearing tall sugar-loaf-shaped hats of gray; others, white turbans, or green ones, indicating that their possessors had made a holy pilgrimage to Mecca. Elegant burnooses, or sleeveless cloaks, of white, black, orange and yellow silks, fluttered in the wind or were gathered at the waist by rich sashes, from which hung great cimeters.

Near an open spot was a stand, or running gallery, enclosed in lattice-work, from behind which the ladies of the harem could witness the sports, themselves unseen. The presence of these invisible beauties was indicated by the stiff, straight forms of the black eunuchs, whose faces appeared above their white cloaks like heads of ebony on statues of alabaster.

Prince Mahomet rode a horse, small but compactly built, with head and mane suggestive of the power of his well-rounded muscles; slim ankles, seemingly better adapted to carry the lighter form of a deer; jet black, in strongest contrast with the white tunic and gaily embroidered jacket of the little prince, as well as with the saddle-cloth of purple silk, in which the star and crescent were wrought with threads of gold. With merry shout the young tyrant chased the boys, who, carrying wands decorated with ribbons, ran ahead of him to clear the way.

"So it will be if he ever comes to the throne," said Selim to a comrade. "Mahomet II. would follow no one. There would be no use of viziers and generals, and he would even attempt to drive the Janizaries like his sheep. It is well that Aladdin is the elder."

"But woe to Aladdin if Mahomet lives after his brother comes to the throne," said the man addressed. "With such fire-boxes about him one could justify the practice of a sovereign inaugurating his reign by the slaughter of his next of kin."[31]

The woinaks brought in several crates, with latticed sides, containing the foxes, which, one by one, were to be let loose for the chase; the boys to act the part of hounds, and drive the game from the thickets, in which they would naturally take refuge, out into the open space, and within arrow range of the prince. Mahomet, by constant practice, had acquired great dexterity in managing his steed, and almost unerring aim in using the bow from the horse's back.

A splendid red fox was thrust out of the crate. For a moment he remained crouching and trembling in his fright at the crowd; then darted suddenly for the underbrush. The boys, imitating the sharp cry or prolonged baying of a pack of hounds, scattered in different directions; some disappearing in the copse; others stationing themselves at the openings or run-ways where they thought the animal would appear. The bugle of the white eunuch, who was constantly near the prince, kept all informed of his position, so that reynard might be driven toward him. In a few moments the arrow of Mahomet laid him low.

A second fox was liberated—like many of the Sultan's nobler creatures—only to fly to his speedy execution. The third animal was an old one, who persisted in taking the direction opposite to that in which the chasers would drive him. Again and again, as the boys closed about him, he dashed through the thickest of their legs, leaving them tumbled together in a heap. At one time he sprang through the opening at which Michael, studying the tricks of the quick-witted brute, had stationed himself. Sudden as were his movements, the young mountaineer's were not less so; for, like a veritable hound, he threw himself bodily upon the prey. Passing his right hand beneath the entire length of the animal's body from the rear, he grasped his front leg and bent it back beneath him; at the same time using his whole weight to keep the animal's head close to the ground, so as to escape his fangs. He had taken more than one beast in a similar way from the holes in the old mountain pass. In the excitement of the sport he now forgot that he was merely to enable another to get the game without effort or danger.

Prince Mahomet rode to the spot toward which the fox had turned, and, in a sudden outburst of anger at this interference with his shot, drove the arrow at the two as they were struggling on the ground. The whirring barb cut the arm of Michael before it entered the heart of the prey. The sharp cry of pain uttered by the lad recalled Mahomet from his insane rage. The rushing attendants showed pity for Michael, but no one ventured a remonstrance against this act of imperial cowardice and cruelty. A moment's examination showed that the lad's wound was not serious, being only a cut through the flesh. But as the pallor of his fright died away from his face, it was followed by a deep flush of anger. Tears of vexation filled his eyes. His glance of scorn was hardly swifter than his leap: for, with a bound, his arms were around the prince's body, while his weight dragged him from the saddle to the ground. Mahomet, rising, drew a jeweled dagger, and made several hasty passes at his assailant, who, however, dextrously avoided them. The posing of the lads would have done justice to the fame of professional gladiators. The prince pressed upon his antagonist with incessant thrusts, which, by skilful retreating and parries with his bare arm, Michael avoided; until, with a ringing blow upon Mahomet's wrist, he sent the weapon from his hand, and closed with him; the prince falling to the ground beneath the greater strength of Michael.

The spectators at this point interfered. As they rose the eunuch grasped the little victor, and shaking him, cried: "I will cut the throat of the Giaour cub of hell."

But the one hand of old Mustapha was upon the eunuch's throat, and his one eye flashed like a discharging culverin, as he cried, "Had I another hand to do it with, I would cut yours, you white-faced imbecile! Don't you know that the boy belongs to the Janizaries? and woe to him who is not a Janizary that lays a hand on him!"

"The prince's honor must be avenged," wheezed out the eunuch between the finger grips of the old soldier. "I care not for the Janizary, though you were the Aga[32] himself, instead of a mutilated slave."

The eunuch had drawn his dagger, and was working his hand into a position whence he could strike, when old Selim's hand grasped his.

"None of that treachery, or we will let out of your leprous skin what manhood is left in you, you blotch on your race! Touch one hair of Black

Khalil's[33] children and you die like the dog you are. Let him go, Mustapha! His coward throat is no place for you to soil a brave hand. We will get a snake to strangle him; a buzzard to pick his grain of a soul out of his vile carcass;[34] an ass to kick him to death. We must observe the proprieties."

"Pardon my heat!" said the eunuch. "My zeal for my prince has led me too far."

"Not at all!" said Selim. "It is pleasant to see that you have some heat in your cold blooded toad nature."

"It is better for us to retire," said the eunuch to Mahomet. "I shall sound the signal for the close of the games."

Mahomet stood stubbornly for awhile; then turning to Michael said in a tone which was strangely without a shade of anger or petulance in it:

"Say, young Giaour, you and I must have this out some day."

Michael could not help a half-smiling recognition of the boyish challenge, and replied:

"I have seen more foxes than you have, and know some tricks I didn't show you to-day."

As they moved out of the park, Yusef delivered a brief lecture to his princely pupil. "Hark thee, my master. I warn thee, that thou have an eye always open and a hand always closed to the Janizaries. They have grown from being the heel to think that they are the head of the state. They dictate to thy father, the Padishah, and snub the very Vizier. I would have killed both those old imbeciles, but that it would not have been politic. I am glad, too, that thou didst not let thy dagger find the heart of the Balkan boy. That would not have been politic. For, Allah grant! thou mayest one day be Padishah. Then this day would be remembered against us."

"But, Yusef, I did not spare the boy. I think he spared me; and if I ever get to be Padishah, I will make him my vizier, for his cleverness. It would be a pity that so brave a man were elsewhere than at my right hand. Though he angered me awfully at the moment, I shall like that fellow. Did you see how he gripped the fox with his bare arms? He must teach me how to do that. Was it between the hind legs he thrust his hand, or across the beast's body? I could not see for my being so mad because he spoiled for me a fine running shot."

"Thou art a strange child, Mahomet. Thou seemest to have forgotten that the boy leaped at thy throat, and would have torn out thine eyes, but that thou wast more valiant than he."

"Well, I should despise him as white-livered and milk-galled if he had not sprung at me," said Mahomet. "Has not every noble fellow quick blood, as well as a prince, Yusef? That boy shall be mine. He shall teach me his tricks, and I shall give him all my sweetmeats; for they get none of such things in the school."

"Ah! my little prince, thy head is as full of wit as a fig is of seeds. Thou art gifted to know and use men. One that is born to rule must make his passion bend to policy. He must not allow himself the pleasure of hating those whom he can use. But take heed of this:—whom he cannot use he must not love."

"But I was not born to rule, Yusef. If so, I would have been born earlier, before my brother Aladdin cried in his nurse's arms, and would not be comforted until they had covered the soft spot on his bare head with a paper crown. Do you believe in omens, Yusef?"

"Not in such; only in dreams," said the eunuch.

"Well; I dreamed that our two heads—yours and mine, Yusef—were together on a pike-staff, grinning at Aladdin's coronation."

"Nonsense, child!" said the eunuch, his white face bleaching a shade whiter under the thought, as they passed through the gateway into the seraglio grounds.

CHAPTER XI

The physical training of the young Janizaries consisted in such daily exercises as would develop strength and tirelessness of muscle, steadiness of nerve, keenness and accuracy of eye, as well as grace of mien. They were also taught by expert workmen all the arts of daily need; to make as well as to use the bow; to trim and balance the arrow; to forge, temper, and sharpen the sword; to shoe the horse; to make and mend their clothing and the entire trappings of their steeds; to build and manage the keelless kaiks[35] which darted like fishes through the surface of the river; to bind rafts into pontoons for the crossing of streams; to reap and grind the grain, and cook their food. Any special talent or adaptability was noted by the instructors, and the Janizaries encouraged to attain to rare expertness in single arts.

The training in arms was especially severe, and under masters in fencing, archery, riding, swimming, marching, deploying—the ablest tacticians, whose wounds or age permitted their absence from active campaigns, being found always at the head of the various departments. The Janizary, while a mere lad in years, was often more than a match in single combat for the most stalwart men in other corps, such as the Piadé and Azabs among footmen, the Ouloufedji and Akindji among troopers.

But, notwithstanding this individual prowess and ambition were stimulated to the highest degree, they were disciplined to abject obedience within the corps. Each one was as a part of some intricate mechanism, all moved by one spring, which was the will of the chief Aga. At a moment's notice they must start, in companies or alone; on military expeditions, or secret service as spies and scouts; it might be to the recesses of Asia or the upper Danube; to assail forts or to conduct intrigues; having always but one incentive, that of the common service and the common glory.

To develop in the same person these two seemingly antagonistic qualities—of intensest individuality and abject subserviency to their order—required the shrewdest manipulation of the mind and will of the cadet from his earliest enrollment in childhood. As certain expert horse-trainers control the spirit of noble steeds, without extinguishing any of their fiery ardor, and tell the secret of their power to those who come after them in the guild, so from the days of Black Khalil this marvellous system of discipline had been perpetuated among the corps, producing but rarely a weakling and as rarely a rebel.

Michael learned his first lesson in subordination upon the return from the hunt. While the Janizary officers were not displeased with the prowess the little fellow had shown, even against the prince, it was foreseen that such an impetuous nature needed the curb. For three days he was confined to a room in solitude and silence. No one spoke or listened to him. His only attendant was an old man, both deaf and dumb, who evidently knew nothing and cared nothing for Michael's offence or its punishment.

During this time the lad's suspense was terrible. Was he to be killed for having assaulted the prince? Would they take him to the torture? Perhaps this old man had been guilty of some such offence, and they had cut his tongue and bored out his ears! He had heard of the searing iron passed before the eyes, and then the life-long darkness. When he slept his overwrought imagination fabricated horrid dreams in which he was the victim of every species of cruelty. He fancied that he was being eaten by a kennel of foxes, to whom he is given every day until their hunger shall be satisfied; then taken away and reserved for their next meal. He tried to compute how many days he would last. Sometimes he imagined that he was exposed naked in the cold, and made to stand day and night on the ice of the Marissa, until he should be frozen: but his heart is so hot with his rebel spirit that it will not freeze. Once he thought that Prince Mahomet came each day and stabbed him with that pearl-set dagger he drew on him at the hunt.

His dreams were too frightful to allow him to sleep long at a time; yet, when awake, his fears were such that he longed to get back again among the terrible creatures of his fancy. Oh, that some one would speak to him, and tell him his fate! He would welcome the worst torture, if only he could be allowed to talk to the torturer.

After a while rage took the place of, or at least began to alternate with, fear. He regretted that he had not killed the impudent prince.

"There stands his horse," he would say to himself—marking a line on the wall—"now I leap; seize his dagger; strike him to the heart; and, before they can stop me, plunge it into my own heart, so! Ah! when I am out of this place I will kill him! I will! and go down to hell with him!" And the little frame would swell, and the eyes gleam with demoniacal light through the dusky chamber.

There are deep places even in a child's soul—ay, bottomless depths—which, when unfretted by temptation, are so tranquil and clear that the kindliness and joy of heaven are reflected in them, warranting the saying of the old Jewish Rabbis, "Every child is a prophet of the pure and loving God." But when disturbed by a sense of wrong and injury, these depths in a child's heart may rage as a caldron hot with the fires of hell; as a geyser pouring out the wrath and hatred which we conceive to be born only in the nether world.

After a time Michael's fury died away. Another feeling took its place—the crushing sense of his impotence. His will seemed to be broken by the violence of its own spasm. He was stunned by his realization of weakness. He fell with his face to the cold stones of the floor, moaning at first, but soon passing into a waking stupor in which only consciousness remained: hopeless, purposeless, without energy to strive, and without strength to cry—a perfectly passive spirit. The centipede that crawled from the dusty crevice of the walls, and raised half his body to look at the strange figure lying there, might have commanded him. The spider might have captured him, and spun about his soul a web of destiny, if only he could have conveyed a thought of it from his tiny eyes. For, as the body faints, so also does the spirit under the pressure of woe.

The old mute brought in the meal on the third day, placed it beside him, and retired. An hour later he returned and found the bread untasted; the child in the same attitude, but not asleep. He touched him with his foot, but evoked no sign that his presence was recognized. He gazed for a few moments; then shook his head like an artisan who, upon inspecting some piece of work he has been making, is not satisfied with it.

He summoned Selim. The old soldier, finding that his entrance did not arouse the lad, crossed his legs upon the floor beside him, and waited. The light from the high window of the room fell upon Selim's wrinkled face. But it seemed as if another light, one from within, blended with it. His harsh features were permeated by a glow and softness, as he gazed upon the exhausted child. His eyes filled with tears; but they were speedily dried by the stare with which he turned and looked first at the blank walls, and then, following back the ray of light, to the window and beyond; his soul transported far away over lands, through years, to a cottage on the banks of the Grau. He saw there a face so beautiful! was it really of one he once called "Mother?" or a dim and hazy recollection of a painting of the Christian Madonna he had seen in his childhood? Happy groups of village children were playing down among the lilies by the water's edge, and over the hills gently sloping back from the river's bank. Their faces were as clear cut there against the blue sky beyond the window, as once—sixty years ago—they were against the green grass of the meadow. He heard again the sweet ring of the chapel bell echoing back from the ragged rocks of the opposite shore. And now the midnight alarm! A fight with strange looking turbaned men! Flames bursting from the houses of the hamlet! Men shrieking with wounds, and women struggling in the arms of captors! And a little child, ah, so lonely and tired with a long march! and that child—himself!—His eyes rested as fondly upon Michael as did ever a father's upon his boy.

But as the wind extinguishes a candle, a movement of Michael sent all the gleams gathered out of former days from old Selim's features. Severity, almost savageness, took the place of kindliness among the wrinkles of his countenance, as naturally as the waters of a rivulet, held back for a moment by a child's hand, fill again their channels.

The boy raised his head. His face was pale; the eyes sunken; their natural brilliance deepened, but as that of the flashing waters is deepened when it is frozen into the glistening icicle. Or shall we say that the dancing flames of the child's eyes had become the steady glow of embered coals;—their life gone out, but the hot core left there, not to cheer, only to burn. Those three days of silence, with their successive dramas of mystery, terror, rage and depression, had wrought more changes in him than many years of merely external discipline would have done.

The close searching glance of Selim detected all this; and also that the child was in a critical condition. The will was broken, but it was not certain that this had not been accomplished by the breaking of the entire spirit; instead of curbing, destroying it: not taming the tiger's daring, but converting it into the sluggishness and timidity of the cat.

"Michael!" cried he.

There was no response except the slight inclination of the head indicating that the word had been heard.

"Follow me!" The lad rose mechanically, showing no interest or attention beyond that required for bodily obedience.

Pausing at the door-way the old man put his hand upon the boy's shoulder and said sternly, yet with a caution ready to change his tone—

"Do you know that we have power to more severely punish you?"

The words made no impression upon the child.

"The bastinado? The cage?" The boy raised his face, but upon it was no evidence of fear; perhaps of scorn. He had suffered so much that threats had no power over him.

Selim was alarmed at these symptoms. His experience with such cases taught him that this lethargic spell must be broken at whatever cost. Feeling must be excited; and if an appeal to the child's imagination failed, physical pain must be inflicted. Something must rouse him, or insanity might ensue.

A peculiar instrument of torture was a frame set with needles pointing inwards. Into this sometimes a culprit was placed, and the frame screwed so close about the person that he could not move from a fixed position without forcing the needles into his flesh. This frame was put about the boy. He stared stupidly at the approaching points, but did not shrink. Selim pressed one of the needles quickly. Instantly the boy uttered a cry of pain. His face blanched with fright. The tears sprang to his eyes, and through them came an agonizing look of entreaty.

Selim's whole manner changed as suddenly. Schooled as he was to harshness; to strike one's head from his shoulders at the command of the Aga without an instant's hesitation; to superintend the slow process of a "discipline" by torture, without a remorseful thought;—yet this was not his nature. And now that better, deeper, truer nature, hitherto unexercised for years, asserted itself. His heart went out to Michael the instant there was no further necessity for its restraint.

"Bravo! my little hero," cried he, catching him to his arms. "You are of the metal of the invincibles, and henceforth only valiant deeds, bright honors and endless pleasures are to be yours. You shall lodge with me tonight."

CHAPTER XII

Selim's apartment was off from the common barracks of the Janizaries. It was luxuriantly furnished in its way. Elegant rugs lay upon the marble floor. A divan, with silken covering, filled one end of the room. The walls were hung with a variety of richly wrought weapons and armor:—short swords, long crescent-shaped cimeters, spears of polished wood headed with glistening steel, helmets, breastplates, greaves. Badges and honorary decorations shone among costly robes which had accumulated since the days when he had been a page to the Sultan Amurath I.

Upon a low table, reaching to the edge of the divan, had been placed salvers holding cups and open dishes of silver. A woinak entered with basins of scented water in which to wash the hands and bathe the face.

Selim placed his little guest by his side upon the divan. Mustapha also appeared, and, removing his shoes, made a profound and dignified salâm—quite in contrast with his usual rough and badgering manner when with Selim—then placed himself beside his comrade upon the cushions. An excellent repast was served. There was hare's flesh chopped and rolled with rice into balls, made more savory with curry sauce. Sweet cakes, pastry of figs and candied orange blossoms excited a thirst for the sweetened water, which was so strongly flavored with the juices of fruits that the more scrupulous Moslems refused to drink it, lest they should disobey the command of the Koran prohibiting the use of wine.

The two old men vied with each other in telling thrilling stories of adventure in battle and on secret service; of the romance of castles and courts; of how they won their honors and got their scars; of the favors of princes and princesses; and of exploits in which, though the rules of their order forbade their marrying, they retaliated the captivity of the maiden's eye by capturing her person. The burden of every story was the praise of the Janizary organization, which alone enabled them to attain such glories and joys. The close brotherhood, which gave to each the help of all the ten thousand, was commended by incidents illustrating it. They told of their Aga or chief, who was more powerful than the Grand Vizier—for sultans made these latter by a word, and unmade them with equal caprice, often with the stroke of the sword; but to touch a hair of the Aga would be for the Sultan to lose the favor of the entire band, whom he regarded as the main support of his throne, as their hands had won it for his fathers. Did not the word of Mustapha and Selim, at the fox-hunt, cow the pride of Yusef, who was next to the Capee Aga or chief of the white eunuchs? Yet

Selim and Mustapha were but captains in the Janizaries. No general in any other arm of the service would have dared to antagonize the eunuch as they did.

As Michael listened, his cheeks flushed and chilled by turns with the excitement of his martial ambition. The dreams he used to have in his mountain home, of being a soldier and coming back covered with badges of honor to claim Morsinia as his bride, seemed to be dissolving into the reality. Nor was his ardor damped when he learned from Selim that the first step toward all this was the total surrender of himself to the service of the brotherhood, in pledging and keeping obedience to its rules; as a part of the body, like the hand, must never be severed from the rest, but keep the contact perfect in every muscle and nerve, in order to have the strength which only the health of the whole body can give to it. Selim explained to him how wrong it had been for him to seize the fox, no matter how excited he was, or how much daring it showed to do so, since he had not been ordered to seize, but only to turn the beast toward the Prince. Besides, to raise a hand against the prince was treason—unless it were ordered by the chief of the Janizaries. Therefore he had been punished according to the Janizary discipline; though they would not have allowed any one else to touch him—no not even the Padishah himself.

Michael's spirit was fully healed with such words. His depression gave way to a hotter ambition and pride of expectation than he had ever felt before, when Selim put upon his head the whitish gray cap, like that worn by the dervishes, and differing from it only in having upon the back a strip of wool which the old man thus explained, as he told the story of the organization of the Janizary corps.

"The death angel, Azrael, has reaped the earth more than five times since the mighty Othman,[36] who founded our empire, entered paradise. His queen, Malkhatoon, the most beautiful of women, had given him two sons. Never since Khalif Omar followed the Prophet was nobler successor than would have been either Alaeddin or Orchan to Othman. The stars shone not with deeper lustre than did the wisdom of Alaeddin. The storm never burst more resistlessly on your Balkan mountains than did the bravery and strength of Orchan beat down the foe. To Orchan the empire came by will of Allah and Othman. But to Alaeddin the new king said, 'Thou art wise, my brother, above all men. Be thou the eyes of the throne, and I will be its arm!' So Alaeddin was the great minister of the mighty Orchan. To Prince Alaeddin we owe our best laws, our system of drilling and marching in all the Ottoman armies.

"But two lights are better known than one. And in a dream the Angel Gabriel, who knows the secrets of Allah regarding men, said to Alaeddin,

'Go look into the eyes of Kara Khalil Tschendereli. We have given him a thought for thee and thy people.' And Kara Khalil said, 'Know, O wise and virtuous Prince Alaeddin, I have been permitted in my dreams to stand upon the wall Al Araf, that runs between paradise and hell. In the third story of the seven which divide perdition I saw the ghosts of the Giaours. But while I watched their torments the spirit of Othman, the Blessed, came to me, and, pointing to a gate in the wall, said, in a voice so sweet that all the birds in paradise echoed it, but so strong that it shook the mighty wall Al Araf as if it would fall, "I charge thee, as thou art a true believer in Mahomet, open that gate that some of the believers in Jesu, Son of Mary, may escape into paradise."

"'"What power have I for such a miracle, O Othman," I cried. But Othman said:

"'"Thou shalt save the souls of the boys among the captives Allah gives thee in battle. Is it not written in the Koran that all the children are at their birth gifted with the true faith. Believe this, and teach the captive boys to trust the Prophet, to breathe the holy Islam of Father Abraham, and to draw the sword for Allah. So shalt thou be a saviour of many souls. And such valor will Allah send these rescued ones, and such blessings shall follow them, that the Giaour children shall conquer for thee the Giaour nations."'

"And so, Michael," added Selim, "the wisdom of earth and heaven appointed our order. We are still the Yeni Tscheri,[37] though a century has gone by since we were founded; for the vigor of perpetual youth is ours.

"When Orchan, at such advice of Alaeddin and Kara Khalil enrolled the first of the new troop—bright Christian boys like yourself, Michael—they were led to the old dervish, Hadji Beytarch, whose sanctity was as the fragrance of paradise itself. The face of the holy man caught the lustre of the prophecy from heaven. As he drew the sleeve of his mantle over each bowed head—and the strip of wool on our cap is the sign of his sleeve—he uttered this benediction: 'Thy face shall be white and shining; thy right arm shall be strong; thy sabre shall be keen; and thine arrows sharp. Thou shalt be fortunate in fight, and thou shalt never leave the battle-field save as a conqueror.'"

"And have they never been conquered?" asked Michael with incredulity.

"Never!" cried Selim.

"Except," added Mustapha, "that they might prepare themselves for some greater victory. Allah sometimes makes known to us his will that we should retreat; then we take up our kismet as joyfully as we would shout the advance. That we may make sure of Allah's will, before retreating we always assault the enemy thrice. If at that sacred number we cannot conquer we know that the victory has been reserved, still held for us, but in the closed hand of Fate."

"But what of those who were killed? I certainly saw many Janizaries lying dead in the snows of the Balkans the day of the fight. Are they not conquered?" asked the boy.

"Nay, more than conquerors," said Mustapha. "If one falls in battle paradise flings wide its gates, and troops of angels and houris come to lead his soul in a triumphal procession into that beautiful land where the earth is like purest musk, and where the great Tuba tree grows—a branch of which shades the kiosk of every believer, and bends down to place its luscious fruit into his hand, if he so much as desires it; where are grapes and pomegranates, and such as for spicy sweetness have never been tasted on earth; where are streams of water and milk and wine and honey, whose bottoms are pebbled with pearls and emeralds and rubies; where the houris, the fairest of maidens, dwell close beside the believer in pavilions of hollow pearls, and serve every wish of the faithful even before he can utter it."[38]

But Michael's eyes were heavy; and as the old veterans diverted the conversation to some matter of business between them, his excited imagination reproduced the description of paradise in his dreams. Only, the pavilion of pearl was shaped like good Uncle Kabilovitsch's cot on the mountains, and the houris were all fair-haired Morsinias.

CHAPTER XIII

Weeks and months passed away, during which the physical exercises of the lads in the Janizary school were varied with lessons in the Turkish language; and, in the case of a select number, in the Arabic, mastering it at least sufficiently to read the Koran, large sections of which they were compelled to commit to memory.

The teachers in the Janizary schools were far from ordinary men. They were highly learned, and, like most Orientals of education, gifted with great eloquence. After the daily tasks had been accomplished the boys were gathered in a semicircle upon the floor about the instructor, who sat cross-legged among them, and narrated in glowing language the history of the Prophet and his successors in the khalifate; inflaming their young minds with the most heroic and romantic legends of Arabia and Egypt, Algiers and Granada, where the Koran had conquered the faith of the people whom the swords of the true Moslems had subdued. Wild stories of the early days of the Turks, before Ertoghral,[39] "The Right-hearted Man," led the tribes from the banks of the Euphrates; and earlier still when Seljuk[40] led his people from north of the Caspian; of the settlement of their remote ancestors in Afghanistan, where the great chief was first called Sultan;[41] of how they had once held the religious faith of Zoroaster. Indeed, myths from the very dawn of known history, when the Turkius did all sorts of valiant deeds in far-off China.[42]

The Christian books were made to appear to the young proselyte as but imperfect suggestions of the completed teaching of the book of Mahomet; while the peculiar dogmas of the Christians were restated with such shrewd perversion that to the child's judgment they seemed puerile or untrue.

"Behold the sky!" one would exclaim. "Is it not one dome, like the canopy of one mighty throne? Behold the light! Does it not pour from one sun and fill all space with one flood? Breathe the air! Is it not the same over all lands and in all lungs? Do not all birds fly with one mechanism of wings? and all men live by the same beating of the heart? How then can there be three Gods, Allah, and Jesu and Mary, as the Christians teach?[43] What does reason say? What does the universe testify? What says the true and wise believer?"

"There is one God and Mahomet is His Prophet," would be the response of the pupils, bowing their heads to the floor.

"Can the less contain or give out the greater? Can a stone bring forth the orange tree? Can a stick give birth to the eagle? A worm be the father of a man? How, then, can we say with the Christians, that Mary of Bethlehem is the mother of God? What says the faithful and wise believer?"

"There is one God, and Mahomet is His prophet," would be the choral response.

"Is God weak? Can men thwart His plans? Shall we then believe that the infidel Jews crucified the Son of God?"

"God is great, and Mahomet is His Prophet," would roll up from the lips of the scholars.

"Shall we, then, kiss the toe of the pope because he calls himself the grand vizier of Allah, when our Janizaries can cut the throats of his soldiers, as our brethren of Arabia destroyed the crusaders? Or shall we kiss the hand of the patriarch of the Greeks, who claims supremacy in the name of Allah, when already our arms have shut up the whole Greek empire within the walls of Constantinople? What says the faithful and wise believer?"

"God is great, and Mahomet is His Prophet," is the reply.

"Who would cringe and beg forgiveness at the feet of a dirty priest, when the sword of every Janizary may open for him who holds it the gate of paradise?"

Not only such arguments, but every event of the day that could emphasize or illustrate the superiority of the Moslem faith, was skilfully brought to bear upon the susceptible minds of the youths. And within the first year of Michael's cadetship one such significant event occurred.

In the year of the Hegira 822,[44] six months after the flight of Scanderbeg, it was solemnly agreed between Christian and Moslem that the sword should have rest for ten years. A stately ceremony was made to seal the compact. Vladislaus of Hungary represented in his person the pledge of kingly honor. Hunyades gave the sanction of a soldier's word. And Cardinal Julian was supposed to have added to the treaty the confirmation of all that was sacred in the religion of which he was so exalted a representative. On behalf of the Christians, the concord was signalized by an oath upon the Gospels. On the other side, Sultan Amurath, in the presence of his generals and the holiest of the Moslem dervishes, swore upon the Koran. This compact, guarded by all that men hold to be honorable on earth and sacred in heaven, lulled the suspicions of the Turks. The rigid drill, the alert espionage, the raids along the border gave way to the indolence of the barracks and the pastimes of the camp. Thousands of horses and their riders were returned to till the fields in the Timars, Ziamets and Beyliks[45] scattered throughout distant provinces. The Sultan retired to meditate religion, or devise the things belonging to permanent peace, in his secluded palace at Magnesia in Asia Minor. The death of his eldest son, Prince Aladdin, led him to put the crown of associate Padishah upon the brow of the young Mahomet that in these quiet times the prince might learn the minor lessons of the art of ruling.

But this sense of security among the Turks offered too strong a temptation to the cupidity of the Christian leaders. King Vladislaus opposed conscientious objections to any breach of the compact. Hunyades maintained his personal honor by at first refusing to draw his sword. But Cardinal Julian stood sponsor to a breach of faith, and announced that principle which has, in the estimate of history, made his scarlet robe the symbol of his scarlet sin—that no faith need be kept with infidels; and, in the name of the Holy Father, granted absolution to the chief actors for what they were about to do.

Without warning, the tide of Christian conquest poured from Servia eastward until it was checked in that direction by the Black Sea. The hordes of Europe then turned southward, seized upon Varna, and pitched their camps amid the pennants of their ill-gotten victory near to its walls. To human sight no power could avert irrevocable disaster to the arms, if not the subversion of the entire empire of the Ottomans in Europe.

In their extremity the lands of the Moslem made their solemn appeal to Allah. Every mosque resounded with reiterated prayers. The camps echoed the pious invocations with loud curses and the rattle of the preparation of armor. Scurrying messengers flew from the centre to the circumference of the Ottoman domain, and hastily gathered legions concentrated for one supreme blow in retaliation for the grossness of the insult, and in vindication of what they believed to be the cause of honor and truth, which, in their minds, was one with that of Allah and the Prophet.

The Sultan hurried from his retreat, and with marvellous celerity marshalled the faithful against the invaders at Varna. Riding at the head of the Janizaries, he caused the document of the violated treaty to be held aloft on a lance-head in the gaze of the two armies, and with a loud voice uttered this prayer—a strange one for a Moslem's lips—"O, Thou insulted Jesu, revenge the wrong done unto Thy good name, and show Thy power upon Thy perjured people!"

Victory hovered long between the contending hosts, but at last rested with the Moslems. To make the intervention of Allah more apparent, it was told everywhere, how, when Amurath believed that he was defeated, and had given the order for retreat, a soldier seized the bridle of the Sultan's horse and turned him back again toward the enemy. The very beast felt the inspiration of heaven, and led the assault upon the breaking columns of the Christians, until the victors returned, bearing upon spear-points the heads of Cardinal Julian and King Vladislaus; while Hunyades fled in disgrace from the field.

It is not to be wondered at that such an event, which led many whole communities to renounce their alliance with the Christian powers, and many of the chiefs of Bosnia and Servia to accept the Moslem faith, should have rooted that faith more deeply in the hearts of those who already held it. A flame of fanaticism ran throughout the Mohammedan world. The most rabid sects increased in the number and fury of their devotees. Many who were engaged in useful occupations left them to became Moslem monks, spending their lives in meditation, if perchance they might receive more fully the blessings which heaven seemed ready to pour upon every true believer; or to become preachers of the jehad—the holy war against the infidels.

In the schools of the Janizaries the fanaticism was fed and fanned to a flame of utmost intensity. The square court within their barracks was transformed into a great prayer place of the dervishes. Here the Howlers formed their circles, and swaying backward and forward with flying hair and glaring eyes, grunted their talismanic words from the Koran, until they fell in convulsions on the pavement. And the Wheelers spun round and round in their mystic motions until, full of the spirit they sought, they dropped in the dizzying dance. Learned sheiks preached the gospel of the sword, and the imams watered the seed thus sown with fervent prayers, until the ardent souls of the youth seemed to have lost their human identity, and to be transformed into sparks and flashes of some celestial fire which was to destroy the lands of the Christians.

Michael's mind was not altogether unimpressed by the religious fanaticism that raged around him. While in quiet moments he was troubled with what he heard against the Christian faith which he had been taught in his mountain home, at other times he was caught in the tide of the general enthusiasm and felt himself borne along with it, swirled around in the rings of the mad maelstrom; not unwilling to yield himself to the excitement, and yet by no definite purpose committing himself to it. If it requires all the strength of an adult mind, with convictions long held and character well formed, to maintain its faith and principles against the attrition of daily temptation in a Christian land, we must not be surprised if the child gave way to the incessant appeal of the Moslem belief, accompanied as it was by extravagant promises of secular pleasure, and counteracted by no word of Christian counsel. But the spiritual impulse in Michael was less active than the martial instinct; and this latter was stimulated to the utmost by the associations of every day and hour. The battles which were fought on the great fields were all refought in the vivid descriptions of the Janizary teachers, and sometimes in the mimic rencounters of the playground. Michael rebelled against his childish years which prevented his joining some of the great expeditions that were fitted out;—against the Greeks of the Peloponnesus, the Giaour lands to the north, and the Albanians on the west, who, under Scanderbeg, had become the chief menace against the Ottoman power.

CHAPTER XIV

The career of Scanderbeg, or Castriot, as the Albanians love to call their great national hero, makes one of the most illustrious pages in history, whether we look for the display of personal courage, astute generalship, or loftiest patriotism. His military renown, already so wide-spread as the commander of the Turks, became universal through the almost incredible skill with which, for many years, his handful of patriots held the mountains of Albania against the countless armies of the Sultan. His superlative devotion to his country, was maintained with such sacrifices as few men have ever rendered to the holiest cause. He resisted the bribes of riches, power and splendor with which the Sultan, baffled by his arms, attempted to seduce his honor. These things went far to atone for the treachery of his defection from the Turkish service.

Upon his arrival in Albania, the citadel of Croia was given into his hands by the commandant, who was either unsuspicious of the false order that was sealed by the now dead hand of the Sultan's secretary, or who had found that the wily Albanians had already access to its gates. Sfetigrade and other prominent fortresses fell rapidly, won by strategy or by the valorous assault of the patriots. The Albanians had been almost instantaneously transformed into an invincible army by the electric thrill which the coming of Castriot had sent everywhere, from the borders of Macedonia to the western sea; and by the skill with which that great captain organized his bands of Epirots and Dibrians. An army of forty thousand Turks was at one time divided by his masterly movements, and slain in detail. A second army met a similar fate. The great Sultan himself attempted the capture of this Arnaout "wild beast," as he had learned to call him. One hundred and fifty thousand men, supplied from the far-reaches of Asia where the Ottoman made most of his levies, swarmed like a plague of locusts through the valleys of Epirus. By sheer momentum of numbers they pressed their way up to the fortress of Sfetigrade.

The defence of this place is one of the most heroic in the annals of war or patriotism. As the glacier melts at the touch of the warm earth in the Alpine valleys so the mighty army of Amurath dissolved in blood as it touched the beleaguered walls. At the same time Scanderbeg, adopting some new expedient in every attack, made his almost nightly raids through the centre of the Turkish host, like a panther through the folds of the sheep, until Amurath cried in sheer vexation among the generals, "Will none of you save us from the fury of that wild beast?" The incessant slaughter that broke the bewildered silence of the generals was the only response.

Thus passed some six years since the time when our story opens; years which, had they stood by themselves, and not been followed by fifteen years more of equal prowess, would have won for Scanderbeg the unstinted praise of that distinguished writer who enrolls him among the seven greatest uncrowned men of the world's history.[46]

During these years Castriot had studied with closest scrutiny the character of his nephew, Amesa. His natural discernment, aided by his long observation of human duplicity while among the Turks—and, indeed by his own experience, as for many years he had masked his own discontent and ultimate purpose—gave him a power of estimating men which may be called a moral clairvoyance. He discovered that in his nephew which led him to credit the story of Kabilovitsch—as the forester Arnaud was still called, although some more than suspected his identity. The chief saw clearly that Amesa's loyalty would be limited by his selfish interests. Those interests now led him to most faithful and apparently patriotic devotion. Besides, the loss or alienation of so influential a young voivode, involving a schism in the house of the Castriots, might be fatal to the Albanian cause. The general, therefore, fed the ambition of his relative, giving him honorable command, for which he was well fitted by reason of both courage and genius. Nor did Amesa disappoint this confidence. His sword was among the sharpest and his deeds most daring. The peasant soldiers often said that Amesa was not unworthy the blood of the Castriots. To Sultan Amurath's proposal of peace on condition of Scanderbeg's simple recognition of the Ottoman's nominal suzerainty, allowing him to retain the full actual possession of all his ancestral holdings, Amesa's voice joined with that of Moses Goleme and the other allied nobles in commending the refusal of their chief.

Amesa's courage and zeal seemed at times to pass the control of his judgment. Thus, in a sharp battle with the Turks, during the temporary absence of Castriot, who was resisting an encroachment of the Venetians on the neighboring country of Montenegro, the fiery young voivode was seized with such blind ferocity that he knew not where he was. He had engaged a group of his own countrymen, apparently not discerning his mistake until he had unhorsed one of them, whom he was on the point of sabering, when his arm was caught by a comrade. The endangered man was Kabilovitsch, who saw that there was a method in Amesa's madness which it behoved him to note.

It was evident to Kabilovitsch not only that he was recognized by Amesa, but also that the young voivode was more than suspicious of the former forester's knowledge of the affair by which the magnificent estate of De Streeses had passed into his hands. The good man's solicitude was intense through fear that Amesa had become aware of the escape of the child heir, and might discover some clue to her whereabouts. Several times Milosch had visited the camp inquiring for Kabilovitsch; and Constantine had made frequent journeys carrying tidings of Morsinia's welfare. Had neither of these been spied upon? Did no one ever pass the little hamlet where she was in covert who recognized in the now daily developing womanly features the likeness of her mother, Mara De Streeses?

A little after this assault of Amesa upon Kabilovitsch, came news which startled the latter. To understand this the reader must penetrate a wild mountainous district a double score of miles from the camp of Castriot.

CHAPTER XV

Out of a broad valley, through which lies the chief highway leading to the north-west of Albania, there opens a narrow ravine which seems to end abruptly against the precipitous front of a mountain range. But, turning into this ravine, one is surprised to find that it winds sharply, following a swift stream, and climbing for many miles through the mountain, until it suddenly debouches into a picturesque valley, which affords grazing space for sheep and enough arable land to sustain the peasants who once dwelt there.

A hamlet nestled in this secluded vale. No road led beyond it, and it was approached only by the narrow and tortuous path we have described. A rude mill sentineled a line of three houses. These dwellings, though simple in their construction, were quite commodious. A room of ample dimensions was enclosed with walls of stone and loam, supporting a conical roof of thatch. On three sides of this room and opening into it were smaller chambers, having detached roofs of their own. The central apartment was the common gathering place for quite an extensive community, consisting of a family in three or four generations; for each son upon marrying brought his wife to the paternal homestead, and built a new chamber connecting with the central one. The three houses contained altogether nearly a hundred souls. The last of these dwellings was of ampler proportions than the others, and was occupied by a branch of an ancient family to which the inhabitants of the other houses were all of kin. By reason of its antiquity as well as the comparative wealth of its occupants, it was regarded as the konak, or village mansion; and the senior member of its little community was recognized as the stargeshina, or chief of the village.

It was the latter part of April; the day before that upon which from time immemorial the peasants among these mountains had observed the festival of Saint George, which they devoted to ceremonies commemorative of the awakening summer life of the world.

It was still early in the afternoon, though the high mountain wall on the west had shut out the sun, whose bright rays, however, still burning far overhead, dropped their benediction of roseate shadows into the valley they were not permitted to enter; loading the atmosphere with as many tints as there were in Buddha's bowl when the poor man threw in the bud of genuine charity, and it burst into a thousand flowers.

A group of maidens gathered at the little mill, each holding an earthen bowl to catch the glistening spray drops which danced from the edge of the clumsy water-wheel. When these were filled they cast into the "witching waters" the early spring flowers, anemones and violets and white coral arbutus, which they had picked during the day. It was a pleasing superstition that the water, having been beaten into spray, received life from the flowers which the renewed vitality of the awakening spring spirit had pressed up through the earth; and that, if one should bathe in this on St. George's day, health and happiness would attend him during the year.

"What is it?" cried one as a crackling in the bushes far above their heads on a steep crag was followed in a moment by the beat of a pebble, as it glanced from ledge to ledge almost to their feet.

"The sheep are not up there!" said another.

"Perhaps the Vili!"[47] suggested a third, "for I am sure that I have seen one this very day."

"What was he like?" exclaimed several at once, while all kept their eyes upon the cliff above.

"There! there! Did you see it?" Several avowed that they saw it stealing along the very brow of the hill; but all agreed that it passed so swiftly that they could not tell just what they saw.

"It was just so with the one I saw to-day," said the former speaker. "I was on the ledge by the old eagle's nest, gathering my flowers. A tall being passed below me on the path, dressed so beautifully that I know it was none of us, and had dealings with none of us. It seemed anxious not to be seen; for my little cry of surprise caused it to vanish as if it melted into the foam of the stream as it plunges into the pool."

"That was just like the Vili," interposed one. "They live under the river's bank. They talk in the murmur of the streams. Old Mirko, who used to work much in the mill, learned to understand what they said. Did this one you saw have long hair? The Vili, Mirko said, always did."

"I cannot say," replied the girl, "for its head was hidden in a blossoming laurel bush between it and me."

"It was one," cried another, "for there are no blossoming laurels yet. It was its long white hair waving in the wind, that you saw."

"Let us go down to the pool!" proposed one, "maybe we can see it again."

"No! No!" cried the others, in a chorus of tremulous voices.

"No, indeed," said one of the larger girls, "for it might be they are eating, or they are dancing the Kolo—which they always do as the sun goes down, and if any body sees them then they get angry, and will come to your house and look at you with the evil eye."

Hasting home with their bowls of water crowned with flowers, they told their story to the stargeshina.

The old man laughed at their credulity:—

"Girls always see strange things on the eve of Saint George."

At the evening meal in the great room of the first house, the patriarch, taking his cue from the story the girls belonging to that household had told of their imagined vision, repeated legend after legend about those strange beings that people the unknown caverns in the mountains, and rise from the brooks, leaving the water-spiders to mark the spot where they emerged so that they may find their way back again, and of the wjeshtiges, who throw off their bodies as easily as others lay aside their clothes, flit through the fire, ride upon the sparks as horses, float on the threads of white smoke—all the time watching the persons gathered about the blazing logs, that they may mark the one who is first to die. "This doomed person," the old man said, "they visit when he has gone to sleep, and, with a magic rod, open his breast; utter in mystic words the day of his death; take out his heart and feast upon it. Then they carefully close up the side, and, though the victim lives on, having no heart, no spring of life in him, sickens and droops until the fatal day; as the streams vanish when cut off from the fountains whence they start."

These stories were followed by songs, the music of which was within a narrow range of notes, and sung to the accompaniment of the gusle—a rude sort of guitar with a single string. The subjects of these songs and the ideas they contained were as limited in their range as the notes by which they were rendered; such as the impossible exploits of heroes, and improbable romances of love. The merit of the singing generally consisted in the additions or variations with which the genius of the performer enabled him to adorn the hackneyed music or original narrative.

"Let Constantine take the gusle, and sing us the song about the peasant maid who conquered the heart of the king," said the stargeshina.

"Constantine is not here," replied a clear and sweet, but commanding sort of voice. "He went out as it began to darken, and has not returned."

The speaker rose as she said it, and went toward the large door of the room to look out. She was a young woman of slender, but superb form, which the costume of the country did not altogether conceal. She was tall and straight, but moved with the graceful freedom of a child, for her straightness was not that of an arrow—rather of the unstrung bow, whose beauty is revealed by its flexibility. Her limbs were rounded perfectly to the feminine model, but were evidently possessed of muscular strength developed by daily exercise incident to her mountain life. A glance at her would disprove that western theory which associates the ideal of female beauty only with softness of fleshly texture and lack of sinew. Her face was commanding, brow high, eyes rather deep-set and blue, mouth small—perhaps too straight for the best expression of amiability—chin full, and suggestive of firmness and courage. As she gazed through the doorway into the night a troubled look knit her features—just enough, however, to make one notice rather the strong, steady and heroic purpose which conquered it. When she turned again to the company the firelight revealed only a girlish sweetness and gentleness of face and manner. She took the gusle and sang a pretty song about the dancing of the witches; her merry voice starting a score of other voices in the simple chorus. Then followed a war song, in which the daughter of a murdered chieftain calls upon the clan to avenge her father, and save their land from an insulting foe. It was largely recitative, and rendered with so much of the realistic in her tones and manner as to draw even the old men to their feet, while, with waving hands and marching stamp, they started the company in the refrain.

Milosch set the example of retiring when the evening was well advanced. Though Constantine was still absent, it gave his father no anxiety, for the boy was accustomed to have his own private business with coons in the forest, and the eels in the pool, and, indeed, with the stars too—for often he would lie for hours looking at them, only Morsinia being allowed to interrupt his conference with the bright-eyed watchers above.

CHAPTER XVI

Constantine, who was now a manly fellow of nearly eighteen years, had left the house when it grew dark. The night was thick, for heavy clouds had spread their pall over the sky. A little space from the house was the kennel. A deep growl greeted his approach to it.

"Still, Balk!" muttered he, as he loosed an enormous mastiff, and led the brute toward the side of the house on which the clijet, or chamber, occupied by Morsinia was located.

"Down, Balk!" he said, as again and again the huge beast rose and placed his paws upon his master's shoulders. Balk was tied within a clump of elder-bushes a little way from the house, and at the opening of a foot-path ascending the mountain. The young man lay down with his head upon the mastiff. Nearly an hour passed; the silence unbroken except by a querulous whine of the dog as his comrade refused to indulge his playful spirit. Suddenly Balk threw up his head and sniffed the air nervously. Yet no sound was heard, but the soughing of the winds through the budding trees, and the murmur of the brook. The animal became restless and would not lie down except at the sternly whispered command.

Leaving him, Constantine opened the shutter of the clijet occupied by his father and himself, and quietly entered. Though in the dark, he strung a strong bow, balanced several arrows in his hand to determine the best, saying to himself as he did so, "I can send these straight in the direction of a sound, thanks to my night hunting!" A dagger was thrust into the top of his leather hose. He wound his head in the strooka—the cloth which answers for both cap and pillow to those who are journeying among those mountains and liable to exposure without bed or roof at night.

The noise though slight awakened Milosch, who had fallen into a light sleep.

"Where now, my boy? No coon will come to you such a night as this."

"Father, I did not tell you, because you laugh at my fears," said Constantine in a low tone. "But the anxiety of Uncle Kabilovitsch and the great captain, too, when I went to camp last week, makes me more cautious about Morsinia. The Vili are about, as the girls said."

"Nonsense, you child! It's a shame that a boy of your years should believe such stuff. Besides what have the Vili to do with our daughter?"

"Look here, father; when I was searching for a rabbit's burrow this afternoon I saw the footprint of one of them, and it wore a soldier's shoe too. That is the sort of Vili I believe in."

"Why, boy!" said Milosch, "your head is so full of soldiering that rabbits' burrows look like soldiers' feet. Or your head is so turned with love for our girl, that you must imitate the Latin knights, and go watch beneath the shutter of your lady's castle. Go, along, then, and let the night dews take the folly out of you. Foolish boy!" added he, as he turned toward the wall.

Constantine went back to the dog. The huge beast had thrust himself as far as the cord would allow him in the direction away from the house, and stood trembling with excitement as he peered into the black shadows which lay against the mountain. Constantine could detect no unusual sound save the creaking of the gigantic limbs of the trees as they rubbed against each other in the rising wind, the sharpening whistle of the breeze, and the crackle of the dead brushwood. Yet the mastiff's excitement increased. He strained the rope with his utmost strength, but the hand of his master upon his neck checked the whining growl.

A branch snapped on the hillside in the direction of the path.

"No wind did that," muttered he. A stone rolled down the declivity.

"No foot familiar with that path did that. You are right, Balk!" and by main strength he pressed the mastiff's head to the ground, and, with his arm about his neck, kept him crouching and silent.

Stealthy steps were heard.

"One! Two!" counted the boy. "You and I are enough for them, eh, Balk?"

The dog licked the face of his master in token that he understood, and would take his man if Constantine would do equally well.

"Three! Four! Five! A large band! Too many for us, Balk! We must rouse the village——"

But at the moment he would have started, his attention was arrested by low voices almost at his side.

"The clijet nearest. When she is taken I will sound the bugle call—the Turkish call, so that your dash through the village will be thought to be one of their dashes. Do as little real damage as you can, keeping the appearance of a genuine raid; but no matter if you have to cut the throats of a half-dozen or more; especially the red-headed fellow you have seen in camp, and the old devil with the paralyzed arm. I and Waldy will carry the girl, and wait for you by the horses on the open road. Let's inspect!"

Two dusky outlines moved toward the house. Constantine cut the rope, and, at a push of his hand the dog crawled a few feet until he was clear of the copse; then sprang into the air. There was a hardly audible exclamation of surprise and terror; a low growl of satisfied rage, as when a tiger seizes the food thrown to him in his cage. One man is down in death grapple with his strange assailant whose teeth are at his throat. A sharp whiz and a cry of pain tell that the arrow of Constantine has not missed its mark.

A second whiz, and the form topples!

The boy stood stupefied with the reaction of the moment. But the multiplying footfalls along the ledge aroused him. He darted into the house, swinging the great bar that turned on a peg in the door post across the entrance, and thus securing it behind him. To arouse the household was the work of a moment. A word explained all. Arms were seized, not only by the men, but also by the women: for even to this day a marauder will meet no more skilful and brave defenders of the villages of Albania than the wives and daughters who encourage the men by their example as well as by their words. Their hands are trained to use the sword, the axe, the dagger; and the cry of danger transforms the most domestic scene into an exhibition of Amazons.

The expected attack was delayed. Fears were excited lest the raiders were about to set fire to the house. If such were the case, the policy of the inmates was to sally forth and cut their way through the assailants, at whatever cost. Some one must go out. It might be to meet death at the door. Standing in a circle they hastily repeated the Pater Noster, each one giving a word in turn; the one to whom the "Amen" came accepting the appointment as directly from God. With drawn weapons they gathered at the door, which was opened suddenly. No enemy appearing, it was closed, leaving the new sentinel without.

After going a few paces the guard stumbled over the dead body of the dog, by the side of which a man was vainly struggling to rise. Drawing his dagger he would have completed the work of the mastiff's fangs,—when he checked the impulse by better judgment—

"No, it's better to have him along with us. He'll come handy before we get through this job!"

So, grasping the two arms of the wounded man in such a way as to prevent his using a weapon, if strength enough should remain, he swung the helpless hulk upon his back, as he had often carried the carcass of a wolf down the mountain; and, giving the preconcerted signal at the door, was instantly re-admitted.

The wounded man wore the Turkish uniform, and was evidently the officer in charge of the raiding party. This fact sufficiently explained the delay in following up the attack, for doubtless his men were still waiting for the order which he would never give.

"We must rouse our neighbors," said the old man, who was recognized as the commandant of the dwelling, and obeyed as such with that reverence for seniority which is to this day a beautiful characteristic of the Albanian people.

Constantine held a hurried, but confidential talk with Milosch, who proposed that Constantine and his sister should undertake the hazardous venture of alarming the next house. All remonstrated against Morsinia's venturing, the patriarch refusing to allow it. Milosch persuaded him with these words, which were not overheard by the others—

"She is the chief object of attack; this I have discovered. If she remains in the house she will be captured. Her only safety is to leave it, and disappear in the darkness. Once out there she can hide near by, or can thread her way up among the crags, where no stranger's foot will ever come. She knows every stone and tree in the dark as well as a mole knows the twists and turns of his burrow."

Morsinia caught at once the spirit of the adventure, and in her eagerness preceded Constantine to the doorway. The thrill of fear on her account gave way to a thrill of applause for her as she stood in readiness. She had donned a helmet of thick half-tanned hides, and a corsage of light iron links, looped together and tied with leathern thongs, about her person. Her arms were left free for the use of the bow and stock which swung from her shoulder, and the klaptigan, or short dagger, which hung in the plaits of her kilt.

"The Holy Virgin protect her!" was the prayer which came from all sides as she flung her arms about the neck of Milosch, and as she afterward bowed her head to receive the kiss of the patriarch upon her forehead. The light in the room was extinguished that their exit might not be noted by any without when the door should open.

For a moment Constantine and Morsinia stood close to the door which had closed behind them. Their keen hearing detected the fact that the house was surrounded, though by persons stationed at a distance, chiefly upon the higher slopes of the hills. The road to the next house was evidently guarded.

Constantine insisted upon Morsinia's concealing herself rather than attempting to go with him to the neighbors; but only after remonstrance with him did she consent to his plan. Silently crossing the road, and without so much as breaking a stick or rustling a dead leaf beneath her feet—a dexterity acquired in approaching the timid game with which the mountains abounded, and which she had often hunted—she disappeared in the dense copse.

Constantine moved cautiously by the wayside, easily eluding the notice of the men whose dark outlines were discerned by him as they stood on guard at intervals along the road. He had nearly approached the neighboring house when the still night air was rent with the shrill note of a Turkish bugle call from the direction of the dwelling they had left.

"Could it be that the captured officer had recovered sufficient reason and strength to break from his captors and give the signal?" thought Constantine. The call sounded again—it was evidently from a distance, beyond the village. A score or more dim forms at the sound gathered in the road; some emerging from the bushes near, others descending from points high up the slopes on either side—their hurried but muffled conversation showed that they were about to make the appointed dash upon the doomed dwelling. But a second blare of trumpets sounded far down toward the entrance of the valley, followed by a clanging of armor and clatter of horses' feet. Torches glared far away. A party was evidently just winding out of the defile into the open space where the hamlet stood. Rescuers doubtless! for the first party of raiders scattered to right and left, and were heard climbing again up the wooded slopes. Morsinia hastened to Constantine, and together they hurried to meet the new comers. But they were not rescuers. They attacked the house with shouts of "Allah! Allah!" They fired it with their torches. Some poured along the road toward the next house.

They were genuine Turks. Unable to conquer Scanderbeg in battle, the great army had spread everywhere to lay waste the country. In fertile meadows, along every stream, wherever a castle or chalet was known to be, raged the numberless soldiers, who, beaten in nobler fight, sought vengeance by becoming murderers of the more helpless, and kidnappers of women and children to fill their harems.

With flying feet Constantine and Morsinia outstripped the riders, alarmed the second house, and ran to the third. Behind them the crackling flames told that it was too late to return. All who could escape gathered at the great konak. Since a similar raid, some years before, this building had been converted into a rude fortification. The wall which surrounded it, as an enclosure for sheep and cattle, had been built up high and strong enough to prevent any approach to the main structure by an anticipated foe, except as the scalers of the wall should be exposed to the missiles of those within. The konak proper was pierced with loop-holes, through which a shower of arrows could be poured by unseen archers.

The court was already filled with the fugitives, while some had entered the building, when it was surrounded by the Turks. Constantine had gained from Morsinia a promise to avoid exposure; and had agreed upon a place of meeting on the mountain, in the event of their both surviving the conflict. But the eagerness of Constantine overcame his discretion, and, heading a group of peasants who had not been able to enter the konak, he mingled in a hand-to-hand fight with the assailants. Morsinia's interest led her to closely watch the fray from the bordering thicket, changing her position from time to time that she might not lose sight of the well-known form of her foster-brother. Seeing him endangered, she could not resist the vain impulse to fly to his assistance; as if her arms could stay those of the stout troopers who surrounded him; or as if a Turk could have respect for a woman's presence. Scarcely had she moved from her covert when strong hands seized her, and, by a quick movement, pinioned her arms behind her back. "Ho! man, guard this girl! If my houri escapes, your head shall be forfeit," cried her captor, an officer, to a common soldier who was holding his horse. In a moment he was lost to sight in the struggling throng.

The wall was carried, and, though many a turban had rolled from the lifeless head of its wearer, the building was finally fired—life being promised to the women who should surrender. Some of these, who were young, were thrust from the door by their kindred, who preferred for them the chances of miserable existence as Turkish prey, to seeing them perish with themselves. Most, however, fought to the last by the side of their husbands and fathers, and were slain in the desperate attempt to make their way from the flames which drove them out.

Constantine, by strange strength and skill, extricated himself from the mêlée. A sharp flesh wound cooled his blind rage; and, realizing that another's life, as dear to him as his own, was involved in his safety, he withdrew from the danger, and sought Morsinia.

Not finding her during the night, he returned in the earliest dawn to the konak. The building was in ruins; the ground strewn with dead and wounded. With broken hearts the few who had escaped were bewailing their loved ones killed or missing. But there was no tidings of Morsinia. In vain the woods were searched; every old trysting place sacred to some happy memory of the years they had spent together—the eagle's crag, the cave in the ravine, the dense copse. But only memories were there. Imagination supplied the rest—a horrid imagination! The poor boy was maddened and crushed; at one moment a fiend; at the next almost lifeless with grief.

An examination at the lower house discovered the body of his father, Milosch. He had been killed outside the house; for his body, though terribly gashed, was not burned, as were those found within the walls of the building.

Constantine had, up to this time, regarded himself as a boy; now he felt that he was a man, with more of life in its desirableness behind than ahead of him: a desperate man, with but a single object to live for, vengeance upon the Turk, and upon those who, worse than Turks, of Albanian blood, had first attempted Morsinia's capture.

Yet there was another thing to live for. Perhaps she might be recaptured. Improbable, but not impossible! That, then, should be his waking dream. Such a hope—hope against hope—was all that could make life endurable, except it were to drain the blood of her captors.

He was driven by the poignancy of his grief and the hot fury of his rage, to make this double object an immediate pursuit. He felt that he could not sleep again until he had tasted some of the vengeance for which he thirsted.

But how could he accomplish it? He must lay his plan, for it were worse than useless to start single-handed without one. He must plot his tragedy before he began to execute it.

He sat down amid the ruins of the hamlet—amid the ruins of his happiness and hopes—to plot. But he could devise nothing. His attempts were like writing on the air. He sat in half stupor; his power to think crushed by the dead weight of mingled grief and the sense of impotency.

But suddenly he started——

"Fool! fool, that I am, to waste the moments! This very night it may be done."

He hastily stripped the body of a dead Turkish soldier, and, rolling the uniform into a compact bundle, plunged with it through the thicket and up the steep mountain side.

CHAPTER XVII

The valley in which the little hamlet lay, as well as the ravine by which it was approached, was exceedingly tortuous. The stream which seemed to have made these in its ceaseless windings, sometimes almost doubled upon itself, as if the spirit of the waters were the prey of the spirit of the hills that closed in upon its path, and thus it sought to elude its pursuer. Though it was fully twenty miles from the demolished konak to where the narrow valley debouched into the open plain, it was not more than a quarter of this distance in a straight line between those points. The interjacent space was, however, impassable to any except those familiar with its trackless rocks. From a distance the mountain lying between seemed a sheer precipice. But Constantine knew every crevice up which a man could climb; the various ledges that were connected, if not by balconies broad enough for the foot, at least by contiguous trunks of trees, balustrades of tough mountain laurel, or ropes of wild vine. He could cross this wall of rock in an hour or two, but the Turkish raiders would occupy the bulk of the day in making the circuit of the road. Indeed they would in all probability not leave the security of the great ravine, and strike the highway, until night-fall; for the terror of Scanderbeg's ubiquity was always before the Turks. It was this thought that had prompted Constantine's sudden action when he started up from his despairing reverie amid the embers of his home.

It was still early in the afternoon when, having passed with the celerity of a goat among the crags, he looked down from the further side of the great barrier upon the Turkish company. He stood upon a ledge almost above their heads; and never did an eagle's eye take in a brood upon which he was about to swoop, more sharply than did Constantine's observe the details of the camp below him.

There were the horses tethered. Yonder was a group of officers playing at dice. In a circle of guards beyond, a few women and children; and among them—could he mistake that form?

The soldiers were preparing their mess. Some were picking the feathers from fowls; others building fires. Then his surmise had been correct, that they would not leave the valley until night.

Constantine donned the Turkish uniform he had brought with him, and climbed down the mountain. Sentinels were posted here and there upon bold points from which they might get a view of the great plain beyond. Toward this they kept a constant watch, as one of them remarked to his comrade upon a neighboring pinnacle of rock: "Lest some of Scanderbeg's lightning might be lying about loose." Posing like a sentinel whenever he was likely to be observed, Constantine passed through their lines, the guards being too far apart to detect one another's faces. Hailed by a sentinel, he gave back the playful salute with a wave of his hand.

Emboldened by the success of his disguise, he descended to a ledge so near the group of officers that he could easily hear their conversation. They did not use the pure Turkish speech, but sometimes interspersed it with Servian, for many of the officers, as well as the men, in the Sultan's armies were from the provinces where the Turkish tongue was hardly known. The common soldiers in this group Constantine observed used the Servian altogether.

"Good!" said he to himself, "point number one in my plot."

"The highest throw wins the choice of the captives," cried one of the officers. "What say you, Oski?"

"Agreed," replied the one addressed, "but she will never be your houri in paradise, Lovitsch?"

"Why not?"

"Because the Koran forbids casting lots?"

"Well," replied his comrade. "I will take my beauty now, in this world, rather than wait for the next. So here goes!"

"By Khalif Omar's big toe! You have won, Oski. Which will you take?" "The little one with the bright black eyes," replied Oski; "unless you can prevail upon Captain Ballaban to give me his. The man who owns that girl will never have any houris in paradise. They would all die for jealousy."

"Captain Ballaban is his name," murmured Constantine to himself. "Good! Point number two in my plot."

"I would not have her for a gift," said Lovitsch, "for she has a strange eye—the evil eye perhaps—at least there is something in it I cannot fathom. She looks straight through a man. I touched her under the chin, when those gentle blue orbs burst with fire. There was as much of a change in her as there is in one of our new-fashioned cannon when it is touched off; quiet one moment, and sending a bullet through you the next. She's the daughter of the devil, sure."

"You are a bold soldier, Lovitsch, to be afraid of a girl," laughed his comrade. "I would like the chance of owning that beauty. If I could not manage her I could sell her. She would bring a bag of gold at Adrianople. Captain Ballaban will probably give her as a present to Prince Mahomet. He can afford to do so, for the prince has shown him wonderful favors. Think of a young Janizary, who has not seen nineteen summers, with a captain's rank, and commanding such greybeards as we!"

"No doubt the prince favors him," replied Lovitsch, "but that will not account for his advance in the Janizary's corps. Nothing but real grit and genius gets ahead among those fellows. The prince can give his jewels and gold, but he could not secure a Janizary's promotion to a soldier any more than he could bring him to disgrace without the consent of the Aga. No, comrade, Ballaban was born a soldier, and has won every thread in his captain's badge by some exploit or sage counsel. But I wish he was back with us. I like not being left in charge of such a motley troop as this. If Scanderbeg should close up the mouth of this ravine with a few score of his spavined cavalry, we would be like so many eggs in a bag, to be smashed together, without Ballaban's wit to get us out."

"I think the captain has returned, for, if I mistake not, I saw his red head a little while ago glowing like a sunset on the crag yonder," replied Oski, looking up toward the spot where Constantine was sitting.

——"Good! said Constantine, holding his council of war with his own thoughts. "The captain looks like me before sunset. Perhaps I can look like him after sunset. One advantage of having a head tiled in red! But I will not show it again. Point number three in my plot."——

"Quite likely the captain has returned, and is prowling about, inspecting everything, from the horses'-tails to our very faces, that he may read our thoughts. That is his way," said Lovitsch, glancing around.

"Which way did he go?"

"You might as well ask which track the Prophet's horse took through the air when he carried his rider on the night journey to heaven. A messenger from the chief Aga met him just as we were finishing the fight last night, and, with a word turning over the command to me, he mounted his horse and was off. Perhaps he heads some other raid to-night; or, for aught I know, may be conferring with Scanderbeg in the disguise of a Frankish general; for that Ballaban's brain is as prolific of schemes and tricks as this ant's nest is full of eggs"—turning over a stone as he spoke.

The afternoon waned, and, as the night fell, preparations were made for the march. When it was dark a light bugle note called in the sentinels, and the company moved forward.

CHAPTER XVIII

In the gathering gloom Constantine approached the extreme edge of the camp, where those who were to bring up the rear had just mounted. A soldier, somewhat separated from the others, was leading several horses; either a relay in case of accident to the others, or those animals whose saddles had been emptied during the fight at the konak. Constantine's appearance was evidently a surprise to the soldier, who eyed him closely, but made no movement indicating suspicion beyond that of a rather pleased curiosity. The man made a low salâm, bowing his turban to the saddle bow, and addressed him—

"Will you not mount, Sire?" Without responding Constantine leaped into a saddle.

"You will pardon me, Captain," continued the soldier. "You are welcome back, for we are in better heart when you are with us."

"Thanks, good fellow," said Constantine, "but I have not returned yet—at least my return must not be known to the troops until the morning. We will take your tongue out if you tell any one I am back without bidding."

The man gave a quick glance as if perplexed. Constantine's hand was upon his dagger. But the soldier's doubt was relieved as he seemed to be confident of the familiar form of his captain; and he explained his apparent suspicion by quickly adding—

"You speak the Servian excellent well, Captain."

"One must get used to it, and every other tongue, in commanding such a mixed crew as the Sultan gathers into his army," said Constantine.

"You Janizaries are wonderful men," replied the soldier. "You know all languages. There was the little Aga I once"—

"No matter about that now," said Constantine, interrupting him. "I want you for a special duty. Can I trust you to do me an errand? If you do it well you will be glad of it hereafter."

"Ay, ay, Sire! with my life; and my lips as mute as the horse's."

"I captured a girl last night. She knows something I would find out by close questioning. I must have her brought to the rear."

"Ay! the girl Koremi holds?"

"Yes, tell Koremi to loiter a little with her until I come up. We must not go far from this defile before I find out what she knows, if I have to discover it with my dagger in her heart; for there are traitors among us. Last night there were Arnaouts dressed as Moslems in the fight."

"That I know," said the soldier, "for I tripped over a fellow myself, hiding in the bushes, who swore at me in as good round Arnaout tongue as they speak in hell. I ran him through and found a Giaour corslet under his jacket. If there are traitors among us we will broil them over our first camp-fire, that they may scent hell before they get there."

"You see then why I must find out what I can at once," said the assumed captain. "Some of our men are in league with the Arnaouts. I can find out from that girl every one of them. Impress this upon Koremi; and if he hesitates to let the girl drift to the rear, you can tell him that he will be suspected of being in league with the rascals."

Constantine took the ropes which held the horses the man was leading; and, bidding him to haste, but be cautious that no one but Koremi should know the message, followed slowly behind.

It was nearly an hour later when the form of the soldier appeared in the road just before him.

"Right!" said Constantine.

"Right!" was the response, first to the assumed captain, then repeated to some one behind him. Two other forms appeared; one of them a woman.

Anticipating his orders, the second trooper untied a rope from about his own waist, and handed it, together with the rein of the horse the woman rode, to Constantine. Then, making a low obeisance, the two troopers withdrew a little distance to the rear. The other end of the rope which Constantine held was about the waist of the captive. Drawing the led horse close to his own, and dropping his turban more over his face, Constantine closely scrutinized the features of the woman. She was Morsinia. It was difficult for him to repress the excitement and delay the revelation of his true person, but the hazard of the least cry of surprise or recognition on her part nerved him to coolness.

"Where are you taking me? If you have the courage, kill me," said the girl.

Constantine replied only by whistling a snatch of an Albanian air.

"Are you an Albanian renegade?" continued the girl. "Could you not be content to sell yourself to fight for the Turk against other enemies, but must be a double traitor, and kill and kidnap your own kind?"

The whistling continued. But as the soldiers were a little removed, he said in a low voice, disguising his natural tones:

"I am an Albanian, and if you will not speak, but only obey, I can save you."

"Jesu grant you are true!" was the tremulous response.

"This will prove it," muttered he, reaching toward her, and with his knife cutting a broad strap which bound her limbs to the saddle. "If tied elsewhere, here is the knife."

The way, which had been narrowed by the projection of the mountains on either side, now widened a little. Constantine knew the spot well. There had once been a mill and peasant's hut there, and now quite a plat of grass was growing from the soft soil. The eye could not discern it, for the darkness was rayless. But Constantine remembered the grassy stretch was just round the point of rock they were passing. The horses were walking slowly, being allowed by their riders to pick their way along the stony road. As they turned the rock a strong wind rushed through the ravine, wailing a requiem over the now deserted settlement and the dead leaves of last year, which it whirled in eddies; and singing a lullaby through the trees to the new-born leaves of the spring time, which were rocked on the cradling branches. This, together with the clatter of the horses' feet before and behind them, enabled Constantine to draw the captive's horse and his own upon the soft turf without being heard. Halting them at a few yards' distance, they allowed the men who had followed them to pass by, and sat in silence until the lessening sound told them that the soldiers had made another turn in the road. Then, wheeling the horses, Constantine gave loose rein back over the track they had come. After a short ride he dismounted, and closely examining the way, led the horses to one side, up a path, and down again to a little plateau, perhaps a furlong from the main road, where a grazing patch would keep them from being betrayed by the neighing. He dreaded the fatigue of further journey to his comrade; for even his own ordinarily tireless frame was beginning to feel the drain of the terrible night and day they had passed through.

Constantine threw off his turban and stretched his strong arms to lift the captive from her horse, exclaiming with delight in his own familiar tones,—

"I am no Albanian, dear Morsinia, but—"

"Constantine!" she cried.

He laid an almost lifeless form upon the turf, for the shock of the revelation had been too much for her jaded nerves and excited brain.

Unrolling the cloth of his turban he spread it over her person, while his own breast was her pillow. Slowly she recovered strength and self-command.

In a few words the mutual stories of the hours of their separation were told. Morsinia had been treated with exceeding kindness and respect, as the captive of the chief officer of the expedition, who seemed to be a person of some distinction, though she had not seen him. Constantine insisted upon his companion's seeking sleep, but by his inquiries, did as much as her own thoughts to keep her awake; so that at the dawn they confessed that the eyes of neither had been closed. The necessity of procuring food led them to start at daybreak for the nearest settlement. They descended to the road and retraced the course of the preceding night; for it was useless to return to the wrecked hamlet. They had gone but a short distance when they heard the sound of a body of cavalry directly in front of them, riding rapidly up the valley. There was no time to avoid the approaching riders either by flight or concealment. Constantine said hastily,

"Remember, if they are Turks, I too am a Turk, and you are my captive. If they are friends, all is well. Stay where you are, and I will ride forward to meet them."

CHAPTER XIX

The newcomers proved to be a detachment of Albanians. Constantine was instantly captured notwithstanding his declaration that his dress was only assumed.

"Aha! you are a Christian now in a Turk's skin, are you? But yesterday you were a Turk in a Christian's feathers," was the taunt with which he was greeted by one of the foremost riders, who continued his bantering. "Your face is honest, if your heart is not, you Moslem devil; for your ugly features will not lie though your tongue does. I would know that square jaw and red head equally well now, were it under the tiara of the pope instead of under the turban; and I would cut your throat if you carried St. Peter's key in your girdle; you change-skinned lizard!"

"Who is he?" cried the horsemen, gathering about.

"Why! the very knave who escaped us about sundown yesterday, after spying our camp; and he has the impudence to ask us to take him prisoner that he may spy us again."

"Let us hamstring him!" cried another, "and, unless St. Christopher has turned Moslem in paradise and helps the rascal, he will find no legs to run away with again."

"Set him up for a mark when we halt," proposed a third. "A ducat to him whose arrow can split his ear without tearing the cheek at forty paces!" Constantine was helpless as they adjusted a halter about his neck, with which to lead him at the side of a horseman, the butt of the scurrilous wit and sharper spear-points of his half mad and half merry captors.

They had gone but a few paces when the colonel commanding the detachment made his way through the troopers to the front. He was a venerable man with long flowing white beard. His bodily strength seemed to come solely from the vitality of nerve and the dominance of his spirit; for he was well worn with years.

"What is this noise about?" he asked sternly.

Before any could reply he stared with a moment's incredulity and wonder at Constantine, who relieved his doubts by recognizing him.

"Colonel Kabilovitsch!" cried he, doffing his turban as if it had been a Christian cap.[48] "Your men are playful fellows, as frolicksome as a cat with a mole."

"But why are you here, my boy? and why this disguise?" interrupted Kabilovitsch.

The explanation was given in a few words;—on the one side the story of the slaughter at the village, and the adventures of Morsinia and Constantine; on the other of how the news of the Turkish raid reached the camp at Sfetigrade about noon, and the rescuing party had started at once under Kabilovitsch's command, and ridden at breakneck speed during the entire night in the hope of meeting the Turks before they emerged from the narrow valley.

Learning now that they were too late for this, Kabilovitsch halted his command, and with Constantine sought the place where Morsinia was in waiting. When the old man heard that the first assailants of the hamlet had been Albanians in disguise his rage was furious; and through his incautious words Morsinia learned more of her relation to the voivode Amesa than her reputed father had ever told her; for the mystery of her family had never been fully explained in her hearing. It had heretofore been deemed best that the girl should not be made the custodian of her own secret, lest her childish prattle might reveal it to others. Yet she had guessed the greater part of the problem of her identity. But Kabilovitsch was now led by the new curiosity which his inadvertent expressions had awakened in her, as well as by the remarkably discreet and cautious judgment she had displayed, to tell her the entire story of her own life. This was not, however, until orders had been passed through the troop for rest, and the fires hastily kindled along the roadside had prepared their refreshing breakfasts.

Removed from the hearing of all others, Kabilovitsch rehearsed to Morsinia and Constantine what the reader already knows of her extraction and early residence in Albania. He advised her to extreme caution against the slightest reference to herself as the young Mara de Streeses, and that she should insist upon her identity as the daughter of the Servian peasant Milosch and the sister of Constantine.

Morsinia buried her fair face in the gray beard of the old man, as years ago she had done when they sat upon the door-stone of their Balkan home, and sobbed as if his words had orphaned her. In a few moments she looked up into his fine but wrinkled face, and drawing it down to hers, kissed him as she used to do, and said lovingly,

"I must believe your words; but my heart holds you as my father: for father you have been to me, and child I shall be to you so long as God gives us to one another."

The old man pressed her temples between his rough hands, and looked long into her deep blue eyes, as he said slowly,

"Ay, father and mother both was I to thee, my child, from that terrible night, sixteen years ago. My rough arms have often cradled thee. But now you have a nobler and stronger protector in our country's father, the great Castriot. To him you must go; for it is no longer safe in these lonely valleys. Under his strong arm and all-watchful eye you will be amply protected. There are nameless enemies of the old house of De Streeses whom we must avoid as vigilantly as we avoid the Turks."

It was determined that Constantine should make a detour with her, and approach Sfetigrade from the south, giving out that they were fugitives from the lower country, which the enemy had also been raiding.

The colonel stated to his under officers, in hearing of the men, that the young Turk was really one of Castriot's scouts, and that the young woman was an accomplice. Borrowing from one and another sufficient Albanian costumes to substitute for Constantine's disguise, Kabilovitsch dismissed the couple.

There was no end to the badgering the officious soldier who had first arrested the scout received at the hands of his comrades. They jeered at his double mistake in taking the fellow yesterday as a Turkish spy in Albanian uniform, because he had slipped away so shrewdly, and now again being duped by him a real Albanian in Turkish disguise. Some threw the halter over the fellow's neck; others made mimic preparation for hamstringing him; while one presented him with an immense scroll of bark purporting to be his commission as chief of the department of secret service, finishing the mock presentation by shivering the bark over the fellow's head. The unhappy man contented himself philosophically:—

"No wonder General Castriot baffles the enemy when his own men cannot understand him. You were all as badly twisted by that fellow's tricks as I was. But I will never interfere with that red head again, though he wears a turban and is cutting the throat of the general himself."

Two days later a beautiful girl accompanied by her brother—who was as unlike her as the thorn bush is unlike the graceful flowering clematis that festoons its limbs, both of them in apparent destitution, refugees from near the Greek border—entered the town of Sfetigrade. By order of the general, to whom their piteous story was told by Kabilovitsch—for he had chanced, so he said, to come upon them as they were inquiring their way to the town—they were quartered with a family whose house was not far from the citadel. For some weeks the girl was an invalid. A raging fever had been induced by over excitement and the subsequent fatigue of the long journey. Colonel Kabilovitsch could not refrain from expressing his interest in the young woman by almost daily calls at the cottage where she lay. One day, when it was supposed by the surgeon that she might not live, the old man was observed to stand long at the cot upon which the sick girl was lying. A look of agony overspread his features when the surgeon, who had been feeling her pulse, laid her almost nerveless hand beneath the blanket.

"Dear, good old man," said the housewife. "I warrant he has laid some pretty one of his own in the ground. Maybe a child, or a lover, sometime back in the years. These things do come to us over and over again."

The brother of the sick girl scarcely noticed the visits of Colonel Kabilovitsch, except to respond to his questions when no one but himself could give the exact information about the patient's condition; for none watched with her so incessantly.

But her marvellous natural vitality enabled the sufferer to outlive the fever; and, as she became convalescent, the old colonel seemed to forget her. His interest was apparently in her suffering rather than in herself.

CHAPTER XX

The battlements of Sfetigrade lay, like a ruffled collar, upon enormous shoulders of rock rising high above the surrounding country. Over them rose, like a massive head, the citadel with its bartizans projecting as a crown about the brow. The rock upon which the fortification stood was scarped toward the valley, so that it could be climbed only with the help of ladders, even though the assailants were unresisted by its defenders. The few spots which nature had left unguarded were now choked with abattis, or overlooked by bastions so skilfully constructed as to need far less courage and strength for their defence than were possessed by the bands of Dibrian and Epirot patriots who fought from behind them.

The assaults which Sultan Amurath launched against the place had been as frequent as the early summer showers, and his armies were beaten to pieces as the rain rebounded in spray and ran in streams from the rocks. The chagrin of the baffled Sultan reflected itself in the discouragement of his generals and the demoralization of their men. The presence of his majesty could not silence the mutual recriminations, the loud and rancorous strife with which brave officers sought to lay upon one another the responsibility for their defeat, rather than confess that the daily disasters were due to the superior genius commanding among their foes. Especially was the envy of the leaders of the other corps and branches of the service excited against the Janizaries, to whose unrivalled training and daring were due whatever minor victories had been won, and whatever exploits worthy of mention had been performed.

A lofty tent, whose projecting centre-pole bore the glittering brass crescent and star, and before the entrance to which a single horse-tail hung from the long spear, denoted the headquarters of a Sanjak Bey. In front of the tent walked two men in eager, and not altogether amiable, conversation. The one was the Bey, whose huge turban of white, inwound with green, indicated that his martial zeal was supplemented by equal enthusiasm for his faith; and that he had added to the fatigue of many campaigns against the infidels the toil of a more monotonous, though more satisfactory, pilgrimage to Mecca. His companion was an Aga of the Janizaries, second only in rank to the chief Aga.

The latter was speaking with a wrath which his courteous words but ill concealed—

"I do not impugn your honor or the sincerity of your motives, Caraza-Bey, in making your accusation against our Captain Ballaban; but the well-known jealousy which is everywhere manifested against our corps compels me to believe not a single word to the discredit of him or any of the Yeni-Tscheri without indubitable proof. I would allow the word of Captain Ballaban—knowing him so well as I do—to outweigh the oaths on the Koran of a score of those who, like yourself, have reason to be jealous of his superior courage."

"But your upstart captain's guilt can be proved, if not to your personal satisfaction, at least before those who will not care to ask your assent to their judgment," replied the other, not attempting to veil his hatred of the Aga, any more than his purpose of crushing the one of whom they were speaking.

"What will the lies of a whole sanjak of your hirelings avail against the honor of a Janizary?" replied the Aga. "If two horse-tails[49] hung from the standard yonder, I would not publicly disgrace Captain Ballaban by so much as ordering an inquiry at your demand. The Janizaries will take no suggestion from any but the Padishah."

"A curse on the brag of the Janizaries! The arrogancy of the Christian renegades needs better warrant than Ballaban can give it," sneered the Bey. "If you like, let the matter rest as it is. The whole army believes that one of your dervish-capped heroes—the best of the brood, I imagine—deserted his comrades in battle, and all for the sake of a captive girl."

"It is a lie!" shouted the Aga, drawing his sword upon him.

The attitude of the two officers drew a crowd, who rushed from all sides to witness the duel. Both were masters of sword play, so that neither obtained any sanguinary advantage before they were separated by the arrival of the chief Aga, who forbade his subaltern to continue the conflict. Upon hearing the occasion of the affray, the chief said:

"The trial of Captain Ballaban shall be had, with the publication of the fact that Caraza-Bey has assumed the position of his accuser; and, in the event of his charge proving false, he shall atone for his malice by submitting to any punishment the captain may indicate; and the force of the Janizaries shall execute it, though they cut the throats of his entire command in order to do it. We must first vindicate the honor of the corps, and then take vengeance upon its detractors. I demand that Caraza-Bey make good his charge to-morrow at the sixth hour, or accept the judgment of coward and vilifier, which our court shall then proclaim to the army."

At the appointed time on the day following, the tent of the chief Aga was the gathering place of the notable officers of the corps. Without, it differed from hundreds of other tents only in its size, and in the pennant indicating the rank of its occupant. Within, it was lined with a canopy of finest silk and woollen tapestries, on the blue background of which crescents and stars, cimeters and lance-heads, battle-axes, shields, turbans and dervish caps were artistically grouped with texts from the Koran, and skilfully wrought in braids and threads of gold. The canvas sides of the tent were now removed, making it an open pavilion, and inviting inspection and audience from any who desired to approach. A divan was at one side, and made a semicircle of about half the tent. Upon this sat the chief Aga, his cushion slightly raised above those at his side, which were occupied by the agas of lower rank. A group of officers filled the space beneath the tent; and soldiers of all grades made a dense crowd for several rods beyond into the open air.

The chief Aga waved his hand to an attendant, and the military court was formally opened. Several cases were disposed of before that of Captain Ballaban was called.

There was led in a stalwart soldier of middle age. Two witnesses deposed that, in a recent assault upon the enemy's works at Sfetigrade, when there was poured upon the assailants a shower of arrows and stones from the battlements above, this man, without orders from his officer, had cried, "Give way! Give way!" and that to this cry and his example were due the confusion of ranks and the retreat which followed.

The chief Aga turned and looked silently upon the man, awaiting his reply to the accusation. The accused was speechless. The chief then turned to the Aga to whose division the culprit belonged, that he might hear any plea that he should be pleased to offer for the soldier; but the Aga's face was stolid with indifference. The chief, without raising his head, sat in silence for a moment, as in solemn act of weighing the case. He then muttered an invocation of Allah as the Supreme Judge. He paused. A gleam of light circled above the man; a hissing sound of the cimeter and a thud were heard. The culprit's head rolled to the ground. His trunk swayed for an instant and fell.

This scene was apparently of little interest to the spectators. A second case only tested their patience. One was charged with having failed to deliver an order from the colonel of his orta, or regiment, to a captain of one of the odas, or companies. Both these officers testified, the one to having sent the order, the other to not having received it, and on this account to have failed to occupy a certain position with his men in a recent engagement with the enemy. The culprit alleged that it was impossible to deliver the order because of the enemy's movements at the time. The Aga of the division, being appealed to by the silent gaze of the judge, simply said:

"The man is brave;" when, by a motion of the hand, the judge dismissed the soldier together with the case.

The expectation not only of common soldiers, but also of officials, led them to crane their necks to look at the next comer. Even the ordinarily immobile features of the chief relaxed into an expression of anxiety as a young man walked down the aisle made by the reverent receding of the crowd to either side. He was not graceful in form. His body was beyond the proportion of his legs; though his arms compensated for any lack in the length of his lower limbs. His neck was thick, the head round, with full development of forehead, though that portion of his face was somewhat concealed by the short, bushy masses of red hair which protruded beneath his rimless Janizary cap. His face was homely, but strongly marked, evincing force of character as clearly as the convolutions of his muscles evinced animal strength and endurance. The brightness of his eye atoned for any lack of beauty in his features; as did his free and manly bearing make ample amends for deficiency in grace of form. Altogether he was a man to attract one's attention and hold it pleasantly.

Though he bent low to the earth in his obeisance to the chief officer of his troop, it was without the suggestion of obsequiousness, with that dignity which betokens real reverence and crowns itself with the honor it would give to another.

The chief Aga announced that, although the witnesses in this case were not of the order of the Yeni-Tscheri, and, therefore, had no claim to the consideration of the court, yet it pleased him in this peculiar case to waive the right to try the matter exclusively among themselves, that the good name of the Yeni-Tscheri might suffer no reproach. "Caraza-Bey," added the chief, "for some reason best known to himself does not accept the privilege we have extended him, to speak in our official presence what he has freely spoken elsewhere. We shall, therefore, hear any witnesses he may have sent."

One Lovitsch, belonging to the irregular auxiliary troops, testified that Captain Ballaban had organized a raid upon an Albanian village, and engaged himself and company for the venture; but had left them in the heat of the fight, not rejoining them until the second day. A common soldier deposed that the captain returned to the company early in the second evening, and induced him, the witness, and Koremi, to whom the captain had entrusted a beautiful captive, to bring the girl to the rear, under plea of getting from her information regarding the enemy; and had then mysteriously disappeared with her. Koremi corroborated this testimony.

Captain Ballaban gave a look of puzzled curiosity as he heard this; but otherwise evinced not the slightest emotion.

The crowd gazed upon the young captain with disappointment while testimony was being given. The agas present being unable to conceal the deep anxiety depicted upon their countenances, as they leaned forward with impatience to hear from his lips some exonerating statement, which, however, they feared could not be given. A few faces wore a look of contemptuous triumph. But two persons maintained composure. It might be expected that the chief Aga, from his familiarity with such scenes, if not from the propriety of his being the formal embodiment of the rigid and remorseless court of the Janizaries, whose decrees he was to announce, would show no emotion, however strong his sympathy with the prisoner.

The endangered man answered his gaze with equal stolidity when the judge turned to him for his defence; but he remained speechless. A shudder of horror ran through the crowd. The executioner stepped forward to the side of the apparently convicted person. A slight ringing sound, as the long curve of the well-tempered blade grazed the ground, sent to every heart the chilling announcement of his readiness. The chief Aga turned to the others, but sought in vain any palliatory suggestion or appeal for mercy, except in the mute agony of their looks. The chief then raised his eyes as if for the invocation of Allah's confirmation of the sentence as just. But his prayer was a strange one:—"Oh, Allah! thou hast given a wondrous spirit to this man; a courage worthy of the soul of Othman himself!" Then rising with excitement he addressed the throng in rapid speech.

"Look upon this man, my brothers of the shining face![50]

"Did he quail at the ring of the executioner's sword? Did he even change color when he heard the damning testimony? A true son of Kara Khalif is he. A word from his lips would have exonerated him, yet he would not speak it lest it should reveal the secrets of our service, which he would keep with dead lips rather than live to tell them. But I shall be his witness; and you, my brothers, shall be his judges. Captain Ballaban was recalled from the raid by our brother Sinam, aga of the division to which the captain belongs. But, alas! the sword of Scanderbeg has loosed Sinam's soul for flight to paradise, and he could not testify to this man's fidelity. But I know the order of Sinam; in this very tent it was written. And though the faithful messenger who carried it was slain in after conflict, the order was executed by Captain Ballaban to every letter: every moment of his absence from the raid is accounted for on my tablets"—tapping his forehead as he spoke.

A loud shout burst from the crowd which made the tent shake as if filled with a rising wind.

"Ballaban! Ballaban!" cried the multitude, lifting the brave fellow upon their shoulders.

"Take that for your grin when you thought he was guilty!" shouted one, as he delivered a tremendous blow upon the face of another.

"Death to Caraza-Bey! Down with the lying villain!" rose the cry, the crowd beginning to move, as if animated by a common spirit, to seek the envious commandant of the neighboring corps. But they halted at the tent side waiting for the sign of permission from their chief, who, by the motion of his hand forbade the assault which would have brought on a terrific battle between the Janizaries and their rivals throughout the army.

"We shall deal with Caraza-Bey hereafter, if his shame does not send him skulking from the camps," said the chief, resuming his sitting posture, and restoring order about him.

"Summon the witnesses again," he proceeded.

"You Lovitsch testified truly as to Captain Ballaban's absence, and may go. But you twin rascals who swore to his escape with the girl, your heads shall go to Caraza-Bey, and your black souls to the seventh hell.[51] Executioner, do your office!"

"Hold!" cried Ballaban, as the man drew his cimeter. "Upon my return to the company I found my fair captive gone, and under such strange circumstances that I can see that these good fellows may be honest in what they have stated. I bespeak thy mercy, Sire, for them."

"Captain Ballaban's will shall be ours," replied the chief, with a wave of his hand dismissing the assemblage. As the crowd withdrew, he said, "My brothers, the agas, will remain, and Captain Ballaban."

The sides of the tent were put up. The guard patrolled without at a distance of sixty paces, that no one might overhear the conversation in the council.

CHAPTER XXI

"Has Captain Ballaban any explanation of this conspiracy against him?" asked one.

"None!" was the laconic reply. But after a moment's pause he added: "Perhaps there was no conspiracy, except as our jealous neighbors are willing to take advantage of every unseemly circumstance that can be twisted to point against any of the Yeni-Tscheri. This may explain something. The girl that I captured at the Giaour village was no common peasant, by the cheek of Ayesha! Her face, as lit by the blazing konak, was of such beauty as I have never seen except in some dreams of my childhood. Her voice and manner in commanding me to liberate her were those of one well-born or used to authority. It was well that I bethought me to give her into the keeping of that dull-headed Koremi, or she might have bewitched me into obeying her and letting her go. My belief is that the girl was rescued. It may be that our men were heavily bribed to give her up, or that some one personated myself and demanded her, and that the story of my return may be thus accounted for, but I cannot see any treachery in Koremi's manner. If she was of any special value to Scanderbeg he would find some way of running her off, though he had to make a league with the devil and assume my shape to do it. The Arnaouts, you know, believe that the Vili are in collusion with Scanderbeg, and that one of them, a he-vili, Radisha, or some such sprite, is his body servant. That will account for it all," added he, laughing at the conceit.

"But," said the second Aga, "Caraza-Bey's insult was none the less, if your surmise be true. We must wash it out in the blood of a hundred or so of his hirelings to-morrow."

The chief shook his head.

"But," continued the second Aga, "the jealousy of our corps must be punished. You see how near it came to losing for us the life of one of our bravest. Caraza-Bey must fight me to-morrow."

"Bravo!" cried all; while one added, "And let the challenge be public, that the entire force of the Yeni-Tscheri be on hand and all the troops of the Beyler Bey of Anatolia, and—" lowering his voice— "we can manage it so that the fight become general, and teach these reptiles of Asiatics that the Yeni-Tscheri are the right hand and the brain of the empire."

"Ay, *are* the empire!" said another. "Let us have a scrimmage that will be interesting. The war with Scanderbeg is getting monotonous. One day he comes into our camp, like a butcher into a slaughter pen, and the next day we are marched out to him, to be slaughtered elsewhere. It requires one to be full of Islam, the Holy Resignation, to stand this sort of life. Yes! let's do a little fighting in our own way and get rid of some of this soldier spawn which the Padishah has brought with him from across the Bosphorus!"

"But you forget, my brothers," said Ballaban, "that this fight with the Sanjak Bey does not belong to any one beside myself. His lie was about me. I then am the man to take off his head; and I think I can do it with as good grace as the executioner was nigh to taking off mine just now."

"No, Captain!" said the chief. "Your rank is as yet below the Bey's, and he would make that an excuse for declining the gage. Besides," said he, lowering his voice, "I have special service for you elsewhere, which cannot be delayed."

When the agas, making the low courtesy, retired, the chief walked with Ballaban.

"Captain, I have heard no report of the errand upon which you were sent."

"No, Sire, I was arrested the moment I returned to camp."

"You succeeded, I know, from the movements of the enemy: although the slowness of the Padishah in ordering an advance, when Scanderbeg was diverted by your ruse, prevented our taking advantage of it."

"Yes," said Ballaban, "I succeeded as well as any one could, not being seconded from headquarters. But I did some service incidentally, and picked up some helpful information. The night after leaving the hamlet we fired, I fell in with a company of Arnaouts who were coming to the rescue. They would have got into the narrow valley before our men got out, had I not managed to trick them. I was in disguise and readily passed for an Arnaout lout, giving them false information about the direction our party had taken, and so lost them an hour or two, and saved the throats of Lovitsch's fellows, a mere rabble, good enough for a raid, but not to be depended upon for a square fight. But we must have no more raids. Scanderbeg has means of communication as quick and subtle as if the clouds were his signals and the stars were his beacons.

"I then came upon a Dibrian settlement, pretending to be a fugitive from the valleys to the north; and entertained the villagers with bug-a-boo stories about the hosts of men with turbans on their heads and little devils on their shoulders who had destroyed all that country, and were now pouring down toward the south.

"By the way," continued Ballaban laughing, "there was an old fellow there, very lame, with a patch over one eye, who could hardly stand leaning on his staff, he was so palsied with age. But the one eye that was open was altogether too bright for his years; and his legs didn't shake enough for one who rattled his staff so much. So I put him down as one of Scanderbeg's lynxes—they are everywhere. I described to him the Moslem movements in such a way as to let a trained soldier believe that we had entirely changed front, with the prospective raising of the siege of Sfetigrade and alliance with the Venetians for carrying the war farther to the north. The old codger took the bait, and asked fifty questions in the tone of a fellow whose head had been used for a mush-pot instead of a brain-holder; but every question was in its meaning as keen as a dagger-thrust into the very ribs of the military situation. Well! I helped him to all the information he wanted; when with a twinkle in his eye, he hobbled away, as wise as an owl when a fresh streak of day-light has struck him: and before night the whole country to the borders of Sternogovia was alive with Scanderbeg's scouts; and every cross-path was a rendezvous of his broken-winded cavalry.

"I saw one thing which gave me a hint I may use some day. At a village the women were carrying water from a spring far down in a ravine, though there was a fine flowing fountain quite near them. It seems that a dog had got into the fountain about a month before, and was drowned. These Dibrians believe that, if any one should drink the water of such a spring before as many days have passed as the dog has hairs on his tail, the water will make his bowels rot, and his soul go into a dog's body when he dies.

"The next night I spent inside the walls of Sfetigrade."

"No!" cried the chief. "Why, man, you must fly the air with the witches!"

"Not at all, I have some acquaintances in that snug little place; and when they go to bed they hang the key of the town on a moonbeam for me. If it is not there, I have only to vault over the walls, or sail over them on the clouds, or burrow under them with the moles, or hold my breath until I turn into a sprite, like the wizards on the Ganges, and lo! I am in. Well! that night I lodged with a worthy family of Sfetigrade, pretending that I was a poor fugitive from the very town we had raided a few nights before. And, by the hair of the beautiful Malkhatoon![52] I saw there the very captive I had taken. She lay asleep on a cot just within a doorway—unless I was asleep myself and dreaming, as I half believe I was."

"Yes, it was a dream of yours, no doubt, Captain," said the chief, "for when a young fellow like you once gets a fair woman in his arms, as you say you had her in yours the night of the raid, she never gets out of the embrace of his imagination. He will see her everywhere, and go about trying to hug her shadow. Beware illusions, Captain! They use up a fellow's thoughts, make him too meek-eyed to see things as a soldier should. The love passion will take the energy out of the best of us, as quickly as the fire takes the temper out of the best Damascene blade."

"I thank you for your counsel, Aga," replied Ballaban, his face coloring as deep as his hair. "But there was one thing I saw with a waking eye."

"And what was that?"

"That there was but one well of water in the town of Sfetigrade; the one in the citadel court. But another thing I didn't see, though I searched the place for it;—and that was a dog to throw into the well; or I would have thirsted the superstitious garrison out. They have eaten up the last cur."

"Then the surrender must come soon," said the Aga.

"No," replied Ballaban, "for the voivode Moses Goleme came into the town as I was leaving, driving a flock of sheep which he had stolen from us; for he had cut off an entire train of provisions which had been sent to our camp from Adrianople."

"Then I must have you off at once on another errand, Captain. You see yonder line of mountains off to the northwest. It may be necessary to shift the war to that region for a while. Ivan Beg,[53] the brother-in-law of Scanderbeg, has raised a pack of wild fiends among those hills of his, and is driving out all our friends. Nothing can stand against him unless it be the breasts of the Yeni-Tscheri. Scanderbeg may compel us to raise the siege of Sfetigrade, for he bleeds us daily like a leech. A diversion after Ivan Beg will at least be more honorable than a return to Adrianople. Now I would know exactly the passes and best places for fortification in Ivan's country; and you, Captain, are the man to find them out. You should be off at once. Take your time and spy thoroughly, making a map and transmitting to me your notes. And while there feel the people. It is rumored that the young voivode, Amesa, is restless under the leadership of Scanderbeg. If a dissension could be created among these Arnaouts, it would be well. Amesa has a large personal following in that north country; for his castle is just on the border of it."

"But," replied Ballaban, "I must first pluck the beard of that cowardly Caraza-Bey!"

"No! I forbid it. Your blood is worth more in your own veins than anywhere else. I should not consent to your risking a drop of it in personal combat with any one except Scanderbeg himself."

The fight between the second Aga and Caraza-Bey did not take place. That worthy was conveniently sent by Sultan Amurath, who had learned of the feud, to look after certain turbulent Caramanians; and leaving behind him a wake of curses upon all Janizaries from the chief to the pot-scourers, he took his departure for the Asiatic provinces.

Had he remained, the Turks would have had enough to occupy them without this gratuitous mêlée. For during the night scouts brought word that Scanderbeg had massed all his forces, that were not behind the walls of Sfetigrade, at a point to the right of the Turkish lines. Hardly had the army been faced to meet this attack, when scouts came from the left, reporting serious depredations on that flank. Amurath, in the uncertainty of the enemy's movement, divided his host. The Asiatics were given the northern and the Janizaries the southern defence; either of them outnumbering any force Scanderbeg could send against them. But, as a tornado cuts its broad swath through a forest, uprooting or snapping the gigantic trees, showing its direction only by the after track of desolation, which it cuts in almost unvarying width, while beyond its well defined lines scarcely a branch is broken or a nest overturned among the swaying foliage—so Scanderbeg swooped from east to west through the very centre of the Turkish encampment, gathering up arms and provisions, and strewing his track with the bodies of the slain. By the time that the Moslems were sufficiently concentrated to offer effective resistance the assailants were gone.

At the head of the victorious band Scanderbeg rode a small and ungainly, but tough and tireless animal—like most of the Albanian horses, which were better adapted to threading their way down the pathless mountain sides, than to curveting in military parade—their lack of natural ballast being made up by the enormous burdens they were trained to carry.

The figure and bearing of Scanderbeg, however, amply compensated the lack of martial picturesqueness in his steed. He was in full armor, except that his sword arm was bared. His beard of commingled yellow and gray fell far down upon the steel plates of his corselet. A helmet stuck far back upon his head, showed the massive brow which seemed of ampler height, from the Albanian custom of clipping short, or shaving the hair off from the upper forehead.

Wheeling his horse, he engaged in conversation with a stout, but awkward soldier.

"You and your beast are well matched, Constantine. You both need better training before you are fit to parade as prisoners of Amurath. You sit your horse as a cat rides a dog, though you do hold on as well with your heel as she with her claws. Your short legs would do better to clamp the belly of a crocodile."

"Yes, we are both accustomed to marching and fighting in our own way, rather than in company," replied Constantine. "But the beast has not failed me by a false step; not when we leaped the fallen oak and landed in the gulch back yonder. The beast came down as safely and softly as on the training lawn."

"And you have done as well yourself," replied the general. "That was a bad play though you had with the Turk as we cut our way through the last knot of them. But for a side thrust which I had time to give at your antagonist, while waiting for the slow motions of my own, I fear that your animal would be lighter now by just your weight. You strike powerfully, but you do not recover yourself skilfully. A good swordsman would get a response into your ribs before you could deal him a second. Here, I will show you! Now thrust! Strike! No, not so; but hard, villainously, at me, as if I were the Turk who stole your girl! So! Again! Again!—Now learn this movement"—pressing his own sword steadily against his companion's, and bending him back until he was almost off his horse. "And this," dealing so tremendous a slash with the back of the sword that Constantine's arm was almost numbed by the effort to resist it.—"And this!" transmitting a twisting motion from his own to his opponent's weapon, so that for one instant they seemed like two serpents writhing together; but at the next Constantine's sword was twirled out his hand.

"You will make a capital swordsman with practice, my boy. And the girl? Keep a sharpened eye for her; and tell me if so much as a new spider's web be woven at her door."

A peasant woman stood by the path as they proceeded, holding out her hand for alms, as she ran beside the general's horse. He leaned toward her to give something; but, as his hand touched hers, she slipped a bit of white rag into it:

"The map of the roads, Sire, twixt this and Monastir!"

"And your son, my good woman?" inquired the general kindly.

"Ah! the Virgin pity me, Sire, for he died. We could not stop the bleeding, for the lance's point had cut a vein. But I have a daughter who can take his place. She knows the signals—for he taught them to her—and can make the beacon as well as he; and is as nimble of foot to climb the crag. But please, Sire, the child did not remember if the enemy going west was to be signalled by lighting the beacon before or after the bright star's setting."

"Just after, good mother. If they go to the east and cross the mountain, fire the beacon just before the star sets. And the brightest of all stars be for your own hope and comfort!"

"And for dear Albania's and thine own!" replied the woman, disappearing in the crowd, as a man dashed close to Scanderbeg on a well-jaded steed.

"The Turkish auxiliaries will be at the entrance to the defile in thirty hours."

"Your estimate of their number, neighbor Stephen?"

"From three to five thousand."

"Not more?"

"Not more in the first detachment. A second of equal size follows, but a day in the rear."

"Good! Take with you our nephew, Musache de Angeline, and five hundred Epirots each. This will be sufficient to prevent the first detachment getting out of the pass. I will strike the second from the rear as soon as they enter the pass. They can not manœuvre in that crooked and narrow defile, and we will destroy them at our leisure. Strike promptly. Farewell!"

"Miserable sheep!" he muttered, "why will these Turks so tempt me to slaughter them?"

CHAPTER XXII

Upon the southern slope of the Black Mountain—that is, on the rising uplands which lead from Albania to Montenegro—lay the ancient and princely estates of the De Streeses. A dense forest of pines spread for miles, like a myriad gigantic pillars in some vast temple. They seemed to support, as it were, some Titanic dome surrounded with pinnacles and turrets, a huge cluster of jagged rocks, which was called by those who gazed upon it from leagues away "The Eyrie." In the midst of these great monoliths, and hardly distinguishable from them, rose the walls of the new castle which the voivode Amesa had built upon the ruins of that destroyed at the time of the massacre of its former possessor.

The horse of the voivode stood within the court, his head drooping, and the white sweat-foam drying upon his heated flanks. His master paced up and down the enclosure, engaged in low but excited conversation with a soldier.

The voivode was of princely mien; tall, but compactly built; face full in its lower development, and somewhat sensual; eyes gray and restless, which gave one at first a sharp, penetrating glance, and then seemed to hide behind the half-closed lids, like some wild animal that inspects the hunter hastily, then takes to covert.

"You are sure, Drakul, that the party which drove you from the hamlet were Turks, and not Arnaouts in disguise, like yourselves?" "I could not mistake," said Drakul, a hard-faced man, one of whose eyebrows was arched higher than the other, and whose entire countenance was distorted from the symmetrical balance of its two sides, giving an expression of duplicity and cruelty. "I could not mistake, noble Amesa, for I have too often eyed those rascals over the point of my sword not to know a Turk in the dark. But all the fiends combined against us that night. We left our two best men dead, and the two we wanted, the boy and the girl, escaped us. The she-witch did not come back to the village the next day; but the red-headed imp did, and raved like a hyena when he found the girl missing. I watched him as he suddenly went off, doubtless, to some spot they both knew of. The young thief stole the clothes off a dead Turk. The next day we spied him again; this time with that Arnaud-Kabilovitsch, Albanian-Servian, forester-colonel, or whatever he may be, who came back when Castriot did. The fellow escaped us a second time."

"Track him! track him!" cried Amesa spitefully. "I will make you rich, Drakul, the day you bring me that fox's brush of red hair from his head."

"I have tracked him and could take you to the very spot where he and the girl are to-day," said the man. "Come this way, my noble Amesa,"—leading him to the side of the court commanding a far stretch of country to the north-west. "Now let your eye follow Skadar[54] along the left shore: then up the great river.[55] Not two leagues from the mountain spur that bends the stream out of your sight, at the hamlet just off the road into your Uncle Ivan's country—"

"The stargeshina has a red goitre like a turkey cock? I know every hut in the hamlet," interrupted Amesa. "But why think you she is there?"

"Why? I have seen her, and him with her. I followed the fellow day after day. Once I saw him yonder on the spur. He clipped the bark of a tree, and in the smoothed spot cut a line. A little beyond he did the same thing again. He spied this way and that way with all the pains one would take to pick a way for an army. Then he took a roll of paper from his bosom, and marked down something for every mark he had made upon the trees. And when he was out of sight I took the range of his marks, and by St. Theckla! they pointed straight to a path which led down the mountain to the ford in the great river that is opposite the old turkey cock's konak."

"But you may have mistaken the man," suggested Amesa.

"Not I, Sire. I know his head as well as a bull knows a red rag; and his duck legs, and his walk like an ambling horse."

"It is he," submitted Amesa. "But how know you that the girl was there in the hamlet?"

"Did I not see her, my noble Amesa? And could I not know her from the look of her father? If I could forget him living, I have never passed a night without seeing his face as it was dead, when we dragged him to the burning beams of the old house that stood on this——""Silence!" cried Amesa in a sudden burst of rage. "How dare you allude to my uncle's death without my bidding?"

There was a pause for a few moments, during which Amesa stamped heavily upon the stone pavement of the court as he walked, like one endeavoring to shake off from his person some noisome thing that troubled him. The man resumed—

"Besides, the children of the village said she was a stray kid there, and not of kin to anybody. And while I was there the same stump-headed fellow who marked the direction came to the hamlet."

"Be ready to accompany me to-morrow, Drakul. You can say that we are scouting."

CHAPTER XXIII

The lake of Skadar lay like an immense *lapis lazuli* within its setting of mountains, which, on the east, were golden with the rays of the declining sun, and on the west, enameled in emerald with the dense shadows their summits dropped upon them. The surface of the water was unbroken, save here and there by black spots where a pair of loons shrieked their marital unhappiness, or a flock of wild ducks floated, like a miniature fleet, about the reed-fringed shores of some little island. Had there been watchers on the fortress of Obod, which lay on the cliff just above where the Tsernoyevitcha enters Skadar, they would have espied a light shallop gliding along the eastern bank of the lake. This contained the voivode Amesa and his attendant. Just at night-fall they reached the cavern, whose hidden recesses begot a hundred legends which the weird shadows of the cave clothed in forms as fantastic as their own, and which still flit among the hamlets of Montenegro. It was said that whoever should sleep within the cave would rest his head on the bosoms of the nymphs:—only let him take care that their love does not prevent his ever waking. Amesa and his companion were courageous, but discretion led them to wind the strooka about their heads, and seek without a couch of pine needles between the enormous roots of the trees which had dropped them.

The dawn had just silvered the east, and the coming sun transformed the cold blue tints of Skadar into amber, when they entered the river. The great stream wound through the broad lowlands of Tsetinie, girdled with rocky hills. Then it dashed in impetuous floods between more straightened banks, or lingered, as if the river spirit would bathe himself in the deep pools that were cooled by the springs at their bottoms. Though familiar with the phenomenon, they loitered that they might watch the schools of fish which were so dense in places as to impede the stroke of the oar blade, and tint the entire stream with their dull silvery gleam.[56] Emerging from a tortuous channel, through which the river twisted itself like a vast shining serpent, they came to a cluster of houses that nestled in a gorge. These houses were made of stone, and so covered with vines as to be hardly distinguishable from the dense shrubbery that clambered over the rocks about them.

Amesa was warmly greeted by the stargeshina who occupied the konak, or principal house. The older people remembered the visitor as the comely lad who, before the return of George Castriot, was almost the only male representative of that noble family left in the land. The voivode was honored with every evidence that the villagers felt themselves complimented by the visit of their guest, whatever business or caprice might have brought him thither.

A simple repast was provided, in which the courtesy of the service on the part of the stargeshina more than compensated any poverty in the display of viands;—though there were set forth meats dried in strips in the smoke of an open fire; eggs; sweet, though black bread; and wine pressed from various mountain berries, and allowed to ferment in skins. As they sat beside a low table at the doorway of the konak, the stargeshina offered a formal salâm, the zdravitsa, which was half a toast and half a prayer, and extended his hand to Amesa in the protestation of personal friendship. At the meal the glories of Castriot and Ivan Beg—or Ivo, as the peasants called him—were duly recited.

"But why," said the old man, rising to his feet with the enthusiasm of the sentiment—"Why should the country sing the praises of George Castriot, who for thirty years was willing to be a Turk and fight for an alien faith? Your shoulders, noble Amesa—Prince Amesa, my loyal heart would call you—could as well have borne the burden of the people's defence. Your arm could strike as good a blow as his for Albania. Your blood is that of the Castriots, and untainted by Moslem touch. Your estates, since you have become heir to the lands of De Streeses, make you our richest and most influential voivode."

These words made the eyes of Amesa flash, not with any novel pleasure, rather with an ambition to which he was no stranger. But the flash was smothered at once by the half-closed eyelids, and he responded—

"I ought not to hear such words, my good friend. My Uncle George is the hero of the hour. The people need a hero in whom they believe; and the very mystery of his life for the thirty years among the Turks, and the romance of his return, make him a convenient hero."

"But Sire, my noble—my Prince Amesa—do you not daily hear such words as I speak? The thought is as common as the Pater Noster, and echoes from Skadar to Ochrida. It was but a week since a young Albanian passed through this border country, whispering everywhere that the land was ready to cry Amesa's name rather than the reformed renegade, George Castriot's; that Scanderbeg, the Lord Alexander, the strutting title the Turks gave him, was an offence to the free hearts of the people."

"Ah! and what sort of a man for look was this Albanian?" asked Amesa in surprise.

"A sturdy youth of, say, twenty summers, with hair like a turban which had been worn by a dozen slaughtered Turks, so blood red is it."

Amesa gave a puzzled look toward Drakul, who was eating his meal at a little distance, but whose ears seemed to prick up like those of a horse at this description.

"It is likely that he may be again in the village this very night. Our neighbor next lodged him. I will ask him if he will return," said the stargeshina, leaving the konak for a little.

"It is he; it's that Constantine," said Drakul, coming nearer to Amesa. "The wily young devil is ready to betray your Uncle George. That will make the matter easier."

"The way is clear, then," replied Amesa. "I am glad that the raid was not successful. It might have led to further blood. With this fellow in league with us, it is straight work and honorable."

The stargeshina reported the man would probably be in again that very night, and added:

"I would you could see him; for though he is fair spoken, there is some mystery in his going day after day among these mountains, like a hound who is looking for a lost scent."

"Perhaps he is attracted here by some of the fair maidens of the hamlets," suggested Amesa, looking at Drakul, who was tearing a bit of jerked meat in his teeth, apparently intent only upon that selfish occupation.

"It may well be, for our neighbor here has harbored a bit of stray womanhood which might tempt a monk to lodge there rather than in his cell," said the old man.

A shout from above them attracted their attention to a merry company which was coming down the mountain. It was the procession of the Dodola. Drought threatened to destroy the scanty grain growing in the narrow valleys, and the vines on the terraces cut out of the steep hills. According to an ancient custom, a young maiden had been taken by her companions into the woods, stripped of her usual garments, and reclothed in the leaves and flowers of the endangered vegetation. Long grasses and stalks of grain were matted in many folds about her person, and served as a base for artistic decoration with every variety of floral beauty. Her feet were buskined in clover blossoms. A kilt of broad-leaved ferns hung from her waist, which was belted with a broad zone of wild roses. White and pink laurel blossoms made her bodice. An ivy wreath upon her brows was starred with white daisies, and plumed with the stems and hanging bells of the columbine.

The Dodola thus appeared as the impersonation of floral nature athirst for the vivifying rains. Her attendants, who led her in a leash of roses, chanted a hymn, the refrain of which was a prayer to Elijah, who, since he brought the rain at Carmel, is supposed by the peasants of Albania to be that saint to whom Providence has committed the shepherding of the clouds. As the procession wound down the terraced paths between the houses, the Dodola was welcomed by the matrons of the hamlet, who stood each in her own doorway, with hair gathered beneath a cap of coins, teeth enameled in black, fingers tipped brownish-red with henna. The maidens sung a verse of their hymn at each cottage; and, at the refrain, the housewife poured upon the head of the leaf-clad Dodola a cup of water; repeating the last line of the chorus, "Good Saint Elias, so send the rain!"

As the Dodola paused before the konak, Amesa said, quite enthusiastically, and designing to be overheard by the fair girl who took the part of thirsting nature, "If Elias can refuse the prayer of so much womanly beauty, I swear, by Jezebel, that I shall hereafter believe, with the Turks, that the austere old prophet has become bewitched with the houris in paradise, and so does not care to look into the faces of earthly damsels."

"You may still keep your Christian faith, for the Dodola has won the favor of the Thunderer,"[57] replied the stargeshina. "Listen to his love-making in response to the witchery of that wild dove! Do you hear it?"

The distant murmur of a coming shower confirmed the credulity of the peasants.

"Yes, soon the Holy Virgin will turn her bright glances upon us,"[58] said he looking at the sky.

"Who is that wild dove who acts the Dodola?" inquired Amesa.

"The one I told you of, who has come into our neighbor's cot," replied the old man. "But only the sharp eyes of the crows saw where she came from. Did she not speak our tongue and know our ways as well as any of us, I should say she was one of the Tsigani who were driven out of the morning land by Timour.[59] Yet it may be that her own story is true. She says she had two lovers in her village; and these two were brothers in God, who had taken the vow before heaven and St. John to help and never to hinder each other in whatever adventure of love or brigandage, at cost of limb or life. But as the hot blood of neither of these lovers could endure to see this nymph in the arms of the other, it was determined that she should be slain by the hand of both, rather than that the sacred brotherhood should be broken. By her own father's hearth the two daggers were struck together at her heart. But the strong arms of the slayers collided, and both blows glanced. She escaped and fled, and came hither."

"And you believe this story?" asked Amesa, with a look of incredulity mingled with triumph, as of one who knew more than the narrator.

"I believe her story, noble Amesa, because—because no one has told me any other. But—" He shook his head.

"Does not the young stranger you spoke of know something of her, that he prowls about this neighborhood?" asked the guest.

"It may be. I had not thought it, but it may well be! Hist—!"

The Dodola passed by, returning to her own cottage. As she did so her bright black eyes glanced coquettishly at the stranger from beneath her disarranged chaplet of flowers and dishevelled hair. She soon returned, having assumed her garments as a peasant maid, but with evident effort to make this simple attire set off the great natural beauty of face and form, of which she was fully conscious. Her forehead was too low; but Pygmalion could not have chiselled a brow and temples upon which glossy black ringlets clustered more bewitchingly. Her eyes flashed too cold a fire light to give one the impression of great amiability in their possessor; but the long lashes which drooped before them, partially veiled their stare so as to give the illusion of coyness, if not of maidenly modesty. Her mouth was perhaps sensuously curved; but was one of those marvellously plastic ones which can tell by the slightest arching or compressing of the lips as much of purpose or feeling as most people can tell in words:—dangerous lips to the possessor, if she be guileless and unsuspicious, for they reveal too much of her soul to others who have no right to know its secrets; dangerous lips to others if she would deceive, for they can lie, consummately, wickedly, without uttering a word. Her complexion was scarcely brunette; rather that indescribable fairness in which the whiteness of alabaster is tinged with the blood of perfect health, slightly bronzed by constant exposure to the sunshine and air—a complexion seldom seen except in Syria, the Greek Islands, or Wales. Her form was faultless,—just at that stage of development when the grace and litheness of childhood are beginning to be lost in the statelier mysteries of womanly beauty; that transition state between two ideals of loveliness, which, from the days of Phidias, has lured, but always eluded, the artist's skill to reproduce.

The girl's face flushed with the consciousness of being gazed at approvingly by the courtly stranger. But the pretty toss of her head showed that the blush was due as much to the conceit of her beauty as to bashfulness. As she talked with the other maidens, she glanced furtively toward the door of the konak, where Amesa sat. The young voivode foresaw that it would not be difficult to entice the girl herself to be the chief agent in any plan he might have for her abduction.

He needed, however, to make more certain of her identity with the object of his search. He could discern no trace of Mara De Streeses in her face; much less in her manner. Since Drakul had suggested it, he imagined a resemblance to De Streeses himself, whose bearing was haughty and his temperament fiery.

The evening brought the young man of whom the stargeshina had spoken. His resemblance to the description given him of Constantine left no doubt in Amesa's mind of his being the mysterious custodian of the heiress to his estates. The young Servian he supposed would at once recognize him as Amesa; for, as a prominent officer in the army, his face would be well known to all who had been in Castriot's camps, even if the gossip of the villagers did not at once inform him of his presence. It were best then, thought Amesa, to boldly confront him; win him, if possible, to his service; if not, destroy him.

The young stranger was at once on frolicksome terms with the village girls and lads; and Amesa thought he observed that through it all the fellow kept a sharp, if not a suspicious, eye upon him. Lest he should escape, the voivode invited him to walk beyond the houses of the village. When out of sight and hearing he suddenly turned upon the young man, and, laying a hand upon his shoulder, exclaimed, "You are known, man!"

Upon the instant the stranger was transformed from the sauntering peasant into a gladiator, with feet firmly planted, the left hand raised as a shield, and the right grasping a yataghan which had been concealed upon his person. Amesa, though the aggressor, was thrown upon the defensive, and was compelled to retreat in order to gain time for the grip of his weapon.

The two men stood glaring into each other's eyes as there each to read his antagonist's movement before his hand began to execute it.

"I did not know that a Servian peasant was so trained," said Amesa, still retreating before the advance of his opponent, who gave him no opportunity to assume the offensive.

"For whom do you take me that you dare to lay a rough hand on me?" said the man, half in menace, and yet apparently willing to discover if his assailant were right in his surmise.

"Arnaud's man and I need not be enemies," said Amesa, seeing no chance of relieving himself from the advantage the other had gained in the sword play. "I can reward you better than he or Castriot."

A smile passed over the man's face, which Amesa might have detected the meaning of had his mind been less occupied with thoughts about his personal safety from the yataghan, whose point was seeking his throat according to the most approved rules of single combat.

"And what if I am Arnaud's man?"

As he said this the yataghan made a thorough reconnoissance of all the vulnerable parts of Amesa's body from the fifth rib upwards, followed by Amesa's dagger in ward.

"You do not deny it?" said the Albanian between breaths.

"I deny nothing. Nor need I confess anything, since you say I am known."

"Shall we be friends?" asked Amesa, cautiously lowering his arm.

"You made war, and can withdraw its declaration, or take the consequences," was the reply.

The two men put up their weapons.

"So good a soldier as you are should not be here guarding a girl," said Amesa.

"Guarding a girl?" said the man in amazement, but, recollecting himself, added, "And why not guard a girl?"

"Come," replied Amesa, "you and I can serve each other. You can do that for me which no other man can; and I can give to you more gold than any other Albanian can."

"And when you are king of Albania, Prince Amesa, you can reward me with high appointment," said the stranger with a slight sneer, which, however, Amesa did not notice, at the moment thinking of what the stargeshina had said of the man's interest in the movement against his uncle's leadership.

"You have but to ask your reward when that event comes," he replied.

"I will swear to serve Amesa against Scanderbeg to the death," said the man offering his hand.

"You know the girl's true story?" asked Amesa.

"Of course," was the cautious reply. "But of that I may not speak a word. I can leave his service whose man you say I am, but I cannot betray anything he may have told me. As you know the girl's story it is needless to tempt me to divulge it," added he, with shrewd non-committal of himself to any information that the other might recognize as erroneous.

"You speak nobly for a Servian," said the voivode.

"How do you know I am a Servian?" asked the stranger.

"Partly from your accent. You have not got our pure Albanian tongue, though it is now six years you have been talking it. And then Arnaud—Colonel Kabilovitsch—came back as a Servian. Is it not so?" asked Amesa, noticing the surprised look which the mention of Kabilovitsch's name brought to the man's face.

For a while the stranger was lost in thought; but with an effort throwing off a sort of reverie, he said:

"Pardon my silence. I have been thinking of your proposal. May I follow you to the village after a little? I would think over how best I can meet your proposition, my Prince Amesa."

"I will await you at the konak. But first let us swear friendship!" said the voivode.

"Heartily!" was the response. "With Amesa as against Scanderbeg."

"You will induce the girl to go with me to my castle. She will fare better there than here, playing Dodola to these ignorant peasants."

"It is agreed."

As Amesa disappeared, the man sat down upon a huge root of a tree, which for lack of earth had twined itself over the rock. He buried his face in his hands—

"Strange! strange! is all this. Kabilovitsch? the girl? Not my little playmate on the Balkans—sweet faced Morsinia. The Dodola here is not she. If Uncle Kabilovitsch is Colonel Kabilovitsch, or this Arnaud he speaks of, then this treacherous Amesa is on the wrong track. Can it be that Constantine—dear little Constantine—is in Albania, and that I am mistaken for him? No, this is impossible. But still I must be wary, and not do that which would harm a golden hair of Morsinia's head, if she be living, or Constantine's, or Uncle Kabilovitsch's. There's some mystery here. Only one thing is certain—Amesa mistakes this pretty impudent Dodola girl for somebody else. To get her off with him may serve that somebody else: for the voivode is a villain: that much is sure. The cursed Giaour serpent! I will help him to get this saucy belle of the hamlet, and so save somebody else, whoever she may be who is the game for which he lays his snares."

An hour later the Dodola, whose name was Elissa, passed Amesa and blushed deeply.

The family at whose house the girl was living made no objection to Amesa's request that she should be transferred to the protection of the voivode. The elders of the village acquiesced; for, said one,

"We do not know who she is, and may get into difficulty through harboring her."

Another averred his belief that she was possessed of the evil eye; for he had observed her staring at the olive tree the day before it was struck by lightning; and he declared that half the young men of the hamlet were bewitched with her.

A sharp-tongued dame remarked that some of the older men would rather listen to the merry tattle of the sprite than to the most serious and wholesome counsel of their own wives.

CHAPTER XXIV

"Do you know the mind of Gauton who commands at the citadel in Sfetigrade?" asked Amesa of his new confederate, as they parted.

"I have talked with him," replied the man. "He is very cautious."

"Discover his opinion on the matter of my advancement," said Amesa.

"Send him some gift," suggested the man, "I will take it to him. He is very fond of dogs, and I learn that he has just lost a valuable mastiff. Could you replace it from your kennels at the castle?"

"No, but I have a greyhound, of straight breed since his ancestors came out of the ark. His jaws are as slender as a heron's beak: chest deep as a lion's: belly thin as a weasel's: a double span of my arms from tip to tail. To-morrow night meet me at the castle. Should I not have arrived, this will give you admission," presenting him with a small knife, on the bone handle of which was a rude carving of the crest of Amesa. "Give it to the warden. He will recognize it."

Long before the arrival of Amesa and Drakul at the castle in company with Elissa, the stranger, whom the reader will recognize as Captain Ballaban dressed as an Albanian peasant, had been admitted. He had wandered about the court, mounted the parapet, inspected the draw-bridge and portcullis, clambered down and up again the almost precipitous scarp of the rock, and asked a hundred questions of the servants regarding the paths by which the castle was approached. The old warden entertained him with stories of Amesa's early life, his acquisition of the estate, and his prowess in battle; in all of which, while the warden intended only the praise of his master, he discovered to the attentive listener all the weaknesses of the voivode's character.

Upon Amesa's arrival late in the day, Ballaban avoided much intercourse with him, except in relation to the selection of the dog. To Elissa he gave a few words of advice, to the effect that she was now the object of the young lord's adoration; and that, in order to secure her advantage, she should make as much as possible a mystery of her previous life. With this council—which was as much as he dared to venture upon in his own ignorance of the exact part he was playing—Ballaban departed, leading a magnificent hound in leash. A little way from the castle he sat down, and drawing from his breast a roll of paper, added certain lines and comments, as he muttered to himself,—

"I have made neater drawings than this for old Bestorf in the school of the Yeni-Tscheri, but none that will please the Aga more. There is not a goat path on the borders that I have not got. A sudden movement of our armies, occupying ground here and here and here, where I have blazed the trees, would hold this country against Ivan Beg and Scanderbeg. And with this black-hearted traitor, Amesa, in my fingers!—Well! Let's see! I will force him into open rebellion against Scanderbeg, unless he is deeper witted than he seems. But which plan would be best in the long run?—to stir up a feud between him and Scanderbeg, and let them cut each other's throats? Or, inveigle him to open alliance with our side, under promise of being made king of Albania? That last would settle all the Moslem trouble with these Giaours. And it could be done. The Padishah offered Scanderbeg the country on condition of paying a nominal tribute, and would offer the same to Amesa. And Amesa would take it, though he had to become Moslem. I will leave these propositions with the Aga," said he, folding up the papers, and putting them back into his bosom. "In either case I shall keep my vow with Amesa to help him against Scanderbeg. But the devil help them both!"

Whistling a snatch of a rude tune, part of which belonged to an Albanian religious hymn he had heard in his rambles, and part to a Turkish love song—swinging his long arms, and striding as far at each step as his short legs would allow him, he went down the mountain.

CHAPTER XXV

"Who comes here?" cried the sentinel at the bottom of the steep road which led up to the gate at the rear of the town of Sfetigrade.

The man thus challenged made no reply except to speak sharply to a large hound he was leading, and which was struggling to break away from him. In his engrossment with the brute he did not seem to have heard the challenge. As he came nearer the sentinel eyed him with a puzzled, but half-comical look, as he soliloquized,—

"Ah, by the devil in the serpent's skin, I know him this time. He is the Albanian Turk we were nigh to hamstringing. If I mistake that red head again it will be when my own head has less brain in it than will balance it on a pike-staff, where Colonel Kabilovitsch would put it if I molested this fellow again. I'll give him the pass word, instead of taking it from him; that will make up for past mistakes."

The sentinel saluted the new comer with a most profound courtesy, and, shouldering his spear, marched hastily past him, ogling him with a sidelong knowing look.

"Tako mi Marie!"[60]

"Tako mi Marie!" responded the man, adding to himself, "but this is fortunate; the fellow must be crazy. I thought I should have had to brain him at least."

As he passed by, the sentinel stood still, watching him, and muttered,

"How should I know but Castriot himself is in that dog's hide."

The dog turned and, attracted by the soldier's attitude, uttered a low growl.

"Tako mi Marie! and all the other saints in heaven too, but I believe it is the general in disguise," said the sentinel.

"Tako mi Marie!" said the stranger saluting the various guards, whom he passed without further challenge, through the town gates and up to the main street.

The great well, from which the beleaguered inhabitants of Sfetigrade drew the only water now accessible, since the Turks had so closely invested the town, was not far from the citadel. It was very deep, having been cut through the great layers of rock upon which the upper town stood. Above it was a great wheel, over the outer edge of which ran an endless band of leather; the lower end dipping into the water that gleamed faintly far below. Leathern sockets attached to this belt answered for buckets, which, as the wheel was turned, lifted the water to the top, whence it ran into a great stone trough. The well was guarded by a curb of stones which had originally been laid compactly together; but many of them had been removed, and used to hurl down from the walls of the citadel upon the heads of the Turks when they tried to scale them.

The dog, panting with the heat, mounted one of the remaining stones, and stretched his long neck far down to sniff the cool water which glistened a hundred feet below him. The man shouted angrily to the beast, and so clumsily attempted to drag him away that both dog and stone were precipitated together into the well.

"A grapple! a rope!" shouted the man to a crowd who had seen the accident from a distance. "Will no one bring one?" he cried with apparent anger at their slow movements—"Then I must get one myself."

The crowd rushed toward the well. The man disappeared in the opposite direction.

It was several hours before the dead dog was taken from the polluted water. The Dibrian soldiers refused to drink from it. The superstition communicated itself like an epidemic, to the other inhabitants. For a day or two bands sallied from Sfetigrade, and brought water from the plain: but it was paid for in blood, for the Turkish armies, aware of the incident almost as soon as it occurred, drew closer their lines, and stationed heavy detachments of Janizaries at the springs and streams for miles around. The horrors of a water-famine were upon the garrison. In vain did the officers rebuke the insane delusion. The common soldiers, not only would not touch the water, but regarded the accident as a direct admonition from heaven that the town must be surrendered. Appeals to heroism, patriotism, honor, were less potent than a silly notion which had grown about the minds of an otherwise noble people—as certain tropical vines grow so tough and in such gradually lessening spirals about a stalwart tree that they choke the ascending sap and kill it. They who would have drunk were prevented by the others who covered the well with heavy pieces of timber, and stood guard about it.

CHAPTER XXVI

In vain did Castriot assault the Turks who were intrenched about the wells and springs in the neighborhood. Now and then a victory over them would be followed by a long procession from the town, rolling casks, carrying buckets, pitchers, leather bottles and dug-out troughs. The amount of water thus procured but scarcely sufficed to keep life in the veins of the defenders: it did not suffice to nourish heart and courage. It was foreseen that Sfetigrade must fall.

Constantine was in the madness of despair about Morsinia. Her fate in the event of capture was simply horrible to contemplate. Yet she could hardly hope to make her way through the Turkish lines. Constantine was at the camp with Castriot when it was announced that the enemy had at length got possession of every approach to the town, so that there was no communication between the Albanians within and those without, except by signaling over the heads of the Turks. Castriot determined upon a final attack, during which, if he should succeed in uncovering any of the gates of the town, the people might find egress.

Constantine begged to be allowed the hazardous duty of entering, by passing in disguise through the Turkish army, and giving the endangered people the exact information of Castriot's purpose. Taking advantage of his former experience, he donned the uniform of a Janizary, easily learned the enemy's password, and at the moment designated to the besieged by Castriot's signal—just as the lower star of the Great Dipper disappeared behind the cliff—he emerged from the dense shadows of an angle of the wall. He was scarcely opposite the gate when the drawbridge lowered and rose quickly. The portcullis was raised and dropped an instant later, and he was within the town.

Throwing off his disguise, he went at once toward the commandant's quarters to deliver despatches from Castriot. But a shout preceded him—

"The destroyer! The destroyer! Death to the destroyer!"

Multitudes, awakened by the shouting, came from the houses and soldiers' quarters. Constantine was seized by the crowd, who yelled:

"To the well with him! Let the dog's soul come into him!"

He was borne along as helplessly as a leaf in the foaming cataract.

"To the well! To the well with the poisoner!"

The cry grew louder and shriller; the multitude maddening under the intense fury of their mutual rage, as each coal is hotter when many glow with it in the fire. Women mingled with soldiers, shrieking their insane vengeance, until the crowd surged with the victim around the well. The planks were torn off by strong hands. The horror of the deed they were about to commit made them pause. Each waited for his neighbor to assume the desperate office of actually perpetrating what was in all their hearts to do.

At length three of the more resolute stepped forward as executioners of the popular will. The struggling form of Constantine was held erect that all might see him. Torches waved above his head. One stood upon the well curb, and, dropping a torch into the dark abyss, cried with a loud voice—

"So let his life be put out who destroys us all!"

"So let it be!" moaned the crowd; the wildness of their wrath somewhat subdued by the impressiveness of the tragedy they were enacting.

The well hissed back its curse as the burning brand sunk into the water.

But a new apparition burst upon the scene. Suddenly, as if it had risen from the well, a form draped in white stood upon the curb. Her long golden hair floated in the strong wind. Her face, from sickness white as her robe, had an unearthly pallor from the excitement, and seemed to be lit with the white heat of her soul. Her sunken eyes gave back the flare of the torches, as if they gleamed with celestial reprobation.

"The Holy Virgin!" cried some.

"One of the Vili!" cried others.

The crowd surged back in ghostly fear.

"Neither saint nor sprite am I," cried Morsinia. "Your own wicked hearts make you fear me. It is your consciences that make you imagine a simple girl to be a vengeful spirit, and shrink from this horrid murder, to the very brink of which your ignorance and wretched superstition have led you. Blessed Mary need not come from Heaven to tell you that a man—a man for whom her Son Jesu died—should not be made to die for the sake of a dead dog. I, a child, can tell you that."

"But the well is accursed and the people die," said a monk, throwing back his cowl, and reaching out his hand to seize her.

"And such words from you, a priest of Jesu!" answered the woman, warding him off by the scathing scorn of her tones. "Did not Jesu say, 'Come unto Me and drink, drink out of My veins as ye do in Holy

Sacrament?' Will He curse and kill, then, for drinking the water which you need, because a dog has fallen into it?"

These words, following the awe awakened by her unexpected appearance, stayed the rage of the crowd for a moment. But soon the murmur rose again—

"To the well!"

"He is a murderer!"

"It is just to take vengeance on a murderer!"

The woman raised her hand as if invoking the witness of Heaven to her cause, and exclaimed—

"But *I* am not a murderer. A curse on him who slays the innocent. I will be the sacrifice. I fear not to drink of this well with my dying gasp. Unhand the man, or, as sure as Heaven sees me, I shall die for him!"

A shudder of horror ran through the crowd as the light form of the young woman raised itself to the very brink of the well. It seemed as if a movement, or a cry, would precipitate her into the black abyss. The crowd was paralyzed. The silence of the dead fell upon them, as she leaned forward for the awful plunge.

Those holding Constantine let go their grip.

At this moment the commandant appeared. He had, indeed, been a silent witness of the scene, and was not unwilling that the superstition of the soldiers should thus have a vent, thinking that with the sacrifice of the supposed offender they might be satisfied, and led to believe that the spirit of the well was appeased. He hoped that thus they might be induced to drink the water. But he recoiled from permitting the sacrifice of this innocent person, lest it should blacken the curse already impending.

"I will judge this case," he cried. "Man, who are you?"

"I bear you orders from General Castriot," replied Constantine, handing him a document.

By the light of a torch the officer read,

"In the event of being unable to hold out, signal and make a sally according to directions to be given verbally by the bearer. Castriot."

Turning to the crowd, the commandant addressed them.

"Brave men! Epirots and Dibrians! We are being led into some mistake. My message makes it evident that on this man's life depends the life of every one of us——"

His voice was drowned by wild cries that came from a distant part of the town. The cries were familiar enough to all their ears; but they had heretofore heard them only from beneath the walls without. They were the Turkish cries of assault. "Allah! Allah! Allah! Allah!" rolled like a hurricane along the streets of Sfetigrade. The gates had been thrown open by some Dibrian, whom superstition and a thirst-fevered brain had transformed into a traitor.

"Quick!" cried Constantine. "Fire three powder flashes from the bastion, and follow me."

"Brave girl!" said he to Morsinia, grasping her hand and drawing her toward the citadel.

"It is too late!" replied the commandant. "All the ports are occupied by the enemy. We can but die in the streets."

"To the north gate, then! Burst it open, and cut your way to the east. Castriot will meet you there. I will to the bastion."

"We must go with them," said Morsinia. "Better die in the streets than be taken here."

"No, you shall not die, my good angel. I have prepared for this. First, I will fire the signal." In a few seconds three flashes illumined the old battlements.

Returning to Morsinia, he said quietly, "I have prepared for this," and unwound from about his body a strong cord, looped at intervals so that it could be used for a ladder. Fastening this securely, he dropped the end over the wall. Descending part way himself, he opened the loops one by one for the feet of his companion; and thus they reached a narrow ledge some twenty feet below the parapet. From this to the next projection broad enough to stand upon, the rock was steep but slanting; so that, while one could not rest upon it, it would largely overcome the momentum of the descent. Fastening a cord securely beneath the arms of Morsinia, he let her down the slope to the lower ledge. Then, tying the rope to that above, he descended himself to her side. From this point the path was not dangerous to one possessed of perfect presence of mind, and accustomed to balance the body on one foot at a time. Thanks to her mountain life, and the strong stimulus to brain and nerve acquired by her familiarity with danger, Morsinia was undizzied by the elevation. Thus they wound their way toward the east side of the wall; and, as they neared the base of the cliff, sat down to reconnoitre.

Above them frowned the walls of the citadel. Just beneath them were many forms, moving like spectres in the darkness which was fast dissolving into the gray morning twilight. The voices which came up to their ears proved that they were Turks. For Morsinia to pass through them without detection would be impossible. To remain long where they were would be equally fatal.

But their anxiety was relieved by a well known bugle-call. At first it sounded far away to the north.

"Iscanderbeg! Iscanderbeg!" cried the Turks, as they were deployed to face the threatening assault. But scarcely had they formed in their new lines when the sound, as of a storm bursting through a forest, indicated that the attack was from the south.

Taking the Turks who were still outside the walls at a disadvantage, Castriot's force made terrible havoc among them, sweeping them back pell-mell past the eastern front and around the northern, so as to leave the north gate clear for the escape of any who might emerge from it.

But, alas, for the valor of the commandant and the noble men who followed him! few succeeded in cutting their way through the swarm of enemies that had already occupied the streets of Sfetigrade.

This movement, however, enabled Constantine and Morsinia to descend from their dangerous eyrie. The apparition of their approach from that direction was a surprise to the general.

"Why, man, do you ride upon bats and night-hawks, that you have flown from yonder crag? I shall henceforth believe in Radisha and his beautiful demon. And may I pray thy care for myself in battle, my fair lady?"

CHAPTER XXVII

The fall of Sfetigrade, while a material loss to the Albanian cause, served rather to exalt than to diminish the prestige of their great general. The fame of Scanderbeg brightened as the gloomy tidings of the fate of the stronghold spread; for that event, due to a circumstance which no human being could control, gave his enemies their first success, after nearly seven years of incessant effort, with measureless armaments, innumerable soldiery and exhaustless treasure.

The adversity also developed in Scanderbeg new qualities of greatness, both military and moral. As the effort to drain a natural spring only evokes its fuller and freer flow, so disappointment augmented his courage, impoverishment in resources enlarged the scheme of his projects, and the defeat of one plan by circumstances suggested other plans more novel and shrewd. The sight of the Turkish ensign floating from the citadel of Sfetigrade disheartened the patriots. The tramp of fresh legions from almost all parts of the Moslem world was not so ominous of further disaster as were the whispers of discontent from more than one who, like Amesa, had ambitions of their own, or, like brave Moses Goleme, were discouraged regarding ultimate success. But the great heart of Castriot sustained the courage of his people, and his genius devised plans for the defence of his land which, for sixteen years yet, were to baffle the skill and weary the energies of the foe.

The chief gave orders that Morsinia, having eluded capture, should occupy for the day his own tent; for the Albanian soldiers, as a rule, were destitute of the luxury of a canvas covering. Returning toward the middle of the morning, and having need to enter, he bade Constantine call her. No response being given, Castriot raised the curtain of the tent. Upon a rude matting, which was raised by rough boards a few inches from the earth, her limbs covered with an exquisitely embroidered Turkish saddle cloth, Morsinia lay asleep. Her neck and shoulders were veiled with her hair, which, rich and abundant, fell in cascades of golden beauty upon the ground.

The great man stood for a moment gazing upon the sleeping girl. His ordinarily immobile features relaxed. His face, generally passionless, unreadable as that of the sphinx, and impressive only for the mystery of the thoughts it concealed, now became suffused with kindly interest. His smile, as if he had been surprised by the fairness of the vision, was followed by a look of fatherly tenderness. The tears shot into his eyes; but with a deep breath he dropped the curtain, and turned away. Of what was he thinking? Of little Mara Cernoviche, his playmate far back in the years? or of himself during those years? Strange that career among the Turks! and equally strange all the years since he had looked upon the little child asleep by the camp fire at the foot of the Balkans! One who gazed into his face at that moment would have discovered that the rough warrior spirit was an outer environment about a gentle and loving nature.

He was interrupted by officers crowding about him, bringing intelligence of the enemy, or asking questions relative to the immediate movements of their own commands. These were answered in laconic sentences, each one a flash of strategic wisdom.

In the first leisure he put his hand fondly upon Constantine's head, and said quietly as he seated himself upon a rock near the tent door—

"Tell me of last night."

As Constantine narrated what the reader is already familiar with, dwelling especially upon Morsinia's part in the scene at the well, and her courage in the descent from the wall, Scanderbeg exclaimed eagerly—

"A true daughter of Musache De Streeses and Mara Cernoviche! The very impersonation of our Albania! Her spirit is that of our heroic people, fair as our lakes and as noble as our mountains! But these scenes are too rough for her. Her soul is strong enough to endure; but so is the diamond strong enough to keep its shape and lustre amid the stones which the freshet washes together. But it is not well that it should be left to do so. Besides, the diamond's strength and inviolable purity will not prevent a robber from stealing it. There are envious eyes upon our treasure. We had better have our diamond cut and set and put away in a casket for a while. We will send her to Constantinople. There she will have opportunity to gain in knowledge of the world, and in the courtly graces which fit her princely nature."

"Would not Italy be better?" suggested Constantine.

"No," said Scanderbeg. "The Italians are uncertain allies. I know not whom to trust across the Adriatic. But Phranza, the chamberlain at Constantinople, is a noble man. I knew him years ago when I was stationed across the Bosphorus, and had committed to me nearly all the Ottoman affairs, so far as they affected the Greek capital. He is one of the few Greeks we may implicitly trust. And, moreover, he agrees with me in seeking a closer alliance between our two peoples. If the Christian power at Constantinople could be roused against the Turk on the east, while we are striking him on the west, we could make the Moslem wish he were well out of Europe. But Italy will do nothing."

"The Holy Father can help, can he not?" asked Constantine.

"The Holy Father does not to-day own himself. He is the mere foot-ball of the secular powers, who kick him against one another in their strife. No, our hope is in putting some life into the old Greek empire at Constantinople. The dolt of an emperor, John, is dead, thanks to Azrael[61]! In Constantine, who has come to the throne, Christendom has hope of something better than to see the heir of the empire of the Cæsars dancing attendance upon Italian dukes; seeking agreement with the Pope upon words of a creed which no one can understand; and demoralizing, with his uncurtained harem, the very Turk. If the new emperor has the sense of a flea he will see that the Moslem power will have Constantinople within a decade, unless the nations can be united in its defence. I would send letters to Phranza, and you must be my envoy. With Morsinia there, we shall be free from anxiety regarding her; for no danger threatens her except here in her own land—to our shame I say it. A Venetian galley touches weekly at Durazzo, and sails through the Corinthian gulf. You will embark upon that to-morrow night."

"But Colonel Kabilovitsch?" inquired Constantine.

"He has already started for Durazzo, and will make all arrangements. Nothing is needed here but a comely garment for Morsinia, who left Sfetigrade with a briefer toilet than most handsome women are willing to make. Colonel Kabilovitsch will see that you are provided with money and detailed instructions for the journey."

A soldier appeared with a bundle. "A rough lady's maid!" said the general, "but a useful one I will warrant."

Unrolling the bundle, it proved to be a rich, but plain, dress, donated from a neighboring castle.

An hour later Scanderbeg held Morsinia by both hands, looking down into her eyes. It was a picture which should have become historic. The giant form of the grim old warrior contrasted fully with that of the maiden, as some gnarled oak with the flower that grows at its base.

"Keep good heart, my daughter," said the general, imprinting a kiss upon her fair brow.

She replied with loving reverence in her tone and look, "I thank you, Sire, for that title; for the father of his country has the keeping of the hearts of all the daughters of Albania."

It were difficult to say whether the sweet loveliness in the lines of her face, or the majesty of character and superb heroism that shone through them, gave her the greater fascination as she added,

"If Jesu wills that among strangers I can best serve my country, there shall be my home."

"But you will not long be among strangers. Your goodness will make them all friends. Beside, God will keep such as you, for he loves the pure and beautiful."

Morsinia blushed as she answered,

"And does God not love the true and the noble? So he will keep thee and Albania. Does not the sun send down her[62] beams as straight over Constantinople as over Croia? and does she not draw the mists by as short a cord of her twisted rays from the Marmora as from the Adriatic? Then God can be as near us there as here; and our prayers for thee and our land will go as speedily to the Great Heart over all. The Blessed Mary keep you, Sire!"

"Ay, the Blessed Mary spake the blessing through your lips, my child," responded Scanderbeg as he lifted her to her horse.

Constantine released himself from the general's hearty embrace, and sprang into the saddle at her side. Preceded and followed by a score of troopers they disappeared in the deep shadows of a mountain path.

CHAPTER XXVIII

Durazzo lies upon a promontory stretching out into the Adriatic. The walls which surrounded it at the time of our story, told, by the weather-wear of their stones, the different ages during which they had guarded the little bay that lies at the promontory's base. A young monk,[63] Barletius, to whom Colonel Kabilovitsch introduced the voyagers, as a travelling companion for a part of their journey, pointed out the great and rudely squared boulders in the lower course of masonry, as the work of the ancient Corcyreans, centuries before the coming of Christ. The upper courses, he said, were stained with the blood of the Greek soldiers of Alexius, when the Norman Robert Guiscard assaulted the place, hundreds and hundreds of years ago.

Indeed, to the monk's historic imagination, the world seemed still wrapped in the mists of the older ages; and, just as the low lying haze, with its mirage effect, contorted the rocks along the shore into domes and pinnacles, so did his fancy invest every object with the greatness of the history with which the old manuscripts had made him familiar.

While Morsinia listened with a strange entertainment to his rhapsodic narrations, Constantine was busy studying the graceful lines of the Venetian half-galley that lay at the base of the cliff, and upon which they were to embark; her low deck, cut down in the centre nearly to the water's edge; her sharp, swan-necked prow raised high in air, and balanced by the broad elevation at the stern; the lateen sail that, furled on its boom, hung diagonally against the slender mast; the rows of holes at the side, through which in calm weather the oars were worked; the gay pennant from the mast-head, and the broad banner at the stern, which spread to the light breeze the Lion of St. Mark.

They were soon gliding out of the harbor of Durazzo, at first under the regularly timed stroke of a score of oarsmen. Rounding the promontory, the west wind filled the sail; and, careening to the leeward, the galley danced toward the south through the light spray of the billows which sung beneath the prow like the strings of a zither.

Perhaps it was this music of the waves—or it may have been that the wind was blowing straight across from Italy; or, possibly, it was the beauty of the maiden reclining upon the cushioned dais of the stern deck—that led the weather-beaten sailing master to take the zither, and sing one after another of Petrarch's love songs to Laura. Though his voice was as hoarse as the wind that crooned through the cordage, and his language scarcely intelligible, the flow of the melody told the sentiment. Constantine's eyes sought the face of his companion, as if for the first time he had detected that she was beautiful. And perhaps for the first time in her life Morsinia felt conscious that Constantine was looking at her;—for she generally withstood his gaze with as little thought of it as she did that of the sky, or of Kabilovitsch. Even the monk turned his eyes from the magnificent shores of Albania, with their beetling headlands and receding bays, to cast furtive glances upon the maiden.

The monk's face was a striking one. He was pale, if not from holy vigil, from pouring over musty secular tomes. He had caught the spirit of the revival of learning which, notwithstanding all the superstition of ecclesiastics, was first felt in the cloisters of the church. His forehead was high, but narrow; his eyes mild, yet lustrous; his lower features almost feminine. One familiar with men would have said, "Here is a man of patient enthusiasm for things intellectual, a devotee to the ideal. He may be a philosopher, a poet, an artist; but he could never make a soldier, a diplomat, or even a lover, except of the most Platonic sort. Just the man for a monk. If all monks were like him, the church would be enriched indeed; but, if all like him were monks, the world would be the poorer."

Among other passengers was a Greek monk, Gennadius. This man's full beard and long curly forelocks hanging in front of his ears, were in odd contrast with the smooth face and shaven head of the Latin monk. Though strangers, they courteously saluted each other. However sharp might be the differences in their religious notions, they soon felt the fraternity such as cultured minds and great souls realize in the presence of the sublimities of nature. They studied each other's faces with agreeable surprise as the glories about them drew from their lips vivid outbursts of descriptive eloquence, in which, speaking the Latin or Greek with almost equal facility, they quoted from the classic poets with which they were equally familiar.

As the galley turned eastward into the Corinthian gulf there burst upon them a panorama of natural splendor combined with classic enchantment, such as no other spot on the earth presents. The mountainous shores lay about the long and narrow sea, like sleeping giants guarding the outflow of some sacred fountain. Back of the northern coast rose, like waking sentinels, the Helicon and Parnassus, towering thousands of feet into the air; their tops helmeted in ice and plumed with fleecy clouds. The western sun poured upon the track of the voyagers floods of golden lustre which lingered on the still waters, flashed in rainbows from the splashing oars, gilded with glory the hither slope of every projection on either shore, and filled the great gorges beyond with dark purple shadows. As Morsinia reclined with her head resting on Constantine's shoulder, and drank in the gorgeous, yet quieting, scene, the two monks stood with uncovered heads and, half embracing, chanted together in Greek one of the oldest known evening hymns of the Christian church. In free translation, it ran thus:—

"O Jesu, the Christ! glad light of the holy!

The brightness of God, the Father in heaven!

At setting of sun, with hearts that are lowly,

We praise Thee for life this day Thou hast given."

"I love that hymn," said Gennadius, "because it was written long before the schism which rent the Holy Church into Latin and Greek."

"We will rejoice, then, that by the inspiration of the Holy Father, Eugenius, and the assent of your patriarch, the wound in the body of Christ has, after six centuries, at last been healed," replied Barletius.

"I fear that the healing is but seeming," said the Greek. "I was a member of the council of Florence, and know the motives of the men who composed it, and the exact meaning of the agreement—which means nothing. Your Pope cares not a scrap of tinsel from his back for the true Christian dogma; and while his ambition led him to desire to become the uniter of Christendom, his own bishops, who know him well, were gathered in synod at Basil, and pronounced him heretic, perjurer and debauchee."

"But you Greeks were doubtless more honest," said Barletius, with a tone and look of sarcasm.

"Humph!" grunted Gennadius, walking away; but turning about quickly he added,

"How could we be honest when, for the sake of the union, we assented to a denial of our most sacred dogmas by allowing the *Filioque*?[64] It is not in the power of men living to change the truth as expressed through all past ages in the creed of the true church. Our emperor yielded the points to the Latins; but holy Mark of Ephesus and Prince Demetrius, our emperor's brother, did not. They retired in disgust from Italy. Why, the very dog of the emperor, that lay on his foot-cloth, scented the heresy to which his master was about to subscribe, and protested against the sacrilege by baying throughout the reading of the act of union. And I learn that the clergy and populace at Byzantium are foaming with rage at this impiety of our Latinizing emperor. I am hasting thither that I may utter my voice, too, in my cell in prayer, and from the pulpit of St. Sophia, against the unholy alliance."

"Yet," said Barletius, with scorn, "your emperor and church authorities subscribed. What sort of a divine spirit do you Greeks possess, that prompts you to confess what you do not believe?"

"I feel your taunt," replied Gennadius. "It is both just and unjust. Have not some of your own prelates lately taught that the end justifies the means? The union, though wrong in itself, was justified—according to Latin ethics—by the result to be secured, the safety of both Greek and Latin churches from being conquered by the Turks. Our Eastern empire, the glory of the later Cæsars, has already become reduced to the suburbs of Byzantium. The empire of Justinian and Theodosius has not to-day ten thousand soldiers to withstand the myriads of the Sultan. There must be union. We must have soldiers, even if we buy them with the price of an article of the creed—nay the loan of the article—for the union will not stand when danger has passed. Conscience alone is one thing: conscience under necessity—I speak the ethics of you Latins—is another thing. But I abhor the deceit. Your bishop, whom you call Pope, has no reverence from our hearts, though we were to kiss his toe. You are idolaters with your images of Mary and the saints. *Filioque* is a lie!" cried the Greek, giving vent to his prejudice and spite.

Barletius in the meantime had felt other emotions than the holiest being kindled within him by these hot words of his companion; and when the Greek had flashed his unseemly denunciation at *Filioque*, the Latin's soul burst in responsive rage. But he was not accustomed to harsh debate. Words were consumed upon his hot lips, or choked in his fury-dried throat. His frame trembled with the pent wrath. His hands clenched until the nails cut into the flesh. But alas for the best saintship, if temptation comes before canonization! The thin hand was raised, and it fell upon the holy brother's face. The blow was returned. But neither of them had been trained to carnal strife, nor had they the skill and strength to do justice to their noble rage. Constantine, who leaped forward to act as peace-maker, stopped to laugh at the strange pose of the antagonists; for the Greek had valiantly seized the cowl of the Latin, and drawn it down over his face; while Barletius' thin fingers were wriggling through Gennadius' beard, and both were prancing as awkwardly as one-day-old calves about the narrow deck, with the imminent prospect of cooling their spirits by immersion in the water.

The presence of this danger led Constantine to separate the scufflers; although his laughter at the contestants had made his limbs almost as limp as theirs. The ecclesiastical champions stood glaring their celestial resentment, the one white, the other red, like two statues of burlesque gladiators carved respectively in marble and porphyry.

The conflict might have been renewed had not Morsinia risen from her cushion, and approached them. But no sooner did Gennadius realize the danger of having so much as his gown touched by a woman, than he bolted to the other end of the galley, and sat down, with fright and shame, upon a coil of ropes. The Greek had been trained at the monastery on Mount Athos. From that masculine paradise the fair daughters of Eve were as carefully excluded as if they were still the agents of Satan, and sent by the devil to work the ruin of those who, by lofty meditation and unnatural asceticism, would return to the pre-marital Adamic state of innocence. During the long twilight, and when the night left only the outlines of the mountains sharply defined high up against the star-lit sky, Gennadius still sat motionless; his legs crossed beneath him; his head dropped upon his bosom. He gave no response to the salutation of the attendant who brought him the evening meal: nor would he touch it. When the sailors sung the songs whose melody floated over the sea, keeping time to the cadences of the light waves which bent but did not break the surface, the monk put his fingers into his ears. He tried to drive out worldly thoughts by recalling those precepts of an ancient saint which, for four hundred years, had been prescribed at Mount Athos for those who would quiet their perturbed souls and rise into the upper light of God. They were such as these. "Seat thyself in a corner; raise thy mind above all things vain and transitory; recline thy beard and chin upon thy breast; turn thy eyes and thoughts toward the middle of thy belly, the region of the navel; and search the place of the heart, the seat of the soul, which when discovered will be involved in a mystic and ethereal light."

Barletius, equally chagrined by his display of temper before the laity, sought relief by inflicting upon himself a task of Pater Nosters, which he tallied off on his beads, made of olive-wood and sent him by a learned monk at Bethlehem.

When his punishment seemed accomplished, Morsinia asked him,

"Good father, why did you quarrel with the stranger?"

Barletius entered into a long explanation of the faith of the Roman Church at the point challenged by the Greek.

"I understand your words," said Morsinia, "but I do not understand their meaning."

"It is not necessary that you should, my child. If Holy Church understands, it is enough. A child may not understand all that the mother knows; yet believes the mother's word. So should you believe what Mother Church says."

"I would believe every word that Mother Church speaks, even though I do not understand why she speaks it," said Morsinia reverently. "But how can one believe another's words when one does not know what they mean; when they give no thought? Now what you say about the 'procession of the spirit,' and the 'begetting of the Son,' I do not get any clear thought about; and how then can I believe it in my heart."

The monk cast a troubled look upon the fair inquirer, and replied—

"Then you must simply believe in Holy Church which believes the truth."

"And say I believe the creed, when I only believe that the Church believes the creed?" queried the girl.

"It is enough. Happy are you if you seek to know no more. Beware of an inquisitive mind. It leads one astray from truth, as a wayward disposition soon departs from virtue. Credo! Credo! Credo! Help thou mine unbelief! should be your prayer. Restrain your thoughts as the helmsman yonder keeps our prow on the narrow way we are going. How soon you would perish if you should attempt to find your way alone out there on the deep! Woe to those who, like these wretched Greeks, depart from truth, and teach men so. Anathema, Maranatha!"

"But, tell me, good father, can that be necessary to be believed, about which whole nations, like the Greeks, differ from other nations, like the Latins? I have seen Greeks at their worship, and bowed with them, and felt that God was near and blessing us all. And I have heard them say, when they were dying, that they saw heaven open; and they reached out their arms to be taken by the angels. Does not Jesu save them, though they may err about that which we trust to be the truth?"

"My child, you must not think of these things," said Barletius kindly. "It is better that you sleep now. The air is growing chill. Wrap your cloak closely even beneath the deck."

He walked away, repeating a line from Virgil as he scanned the star-gemmed heavens.

"Suadentque cadentia sidera somnos."

Wrapping his hood close over his face, he lay down upon the deck.

CHAPTER XXIX

Two new comers joined the party at Corinth, where, crossing the isthmus on horses, they re-embarked. One was Giustiniani, a Genoese, of commanding form and noble features, the very type of chivalric gentility, bronzed by journeyings under various skies, and scarred with the memorials of heroic soldiership on many fields. The other was a Dacian, short of stature, with broad and square forehead, and a crooked neck which added to the sinister effect of his squinting eyes.

"Well, Urban," said the Genoese, "you still have confidence in your new ordnance, and think that saltpetre and charcoal are to take the place of the sword, and that every lout who can strike a fire will soon be a match for a band of archers:—Eh!"

"Yes, Sire, and if the emperor would only allow me a few hundred ducats, I would cast him a gun which, from yonder knoll, would heave a stone of five talents'[65] weight, and crash through any galley ever floated from the docks of Genoa or Venice. Four such guns on either side would protect this isthmus from a fleet. But, I tell you, noble Giustiniani, that without taking advantage of our new science, the emperor cannot hold out long against the Turk. The Turk is using gunpowder. He is willing to learn, and has already learned, what the emperor will find out to his cost, that the walls of Constantinople itself cannot long endure the battering of heavy cannon."

"You are right, Urban," replied the Genoese. "The Turk is also ahead of us in the art of approaching citadels. I have no doubt that his zigzag trenches[66] give the assailant almost equality with the besieged in point of safety. I will gladly use my influence at the court of Byzantium in behalf of your scheme for founding large cannon, Urban; if, perchance, the defence of the empire may receive a tithe of the treasure now squandered in princely parades and useless embassages."

The galley glided smoothly through the little gulf of Ægina, with its historic bays of Eleusis and Salamis. Giustiniani and Urban discussed the disposition of the Greek and Persian fleets during the ancient fight at Salamis, as they moved under the steep rocky hill on which Xerxes sat to witness the battle. They soon rounded the headland, opposite the tomb of Themistocles, and anchored in the harbor of the Piræus.

This port of Athens was crowded with shipping. There were Spanish galleasses like floating castles, with huge turrets at stem and stern, rowed by hundreds of galley slaves. Other vessels of smaller size floated the standard of France. Those of the maritime cities of Italy vied with one another in the exquisite carving of their prows and the gaiety of their banners.

The chief attention was centred upon a splendid galley of Byzantium, whose deck was covered with silken awnings, beneath which a band of music floated sweet strains over the waters. This was the vessel of the imperial chamberlain, Phranza, who, having been entertained in Athens with honors befitting his dignity, was now about to return to Constantinople.

Giustiniani ordered his galley alongside of that of the chamberlain, by whom he was received with distinguishing favors. Constantine took this opportunity to deliver, through the Genoese, Scanderbeg's letters to Phranza. They were read with evident gratification by the chamberlain. With a hearty welcome, not devoid of some curiosity on his part, as he scrutinized the appearance of the strangers, he invited Constantine and his companion to complete their journey in his galley. Morsinia was at first as much dazed by the splendor, as she was mortified by her ignorance of the formalities, with which she was received. But the natural dignity of her bearing stood her in good stead of more courtly graces: for these modern Greeks emulated those of ancient times in the reverence they paid to womanly beauty. The chamberlain was somewhat past middle life. He was a man whose studious habits, as the great historian of his times, did not dull his brilliancy as the master of etiquette. Nor had his astuteness as a statesman been acquired by any sacrifice of his taste for social intrigues. The diversions from the cares of state, which other great men have found at the gaming-table or in their cups, Phranza sought in studying the mysteries of female character; admiring its virtues, and yet not averse to finding entertainment in its foibles. A true Greek, he believed that physical beauty was the index of the rarer qualities of mind and heart. He would have been a consenting judge at the trial of that beautiful woman in the classic story, the perfection of whose unrobed form disproved the charge of her crime. He was such an ardent advocate of the absolute authority of the emperor that, though of decided aristocratic tendencies, he held that no marriage alliance, however high the rank of the bride, could add to the dignity of the throne: indeed, that beauty alone could grace the couch of a king; that the first of men should wed the fairest of women, and thus combine the aristocracy of rank with the aristocracy of nature. He had frequent opportunities to express his peculiar views on this subject; for, among the problems which then perplexed his statecraft, was that of the marriage of the emperor—that the succession might not be left to the hazard of strife among the families of the blood of the Palæologi. Had the choice of the royal spouse been left entirely in his hands, he would have made the selection on no other principle than that adopted by the purveyor of plumage for the court, who seeks the rarest colors without regard to the nesting-place of the bird.

The genuine politeness of the courtier, together with Morsinia's womanly tact in adapting herself to her new environment, soon relieved her from the feeling of restraint, and the hours of the voyage passed pleasantly. Her conversation, which was free from the conventionalities of the day, was, for this very reason, as refreshing to Phranza as the simple forms of nature—the mountain stream, the tangles of vines and wild flowers—are to the habitués of cities. There was a native poetry in her diction, an artlessness in her questions, and a transparent honesty in her responses. Indeed, her very manner unveiled the features of so exalted and healthy a mind, of a disposition so frank and ingenuous, of a character so delicately pure and exquisitely beautiful, that they compensated many fold any lack of artificial culture. The great critic of woman forgot to study her face: he only gazed upon it. He ceased to analyze her character: he simply felt her worth.

But no fairness of a maiden, be she Albanian or Greek, can long monopolize the attention of an elderly man whose swift vessel bears him through the clustering glories of the Ægean. Nor could any awe for his rank, or interest in his learned conversation, absorb Morsinia from these splendors which glowed around her. They gazed in silence upon the smooth and scarcely bending sea, which, like a celestial mirror, reflected all the hues of the sky—steely blue dissolving into softest purple; white mists transfused by sunset's glow into billows of fire; monolithic islands flashing with the colors of mighty agates in the prismatic air; clouds white as snow and clear cut as diamonds, lifting themselves from the horizon like the "great white throne" that St. John saw from the cliffs of Patmos yonder.

Crossing the Ægean, the voyagers hugged the old Trojan coast until off the straits of the Hellespont. They lay during a day under the lee of Yeni Sheyr shoals, and at night ran the gauntlet of the new Turkish forts, Khanak-Kalesi and Khalid-Bahar, at the entrance to the Sea of Marmora. Two days later there broke upon the view that most queenly of cities, Byzantium, reclining upon the tufted couch of her seven hills, by the most lovely of seas, like a nymph beside her favorite fountain. The galley glided swiftly by the "Seven Towers," which guard on Marmora the southern end of the enormous triple wall. The bastions and towers of this famous line of defenses cut their bold profile against the sky for a distance of five or six miles in a straight line, until the wall met the extremity of the Golden Horn on the north; thus making the city in shape like a triangle—the base of gigantic masonry; the sides of protecting seas.

Gay barges and kaiks shot out from the shore to form a welcoming pageant to the returning chamberlain. With easy oars they drifted almost in the shadows of the cypress trees which lined the bank and hid the residences of wealthy Greek merchants and the pavilions of princes. The lofty dome of St. Sophia flashed its benediction upon the travelers, and its challenge of a better faith far across the Bosphorus to the Asiatic Moslem, whose minarets gleamed like spear-heads from beside their mosques. From the point where the Golden Horn meets the strait of the Bosphorus and the sea of Marmora, rose the palace of the emperor, embowered in trees, and surrounded with gardens which loaded the air with the perfume of rarest flowers and the song of birds. Rounding the point into the Golden Horn, the grim old Genoese tower of Galata, on the opposite bank, saluted them with its drooping banner. They dropped anchor in the lovely harbor. Strong arms with a few strokes sent the tipsy kaiks from the galley through the rippling water to the landing. An elegant palanquin brought the wife of Phranza to meet her lord. Another, which was designed for the chamberlain, he courteously assigned to Morsinia; while Constantine and the gentlemen of the suite mounted the gaily caparisoned horses that were in readiness. The chamberlain insisted upon Morsinia and Constantine becoming his guests, at least until their familiarity with the city should make it convenient for them to reside elsewhere.

CHAPTER XXX

The house of Phranza was rather a series of houses built about a square court, in which were parterres of rarest plants, divided from each other by walks of variegated marble, and moistened by the spray of fountains.

Morsinia's palanquin was let down just within the gateway. A young woman assisted her to alight, and conducted her to apartments elegantly furnished with all that could please a woman's eye, though she were the reigning beauty of a court, instead of one brought up as a peasant in a distant province, and largely ignorant of the arts of the toilet. She was bewildered with the strangeness of her surroundings, and sat down speechless upon the cushion to gaze about her. Was she herself? It required the remembrance that Constantine was somewhere near her to enable her to realize her own identity, and that she had not been changed by some fairy's wand into a real princess.

"Will my lady rest?" said the attendant, in softest Greek.

Morsinia was familiar with this language, which was used more or less everywhere in Servia and Albania; but she had never heard it spoken with such sweetness. The words would have been restful to hear, though she had not understood their meaning. Without hesitation she resigned herself to the hands of the servant, who relieved her of her outer apparel. Another maiden brought a tray of delicate wafers of wheat, and flasks of light wine, with figs and dates. A curtain in the wall, being drawn, exposed the bath; a great basin of mottled marble, and a little fountain scattering a spray scented with roses.

Morsinia began to fear that she had been mistaken for some great lady, whose wardrobe was expected to be brought in massive chests, and whose personal ornaments would rival the toilet treasures of the Queen of Sheba. There entered opportunely several tire-women, laden with silks and linens, laces and shawls, every portion of female attire, in every variety of color and shape—from the strong buskin to the gauze veil so light that it will hide from the eye less than it reveals to the imagination.

The guest was about to question her attendants, when one gave her a note, hastily written by Constantine, and simply saying—

"Be surprised at nothing." Phranza had expressed to Constantine the deep interest of the emperor in the career of Scanderbeg, and his plans for Morsinia.

"Scanderbeg," said he, "is the one hero of our degenerate age; the only arm not beaten nerveless by the blows of the Turk. I have asked nothing concerning yourself, my young man; nor need I know more than that such a chieftain is interested in you and your charge. Your great captain informs me (reading from a letter), that any service we may render you here will be counted as service to Albania; and that any favor we may bestow upon the lady will be as if shown to his own child. Is she of any kin to him?"

"I may not speak of that," replied the youth, "except to tell that her blood is noble, and that General Castriot has made her safety his care. An Albanian needs but to know that this is the will of our loving and wise chieftain, to defend Morsinia with his life."

"You speak her name with familiarity," said Phranza.

"It is the custom of our people," replied Constantine, coloring. "The trials of our country have thrown nobles and peasants into more intimate relations than would perhaps be allowed in a settled condition. This, too, may have influenced General Castriot in sending her here, where her life may be more suitable to her gentle blood."

"It is enough!" exclaimed Phranza. "If our distance from Albania, and our own pressing difficulties and dangers do not allow us to send aid to your hero, we can show him our respect and gratitude by treating her, whom he would have as his child, as if she were our own. And now for yourself—well! you shall have what, if I mistake you not, your discreet mind and lusty muscles most crave—an opportunity 'to win your spurs,' as the western knights would say. Events are thickening into a crash, the outcome of which no one can foresee, except that the Moslem or the Christian shall hold all from the Euxine to the Adriatic. This double empire cannot long exist. Scanderbeg's arms alone are keeping the Sultan from trying again the strength of our walls. A disaster there; an assault here! You serve the one cause whether here or there."

"I give my fealty to the emperor as I would to my general," replied the young man warmly.

Constantine found himself arrayed before night in the costume of a subaltern officer of the imperial guard, and assigned to quarters at the barracks in the section of the city near to the house of the chamberlain. His brief training under the eye of Castriot, and his hazardous service, had developed his great natural talent for soldiership into marvellous acquirements for one of his years. With the foils, in the saddle, in mastery of tactics, in engineering ability displayed at the walls—which were being constantly strengthened—he soon took rank with the most promising. By courtesy of the chamberlain he was allowed the freest communication with

Morsinia, and was often the guest of her host; especially upon excursions of pleasure up the Golden Horn to the "Sweet Waters," along the western shore of the Bosphorus, to the Princess Island, and such other spots on the sea of Marmora as were uninfested by piratical Turks.

Morsinia became the favorite not only of the wife of Phranza, but of the ladies of the court, and the object of especial devotion on the part of the nobles and officers of the emperor's suite.

But it would have required more saintliness of female disposition than was ever found in the court of a Byzantine emperor, to have smothered the fires of jealousy, when, at a banquet given at the palace, Morsinia was placed at the emperor's right hand. It might not be just to Phranza to say that to his suggestion was due the praise of Morsinia's beauty and queenly bearing, which the emperor overheard from many of the courtiers' lips. Perhaps the charms of her person forced this spontaneous commendation from them: as it was asserted by some of the more elderly of the ladies—whom long study had made proficient in the art of reading kings' hearts from their faces, that the monarch found an Esther in the Albanian.

The reigning beauty at the court of Constantine Palælogus at this time was the daughter of a Genoese admiral. Though not reputed for amiability, she won the friendship of Morsinia by many delicate attentions. Gifts of articles of dress, ornaments and such souvenirs as only one woman can select for another, seemed to mark her increasing attachment. A box of ebony, richly inlaid with mother of pearl, and filled with delicious confections, was one day the offering upon the shrine of her sisterly regard. The wife of Phranza, in whose presence the box was opened, on learning the name of the donor, besought Morsinia not to taste the contents; and giving a candied fig to a pet ape, the brute sickened and died before the night.

An event contributed to the rumors which associated the name of the fair Albanian with the special favors of the emperor. An embassage from the Doge of Venice had brightened the harbor with their galleys. A gondola sheathed in silver, floated upon the waters of the Golden Horn, like a white swan, and was moored at the foot of the palace garden—the gift of the Doge. Another, its counterpart, was in the harbor of Venice—the possession of the daughter of the Doge; but waiting to join its companion, if the imperial heart could be persuaded to accept with it the person of its princely owner. Better than the ideal marriage of Venice with the sea—the ceremony of which was annually observed—would be the marriage of the two seas, the Adriatic and the Ægean; and the reunion of their families of confluent waters under the double banner of St. Mark and Byzantium. But the Grand Duke Lucas Notaris, who was also grand admiral of the empire, declared openly that he would sooner hold alliance with the Turk than with a power representing that schismatic Latin Church. The hereditary nobles protested against such a menace to social order as, in their estimate, a recognition of a republic like Venice would be. But it was believed that more potent in its influence over the emperor than these outcries, was the whisper of Phranza that the silver gondola of Venice was fairer than its possessor; and that queenly beauty awaited elsewhere the imperial embrace.

No habitué of the court knew less of this gossip than Morsinia herself; nor did she suspect any unusual attention paid her by the emperor to be other than an expression of regard for Castriot, whose ward she was known to be. Or if, when they were alone, his manner betrayed a fondness, she attributed it to his natural kindliness of disposition, or to that desire for recreation which persons in middle life, burdened with cares, find in the society of the young and beautiful; for no purpose of modesty could hide from Morsinia the knowledge which her mirror revealed. She had, too, the highest respect for the piety of the emperor; the deepest sympathy with him in his distress for the evils which were swarming about his realm; and a true admiration for the courage of heart with which he bore up against them. It was therefore with a commingling of religious, patriotic, and personal interest that she gave herself up to his entertainment whenever he sought her society. That she might understand him the better, and be able to converse with him, she learned from Phranza much of the history of recent movements, both without and within the empire. So expert had she become in these matters that the chamberlain playfully called her his prime minister.

CHAPTER XXXI

One evening the lower Bosphorus and the Golden Horn were alive with barges and skiffs, which cut the glowing water with their spray-plumed prows and flashing blades. Thus the tired day toilers were accustomed to seek rest, and the idlers of fashion endeavored to quicken their blood in the cool wind which, from the heights of the Phrygian Olympus, poured across the sea of Marmora. The Emperor, attended by one of his favorite pages, appeared upon the rocky slope which is now known as Seraglio Point. A number of boats, containing the ladies and gentlemen of the court, drew near to the shore. It was the custom of his majesty to accept the brief hospitality of one and another of these parties, and for the others to keep company with him; so that the evening sail was not unlike a saloon reception upon the water. The dais of Phranza's boat was, on the evening to which we refer, occupied by Morsinia alone; and, as the rowers raised the oars in salute of his majesty, he waved his hand playfully to the others, saying:

"The chamberlain is so occupied to-day that he has no time to attend to his own household. I will take his place, with the permission of the dove of Albania."

"Your Majesty needs rest," said Morsinia, making place for him at her side on the dais, which filled the stern of the barge, and over which hung a silken awning. "Your face, Sire, betokens too much thought to-day."

Throwing himself down, he replied lazily: "I would that our boat were seized by some sea sprite, and borne swift as the lightnings to where the sun yonder is making his rest, beyond the Hellespont, beyond the pillars of Hercules, beyond the world! But you shall be my sprite for the hour. Your conversation, so different to that of the court, your charming Arnaout accent, and thoughts as natural as your mountain flowers, always lead me away from myself."

"I thank heaven, Sire, if Jesu gives to me that holy ministry," replied she blushing deeply and diverting the conversation. "But why are you so sad when everything is so beautiful about us? Is it right to carry always the burden of empire upon your heart?"

"Alas!" replied he, "I must carry the burden while I can, for the time may not be far distant when I shall have no empire to burden me. Events are untoward. While Sultan Amurath lives our treaty will prevent any attack upon the city. But if another should direct the Moslem affairs, our walls yonder would soon shake with the assault of the enemy of Christendom. Nothing but the union of the Christian powers can save us."

"And you have the union with Rome?" suggested Morsinia.

"A union of shadows to withstand an avalanche," replied the Emperor. "The Pope is impotent. He can only promise a score of galleys and his good offices with the powers. At the same time our monks have almost raised an insurrection against the throne for listening to the proposition of alliance to which my lamented brother subscribed during the last days of his reign."

"But God," replied Morsinia, "is wiser than we, and will not allow the throne of the righteous to be shaken. I have looked to-day at the marvellous dome of St. Sophia. As I gazed into its mighty vault, and thought of the great weight of the stones which made it, I looked about to see upon what it rested. The light columns and walls, far spread, seemed all insufficient to support it. As I stood looking, I was at first so filled with fear that I dared not linger. But then I remembered that a great architect had made it; and that so it had stood for many centuries, and had trembled with songs of praise from millions upon millions of worshippers who in all these generations have gathered under it. Then I stood as quietly beneath it as I am now under the great vault of the sky. And surely, Sire, this Christian empire was founded in deeper wisdom than that of the architect. Are not the pillars of God's promises its sure support? Have not holy men said that so long as the face of Jesu[67] looks down from above the great altar, the sceptre shall not depart from him who worships before it?"

"But," said Palælogus, "God rejects His people for their sins. The empire's misfortunes have not been greater than its crimes. As the rising mists return in rain, so the sins of Constantinople, rising for centuries, will return with storms of righteous retribution. And I fear it will be in our day; for the clouds hang low, and mutter ominously, and there is no bright spot within the horizon."

"Say not so, my Emperor!" cried Morsinia earnestly. "A breath of wind is now scattering yonder cloud over Olympus; and the lightest moving of God's will can do more. Do you not remember the words of a holy father, which I have often heard one of our Latin priests repeat to those fearful because of their past lives;—'Beware lest thou carry compunctions for the past after thou hast repented and prayed. That is to doubt God's grace.' But I am a child, Sire, and should not speak thus to the Emperor."

"A child?" said his majesty, gazing upon her superb form and strong womanly features. "Well! a child can see as far into the sky as the most learned and venerable; and your faith, my child, rests me more than all the earth-drawn assurances of my counsellors. Where have you learned so to trust? I would willingly spend my days in the convent of Athos or Monastir to learn it! But I fear me the holy monks have it not of so strong and serene a sort as yours."

"I have learned it, Sire, as my heart has read it from my own life. My years are scarcely more numerous than my rescues have been, when to human sight there was no escape from death, or what I dreaded worse than death. I have learned to hold a hand that I see not; and it has never failed. Nor will it fail the anointed of the Lord; for such thou art. But see! yonder comes my brother Constantine. I know him from his rowing. They who learn the oars on mountain lakes never get the stroke they have who learn it at the sea."

The Emperor turning in the direction indicated, frowned, and said angrily,

"Your brother has forgotten the regulations, and is in danger of discipline for rowing within the lines allowed only to the court."

The boat came nearer; not steadily, but turning to right and left, stopping and starting as if directed by something at a distance which the rower was watching.

The Emperor's attention was turned almost at the same instant to a light boat shooting toward them from an opposite direction. The occupant of this was a monk. His black locks, mingled with his black beard, gave a wildness to his appearance, which was increased by the excited and rapid manner of his propelling the craft. "Something unusual has occurred, or they would wait the finding of another messenger than he," said the Emperor.

The monk's boat glided swiftly. When within a few yards of the barge in which the Emperor was the man stood up, his eyes flashing, and his whole attitude that of some vengeful fiend. "Hold!" shouted the rowers of the royal barge, endeavoring to turn the craft so as to avoid a collision.

"The man is crazed!" said Morsinia.

But at the instant when the two boats would have come together, another, that of Constantine, shot between them and received the blow. Its thin sides were broken by the shock.

The monk who had come to the very prow, and drawn a knife from his bosom, cried out, "To the devil with the Prince of the Azymites."[68]

He leaped upon Constantine's boat in order to reach that containing the Emperor: but was caught in the strong arms of Constantine who fell with him into the water. The monk gripped with his antagonist so that they sank together. In a few seconds, however, Constantine emerged. A thin streamer of blood floated from him. He was drawn upon the barge. Morsinia's hand tore off the loose gold-laced jacket, and found the wound to be a deep, but not dangerous flesh cut across the shoulder. It was several moments before the monk appeared. He gasped and sank again forever.

Constantine stated that the day before, while aiding in the erection of a platform for some small culverin that Urban had cast, the latter spoke to him of the marvellous mosaic ornamentation in the vestibule of the little church just beyond the walls, and took him thither. The monk was there, and passed in and out, evidently demented, and muttering to himself curses upon the Latinizers. Constantine thought little of this at the time; for a mad monk was not an uncommon sight in the city. But observing the same man at the quay hiring a boat, he determined to watch him. Hence the sequel.

CHAPTER XXXII

The members of Phranza's family were dining, as was their custom on pleasant days, under the great fig tree in the garden; a favorite spot with the chamberlain when allowed that privacy of life and domestic retirement which were seldom enjoyed by one whose duty it was to show the courtesies of the empire to ambassadors and distinguished visitors from the ends of the earth.

"I would willingly exchange conditions with old Guerko, the gate keeper, to-day," said Phranza, pushing from him the untasted viands. "The gate-keeper of an empire has less liberty and rest."

"What new burden has the council put upon you, my lord?" said his wife. "Remember that your little prime minister will help you," interposed Morsinia playfully.

Phranza glanced with a kindly but troubled look at her——

"The wheels of the public good grind up the hearts of individuals remorselessly," continued the good man. "Here am I with a spouse as fair as Juno; yet I must leave her for months, and maybe years, that I may seek a spouse for the Emperor. I am to make a tour of all Christian courts; sampling delicate bits of female loveliness, and weighing paternal purses. But sacred policy takes the place of holy matrimony among the great. An emperor and empress are not to be man and wife, but only the welding points of two kingdoms, though their hearts are burned and crushed in the nuptials. I had hoped that his majesty would assert his sovereignty sufficiently to declare that, in this matter, he would exercise the liberty which the commonest boor possesses, and choose who should share his couch, and be the mother of his children. But the very day after his escape from the mad monk, he put the keeping of his royal heart into the hands of his ministers. The shock of the attempt upon his life, or something else (glancing at Morsinia), seems to have turned his head with fear for the succession. So, to-morrow I sail to the Euxine to inspect the Circassian beauties, who are said to bloom along its eastern shore. But my dear wife will be consoled for my absence by the return of our nephew Alexis, who, I learn from my letters, is already at Athens, having wearied of his sojourn among the Italians, and will be with you before many days. Heaven grant that he has not become tainted with the vices of the Italians, which are even worse than those of the Byzantines. I trust he will find his aunt's care, and the sisterly offices of our Albanian daughter, more potently helpful than my counsel would have been."

The magnificent retinue, the splendid galleys, the untold treasures scraped from the bottom of the imperial coffers, with which, on the following day, the chamberlain sailed away through the Bosphorus to the Euxine, were but poor compensation to his loving household for his prolonged absence. Nor was his place adequately filled by Alexis with his fine form and western elegance of manners. In one respect Phranza's wish was met; for if the care of his aunt was not appreciated by the young man, the sisterly offices of the fair Albanian were.

Morsinia's respect for the absent Phranza led her to allow more attention from Alexis than her heart, or even her judgment, would have suggested. The young nobleman soon entangled himself in the web of her unconscious fascination. It was not until with passionate ardor he told his love, that Morsinia realized her fatal power over him. But with a true woman's frankness and firmness, she endeavored to dispel the illusion his ardent fancy had created.

"If I have not yet won you," cried the impetuous youth, "do not tell me that my suit is hopeless. It was folly in me to dream that you would see in me anything worthy of your love, so soon as your transcendent beauty of face and soul made me feel that you were all worthy of mine. Let me prove myself by months or years of devotion, if you will. If I do not now merit your esteem, surely the charm of daily looking upon you will make me better; the sweetness of your spirit will change mine; then as you see in me some impression of your own goodness, you will not scorn and repel me. I beg that you will make of me what you will, and love me as you can. I am not harder than the marble of which Pygmalion made the statue he loved. Mould me, Morsinia!"

"It is not that you are not worthy of me, Alexis. The nephew of Phranza need not humiliate himself at the feet of any king's daughter. But—but—it may not be! It cannot be!" and, gently releasing the hand she had allowed him to seize, she withdrew to her own chamber.

Alexis stood for a moment as if stupefied with his disappointment. This feeling was followed by a chagrin, which showed itself in the deep color mounting his haughty face. Then rage ensued, and he stamped upon the ground as if crushing some helpless thing beneath his feet, and muttered to himself:

"If not I, no man shall have her and live. Can it be that Albanian Constantine? Who is that vagrant? that menial? that hell-headed hireling who follows her? Angels and toads do not brood together; and he is of no kin to her."

CHAPTER XXXIII

Through a narrow street, lighted by the lanterns which hung before the doors of the few wine shops that were still open—for the hour was late—a man, wrapped in a hooded cloak, went stumbling over the dogs that were asleep in the middle of the way, and not unfrequently over the watchmen lying upon the mats before the closed entrances to the bazaars they were guarding. He entered one wine shop after another, muttering an oath of disappointment as he withdrew from each. At length he turned into an alley, which seemed like a mere crevice in the compact mass of houses, and threaded his way between windowless and doorless walls, until the passage widened into a small and filthy court. At the extreme rear of this a lamp was just flickering with its exhausted oil, and only sufficed to show him a doorway. Rapping gently he called in Italian:

"Pedro! Giovan!"

The door was opened by a short, stout man with bullet head, who spread himself across the entrance and peered into the face of the late comer. Two villainous looking men stared through the lurid glare of a rush light on a low table, at which, squatted on the ground, they were playing dice. A purse or pouch of gold thread, decorated with some device wrought with pearls and various precious stones, lay beside them.

"Ah, the gentleman from Genoa!" exclaimed one. "You are quite welcome to our castle. Ricardo, where is the stool? Well! if you can't find it, lie down, and let the gentleman sit on your head."

"You appear to be in luck, Pedro, if I am to judge from the purse yonder," said the visitor. "Your lady has taken you back to her affection, and given you this as a love token, I suppose."

"I'll tell you the secrets of my lady's chamber, Signior, when you tell me those of yours," replied Pedro.

"Perhaps," interposed Giovan, "the gentleman would have us help him in to the secrets of his lady's chamber. How now, Signior Alexis, have you trapped a new beauty so soon in Byzantium?"

"Let's throw for this before we talk," interposed Ricardo, holding the purse in one hand and a dice cup in the other. "One business at a time."

The three men threw. The stake fell to Ricardo, who thrust the rich prize into his dirty pocket, where a third of the contents of the purse had previously been deposited.

"May I see the little bag?" asked Alexis.

"No!" was the surly response.

"You see, Signior," interposed Giovan, in an attempt to mitigate the rudeness of his comrade, "You see it was a trust from—from a dead man, who was afraid to take it with him to purgatory, lest the fire might tarnish it. So we keep it for him until he comes back. And we are still in the trust business, Signior! Our credit is without a stain. You know it was just a suspicion of our integrity—we would not have our honor even suspected by the police—that led us to leave Genoa. Will you trust us with any little business?" "Do you know the Albanian officer in the emperor's guards?" asked Alexis.

"No, and want to know nothing about officers of any sort," growled Giovan.

"Ay!" interposed Ricardo, "the red-topped fellow, with a body like Giovan's, and the neck the right height to come under my sword arm?" making the gesture of cutting off one's head with a sabre. "Does he disturb you?"

"Yes!"

"It will be worth a hundred ducats," said Giovan.

"A hundred and fifty," said Ricardo; and, lowering his voice to the others, added, "I need fifty, and I would take only my even share."

"You shall have it," said Alexis, counting out the gold. "If you deceive me, you know that one word from me here in Byzantium will cost you your heads. Good night!"

When he had gone, Giovan said in low voice:

"I say, Pedro, we will divide a thousand ducats out of this."

"How?" exclaimed the two.

"The young officer is brother to the lady at the grand chamberlain's. She will pay heavy ransom if we deliver him instead of—" drawing his finger across his throat. "Of course we should have to leave Byzantium. But Ricardo and I have concluded that it were best to be gone anyhow; for the people here are so poor that our business does not thrive. This purse once held ducats, but when we took it, it had only silver bits. We pocket-bankers need better constituency." "Yes, we had better get out of this," said Pedro. "General Giustiniani has come to live in Galata.[69] He got his weasel-eyes on me yesterday as I was doing a little business by the old wharf. That man knows too much, he does. But he'll never get me on the galley benches again. I'd crawl like a mud turtle on the bottom of Marmora before I'd go under the hatches a second time. I like freedom and fresh air, I do—" blowing out of his face the thick smoke emitted by the wick floating on the surface of a saucer of oil.

"Right!" said Giovan. "Let's get out of this if we can do so with enough gold to pay our royal travelling expenses. But if we spare the neck of that fellow who is in Signior Alexis' way, where will we keep him that Alexis will not know it?"

"Our mansion here is hardly commodious enough for so distinguished and lively a guest as the young officer will be likely to be," said Ricardo, scraping the spiders' webs from the low ceiling of the room with his cap.

"Try the old water vault," suggested Pedro.

"Good!" said Ricardo, "when the Albanian goes to the walls, as he does every day, he will pass near to the opening."

CHAPTER XXXIV

The day following the three ruffians lingered about the site of the old Hippodrome—through the open space of which the citizens passed in going from one part of the city to another. Toward evening a stone was thrown against the bronze-sheathed column, or walled pyramid, which still held some of the great plates that in the palmy days of Byzantium made it one of the wonders of the city. It was the signal for alertness. A short-bodied, long-armed, red-haired man, dressed in the white kilt and gold-embroidered jacket of a citizen, sauntered leisurely through the Hippodrome. He measured with his eye the space which once blazed with the splendor of fashion, when, beneath the imperial eye of a Justinian or Theodosius, the horses of Araby and Thracia ran, and the factions of "the Blues" and "the Greens" shouted, and the whirling wheels of the golden chariots sprinkled the dust upon the multitudes.

The man paused to gaze at the bronze column of three intertwined serpents, with silver-crested heads, which was believed to have been brought from the temple at Delphi to his new city by the great Constantine. He stood reverently before the tall Egyptian obelisk of rose-granite, whose light red glowed with deeper hue in the eastern flush of the twilight sky; puzzled over its vertical lines of hieroglyphs which thirty centuries had not obliterated, and studied the figures on its marble base, representing the machines used by the engineers of Theodosius in hoisting the great monolith to its place, a thousand years ago. Broken statues—the spoil of conquered cities in generations of Greek prowess which shamed the supineness of the present, stood or lay about the grand pillar of porphyry, which was once surmounted by the statue of Apollo wrought by Phidias.

"Shame for such neglect!" muttered the man. "A people that cannot keep its art from cracking to pieces with age, cannot long keep the old empire of the Cæsars."

The narrow street to the north of the Hippodrome square shut out the remnant of daylight as the man turned into it. His attention was drawn by the groaning of some poor outcast crouching in the dark shadow of an angle in the wall. As he stooped to inspect this object a stunning blow fell upon his head. Two stalwart men instantly pinioned his arms. They rolled his helpless body a few yards, and carried or slid it down a flight of steps into a dark cavern, whose sides echoed their footfalls and whispers, as if it were the place of the last Judgment where the secrets of life are all to be proclaimed. Reaching the bottom, one of the men produced a light. The glare seemed to excavate a hollow sphere out of the thick darkness, but revealed nothing, except the spectral flash of the bats flitting around the heads of the intruders, and the damp earthen floor upon which the men had thrown their victim. At length great forms rose through the gloom, like the trunks of a forest. The water of a subterranean lake gleamed from near their feet, but its smooth black sheen was soon lost in the darkness. A small boat, or raft, was near, into which the man was lifted; one of the ruffians sitting on his feet, the other by his head, while the third propelled the craft by pushing against great granite pillars between which they passed. After going some distance the boat ground its bottom against a mass of fallen masonry and dirt, which made a sort of island, perhaps twenty feet across. Here they landed, and dragged their victim.

"What would you have with me?" said the prostrate man.

"It is enough that we have you," said Pedro, in broken Greek. "We want nothing more; not even to keep your miserable carcass, since we have already got our pay for burying it. I'll be your father-confessor and shrive you. If you like the Latin—Absolvo te! and away go your sins as easily as I can strip this gold-laced jacket off your back. Or if you prefer the Greek—By the horns of Nebuchadnezzar, I've forgotten the priestly words! But I'll shrive you all the same without the holy mumble. And if you want to pray a bit yourself, why fold your feet in front of your nose and kneel on your back."

"Why do you kill me?" said the man. "I am nothing to you."

"Nothing to us, but something to him who has hired us. As honest men we must do what we were paid to do."

"Unless I can pay you more," said the man, instantly taking a hopeful hint.

"Do you wear the belt of Phranza, that you think you can pay so much?" replied one of the ruffians, feeling about the person of the helpless man.

"What I have I give—a hundred ducats."

"A hundred! Are you love-crossed that you value life so little? You'll skin well, my gentle lambkin; and as you are half tanned already, we will sell your hide to the buskin maker for almost that sum; and your fat (feeling his ribs) will grease a hundred galley masts. A thousand ducats is your value, you Albanian imp!"

"I do not possess so much," said the victim.

"But your sister does," said the ruffian; and not noting the surprised look of the man, continued: "We have arranged for that. Your life is worth to us just one thousand ducats of gold. Sign this!" producing a bit of paper on which was something written.

"I cannot read it in this light. You read it. I may trust such honest fellows as you are."

The man read—"To my sister, the Albanian, at the house of Phranza. I am in danger from which I can escape only if you will give the bearer one thousand ducats. Speak not to any one of it, or my life is forfeit. That you may know this is genuine the bearer will show you my ring and a clip of my hair."

"Give me your ring; and, comrade, warm the wax to seal the letter," said Giovan.

"But I am not the man you seek," said the victim.

"And who in the devil's name are you then?"

"A mere stranger."

"Prove it!"

"Take the ring, and the lady will not recognize it."

"We shall see," said the ruffian, "but we will take the hundred ducats now to pay for any trouble you have put us to."

His belt was stripped off, and its golden contents ripped out. The victim was untied, first having been completely disarmed. The three men entering the boat, pushed off in the direction from which they had entered.

The island prisoner watched the receding light as it flashed its long rays on the water, illumined the arches of the roof, and lit the crouching figures in the boat. The multiplying pillars became like a solid wall as the light receded, until at length the darkness was complete. The sound of the boat as it scratched against the stone at the landing, gave place to the most oppressive silence.

To attempt escape in the direction of the entrance would be folly. If he could find his way his captors would doubtless be on guard and easily overpower him, as he would have to wade or swim. But to remain where he was would be as hazardous, for the wretches would not risk exposure for the sake of the hundred ducats they had secured; but would probably return and put him out of the way of witnessing against them.

As he meditated, a low rumble like distant thunder, ran along the arches. "Some passing vehicle in the city above," he concluded.

A light drip, as of a bat's wing touching the water! Another! and another! "Strange that they should be so regular!" thought the man. "There must be some inlet: I will explore."

He walked cautiously into the water in the direction of the sound. Soon he was beyond his depth; but, being an expert swimmer, kept on; his outstretched arms answering as antennæ of some huge water-spider, and guarding him from collision with the pillars.

The dripping sound became louder. Now it was just above his head. He felt his way with his hands until it became evident that he was at the end or side of the subterranean lake. But the shore was steep; indeed, a wall. Fixing his fingers into the crevices between the stones, he was able to raise himself half out of the water. Reaching up with one hand he felt the curved edge of a viaduct, by which the dark lake was evidently fed, or had been in earlier days. But, bah! The water now trickling through it was foul. The spring had been stopped, and the viaduct become a sewer; fed doubtless through its rents with the soakage of the city.

But might there not be an opening into the upper air? If not, a great human mole—especially if, to blind scratching power, he adds the skill of one trained in the art of engineering—can possibly make an opening.

The prisoner climbed into the viaduct. It was large enough to allow him to crawl a short distance. A faint glimmer of light proved the correctness of his surmise that it was connected with the surface. But fallen stones blocked his way. As he lay planning with fingers and brain for his further progress, voices sounded from the reservoir. They were those of two of the cut-throats returning. He pushed himself back to the opening. His captors had missed him at the island. If they knew of this sluice, or chanced to come upon it in their search, he was lost in his present position; for a pair of bare heels was the only weapon he could show against their sharp daggers. He let himself down into the water, and swam silently away. The light, however, from his captors' lamp came nearer.

"Hist!" said one. "He is yonder; perhaps by the devil's window."

The boat pushed directly toward the viaduct he had left.

While they explored the opening, which might well be called the window into the blackness of darkness of the nether world, their victim swam rapidly, keeping always in the shadow of the great pillars. But the boat was upon his track again.

The fugitive now made a fortunate discovery. Several feet below the surface of the water the base of each pillar projected far enough for standing room. This base had probably marked the height to which the

- 158 -

water was originally allowed to rise. By standing upon one of these projections, he was able to move round the pillar, so as to keep its huge block between himself and his pursuers. Thus they passed him. By the light in the boat he could discern the ground or shore near which was the entrance.

Returning to coast the other side of the cavern, they had passed close by him, when, his foot slipping, he was projected into the water. The wretches hailed with grim joy the splash, and turned the boat in the direction of the noise. But, dropping beneath the surface, the man swam to a pillar near by, from which he watched their baffled circuit of his former retreat. This chase could not be kept up endlessly. Plunging again under the water, he swam directly to the boat. Rising suddenly, he grasped its side with main weight and overturned it. The cries of the men and the splashing of the boat echoed a hundred times among the arches; while the hissing oil of the open lamp, which, poured on the surface of the water, blazed for a moment, made as near a representation of pandemonium as this world ever affords, except in the brain of the demented.

Though the captive had endeavored to keep his bearings, and had not lost for an instant his presence of mind, the swirling of the boat had destroyed all impression of the direction he should take. He remembered that on one of the pillars the projecting base was broken. It was that on which he had stood when he caught a glimpse of the ground near the entrance. If he could find that pillar again he could take his bearings as readily as if a star guided him. Several pillars were tried before the talismanic one was discovered. Feeling the broken place, and recalling the way in which he stood upon the narrow ledge when he saw the entrance, he took his course accordingly, and swam on.

One of his pursuers had evidently found a lodgment somewhere, and was calling lustily to his comrade for help. But there came back no answer to his call.

On went the swimmer until the light of the outer world gleamed through the crevice of the door, twenty or thirty feet above him, and he crawled upon the ground.

Squeezing the water from his garments, he climbed the stairway, and, opening the heavy and worm-eaten doors, peered out. The street was crowded with passers; for another day had come since his entrance to the old reservoir. In his half naked and bedrabbled condition he hesitated to make his exit, and returned to the bottom of the stairs. A hand on the door above made him leap to one side.

Giovan entered. Peering intensely into the shadows, he descended the steps. Pausing a moment he whistled through his teeth. There was no response. He whistled louder on his fingers. A shout came back.

"Help! Giovan—help!"

Giovan's dagger protruded from his belt. Another's hand suddenly drew it, and, before he had recovered from his surprise, it entered his neck to the haft. The Italian's short breeches, velveteen jacket and skull cap were made to take the place of the remnant of the prisoner's once most reputable wardrobe, and he sallied forth.

CHAPTER XXXV

Later in the day the gate keeper at Phranza's mansion put into Morsinia's hand a letter left with him by an Italian laboring man. It was addressed—"To the Albanian lady," and read thus:

"Your brother's life is threatened by some secret enemy. Let him exercise an Albanian's caution! This is the advice of a stranger."

A little before this, as the "poor Italian" was moving away from the gate of Phranza, a gorgeous palanquin, with silken canopy and sides latticed with silver rods, was borne in by four stout and well-formed men, with bare legs and arms, purple short trousers, embroidered jackets, and jaunty red caps, whose long tassels hung far down their backs.

The "Italian" stepped into an angle that the palanquin might pass; and stood gazing a long time after it had disappeared. At length, turning away, he said to himself:

"Strange! It must be that my imagination has been disturbed by the scenes of last night. But the lady in yonder palanquin is my dream made real. The pretty face of the child with whom I once played on the mountains must have cut its outlines somewhere on my brain, for I seem to see it everywhere. My captive in the mountains of Albania had the same features—though I saw them only under the flash of a torch. Imagination that, surely! The girl at Sfetigrade was similar. And now this one! The aga's advice to beware female illusions was good. But she may be the Albanian lady after all. Impossible! Stupidity! Perhaps my chosen houri in paradise is only flashing her beauty upon my soul from these fair earthly faces, and so training me first to love her as an ideal, that the joy of the realization may be perfect. But, tut! tut! silly boy that I am!"

Whistling monotonously he turned down a street.

A short, crooked-necked officer passed along. His face at the moment was the picture of dissatisfaction. The "Italian" stopped him, and, with a courtesy which belied his common apparel, addressed him:—

"Captain Urban of the engineers, is it not?"

"And who are you?" was the surly, yet half respectful, reply, as the one addressed glanced into the other's face.

"One who knows that the cannon you are casting are not heavy enough to lodge a ball against the old tower of Galata yonder across the Golden

Horn, much less breach a fortification; and further, that all you can cast at this rate from now until the Turks take Byzantium would not enable you to throw ten shot an hour."

"By the brass toe of St. Peter! man, I was just saying the same thing to myself," replied Urban.

"And the Emperor's treasury, when he has bought himself a wife, will not have enough left to buy saltpetre with which to fire the guns, if he should allow you brass enough for the casting," added the stranger.

"True again, my man; and the Emperor's service in the meantime does not yield stipend enough for an officer to live upon decently. If you were better dressed, my prince of lazaroni, I couldn't afford to ask you to drink with me; but this cheap shop will shame neither your looks nor my purse. Come in."

"Who are you, my good fellow?" asked Urban, as he drained a cup of mastic-flavored wine. "Were not your voice different, and your pronunciation of Greek rather provincial, with a slight Servian brogue, I would take you for one of our young engineers. You are not an Italian, spite of your garb."

"No," was the reply, "I was once in the employ of the Despot of Servia, engineer and artillery-man; but I think of entering the service of the Sultan. He pays finely, and gives one who loves the science of war a chance to use his genius."

"For such a chance and good pay I would serve the devil," said Urban. "The Greek emperor here is no saint, and yet I have served him for a crust. I am not bound to him by any tie. If you find good quarters with the Turks, give me a hint, and I will join you."

The stranger eyed him closely as he said this, and replied in low tones— "Captain Urban, I am a Moslem; Captain Ballaban of the Janizary corps. And I bear you a commission from the Padishah. To seek you is a part of my business in Constantinople. I do not ask you to take my word for this, but if you will accompany me, I will give you proof of my authority. A thousand ducats I will put into your hand within an hour, with which you may taste the Padishah's liberality and imagine what it shall be when you accompany me to Adrianople."

The two men left the wine shop together and entered a bazaar. The stranger whispered to the merchant who was nearly buried amid huge piles of goods of every antique description; strange patterned tapestries, rugs of all hues and sizes, ebony boxes inlaid with silver and ivory, shields bossed and graven, spear-heads, cimeters and daggers. The salesman made as low a salâm as his crowding wares would permit, and, opening a way through the heaps of merchandise, conducted the visitors into an inner room.

CHAPTER XXXVI

To better understand the events just recited, we must trace some scenes which had been enacted elsewhere.

During the sojourn of Constantine and Morsinia in Constantinople, the Turks had made no progress toward the conquest of Albania. The walls of Croia, upon which they turned their thousands of men, and exhaustless resources of siege apparatus, served only to display the valor and skill of the assailants, the superior genius of Castriot, and the endurance of his bands of patriots.

The haughty Sultan Amurath, broken in health, more by the chagrin of his ill success than by exposures or casual disease, retired to Adrianople, in company with his son, Prince Mahomet, who was satisfied with a few lessons in the science of military manœuvering as taught by the dripping sword of Castriot; and preferred to practice his acquirements upon other and less dangerous antagonists. Prince Mahomet had scarcely withdrawn to Magnesia in Asia Minor, and celebrated his nuptials with the daughter of the Turkoman Emir, when news was brought of the death of his father.

The prince was hardly twenty-one years of age; but his first act was ominous of the promptitude, self-assertion and diligence of the whole subsequent career of this man, whose success on the field and in the divan made him the foremost monarch of his age. On hearing the news he turned to Captain Ballaban, for whom the young Padishah entertained the fondest affection, and who had accompanied him to Magnesia in the capacity of kavass.—

"I shall leave to you, Captain, the duty of representing me at the burial of my royal father at Brusa, after which meet me at Adrianople."

Leaping into the saddle, he cried to the company about him, "Let those who love me, follow me!" and spurred his Arab steed to the Hellespont.

The magnificent cortege of the dead Sultan moved rapidly from the European capital of the Turks to their ancient one in Asia Minor. The thoughts of the attendants were more toward the new hand which would distribute the favors or terrors of empire, than toward the hand which was now cold.

Captain Ballaban was in time to join the reverent circle which committed the royal body to its ancestral resting place. They buried it with simple sepulchral rites, in the open field, unshadowed by minaret or costly mosque or memorial column; that, as the dying Padishah had said, "the mercy and blessing of God might come unto him by the shining of the sun and moon, and the falling of the rain and dew of heaven upon his grave."

Sultan Mahomet II. was scarcely within the seraglio at Adrianople when Captain Ballaban reported for duty. Passing through the outer or common court, he entered by the second gate into the square surrounded by the barracks of the Janizaries, who, as the body guard of the monarch, occupied quarters abutting on those of the Sultan. Near the third gate was gathered a crowd of Janizaries, in angry debate; for as soon as they realized that the firm and experienced hand of Amurath was no longer on the helm, the pride and audacity of this corps inaugurated rebellion.

"The Janizaries have saved the empire, let them enjoy it," cried one.

"Our swords extended the Moslem power, so will we have extension of privilege," cried another.

"Why should Kalil Pasha be Grand Vizier instead of our chief Aga? Kalil is one of the Giaour Ortachi.[70]

"Down with the Vizier!" rang among the barracks.

"A mere child is Padishah! one of no judgment the Hunkiar!"

"My brothers," said Captain Ballaban. "You know not the new Padishah. Well might Amurath have said to him what Othman said to Orchan: 'My son, I am dying: and I die without regret, because I leave such a successor as thou art.' Believe me, my brothers, if Mahomet is young, he is strong. If he is inexperienced in the methods of government, it is because heaven wills that he shall invent better ones."

"Your head is turned by the Padishah's favors," muttered an old guardsman.

"But am I not a Janizary?" cried the captain, "and it is as a Janizary that the Padishah loves me, as he loves us all. I once heard him say that the white wool on a Janizary's cap was more honorable than the horse tail on the tent spear of another. Old Selim here can tell you that, as a child, Mahomet was fonder of the Janizary's mess than of the feast in the harem."

"Yes," said old Selim, with voice trembling through age, but loud with the enthusiasm excited by the captain's appeal. "My hands taught Mahomet his first parries and thrusts; and he would sit by our fire to listen to the stories of the valor of our corps, and clap his hands, and cry 'good Selim, I would rather be a Janizary than be a prince.'" The old man's eyes filled with tears as he added, "And all the four thousand prophets bless the Padishah!"

While this scene was being enacted without, the young Sultan was reclining, with the full sense of his new dignity, upon the sofa which had never been pressed except by the person of royalty. It was covered with a cloth of gold and crimson velvet, relieved by fringes of pearls. Before it was spread a carpet of silk, an inch thick, whose softness, both of texture and tints, made a luxuriant contrast with its border, which was crocheted with cords of silver and gold. The walls of his chamber were enriched with tiles of alabaster, agate, and turquoise. The ceiling was plated with beaten silver, hatched at intervals with mouldings of gold; near to which were windows of stained glass made of hundreds of pieces closely joined to form transparent mosaic pictures, through which the variegated light flooded the apartment.

Mahomet was himself in striking contrast with his surroundings. He was dressed in négligé, with loose gown, large slippers, and white skull cap.

Before the Sultan stood the Grand Vizier, Kalil, bedizened in the costume of his office:—an enormous turban in whose twisted folds was a band of gold; a bournous of brocade, enlivened by flowers wrought upon it in green and red; and a cashmere sash gleaming with the jewelled handle of his yataghan.

"They are even now in revolt, your Majesty," said the Vizier. "Your safety will be best served by severe measures. They say the iron has not grown into your nerves yet."

The Sultan colored. After a moment's pause he replied. "When Captain Ballaban comes we will think of that matter."

"The captain had just arrived as I entered, Sire."

"Then announce to the Janizaries that the seven thousand falconers and game keepers which my father allowed to eat up our revenue, as the bugs infest the trees, are abolished; and their income appropriated to the better equipment of the Janizaries."

"But, Sire, would you sharpen the fangs of——"

"Silence! I have said it," said Mahomet, striking his hand on his knee. "But what is this demand from Constantinople?"

"That the pay for the detention of your Cousin Orkran at Constantinople shall be doubled, or the Greeks will let him loose to contest the throne with your Majesty."

"Assent to the demand," said the Sultan. "The time will the sooner come to avenge the insult, if we seem not to see it."

The Vizier continued looking at his tablets. "Maria Sultana[71] asks, through the Kislar Aga, that she may be allowed, since the death of her lord, to return to her kindred."

"Let her go! She is a Giaour whose cursed blood was not bettered by six and twenty years' habitation with my father. She is fair enough in her wrinkles for some Christian prince, and George Brankovitch needs to make new alliances."

"Hunyades"—said the Vizier.

"Ay, make peace with him, and with Scanderbeg, too, if that wild beast can be tamed, which I much doubt."

The Sultan rose from his cushion, his form animated with strong excitement, and, putting his hand upon the shoulders of the Vizier—who drew back at the strange familiarity—and looking him fixedly in the face, he whispered: "Everything must wait,"—and the words hissed in the hot eagerness with which he said them—"until—I have Constantinople."

Turning upon his heel, he withdrew toward his private chamber.

The Sultan threw himself upon his bed. The Capee Aga, or chief of the white eunuchs, whose duty it was to act as valet-de-chambre, as well as to stand at the right hand of the Sultan on state occasions, began to draw the curtains around the silver posts upon which the bed rested.

"You may leave me," said his majesty. "Nay, hold! Send Captain Ballaban of the Janizaries."

As the young officer entered, the face of the Sultan relaxed.

"You make me a man again, comrade," said he, grasping his hand. "These few days playing Sultan make me feel as old as the empire. I hate this parade of boring viziers and mincing eunuchs; and to be shut up here with these palace proprieties is as irksome to me as Timour's iron cage was to my grandfather Bajazet. I think I shall put my harem on horse-back, and take to the fields. Scudding out of Albania with Scanderbeg at one's heels were preferable to this busy idleness. You have had a rapid ride to get from Brusa so soon, and look winded. Roll yourself on that wolf's skin. I killed that fellow in Caramania. By the turban of Abraham! your red head looks well against the black hide. But why don't you laugh? Have they made a Padishah of you, too, that you must mask your face with care?"

"I have a care, Sire," said the soldier.

"Tell me it," said the Sultan, "and I'll make it fly away as fast as the Prophet's horse took him to the seventh heaven."

"The Janizaries are restless, Sire."

"Does not the donative I have announced pacify them?"

"I have not heard of it," said the officer.

"Listen! Is not that their shout?" Shout after shout rent the air from the court without.

The Janizary turned pale; but in a moment said, "Your donative has been announced. They are cheering your Majesty."

"Long live the Padishah!" "Long life to Mahomet!" rang again and again.

"I thank you, Sire," eagerly cried the young man, kissing the hand of the Sultan.

"What else would they have?" asked he. "Nothing but chance to show their gratitude by valiant service," was the reply.

"This they shall have, with you to lead them," putting his hand on the young officer's shoulder.

"Nay, Sire, I may not supplant those who are my superiors by virtue of service already rendered."

"But I command it. The corps shall to-morrow be put under your orders as their chief Aga."

"I beg your Majesty to desist from this purpose," said Ballaban. "The spirit of the corps, its efficiency, depends upon the strictest observance of the ancient rules of Orchan and Aladdin. By them we have been made what we are."

"But," cried Mahomet angrily, "there shall be no other will than mine throughout the army."

"I would have no other will than thine, Sire," was the response; "but it were well if your will should be to leave the Janizaries' rule untouched."

"You young rebel!" cried Mahomet, half vexed yet half pleased as, bursting into a laugh, he dashed over the face of his friend a jar of iced sherbet which was upon a lacquered stand at his side.

"You may thank the devil that it wasn't the arrow I once shot you with," said the playful tyrant, as Ballaban jumped to his feet.

"If you were not the Sultan now, I would pull you from the bed, as I pulled you from your horse that day," replied the good-natured favorite, making a motion as if to execute the threat.

"You are right," said Mahomet rising. "I am Sultan! Sultan? pshaw! Yet Sultan, surely." He paced the floor in deep agitation, and at length said, "I have a duty to perform, than which I would rather cut off my arms."

"Let me do the deed, though it takes my arm and my life," said Ballaban eagerly.

"You know not what it is, my old comrade."

"But I pledge before I know," was the response which came from stiffened lips and bowed head, as the captain made his obeisance.

The Sultan looked him in the face long and earnestly, and then, turning away, said:

"No! no! there are hands less noble than yours."

"But try me, Sire."

"You know the custom of our ancestors, approved by the wisdom of divans, as an expedient essential to the peace and safety of the empire, that—But I can not speak it: nor will I ask it of you. Leave me, Captain. Come to-morrow at this hour. I shall need the relief of your company then, even more than to-day."

CHAPTER XXXVII

An hour later the Kislar Aga, chief of the black eunuchs in charge of the royal harem, was announced.

"Well, Sinam, have any of your herd of gazelles escaped?" asked the Sultan.

"None. But Mira Sultana would pay her homage at your Majesty's feet."
"Mira, the Greek?" said Mahomet, the deep color rising to his temples.

Lowering his tone to a whisper, he conversed for a few moments with the eunuch, who prostrated himself upon the ground, and with harsh, yet thin voice, said:

"Your Majesty is wise, very wise. Your will is that of Allah, the Great Hunkiar. It shall be done."

Mira was a beautiful woman. The light texture of her robe revealed a perfect form; and the thin veil lent a charm to her face, such as shadows send across the landscape.

Mahomet shuddered, as the kneeling woman embraced his feet. The words of her congratulation to the young monarch, her protestation of devotion to him as to his father, though uttered with the sweetest voice he had ever heard, and with evident honesty, sent a visible tremor through the frame of her listener. And when she added, "My child, Ahmed, the image of his noble father and thine, will serve thee with his life, and"—

"It is well! It is well," interrupted the Sultan. "Be gone now!"

The morning following was one in which the hearts of the citizens of Adrianople stood almost throbless with horror. Mothers clasped their babes with a shudder to their breasts; and fathers stroked the fair hair of their boys, and thanked Allah that no tide of royal blood ran in their veins. A story afterward floated over the lands of Moslem and Christian, as terrible as a cloud of blood, dropping its shadow into palace and cottage, and dyeing that page of history on which Mahomet's name is written with a damning blot. While Mira Sultana was bowing at the feet of the new monarch, congratulating him upon his accession to the throne, her infant son, Ahmed, half brother to Mahomet, was being strangled in the bath by his orders. Another son of Amurath, Calapin, had, through his mother's timely suspicion, escaped to the land of the Christians.

It was late in the day when Captain Ballaban appeared for audience with the Sultan. His Majesty was apparently in the gayest of moods.

"Come, toss me the dice! We have not played since I laid aside my manhood and put on the Padishah's cloak. Come! What? Have you no stake to put up? Then I will stake for both. A Turkoman, the father of my own bride, has sent me a bevy of women, Georgians, with faces as fair as the shell of an ostrich's egg,[72] and voices as sweet as of the birds which sang to the harp of David.[73] The choice to him who wins! What! does not that tempt the cloud to drift off your face? Then have your choice without the toss. What! still brooding?" added he, growing angry. "By the holy house at Mecca! I'll make you laugh if I tickle your ribs with my dagger's point."

"You made me promise that I would be true to you, my Padishah, and if I should laugh to-day I would not be true," replied Ballaban quietly. "My face wears the shadows which the people have thrown into it."

"The people?" said Mahomet growing pale.

"Ay, the people have heard the wailing of the Sultana."

"For what? Tell me for what?" asked the Sultan with feigned surprise.

Ballaban narrated the story which was on every one's lips.

"It is treason against me," cried the monarch. Summoning the Capee Aga he bade him call the divan.

The great personages of the empire were speedily gathered in the audience room. At the right of the Sultan stood the Grand Vizier and three subordinate viziers. On his left was the Kadiasker, the chief of the judges, with other members of the ulema or guild of lawyers, constituting the high court. The Reis-Effendi, or clerk, stood with his tablets before the seat of the Sultan. The rear of the room was filled with various princes and high officials.

Turning to the Kadiasker, the Sultan asked:

"What is the denomination of the crime, and the penalty of him who, unbidden by the Padishah, shall put to death a child of royal blood?"

The Kadiasker, after a moment's evident surprise at the question, pronounced slowly the following decision:

"It were a double crime, Sire, being both murder and treason. And if perchance the child were fatherless, let a triple curse come upon the slayer. For what saith the Book of the Prophet?[74] 'They who devour the possessions of orphans unjustly, shall swallow down nothing but fire into their bellies, and shall broil in raging flames.' If such be the curse of Allah upon him who shall despoil the child of his rightful goods, much more does Allah bid us visit with vengeance one who despoils the child of that chiefest possession—his life. Such is the law, O Zil Ullah."[75]

Turning to the Kislar Aga, Mahomet commanded him to give testimony.

The Nubian trembled as he looked into the blanched face of the Sultan; but soon recovered his self possession sufficiently to read his master's thoughts, and said,

"The child of Mira Sultana was found dead at the bath while in the hands of Sayid."

"Was Sayid the child's appointed attendant?" asked the Kadiasker.

"He was not," was the response.

"Let him die!" said the judge slowly.

"Let him die!" repeated the Grand Vizier.

The Sultan bowed in assent and withdrew.

The swift vengeance of the Padishah was hailed with applause by the officials, as if it had erased the blood guilt from the robe of royal honor; but the people shook their heads, and kept shadows on their faces for many days.

"I tire of this life in the barracks," said Captain Ballaban to the Sultan, shortly after this event.

"Speak honestly, man," was the reply. "You tire of me; my heart is not large enough to entertain one of such ambition."

"Nay, Sire, but I would get nearer to the innermost core of your heart, into that which is your deepest desire."

"And where, think you, is that spot?" said the Sultan smiling.

"Constantinople," was the laconic response.

"Ah! true lover of mine art thou, if you would be there. Until I put the Mihrab[76] in the walls of St. Sophia, I shall not sleep without the dream that I have done it. Know you not the dream of Othman? how the leaves of the tree which sprang from his bosom when the fair Malkhatoon, the mother of all the Padishahs, sank upon it, were shaped like cimeters, and every wind turned their points toward Constantinople? My waking and sleeping thoughts are the leaves. The spirit of Othman breathes through my soul and turns them thither. Go! and prepare my coming. The walls withstood my father Amurath. Discover why? I hear that Urban, the cannon founder, is in the pay of the Greeks. He who discovered a way to turn the Dibrians against Sfetigrade can find a way to turn a foreigner's eyes from the battered crown of the Cæsars to something brighter—Go, and Allah give you wisdom!"

The reader is acquainted with the immediate sequel of Captain Ballaban's departure, his adventure with the Italian desperadoes at the old reservoir, and his success with Urban.

CHAPTER XXXVIII

The siege and capture of Constantinople by the Turks in 1453, was, with the exception of the discovery of America, the most significant event of the fifteenth century. The Eastern Roman Empire then perished, after eleven centuries of glory and shame; of heroic conquests, and pusillanimous compromises with other powers for the privilege of existence; exhibiting on its throne the virtues and wisdom of Theodosius and Justinian, and the vices and follies of emperors and empresses whose names it were well that the world should forget.

But the historic importance of the siege was matched by the thrilling interest which attaches to its scenes.

The last of the Constantines, from whose hands the queenly city was wrested, was worthy the name borne by its great founder, not, perhaps, for his display of genius in government and command, but for the pious devotion and sacrificial courage with which he defended his trust. A band of less than ten thousand Christians, mostly Greeks, and a few Latins whose love for the essential truth of their religion was stronger than their bigotry for sect, withstood for many weeks the horrors which were poured upon them by a quarter of a million Moslems. These foes were made presumptuous by nearly a century of unchecked conquest; their hot blood boiled with fury and daring excited by the promises of their religion, which opened paradise to those that perished with the sword; and they were led by the first flashings of the startling genius and audacity of Mahomet II.

The Bosphorus was blockaded six miles above the city by the new fortress, Rumili-Hissar, the Castle of Europe; answering across the narrow strait to Anadolu-Hissari—the Castles of Asia.

A fleet of three hundred Moslem vessels crowded the entrance to the Bosphorus, to resist any Western ally of the Christians that might have run the gauntlet of forts which guarded the lower entrance to Marmora. At the same time this naval force threatened the long water front of the city with overwhelming assault. The wall which lay between the sea of Marmora and the Golden Horn, and made the city a triangle, looked down upon armies gathered from the many lands between the Euphrates and Danube;—the feudal chivalry from their ziamets under magnificently accoutred beys; the terrible Akindji, the mounted scourge of the borders of Christendom; the motley hordes of Azabs, light irregular foot-soldiers,—these filling the plains for miles away:—while about the tents of the Sultan were the Royal Horse Guards, the Spahis, Salihdars, Ouloufedji and Ghoureba, rivals for the applause of the nations, as the most daring of riders and most skilful of swordsmen: and the Janizaries, who boasted that their tread was as resistless as the waves of an earthquake.

Miners from Servia were ready to burrow beneath the walls. A great cannon cast by Urban, the Dacian, who had deserted from the Christian to the Moslem camp, gaped ready to hurl its stone balls of six hundred pounds weight. It was flanked by two almost equally enormous fire-vomiting dragons, as the new artillery was called: while fourteen other batteries of lesser ordnance were waiting to pour their still novel destruction upon the works. Ancient art blended with modern science in the attack; for battering rams supplemented cannon, and trenches breast-deep completed the lines of shields. Moving forts of wood antagonized, across the deep moat, the old stone towers, which during the centuries had hurled back their assailants in more than twenty sieges. The various hosts of besiegers in their daily movements were like the folds of an enormous serpent, writhing in ever contracting circles about the body of some helpless prey. From dawn to dark the walls crumbled beneath the pounding of the artillery; but from dark to dawn they rose again under the toil of the sleepless defenders.

Thousands, impelled by the commands of the Sultan, and more, perhaps, by the prospect of reward in this world, and in another, out of which bright-eyed houris were watching their prospective lords, mounted the scaling ladders only to fill with their bodies the moat beneath. At the point of greatest danger the besieged were inspired with the courage of their Emperor, and by the aid of the bands of Italians whom the purse and the appeals of John Giustiniani had brought as the last offering of the common faith of Christendom upon the great altar already dripping with a nation's blood.

Sometimes when the Christians, whose fewness compared with the assailants compelled them to serve both day and night, were discouraged by incessant danger and fatigue, a light form in helmet and breastplate moved among them, regardless of arrows and bullets of lead: now stooping to staunch the wounds of the fallen; now mounting the parapet, where scores of stout soldiers shielded her with their bodies, and hailed her presence with the shout of "The Albanian! The Albanian!" The reverence which the soldiers gave to the devoted nuns, who were incessant in their ministry of mercy, was surpassed by that with which they regarded Morsinia. She had become in their eyes the impersonation of the cause for which they were struggling.

The interruption by the war of the negotiations with the Emir of Trebizond, whose daughter had been selected as the imperial spouse, revived the rumors which had once associated the fair Albanian's name with that of his Majesty; and gave rise to a nick-name, "the Little Empress," which, among the soldiers, came to be spoken with almost as much loyalty of personal devotion, as if it had received the imperial sanction.

Constantine's solicitude led him to remonstrate with Morsinia for the exposure of her person to the dangers of the wall: but she replied—

"Have you not said, my dear brother, that the defence is hopeless? that the city must fall? What fate then awaits me? The Turks have service for men whom they capture, which, though hard, is not damning to body and soul. What if they send you to the mines, to the galleys? What if they slay you? You can endure that. Yet I know that you yourself would perish in the fight before you would submit to even such a fate. But what is the destiny of a woman who shall fall into their hands? It is better to die than to be taken captive. And is not yonder breach where the men of the true God are giving their lives for their faith, as sacred as was ever an altar on earth? Is not the crown of martyrdom better than a living death in the harem of the infidel? The arrow that finds me there on the wall shall be to me as an angel from heaven; and a death-wound received there will be as painless to my soul as the kiss of God."

"But this must not be!" cried Constantine. "Our valor, if it does not save the city, may lead to surrender upon terms which shall save all the lives of the people."

"It is impossible," replied she. "His Majesty informed me yesterday that Mahomet had pledged to his soldiers the spoil of the city, with unlimited license to pillage."

Constantine was silent, but at length added. "If worst comes, it will then be time enough to expose your life."

"But the end is near, dear Constantine. The city is badly provisioned. The poor are already starving. The garrison is on allowance which can sustain it but a few days. Besides, as you have told me, the Italians are at feud with the Greeks, and ready to open the gates if famine presses upon them."

"Yes, curses on the head of that monk Gennadius, who sends insult to our allies every day from his cell!" muttered Constantine. "But I cannot see you in danger, Morsinia. Promise me—for your life is dearer to me than my own—that you will not go upon the walls. I need not the solemn oath to our brave Castriot, and that to our father Kabilovitsch, that I will guard you. But, if not for my sake, then for their sake, take my counsel. I know that you are under the special care of the Blessed Jesu. Has He not shielded us both—me for your sake—many times before?"

"Your words are wise, my brother. You need not urge the will of Castriot and father Kabilovitsch, for your own wish is to me as sacred as that of any one on earth," said she, looking him in the eyes with the reverence of affection, and yielding to his embrace as he kissed her forehead.

"But," added she, "I must exact of you one promise."

"Any thing, my darling, that is consistent with your safety," was the quick reply.

"It is this. Promise me, by the Virgin Mother of God, that you will not allow me to become a living captive to the Turk."

"Not if my life can shield you. This you know!"

"Yes, I would not ask that, but something harder than that you should die for me."

A pallor spread over the face of Constantine, for he suspected her meaning, yet asked, "And what—what may that be?"

"Take my life with your own hand, rather than that a Turk should touch me," said Morsinia, without the slightest tremor in her voice.

Constantine stood aghast. Morsinia continued, taking his strong right hand in hers, and raising it to her lips—

"That were joy, indeed, if the hand of him who loves me, the hand which has saved me from danger so often—could redeem me from this which I fear more than a thousand deaths! Promise me for love's sake!"

"I may not promise such a thing," said the young lover, with a voice which showed that her request had cut him to the heart.

"Then you love me not," said the girl, turning away.

But the look upon Constantine's face showed the terrible tragedy which was in his soul, and that such an accusation brought it too near its culmination. Instantly she threw herself into his arms.

"Forgive me! forgive me!" cried she. "I will not impugn that love which has proved itself too often. But let us speak calmly of it. Why should you shrink from this?" she asked, leading him to a seat beside her.

"Because I love you. My hand would become paralyzed sooner than touch rudely a hair of your head."

"Nay, in that you do not know yourself," said Morsinia. "Would you not pluck a mole from my face if I was marred by it in your eyes!"

"But that would be to perfect, not to harm you," said Constantine.

"And did you not hold the hand of the poor soldier to-day, while the leech was cutting him, lest the gangrene should infect his whole body with poison? And would you not have done so had he been your long lost brother, Michael, whom you loved? And would you not have done it more willingly because you loved him?"

"Yes," said Constantine, "but that would be to save life, not to destroy it."

"But what, my brother dear, is the fairness of a face compared with the fairness of honor? What the breath of the body, when both the body and the soul in it are threatened with contamination of such an existence as every woman receives from the Turk?"

"I cannot argue with you, Morsinia. My nature rebels against the deed you propose."

"But," replied she, "is not love nobler, and should it not be stronger, than nature? If nature should rebel against love, let love crush the rebellion, and show its sovereignty. If my hand should tremble to do aught that your true service required, I would accuse my hand of lack of devotion. But I think that men do not know the fulness of love as women do."

"Let me ask the question of you, Morsinia," replied the young lover after a pause. "Could you take my life as I lie here? Will your hand mix the poison to put to my lips in the event of the Turk entering the city? My life will be worse than death in its bitterness if you are lost to me."

Morsinia pondered the question, growing pale with the fearfulness of the thought. For a while she was speechless. The imagination started by Constantine's question seemed to stun her. She stared at the vague distance. At length she burst into tears, and laying her head upon her companion's shoulder, said:

"I love you too dearly, Constantine, to ask that of you which you shrink from doing. There is another who can render me the service."

"Who would dare?" said Constantine, rising and gazing wildly at her. "Who would dare to touch you, even at your own bidding?"

"I would," said Morsinia quietly. "And this I shall save for the moment when I need the last friend on earth," she added, drawing from her dress the bright blade of an Italian stiletto. "Perhaps, my heart would tremble, and my flesh shrink from the sharp point, though I love not myself as I love you."

"Let us talk no more of this," said Constantine, "but leave it for the hour of necessity, which happily I think will not soon come. I must tell you now for what I sought you. I have been ordered this very night to aid in a venture which, heaven grant! shall re-provision the city. Several large galleys, laden with corn and oil, are now coming up the sea from Genoa. If they see the cordon of the enemy's ships drawn across the harbor, not knowing the extremity to which the city is reduced, they may return without venturing an encounter. I am to reach them, and, if possible, induce them to cut their way through. The great chain at the entrance to the Golden Horn will be lowered at the opportune moment, and all the shipping in the harbor will make an attack upon the enemy's fleet. Of this our allies must be informed. As soon as it is dark I shall drift in a swift little skiff between these Turkish boats; and before the dawn I shall be far down on Marmora. To-morrow night, if your prayers are offered, Jesu will grant us success." With a kiss he released himself from her embrace and was gone.

CHAPTER XXXIX

Constantine eluded the heavy boats of the Turks, which were anchored to prevent their drifting away upon the swift current with which the Black Sea discharges itself through the Bosphorus into Marmora. Upon meeting the befriending galleys, it was with little difficulty that he persuaded the Genoese captains to risk the encounter with the Turkish fleet. As Constantine pointed out to the Italian captains, the enormous navy of the blockaders, formed in the shape of a crescent, and stretched from the wall of the city across to the Asiatic shore, presented a more formidable obstacle to the eye than to the swift and skilfully manned Genoese galleys. The Turkish boats were generally but small craft, and laden down to the water's edge with men. The Genoese had four galleys, together with one which belonged to Byzantium.

These were vessels of the largest size, constructed by men who had learned to assert their prowess as lords of the sea. They were armed with cannon adapted to sweep the deck of an adversary at short range:—a weapon which the Turks had not yet floated, though they were in advance of the Christians in using such artillery on land. The high sides of the Christian galleys, moreover, prevented their being boarded except with dangerous climbing, while the defenders stood ready to pour the famous liquid called "Greek fire" upon the heads of those who should attempt it. Besides, heaven favored the Christians; for a strong gale was blowing, which, while it tossed the boats of their adversaries beyond their easy control, filled the sails of the Genoese, and sent them bounding over the waves: the oarsmen sitting ready to catch deftly into the bending billows with their blades. Each of the five vessels chose for a target a large one of the Turks, and clove it with its iron prow: while the cannon swept the Turkish soldiers by hundreds from other boats near to them. Passing through the thin crescent, the Christian galleys skilfully tacked, and, careening upon their sides, again assailed the Turks before they could evade their swift and resistless momentum. Again and again the galleys passed, like shuttles on a loom, through the line of the enemy, sinking the unwieldy hulks and drowning the crowded crews.

From the walls and house tops of the city went up huzzas for the victors and praises to heaven. From the shores of Asia, and from below the city wall, thousands of Moslems groaned their imprecations. The Sultan raged upon the beach, as he saw one after another of his pennants sink beneath the waves. Dashing far into the sea upon his horse, he vented his impotent fury in beating the water with his mace, shrieking maledictions into the laughing winds, and invoking upon the Christians curses from all the Pagan gods and Moslem saints.

At one moment the Byzantine galley was nearly overcome, having been caught in a group of Turkish boats, whose occupants climbed her sides, and did murderous work among the crew. Though ultimately rescued by the Genoese, it was only after severe loss.

But above all other casualties the Christians mourned the fate of young Constantine. With almost superhuman strength he had cut down several assailants; but was finally set upon by such odds that he was pressed over the low bulwarks, and fell into the sea. The galley with its consorts made way to the chain at the entrance to the Golden Horn, where the rich stores, a thousand times richer now in the necessity which they relieved, were received amid the acclamations of the grateful Greeks.

But woe,—Oh, so heavy! crushed one solitary heart. Her eyes stared wildly at the messenger who brought the fatal tidings; and stared, hour by hour, in their stony grief, upon the wall of her apartment. Kind attendants spoke to her, but she heard them not. Her soul seemed to have gone seeking in other worlds the soul of her lover. The servants, awed by the majesty of her sorrow, sat down in the court without, and waited: but she called them not. Daylight faded into darkness. The lamp which was brought she waved with her hand to have taken away. The maidens who came to disrobe her for the night found her bowed with her face upon the couch; and, receiving no response to their proffered offices, retired again to wait.

The morning came; and the cheer of the sunlight which, quickening the outer world, poured through the windows high in the walls of her apartment, seemed to awaken her from her trance. But how changed in appearance! The ruddy hue of health, and the bronzing of daily exposure to the open air, seemed alike to have been blanched by that which had taken hope from her soul. Her eyes were sunken, and the lustre in them, though not lessened, now seemed to come from an infinite depth—from some distant, inner world which had lost all relation to this, as a passing star. Morsinia rose, weak at first; but her limbs grew strong with the imparted strength of her will. She ate; and speaking aloud—but more in addressing herself than her attendants—said: "I will away to the walls!"

Through the masses of debris, and among the groups of men who were resting and waiting to take the places of their wearied comrades on the ramparts, she went straight to the gate of St. Romanus, where the assaults were most incessant. The cry of "The Little Empress!" gave way to that of "The Panurgia! The Panurgia!"[77] as some, though familiar with her form, were startled by the almost unearthly change of her countenance. She returned no salutation as was usual with her, but, as if impelled by some superhuman purpose, her beauty lit as with a halo by the majesty of a celestial passion, she climbed the steps into the tottering tower above the gate. A strong, but gentle hand was put upon her arm. It was that of the Emperor.

"My daughter, you must not be here. Come away!"

She looked at him for an instant in hesitation; and then, bowing her head, responded in scarcely audible voice:

"I will obey you, Sire," and added, speaking to herself—

"It is *his* will too."

"I know your grief," said his majesty kindly, "and now, as your Emperor, I must protect you against yourself."

"I want no protection," cried the broken-hearted girl. "Oh, let me die! For what should I live?"

"My dear child," said the Emperor with trembling voice, while the tears filled his eyes. "In other days your holy faith taught me how to be strong. Now, in your necessity, let me repeat to you the lesson. For what shall *you* live? For what should *I* live? I am Emperor, but my empire is doomed. I live no longer for earthly hope, but solely to do duty; nothing but duty, stern duty, painful every instant, crushing always, but a burden heaven imposed on a breaking heart. That heaven appoints it—that, and that alone—makes me willing to live and do it. When the time comes I shall seek death where the slain lie the thickest. But not to-day; for to-day I can serve. Live for duty! Live for God! The days may not be many before we shall clasp hands with those who, now invisible, are looking upon us. Let us go and cheer the living before we seek the companionship of the dead."

As the Emperor spoke, his face glowed with a majesty of soul which made the symbol of earthly majesty that adorned his brow seem poor indeed.

Gazing a moment with reverent amazement at the man who had already received the divine anointing for the sacrifice of martyrdom he was so soon to offer, Morsinia responded:

"Your words, Sire, come to me as from the lips of God. I will go and pray, and then—then I shall live for duty."

CHAPTER XL

Mahomet had not expended all his petulant rage upon feelingless waves and distant Christians. He summoned to his presence the Admiral of his defeated fleet, Baltaoghli, and ordered that he should be impaled.

The Admiral had shown as much naval skill as could, perhaps, have been exhibited with the unwieldy boats at his command; and, moreover, had brought from the fight an eyeless socket to attest his bravery and devotion. The penalty, therefore, which Mahomet attached to his misfortune, brought cries of entreaty in his behalf from other brave officers, especially from the leading Janizaries. This opposition at first confirmed the determination of the irate despot. But soon the petition of the honored corps swelled into a murmur, which the more experienced of his advisers persuaded Mahomet to heed.

The Sultan had schooled himself to obey the precept which Yusef, the eunuch, who instructed his childhood, had imparted, viz, "Make passion bend to policy." He therefore apparently yielded, so far at least as to compromise with those whom he feared to offend, and commuted the Admiral's sentence to a flogging.

The brave man was stretched upon the ground by four slaves. Turning to Captain Ballaban, the Sultan bade him lay on the lash. Ballaban hesitated. Drawing near to Mahomet, he said respectfully, but firmly,

"The Janizaries are soldiers, not executioners, Sire."

Mahomet's rage burst as suddenly as powder under the spark.

"Away with the rebel!" cried he. "We will find the executioner for him, too, who dares to disobey our orders."

Seizing his golden mace, the Sultan himself beat the prostrate form of the Admiral until it was senseless.

Wearying of his bloody work, Mahomet glared like a half satiated beast upon those about him.

"Where is the damned rebel who dares dispute my will? Did no one arrest him?"

"The order was not so understood," said an Aga who was near.

"You understand it now," growled the infuriated, yet half-ashamed, monarch. "Arrest him!—But no! Let these slaves go search for the runaway. It shall be their office to deal with one who dares to break with my will."

The Janizaries returned to their places near the walls.

Mahomet was ill at ease when his better judgment displaced his unwise passion. His love for Ballaban, the manliness of the captain's reply to the unreasonable order, and the danger of injuring one who stood so high in the estimate of the entire Janizary corps, were not outweighed even by the sense of the indignity which the act of disobedience had put upon the royal authority.

The slaves, not daring to venture among the Janizaries in their search for Captain Ballaban, easily persuaded themselves that he must have fled; and that, perhaps, he might be lurking somewhere on the shore, as this was the only way of escape. Their search was rewarded. Though in the disguise of scant garments, utterly exhausted so that he could make no resistance, their victim was readily recognized by his form and features, which were too peculiar to be mistaken. The captain had apparently attempted to escape by water; perhaps, had ventured upon some chance kaik or raft, and been wrecked in the caldron which the strong south wind made with the current pouring from the north.

His wet garments, such as he had not stripped off, and his exhausted look confirmed their theory.

One of their number brought the report to the Grand Vizier, Kalil, who repeated it to the Sultan.

"I will deal with him in person. Let no one know of the capture until I have seen him," said Mahomet, seeking an opportunity to revoke the threat against his friend, which he had uttered in insane rage; and, at the same time, to cover his imperial dignity by the semblance of a trial.

The culprit was brought in the early evening to the Sultan's tent. A large lantern of various colored crystals hung from the ridge-pole, and threw its beautiful, but partly obscured, light over the arraigned man.

His captors had clothed him in the uniform of the Janizaries.

"His face has a strange look, as if another's soul had taken lodging behind the familiar lineaments," the Sultan remarked to Kalil as he scanned the culprit closely.

"Do you know, knave, in whose presence you are?" said Mahomet, sternly.

"I know not, Sire, except that the excellent adornment of your person and pavilion suggest that I am in the presence of his majesty the—"

"Silence, villain! do you mock me?" cried the Padishah, in surprise at the man's assumed ignorance.

"I mock thee not, Sire," said the victim, bowing with courtly reverence, and speaking in a sort of patois of Greek and Turkish. "But I was about to say that I know thee not, except that from the excellence of thy person and estate thou art none less"——

"Silence, you dog! This is no time for your familiar jesting, Ballaban. Speak pure tongue, or I'll cut thine from thy head!" interrupted the Padishah.

"I speak as best I can," replied the man, "for I was not brought up to the Turkish tongue. I presume that I address the king of the Turks."

"Miserable wretch!" hissed his majesty, drawing his jewelled sword. "Dare you call me king of the *Turks*? TURKS! thou circumcised Christian dog! thou pup of Nazarene parentage! thou damned infidel, beplastered with Moslem favors!"[78]

"It would seem that I needed Moslem favors, which in my destitute condition and imminent danger, I most humbly crave," replied the object of this contumely.

"Are you mad?" shrieked the Sultan, rising and glaring into the other's face. "You *are* mad, man. Poor soul! Ay! Ay! I see it now. Some demon has possessed you. Some witch has blown on the knots against you."[79]

"I am not mad, Sire," said the culprit, "but a poor castaway on your coast."

"Hear him, poor fellow! so mad that he knows not himself. Well! well! I must forgive you then for not knowing me," said Mahomet, with genuine pity. "Did you love me so, old comrade, that my harsh words knocked over your reason? or did your reason, toppling over, lead you to challenge me as you did? We must cure this malady, though it takes the treasure of the empire to do it." Lowering his voice he addressed the Vizier:

"I could not believe that my faithful comrade would have rebelled. It was not he, but the demon who has possessed him. Think you not so, good Kalil?"

The Vizier bowed in assent to the Sultan's theory, and whispered, "It provides a wise escape from antagonizing the Janizaries. But you should summon a physician."

Clapping his hands, an attendant appeared, who was dispatched for the court physician; a man of fame in his profession, whose duty it was to be always within call of the Sultan.

The physician entering, examined the culprit, looking into his eyes, balancing his head between his hands to determine if there were any sudden disturbance of the proportionate avoirdupois; noting if his tongue lay in the middle of his mouth, and feeling his pulse. At length he said in low voice to the Sultan and Vizier:

"There is, Sire, no outward evidences of lacking wit. I would have him speak."

"He is the Janizary, Captain Ballaban," whispered the Vizier. "You will observe that the wit is clean gone from him. Tell us your story, Ballaban, or whoever you are."

"I beg the favor of your excellency, your lordship, Sire; for, since you deny that you are the king of the Turks, I know not what title to give to your authority. I am your prisoner. I fought on the Byzantine galley as Jesu gave me strength, but was unfortunate enough to fall overboard, and fortunate enough to avoid capture by the Turkish boats, as I dived beneath them, or rested myself below their sterns until I reached the shore. But as heaven willed it, I landed below the walls of the city. I was altogether weaponless, having shuffled off my armor that I might swim—and altogether blown by my effort—or, by the bones of Abraham! I had never been captured by the cowardly slaves you sent. I ask only the treatment of an honorable enemy."

"By the beard of the Prophet!" exclaimed Mahomet, "if he were a Christian I would give him liberty for the valor of his speech. Some of the spirit of our gallant Ballaban is still left in him. The witches could not take the great heart out of him, though they stole away his wits. What say you, Sage Murta?" The physician replied, knitting his brows and stroking his chin—

"The Padishah is wise. The man is mad. But since his heart is not touched by the demon, but only his memory erased and his imagination distorted, my science tells me there is hope of his cure."

"What medicament have you for a diseased mind?" asked the Sultan.

With reverent pomposity, but in low voice not overheard by the patient, the physician uttered the prescription:

"First, we have the religious cure—if so be that the man is under the charm of the evil spirits—Find thee a cord with eleven knots tied on it:—for such was the number on the cord with which the daughters of Lobeid, the Jew, bewitched the Prophet. As thou untiest the knots repeat the last two chapters of the Koran, which the Angel Gabriel revealed as the talisman, saying—

"'I fly for refuge unto the Lord of the daybreak, that he may deliver me from the mischief of the night, when it cometh on; and from the mischief of women, blowing on the knots; and from the mischief of the envious; and from the mischief of the whisperer, the devil, who slyly withdraweth, who whispereth evil suggestions into the breasts of men: and from genii and men.'

"If this should fail—as I have known it to fail in the case of those who were not born in the sacred family of Islâm—we should try the virtues of the heritage bowl, which is much esteemed among the Giaours. I have possessed myself of one, once the property of an ancient family. It is made of silver, and engraved with forty-one padlocks. A decoction mixed in this bowl, and poured on the head of the patient any time within seven weeks after the day on which they celebrate the imagined rising of Jesu, son of Mary, from the dead, will often break the most malignant spell. The Christian Paska[80] is just past; so that it will be opportune."

"But should this likewise fail?" asked Mahomet, impatient with the sage's prolixity.

"Ah! we shall then have to try our strictly human remedies. This ailment is called by the Latin disciples of Galen, *dementia*, which signifieth that the man's mind, his natural thoughts, have gone away from him. We must recall them. For this we must have some strong appeal to that which was his hottest passion or interest before his mind flew away from him. Do you know the absorbing humor of this man? Was he a lover? If so, we must find the fair one who has robbed him of his better part, and, restoring her to him, we shall restore him to himself."

"Nay," said Mahomet. "Captain Ballaban was never enamored of woman. The maid who lured the Prophet from the charms of Ayesha and Hafsa,[81] would not have turned Ballaban's head. I once offered him the choice of a bevy of Georgians; but he would not even look at them. He is a soldier; from tassel to shoe-thong a soldier."

"Ah! then we have the remedy at hand," said Murta, rolling his eyes as if reading the prescription in the air. "Give him command; military excitement; honors of the field. When the cimeters gleam then will reason flash again. And my science is at fault if the simple summons to some high duty work not a counter charm to break the spell that is on him, though it were woven by the mystic dance of all the genii and devils."

"We will try this last remedy first," said Mahomet. "Dismiss him. Let him go as he will, without hindrance or seeming to follow, until my orders be brought him by his Aga. In the meantime search the shore for the knotted cord the witches may have blown upon. And, good Murta, send for the silver bowl; for my brain is that hot that I fear me the Giaour ghosts we have sent gibbering to hell during the last few days have left the spell of their evil eyes upon me too."

The following day was not far advanced when Captain Ballaban was summoned to the Sultan's tent, the rumor of his restoration to royal favor having been made to precede the summons. In fact, after the affair of the preceding afternoon, Ballaban had not gone to the sea shore, but retired to his own quarters, where he loyally awaited either his death summons, or an invitation for some wild frolic with the Padishah; he knew not which, so thought about neither; but busied himself over a plan for a new gun-carriage he was going to submit to Urban.

With assumed stolidity he entered the royal tent. As he rose from his obeisance upon the earth, his majesty embraced him with boyish delight.

"Your old self again: I see your soul in your face. I'd give half the horse-tails in the empire rather than lose that shock of hair from my sight, or the glowing brain that is under it from my councils, my red-headed angel!"

"There is no need to lose it, except by cutting it off at my shoulders," said Ballaban, falling in with the humor of the Sultan, yet watchful not to be taken unawares, if, in its fitfulness, that humor should turn.

"I have a grand service for you, if you have skill and courage enough to execute it," said Mahomet, watching the effect on his friend.

The captain's eyes flashed with the prospect, as he said:

"I wait your plan, Sire; only let it be bold."

"I have no plan, you must make one. I would see if your brain is as square as the pot you keep it in," said the Sultan, tapping him on the head with a jewelled whip staff, and adding,

"It is evident, Captain, that we must get possession of the Golden Horn; for so long as the enemy hold that for their harbor, we cannot prevent their reprovisioning the city as they did yesterday; and a few more such auxiliaries as they brought, indeed, another such leader as the Genoese Giustiniani, would compel us to raise the siege. How can we take the harbor? Our boats can never raise the chain at the mouth."

"That has been my problem since the siege began," said Ballaban. "I remember while in Albania, as I lodged one night in a village, I met with some Italian officers, who had come to offer their swords to Castriot. They told how they moved their fleet overland, several miles on a roadway of timbers.[82] We can use that device. The thing is not impracticable; for there is a depression to the north of Galata, through which from the Bosphorus to the inland extremity of the Golden Horn is but five or six miles. Our vessels are not large; could be transported with the multitudes of our troops, and on the still water of the harbor would soon, by superior numbers, capture those of the Christians."

"A good conception!" said Mahomet, "and if my reading has not been at fault, the Roman Augustus did something similar.[83] It shall be done. Let it not be said that the Ottoman was surpassed in daring or difficulty of enterprise by Pagan or Christian. You shall perform it, Ballaban. The woods above Galata will serve for planking, and the engineers can be spared from before the walls until it is accomplished."

A few days later a large fleet of the Moslems was conveyed overland, by means of a roadway of greased timbers. To the amazement of the Christians their adversary's navy no longer lay idly upon the Bosphorus, but was transformed into a line of floating batteries within the harbor of the Golden Horn, and from their rear soon destroyed the fleet of the defenders.

CHAPTER XLI

The city was now completely invested. Menaced from all sides, the defenders were not sufficient in numbers to guard the many approaches. Yet the daily fighting was desperate, for the Moslems were inspired by the certainty of success, while the Christians were nerved with the energy of despair. To end the siege Mahomet designated a time for a combined assault from sea and land.

As the fatal day dawned, numberless hordes moved towards the walls. The great ditches were soon filled with the dead bodies of thousands of the least serviceable soldiers, who had been driven from behind by the lances of the trained bands, that they might thus worry the patience and exhaust the resources of the brave defenders, without taxing the best of the Moslem troops. The carcasses of the slain made a highway for the living, over which they poured against the gate of St. Romanus. The four grim towers toppled beneath the pounding of great stone balls hurled from the cannon of Urban. The defenders were driven off the adjacent walls by the storms of bullets and arrows that swept them. At the critical moment the Janizaries, unwearied as yet by watching or fighting, twelve thousand strong, as compact a mass beneath the eye of the Sultan as the weapon he held in his hand, moved to where the breach was widest.

"The spoil to all! A province to him who first enters!" cried the Sultan, waving his iron battle mace. Hassan, the giant, first mounted the rampart, and fell pierced with arrows and crushed with stones. But through the gap his dying valor had made in the ranks of the foe first rushed the company of Ballaban.

In vain did the people crowd beneath the dome of St. Sophia, grasping with hopeless hope an ancient prophecy that at the extreme moment an angel would descend to rescue the city. Alas! only the angel of death came that day; and to none brought he more welcome news than to the Emperor,—"Thy prayer is answered; for thou hast fallen where the dead lie thickest!" Near the gateway of St. Romanus, where he had met the first of the invaders, under the piles of the dead, gashed by sabre strokes and crushed beneath the feet of the victors, lay the body of Constantine Palæologus, the noblest of the Cæsars of the Eastern Empire!

The Turks placed his ghastly head between the feet of the bronze horse, a part of the equestrian statue of Justinian, where it was reverently saluted even by the Moslems, who paused in the rage of the sack to think upon the virtue and courage of the unfortunate monarch.

Captain Ballaban had pressed rapidly through the city to the doors of St. Sophia. The oaken gates flew back under the axes of the Moslems. Monks and matrons, children and nuns, lords and beggars were crowded together, not knowing whether the grand dome would melt away and a legion of angels descend for their relief, or the vast enclosure would become a pen of indiscriminate slaughter. The motley and helpless misery excited the pity of the captors. Ballaban's voice rang through the arches, proclaiming safely to those who should submit. That he might the better command the scene, he made his way to the chancel in front of the grand altar. It was filled with the nuns, repeating their prayers. Among them was the fair Albanian. Her face was but partly toward him, yet he could never mistake that queenly head. She was addressing the Sisters. Holding aloft the bright shaft of a stiletto, she cried,—

"Let us give ourselves to heaven, but never to the harem!"

Ballaban paused an instant. But that instant seemed to him many minutes. As, under the lightning's flash, the whole moving panorama of the wide landscape seems to stand still, and paints vividly its prominent objects, however scattered, upon the startled eye of the beholders; so his mind marvellously quickened by the excitement, took in at once the long track of his own life. He saw a little child's hand wreathing him with flowers plucked beside a cottage on the Balkans; a lovely captive whose face was lit by the blazing home in a hamlet of Albania; a form of one at Sfetigrade lying still and faint with sickness, but radiant as with the beginning of transfiguration for the spirit life; and the queenly being who was borne in the palanquin through the gate of Phranza. But how changed! How much more glorious now! Earthly beauty had become haloed with the heavenly. He never had conceived of such majesty, such glory of personality, such splendor of character, as were revealed by her attitude, her eye, her voice, her purpose.

"But now," thought he, "the descending blade will change this utmost sublimity of being into a little heap of gory dust!"

All this flashed through his mind. In another instant his strong hand had caught the arm of the voluntary sacrifice. The stiletto, falling, caught in the folds of her garments, and then rang upon the marble floor of the chancel. Morsinia uttered a shriek and fell, apparently as lifeless as if the blade had entered her heart.

The Janizary stood astounded. A tide of feeling strange to him poured through his soul. For the first time in his life he felt a horror of war. Not thousands writhing on the battle field could blanch his cheek with pity for their pangs: but that one voice rang through and through him, and rent his heart with sympathetic agony. Her cry had become a cry of his own soul too.

For the first time he realized the dignity of woman's character. This woman was not even wounded. She had fallen beneath the stroke of a thought, a sentiment, a woman's notion of her honor! The women he had known had no such fatal scruples. Other captive beauties soon became accustomed to their new surroundings. Many even offered to buy with their charms an exchange of poverty for the luxuries of the harem of Pashas and wealthy Moslems. Was this a solitary woman's tragedy of virtue? Or was it some peculiar teaching of the Christian's faith that inspired her to such heroism? However it came, the man knew that with her it was a mighty reality; this instinct of virtue; this sanctity of person.

And this woman was his dream made real! A celestial ideal which he had touched!

The man's brain reeled with the shock of these tenderer and deeper feelings, coming after the wildness of the battle rage. He grasped the altar for support. The blood seemed to have ceased to bound in his veins, the temples to be pulseless; a band to have been drawn tightly about his brain so as to paralyze its action. He felt himself falling. A deathly sickness spread through his frame. He was sure he had fainted. He thought he must have been unconscious for a while. Yet when he opened his eyes, the soldier near him was in the same attitude of dragging a nun by her wrists as when he last saw him. Time had stood still with his pulses. He shuddered at the cruelty on every side, as the shrieks from the high galleries were answered by those in distant alcoves and from the deep crypt. He watched the groups of old men and children, monks and senators, nuns and courtesans, tied together and dragged away, some for slaughter, some for princely ransom, some for shame.

The building was well emptied when the Sultan entered.

He at once advanced to the altar and proclaimed:

"God is God; there is but one God, and Mahomet is the apostle of God!"

"But whom have we here, Captain Ballaban?" "Your Majesty, I am guarding a beautiful captive whom I would not have fall into the hands of the common soldiers; I take it, of high estate," replied the Janizary, knowing that such an introduction to the royal attention alone could save her from the fate which awaited the unhappy maidens, most of whom were liable to be sold to brutal masters and transported to distant provinces.

The Sultan gazed upon the partly conscious woman, and commanded,——

"Let her be veiled! Seek out a goodly house. Find the Eunuch Tamlich." Ballaban shuddered at this command, and was about to reply, when his judgment suggested that he was impotent to dispute the royal will except by endangering the life or the welfare of his captive.

The safest place for her was, after all, with the maidens who were known to be the choice of the Sultan, and thus beyond insult by any except the imperial debauchee.

Mahomet II. gave orders for the immediate transformation of the Christian temple of St. Sophia into a Mosque. In a few hours desolation reigned in those "Courts of the Lord's House," which, when first completed, ages ago, drew from the imperial founder, the remark: "Oh, Solomon! I have surpassed thee!" and which, though the poverty of later monarchs had allowed it to become sadly impaired, was yet regarded by the Greek Christians as worthy of being the vestibule of heaven.

The command of the Sultan: "Take away every trace of the idolatry of the infidel!" was obeyed in demolishing the rarest gems of Christian art to which attached the least symbolism of the now abolished worship. The arms were chiseled off the marble crosses which stood out in relief from the side walls, and from the bases of the gigantic pillars. The rare mosaics which lined the church as if it were a vast casket—the fitting gift of the princes of the earth to the King of Kings—were plastered or painted over. The altar, that marvellous combination of gold and silver and bronze, conglomerate with a thousand precious stones, was torn away, that the red slab of the Mihrab might point the prayers of the new devotees toward Mecca. The furniture, from that upon the grand altar to the banners and mementoes of a thousand years, the donations of Greek emperors and sovereigns of other lands, was broken or torn into pieces. There remained only the grand proportions of the building—its chief glory—enriched by polished surfaces of marble and porphyry slabs; the superb pillars brought by the reverent cupidity of earlier ages from the ruined temple of Diana at Ephesus, the temple of the Sun at Palmyra, the temple on the Acro-Corinthus, and the mythologic urn from Pergamus, which latter, having been used as a baptismal font by the followers of Jesus, was now devoted to the ablutions of the Moslems.

From St. Sophia the Sultan passed to the palace of the Greek Cæsars.

"Truly! truly!" said he "The spider's web is the royal curtain; the owl sounds the watch cry on the towers of Afrasiab," quoting from the Persian poet Firdusi, as he gazed about the deserted halls. He issued his mandate which should summon architects and decorators, not only from his dominions, but from Christian nations, to adorn the splendid headland with the palatial motley of walls and kiosks which were to constitute his new seraglio.

The considerateness of Ballaban led him to select the house of Phranza as the place to which Morsinia was taken. The noble site and substantial structure of the mansion of the late chamberlain commended it to the Sultan for the temporary haremlik; and the familiar rooms alleviated, like the faces of mute friends, the wildness of the grief of their only familiar captive.

CHAPTER XLII

Constantine, after his escape from the Sultan's tent, where he had been taken for the demented Ballaban, was unable to enter Constantinople before it fell. His heart was torn with agonizing solicitude for the fate of Morsinia. He knew too well the determination of the dauntless girl in the event of her falling into the hands of the Turks. Filling his dreams at night, and rising before him as a terrible apparition by day, was that loved form, a suicide empurpled with its own gore. Yet love and duty led him to seek her, or at least to seek the certainty of her fate. He therefore disguised himself as a Moslem and mingled with the throng of soldiers and adventurers who entered the city under its new possessors. He wandered for hours about the familiar streets, that, perchance, he might come upon some memorial of her. The secrets of the royal harem he could not explore, even if suspicion led his thought thither. The proximity of the residence of Phranza was guarded by the immediate servants of the Sultan, so that he was deprived of even the fond misery of visiting the scenes so associated with his former joy.

In passing through one of the narrowest and foulest streets—the only ones that had been left undisturbed by the Vandalism of the conquerors—he came upon an old woman, hideous in face and decrepit, whom he remembered as a beggar at the gate of Phranza. From her he learned many stories of the last hours of the siege.

According to her story she had gone among the first to St. Sophia. When the Moslems entered they tied her by a silken girdle to the person of the Grand Chamberlain, and, amid the jeers of the soldiers, marched them together to the Hippodrome. She remembered the Sultan as he rode on his horse,—how he struck with his battle hammer one of the silver heads of the bronze serpents, and cried: "So I smite the heads of the kingdoms!" Just as he did so he turned, and saw her in her rags tied to the courtly-robed lord, and in an angry voice commanded that the princely man be loosed from contact with the filthy hag. Phranza was taken away: but nobody cared to take her away. She was trampled by the crowd, but lived. And nobody thought of turning her out of her hovel home. She was as safe as is a rat when the robbers have killed the nobler inmates of a house.

The woman said that she had heard that the daughter of Phranza was sent away somewhere to an island home. But the Albanian Princess,—Yes, she knew her well; for no hand used to drop so bountifully the alms she asked, or said so kindly "Jesu pity you, my good woman!" as did that beautiful lady. The beggar declared that she stood near her by the altar in St. Sophia. "She looked so saintly there! There was a real aureole about her head as she prayed, so she was a saint indeed. Then she raised her dagger!" But the wretched watcher could watch no longer, though she heard her cry, so wild that she would never cease to hear it.

The beggar ceased her story; all her words had cut through her listener's heart as if they had been daggers.

"It is well!" he said, "I will go to Albania. Among those who loved her I will worship her memory; and, under Castriot, I will seek my revenge."

CHAPTER XLIII

Morsinia's fears, and her horror at the anticipated life in the harem, were not confirmed by its actual scenes. Except for the constant surveillance of the Nubian eunuchs and female attendants, there was no restriction upon her liberty. She passed through the familiar corridors, and rested upon the divan in what had been her own chamber in better days. Other female captives became her companions; but among them were none of those belonging to Constantinople. Suburban villages were represented; but most of the odalisks[84] were Circassian beauties, whose conduct did not indicate that they felt any shame in their condition. They indulged in jealous rivalry, estimating their own worth by the sums which the agents of the Sultan had paid their parents for their possession; or bantering one another as to who of their number would first meet the fancy of their royal master. There were several Greeks, who, with more modesty of speech, spared none of the arts of the toilet to prepare themselves to better their condition in the only way that was now open to them. A Coptic girl had been sent by Eenal, the Borghite Khalif of Egypt, as a present to the Sultan. Her form was slight, and without the fullness of development which other races associate with female beauty, but of wonderful grace of pose and motion; her face was broad; eyes wide and expressionless; mouth straight. Yet her features had that symmetry and balance which gave to them a strange fascination. The Turcoman Emir who had already given his daughter to Mahomet—the nuptials with whom he was celebrating when called to the throne—exercised still further his fatherly office in presenting to his son-in-law as fine a pair of black eyes as ever flashed their cruel commands to an amative heart. To study this physiognomical museum afforded Morsinia an entertaining relief from the otherwise constant torture of her thoughts.

To her further diversion one was introduced into the harem who spoke her own Albanian tongue. This new comer was of undoubted beauty, so far as that quality could be the product of merely physical elements. It was of the kind that might bind a god on earth, but could never help a soul to heaven. Her lower face, with full red lips arching the pearliest teeth, and complexion ruddy with the glow of health, shading into the snowy bosom, might perhaps serve to make a Venus; but her upper features, the low forehead and dilated nostrils, could never have been made to bespeak the thoughtful Minerva in this retreat of those, who, to the Moslem imagination, are the types of heavenly perfection. Her eyes were bright, but only with surface lustre. Her nature evidently contained no depths which could hold either noble resentment or self sacrificing love; either grand earthly passion or heavenly faith.

This woman's vanity did not long keep back the story of her life. She told of her conquest of the village swains who fought for the possession of her charms; of the devotion of an Albanian prince who took her dowerless in preference to the ladies of great family and fortune, and would have bestowed upon her the heirship to his estates: of how she was stolen away from the great castle by a company of Turkish officers, who afterward fought among themselves for the privilege of presenting her to the Validé Sultana;[85] for it was about the time of the Ramedan feast when the Sultan's mother made an annual gift to her son of the most beautiful woman she could secure. The vain captive declared that the jealousy of the odalisks at Adrianople had led the Kislar Aga to send her here to Constantinople.

"And who was the Albanian nobleman whose bride you had become?" asked Morsinia.

"Oh, one who is to be king of Albania one day, the Voivode Amesa."

"Ah!" said Morsinia, "this is news from my country. When was it determined that Amesa should be king?"

"Oh! every one speaks of it at the castle as if it were well understood. And when he becomes king then he will claim me again from Mahomet, though he must ransom me with half his kingdom. Yes, I am to be a queen; and indeed I may be one already, for perhaps Lord Amesa is now on the throne. And that is the reason I wear the cord of gold in my hair; for one day my royal lover will put the crown here."

The bedizened beauty rose and paced to and fro through the great salôn. The pride which gave the majestic toss to her head, however it would have marred that ethereal form which the inner eye of the moralist or the Christian always sees, and which is called character, only gave an additional charm to her;—as the delicate yet stately comb of the peacock adds to the fascination of that bird. Her carriage combined the gracefulness of perfect anatomy and health with the dignity which conceit, thoroughly diffused in muscle and nerve, lent to all her movements. With that step upon it no carpet beneath a throne would have been dishonored. Her dress was in exquisite keeping with her person. The close fitting zone or girdle about her waist left the bust uncontorted; a model which needed no device to supplement the perfection of nature. A robe of purple velvet trailed luxuriantly behind; but in front was looped so as to display the loose trousers of white silk which were gathered below the knee and fell in full ruffles about the unstockinged ankles, but not so low as to conceal the rings of silver which clasped them, and the slippers of yellow satin, ending in long and curved points, which protruded from beneath.

As the other women gazed at this self-assumed queen of the harem the green fire of jealousy flashed alike from black eyes and blue. The straight thin noses of the Greeks for the moment forgot their classic models, and dilated as if in rivalry of that flattened feature of the Egyptian; while the straight mouth of the daughter of the Nile writhed in indescribable curves, indicative of commingled wrath, hatred, pique and scorn.

This parade would have produced in Morsinia the feeling of contempt, were it not for that sisterly interest which was awakened by the fact that she was her own country-woman. Morsinia's face, usually calm in its great dignity and reserve, now flushed with the struggle between indignation and pity for the girl.

At this moment the purple hangings which separated the salôn from the open court were held aside by the silver staff of the eunuch in charge; and the young Padishah stood as a spectator of the scene.

"Ah! Tamlich," cried he, addressing the black eunuch, "you were right in saying that the great haremlik at Adrianople, with its thousand goddesses, could not rival this temporary one for the fairness of the birds you have caged in it." The women made the temineh—a salutation with the right hand just sweeping the floor, and then pressed consecutively to the heart, the lips and the forehead; a movement denoting reverence, and, at the same time, giving field for the display of the utmost grace of motion.

The Padishah passed among these his slaves with the license which betokened his absolute ownership; stroking their hair and toying with their persons according to his amiable or insolent caprice. Morsinia, however, was spared this familiarity. The Sultan himself colored slightly as he addressed her a few words in Greek, of which language, in common with several others, he knew enough to act as his own interpreter. His questions were respectful, all limited to her comfort in her new home. With Elissa, the queenly Albanian, he was at once on terms of intimacy. Her manner betokened that she gave to him only too willingly whatever he might be disposed to take.

As the Sultan withdrew, the eunuch Tamlich remarked to him:

"My surmise of your Excellency's judgment was verified. Said I not that the two Arnaouts were the fairest? And did I not behold your Majesty gaze longest upon them?"

"I commend your taste, Tamlich," replied Mahomet. "But those two are as unlike as a ruby and a pearl."

"But as fair as either, are they not? The chief hamamjina[86] declares that the blue-eyed one has the most perfect form she ever saw; and that it is a form which will improve with years. Morsinia Hanoum[87] will be more fit for Paradise, while Elissa Hanoum may lose the grace of the maiden as a matron. But the cherry is ripe for the plucking now."

"I like the ruby better than the pearl," said the Sultan. "I cannot quite fathom the deep eye of the latter. She thinks too much. I would not have women think. They are to make us stop thinking. The problems of state are sufficiently perplexing: I want no human problem in my arms."

"But one who thinks may have some skill in affording amusement. Have I not heard thee say, Sire, 'Blessed is the one who can invent a new recreation?' That requires thinking."

"Right, Tamlich! can she sing?"

"Ay! your Majesty, to the Greek cythera; and such songs that, though they know not a word of them—for the songs are in her own Arnaout tongue—the odalisks all fall to weeping."

"I like not such singing," said Mahomet. "To make people think with her thoughtful eyes is bad enough in a woman. To make them weep with her voice is wicked, is Christian. I will give her away to some one who wants a wife that thinks. There is Hamed Bey, one of the muderris[88] who is to be put at the head of my new chain of Ulemas.[89] He will want a wife who thinks; and his eyes are that blind with dry study that it will do him good to weep. But who is the woman? I think I saw her face in St. Sophia the day of our entry."

"She belonged to the house-hold of Phranza, the Chamberlain, who possessed this very house," replied the eunuch. "And I think, from its goodly size and decoration, he must have used the treasury of the empire freely."

"To Phranza! Why, I have a daughter of his in the nursery at Adrianople. His wife I have given to the Master of the Horse.[90] His son I have this day sent to hell for his insolence. But she is an Arnaout; therefore not of kin to Phranza. Search out her story, Tamlich! For a member of the family of Phranza, and not of his blood, may be of some political consequence. I will keep her. But get her story, Tamlich, get her story!"

"I have it already, Sire," replied the eunuch.

"Ah!"

"She is a ward of Scanderbeg, the Arnaout traitor, sent to Constantinople to escape the danger of capture by thine all-conquering arms. But the bird fled from the fowler into the snare."

"Perhaps a child of Scanderbeg! Eh, Tamlich? One at least whose life is of great value to him, and was to the Greek empire. I will inform Scanderbeg that she is in my possession. By the dread of what may happen to her I shall the easier force that ravening brute to make terms; for I am tired of battering my sword against his rocks, trying to prick his skin. Keep her close, Tamlich, keep her close!"

CHAPTER XLIV

Late in the day the Sultan retired to a neighboring mansion, once possessed by the Greek Grand Duke, Lucas Notaras, and there sought relaxation from the incessant cares of the empire. The day had been wearisome. Architects had submitted plans for the detailed ornamentation of the new seraglio which was rising on the Byzantine Point. One of the plans led to dispute between the Padishah and the chief Mufti, the expounder of the Moslem law. It was occasioned thus. The porphyry column[91] which stood hard by the palace of the Greek emperors, had once served to hold aloft the bronze statue of Apollo, a precious relic of ancient Greek mythology. This was afterward reverenced by the people as the figure of the Emperor Constantine the Great, or worshipped by them as that of Christ. An architect proposed that the time-glorious shaft should now be surmounted by the colossal statue of Mahomet II. The Mufti declared the project to be impious, as tempting to idolatry, against which the Koran was so clear and denunciatory, and also the Sounna or traditional sayings of the Prophet. The Sultan's pride rebelled against this assumption of an authority above his own. But the Sultan's superstitious regard for the faith among the people, which led him to wash his hands and face openly whenever he spoke with the architect, who was a Christian engaged at great cost from Italy, also led him to fear to break with the prescriptions and customs of his religion in this matter. He contented himself with an oath that he had sooner lost the honor of a campaign than the privilege of seeing himself represented as the conqueror of both Constantine and Christ. Generals, too, had been in council with him that day regarding the conduct of intrigues for the possession of the Peloponnesus, and about the wars in Servia, Boznia and Trebizond. Ill tidings had come from Albania, where Scanderbeg was consuming the Turkish armies, as a great spider entraps in his webs and at his leisure devours a swarm of hornets, which, could they have free access to him, would instantly sting him to death. The messenger who brought this news was rewarded by having hurled at his head an immense vase of malachite, in the exertion of lifting which the imperial wrath was sufficiently eased to allow of his turning to other business. A plan for the reception of the inmates of the grand harem at Adrianople, when they should be transported to the spacious buildings being constructed for them in the seraglio, was also a pleasing diversion, and led the Sultan to make the brief visit to the fair ones at the house of Phranza, which has been described. But the nettled spirit of the Padishah was far from subdued. He had during the day given an order, the sequel to which we must relate, and which, while it disturbed his conscience and flooded him at moments with the sense of self-contempt, also inflamed his natural passion for cruelty. He determined to drown the noble, and to satiate the the vicious, craving by an hour or two of unrestrained debauch.

In the court of the house of the Grand Duke Notaras was spread the royal banquet. Rarest viands were flanked by flagons of costliest wines. Upon the momentary surprise of the steward when he received the order to provide the wines, the monarch cried in a contemptuous tone:

"Ah! I know your thoughts. It is not according to the Koran that wine should be drunk. But by the staff of Moses,[92] which they found in the palace of the Cæsars yonder, I swear that Mahomet the Emperor shall not yield to Mahomet the Prophet in everything. The Prophet made laws to suit his own taste, so will I[93]. He can have Mecca and Medina and Jerusalem; but I shall reign without him in my own palace in Stamboul, which I have captured with my own hand. Bring the wine, or I'll spill your black blood as a beverage to those in hell! It will be sweet enough for your kin who are black with roasting. I will have wine to-day! Cool it in all the snows from Mount Olympus yonder; for my blood is as hot as if I were shod with fire; and my skull boils like a pot."[94]

About the table were divans cushioned with down and covered with yellow silk. The Padishah took his seat upon the highest cushion. By his side stood the chief of the black eunuchs, splendidly[95] attired in the waistcoat of flower embroidered brocade, tunic of scarlet, flowing trousers, red turban, and half boots of bronzed leather. He held a wand of silver covered with elegant tracery and topped in filagree. As he waved this symbol of his office, there came from the various doors opening into the court groups of the harem women. They were draped in gauze, in the folds of which sparkled diamonds and glowed the hues of precious stones selected by the taste of the chief eunuch to set off the complexion and hair of their various wearers, and at the same time to facilitate their grouping into sets of dancers. The court was made radiant with these beautiful forms, which moved in circles or in spirals about the fountains and under the orange trees, whose white blossoms and golden fruit in simultaneous fulness completed the picture for the eye, while their fragrance loaded the air with its delicate delight.

The Kislar Aga had arranged a scene which especially pleased the monarch, whose head was already swimming with the combined effect of the mazy dance and the fumes of the wine. An attendant led into the court, held partly by a strong leash and partly by the voice of his trainer, a magnificent leopard. With utmost grace the beast leaped over the ribboned wand, falling so softly to the ground that, though of enormous weight, he would not seemingly have broken a twig had it lain beneath his feet. In imitation of this, a eunuch led into the court by a leash of roses a Circassian dancer, the gift of a Caramanian prince. Her form was as free from the hindrances of dress as that of her spotted competitor; except that a bright gem burned upon her forehead, in the node which gathered a part of her hair; while the abundance of her tresses was either held out on her snowy arms, or fell about her as a veil almost to her feet. With a hundred variations the girl repeated the motions of the leopard, leaping the wands with equal grace as she came to them in the measures of the dance.

The great brute had laid his head in the lap of his trainer, and was watching his beautiful rival with apparent enjoyment; only now and then uttering a low growl as if in jealousy, when the Bravo! of the Sultan rewarded some especially fascinating movement. The girl came to the side of the magnificent monster and dropped her long hair over his head. The brute closed his eyes as if soothed by the wooing of the maiden. Cautiously, but encouraged by the low voice of the trainer, she placed her head upon the mottled and living pillow. A great paw was thrown about her shoulder.

The Sultan was in ecstasy of applause, and shouted:

"A collar of gold for each of them!"

The girl attempted to rise, but her splendid lover seemed to have become really enamored of the beautiful form he held. Her slightest motion was answered by a growl; while the swaying of his tail indicated that, as among human kind, so with the brutes, the softest sentiments were to be guarded by those of a severer nature; that baffled love must meet the avenging of cruel wrath. Like the affection of some men, that of the leopard was limited to its own gratification, and utterly regardless of the comfort of its object; for the fondness of the brute was not such as to prevent his long nails protruding through their velvet covering, and entering the bare flesh of the girl. She quivered with pain, yet, at the quick warning of the trainer, she made no outcry. The man drew from his pocket a small bit of raw flesh, and diverted the eyes of the brute from the blood streaming at each claw-puncture on the neck and bosom of his victim. The leopard savagely snapped at the morsel, and, at the same instant struck it with his paw, and leaped to seize it as it was hurled many feet away. The girl as quickly darted to a safe distance. Attendants instantly appeared and surrounded the beast with their spear points. He crouched at the feet of the trainer, and whined in fear until he was led out.

The girls then encircled the seat of the Sultan, and vied with one another in the simulated attempt to throw over him a spell. Nor was the attempt merely simulated, as each one displayed the utmost art of beauty and manner to win from the half-drunken tyrant some token of his favor.

When Elissa came near the Sultan, he bade her play with him as the Circassian did with the leopard. He held her and exclaimed to the others:

"Beware your leopard when he growls! but where is the other Arnaout? I will have the pearl with the ruby of the harem! where is she, I say? Did I not order you to bring all the odalisks to my feast?"

"From your Majesty's orders but lately, Sire, I supposed—" began the eunuch.

"Supposed? You are to obey, not to suppose," cried the demented man, slashing at him with the cimeter that lay at his feet. "But she is not robed for the feast."

"Bring her as she is, and robe her here. You said that she was fairer than this one. If she is not fairer than this one, the leopard's claws will grip her, and the beast shall have your black body for his next supper. Bring her!"

The eunuch soon returned with Morsinia. She wore a sombre feridjé, or cloak completely enveloping the person. This she had on at the moment she was summoned, and the eunuch obeyed literally the mandate of the monarch to bring her as she was.

As she stood before the Sultan she appeared, in contrast with her half naked and bejeweled sisters, like a prophetess; some female Elijah before Ahab surrounded by his household of Jezebels. Throwing back the yashmak, or long veil—the one Moslem costume she had very willingly assumed after her captivity—she gazed upon the tyrant with a look of amazed inquiry of his meaning in summoning her to such a place. The sovereignty of her soul asserted and expressed itself in her noble brow, her clear and steady eye, her dauntless bearing.

"Sire, I have obeyed," said she, making the obeisance which in form was obsequious, but which she executed with such dignity that even the dull wit of the reveller felt that she had not really humbled herself before him by so much as the shadow of a thought.

"Disrobe her!" cried the monarch.

The woman stepped back, as if to avoid the contact of her person with the black eunuch; but as suddenly threw off the feridjé herself. If she had seemed a gloomy prophetess before, her appearance now would have suggested to an ancient Greek the apparition of Pudicitia, the goddess of modesty. Her gown of rich pearl-tinted cloth covered her shoulders; and, though opened upon the bosom, it was to show only the thick folds of white lace which embraced the throat in a ruffle, and was clasped with a single gem—a cameo presented to her by the Greek Emperor.

The bearing of the woman gave a temporary check to the abominable rage of the royal wretch, and recalled him to his better judgment. For it was a peculiarity of Mahomet that no passion or debauch could completely divert him from carrying out any plan he had devised pertaining to his imperial ambition. As certain musicians perform without the sacrifice of a note the most difficult pieces, when too drunk to hold a goblet steadily to their lips, and as certain noted generals have staggered through the battle without the slightest strategic mistake, so Mahomet never lost sight of a political or military purpose he had formed. While sleeping and waking, in the wildest revelry and in the privacy of his unspeakable sensuality, that project blazed before him like a strong fire-light through the haze.

"Take her away! Take her away!" said he to the eunuch, recollecting his purpose of using her in his negotiations with Scanderbeg; and covering his retreat from his original command by the remark, "She is the woman who thinks, I want none such to put her head against my heart. She might discover my thoughts; and by the secrets of Allah! if a hair of my beard knew one of my thoughts I would pluck it out and burn it."[96]

As Morsinia withdrew, a eunuch approached and whispered to the Sultan.

"Ah! it is good! good!" cried the Monarch. "My Lord, the Grand Duke Notaras, will revisit his mansion. For him we have provided a feast such as his master Palæologus never gave him. Ah! my lovely Arnaout shall sit at my right hand—for the queen of beauty has precedence to-day," said he, addressing Elissa. "And the Egyptian shall make me merry with the music of her voice, which I doubt not is sweeter than the strains of her native Memnon. And, Tamlich, you shall do me the honor of representing the king of Nubia, and lie there opposite."

The eunuch stood bewildered; for never before had a Moslem proposed to introduce into his harem the person of any man, as now the Duke of Notaras was to look upon the beauties who should be reserved solely for the feasting of the Padishah's eyes.

Mahomet, knowing his thoughts, bade him obey, and cried,

"Let the fair houris veil their faces with their blushes. Bring in Notaras!"

Three blacks entered, each bearing a great salver, on which was a covered dish of gold.

"To Tamlich I demit the honors of the board," said he, waving the foremost waiter toward the eunuch, whose face almost blanched at the strange turn affairs were taking, or perhaps with the suspicion that to-morrow his head would fall from his shoulders as the penalty of having witnessed the Padishah disgrace himself.

The attendants placed the dishes before the eunuch and the two favored beauties. The covers removed revealed the ghastly sight of three human heads, their unclosed eyes staring upward from their distorted faces and gory locks. The eunuch leaped from the divan. The women fell back shrieking and fainting. They were the heads of the Grand Duke Notaras and his two children.

Well did the Sultan need the strong diversion of the drunken revelry to drown the thoughts of what he knew to be transpiring at the hour. In spite of his royal word to the distinguished captive who had made his submission absolute, except to the extent of seeing his children dishonored to the vilest purposes, Mahomet had ordered that Notaras should be beheaded at the Hippodrome, having been first compelled to witness the decapitation of his family.

Even Mahomet was sobered by the horrid ghoulism he had devised, and dismissed the terror-stricken revelers with a volley of curses.

CHAPTER XLV

The courage of Morsinia when she appeared before Mahomet had been stimulated by an event which occurred a little before her summons.

She was sitting by the latticed window in the house of Phranza. It overlooked the wall surrounding the garden, which on that side was a narrow enclosure. This had been her favorite resort in brighter days. From it she could see what passed in the broad highway beyond, while the close latticed woodwork prevented her being seen by those without. While musing there she was strangely attracted by an officer who frequently passed. His shape and stature reminded her strongly of Constantine. As he turned his face toward the mansion the features seemed identical with those of her foster brother. Recovering from the stroke of surprise this apparition gave her, Morsinia rubbed her eyes to make sure she was not dreaming, and looked again. He was in conversation with another. It could not be Constantine, for, aside from the general belief in Constantine's death before the termination of the siege, this person was saluted with great reverence by the soldiers who passed by, and approached with familiarity by other officers of rank.

The sight brought into vivid conviction what had long been her day dream, namely, that Michael, her childhood playmate, might be living, and if so, would probably be among the Turkish soldiers; for his goodly physique and talent, displayed as a lad, would certainly have been cultivated by his captors. She now felt certain of her theory. So strong was the impression, and so active and exciting her thoughts as she endeavored to devise a way by which the discovery might be utilized to the advantage of both, that even the loathsome splendor of the Sultan's garden party, had not impressed her as it otherwise would have done.

For several days after she was almost oblivious to the monotony of the harem life; so busy was she with her new problem. She determined that, at any cost, she would bring herself into communication with the officer, and, if her theory should be confirmed, declare herself, and boldly propose that he should rescue her. For she could not conceive that, however much he had become accustomed to Turkish life, he had lost all yearning for his liberty and all impression of his Christian faith.

But how could she convey any intelligence to him? Except through the eunuchs, the inmates of the harem had little communication with the outer world. The customs of life there were as inflexible as the walls.

To her natural ingenuity, now so quickened by necessity and hope, there at length appeared an end thread of the tangle. The women of the harem relieved the tedium of their existence by making various articles, the construction of which might not mar the delicacy of their fingers; such as needlework upon their own clothing, coverings for cushions, curtains, tapestried hangings, spreads for couches, cases in which the Koran could be kept so that even when being read it need not be touched by the fingers, bags of scented powders, and the like. Many of these articles were disposed of at the bazaars of the city, and the proceeds spent by the odalisks at their own caprice; generally for confections and gew-gaws. At the time there was quite a demand for articles made in the harem. Many thousands of Moslems had been imported from Asia Minor to take the place of the rapidly disappearing Greek population. Large stores of articles were sent from the great harem at Adrianople, and sold for fabulous prices in the bazaars of Stamboul, as the new capital was called by the Turks. The agents for the sale of these things were generally the female attendants at the harem, who had free association with the bazaar keepers. Sometimes these women sold directly to the individual purchasers without going to the trade places. An officer or young citizen was often inveigled into buying, and paying exorbitant prices too, on hearing that some odalisk had set longing eyes upon him, and wrought the purse or belt, the dagger-sheath or embroidered jacket, as a special evidence of her favor. Many were the stories which the gallants of the city and garrison were accustomed to tell, as they displayed their purchases, about nocturnal adventures, in which they were guided only by a pair of bright eyes, and of favors received from beauties whose names, of course, prudence forbade them to mention. All the traditions of lovers, romances of moon-shadowed grottoes, and all the stories of castles with the thread at the window, that have been told from the beginning of the world, had their counterpart in those the swains of Stamboul told about the Sultan's earthly paradise at Adrianople, or those which, in their amatory bantering, they had made to cluster about the villa of the late Phranza at the new capital.

An old woman, who, formerly a servant in the harem, had been given by the Validé Sultana, the mother of Amurath, to a subaltern officer as wife, but had long been a widow, was permitted freely to enter the haremlik, and engaged as a convenient broker between those within and those without. One day Morsinia, in giving her some of her handiwork for sale, held up an elegant case of silk containing several little crystals, or phials, of atar of roses.

"Kala-Hanoum, do you know the young Captain Ballaban?"

"Ay, the Knight of the Golden Horn?" asked the woman.

"And why do they call him that?"

"Because," she replied, "his head glows like one, I suppose."

"Yes, he is the man—Well! find him—Tell him any story you please about my beauty."

"I need not invent one; I must only tell the truth to bewitch him," replied the old dame, with real fondness and admiration. "But that will be difficult. I can invent a lie better than describe the truth, unless you help me."

"Well," said Morsinia, "tell him as much truth about my appearance as you can, and invent the rest. Tell him—let me see—that my eyes are as bright as the stars that shine above the Balkans."

"Do they shine there more brilliantly than here where they make their toilet in the Bosphorus?" asked the woman.

"Oh! yes," said Morsinia, "for the air is clearest there of any place on the earth. Tell him, too, that my teeth are as white as the snows that lie in the pass of Slatiza."

"Where is that?" queried the messenger.

"Oh! it is a grotto I have heard of, that lies very high up toward the sky, where the snows are unsoiled by passing through the clouds, which, you know, always tints them. And then tell him that altogether I am as queenly as—as—well! as the wonderful Elizabeth Morsiney, the bride of the Christian king Sigismund."

"Elizabeth Morsiney? yes, I will remember that name, if some day you will tell me her story."

"That I will," said Morsinia. "And tell the young officer that the odalisk who made this lovely case has dreamed of him ever since she was a child."

"He cannot resist that," said the woman.

"But you must sell it to no one else. And see this elegant sash of cashmere! I will give it to you to sell on your own account, Hanoum, if you bring me some sure evidence that he has bought the case of perfume. And be sure to tell him that just when the sun is setting he must go somewhere alone, and look at the sun through each of the little phials, and he may see the face of her who sent them; for you know that a true lover can always see the one who sends a phial of atar of roses in the sun glints from its sides. And when you bring me evidence that he has bought it, then, good Kala, you shall have the sash of cashmere." The old woman's cupidity hastened her feet upon her errand.

CHAPTER XLVI

"Peace be with thee!" said the old woman, dropping a low courtesy to the officer, as he walked near the new buildings of the seraglio.

"Peace be unto *thee*, and the mercy of God and His blessing,[97] good woman!" replied the soldier; but waving his hand, added kindly, "I have no need of your harem trumpery."

"But see this!" said she, showing the elegant case of perfumery. "This holds the essence of the flowers of paradise."

"Go along, old mother! I would have no taste for it if it contained the sweat of the houris."[98]

"But this case was made especially for you, Captain Ballaban."

"Or for any other man whose purse will buy it," replied he, moving away.

The woman followed closely, chattering into his deaf ears.

"But, could you see her that made it, you would not decline to buy, though you gave for it half the gold you found in the coffers of the rich Greeks the day your valor won the city, brave Captain; and the cost of it is but a lira;[99] and the maiden is dying of love for you."

"Then why does she not give it to me as a present? Love asks no price," said he, just turning his head.

"That she would, but for fear of offending your honor by slighting your purse," said the quick-witted woman.

"Well said, mother! I warrant that the Beyler Bey, or the noble Kaikji,[100] who made love to you never got you for nothing."

"Indeed, no! He paid the Validé Sultana ten provinces, and a brass buckle besides, to prevent her giving me to Timour; who took it so hard that he would have broken his heart, but that the grief went the wrong way and cracked his legs, and so they call him Timour-lenk. That was the reason he made war on the Ottomans. It was all out of jealousy for me," said she, making a low and mock courtesy. "But if you could see the beautiful odalisk who made this! Her form is as stately as the dome of St. Sophia."

"She's too big and squatty, if she's like that," laughed the officer.

"Her face glows in complexion like the mother of pearl," went on the enthusiastic saleswoman.

"Too hard of cheek!" sneered the other. "Even yours, Hanoum, is not so hard as mother of pearl."

"A neck like alabaster——"

"Cold! too cold! I would as soon think of making love to a gravestone," was the officer's comment.

"And such melting lips——"

"Yes, with blisters! I tell you, old Hanoum, I'm woman proof. Go away!"

"And her eyes shine through her long lashes like the stars through the fir trees on the Balkans."

"Tut! Woman, you never saw the stars shine on the Balkans. They do shine there, though, like the very eyes of Allah. A woman with such eyes would frighten the Padishah himself."

Kala Hanoum took courage at this first evidence of interest on the part of the officer, and plied her advantage.

"And her teeth are as white as the snows in the grotto of Slatiza—"

"The grotto of Slatiza? You mean some bear's cave. But the snows are white there, whiter and purer than anywhere else on earth, except as I once saw them, so red with blood, there in the Pass of Slatiza. But how know you of Slatiza, my good woman?"

"And altogether she is as fair as the bride of Sigismund of Hungary," said Kala, without regarding his question.

"And who was she, Hanoum?" asked the man, with curiosity fully aroused.

"Why, Elizabeth Morsiney, of course."

The officer turned fully toward the woman, and scanned closely her features as if to discover something familiar. Was there not some hint to be picked from these words?

"Hanoum, who told you to say that?"

The woman in turn studied his face before she replied. She would learn whether the allusions had excited a pleasant interest, or roused antagonism in him. It required but a moment for her to discover that Morsinia had given her some clue that the man would willingly follow, so she boldly replied:

"The odalisk herself has talked to me of these things."

"The odalisk! What is she like?" said he eagerly. "Describe her to me."

"Why, I have been describing her for this half-hour; but you would not listen. So I will go off and do my next errand."

The woman turned away, but, as she intended it should be, the officer was now in the attitude of the beggar.

"Hold, Hanoum, I will buy your perfume—But tell me what she is like in plain words. Is she of light hair?"

"Ay, as if she washed it in the sunshine and dried it in the moonlight, and as glossy as the beams of both."

"Think you she belonged to Stamboul before the siege?"

"Ay, and to the great Scanderbeg before that."

The officer was bewildered and stood thinking, until Kala interrupted him.

"But you said you would buy it, Captain."

"Did I? Well, take your lira."

As the woman took the piece of money she added: "And don't forget that the odalisk said she had dreamed of you since she was a child, and that at sunset if you looked through the phials you would see her face."

"Nonsense, woman!"

"But try it, Sire, and maybe the noble Captain would send something to the beautiful odalisk?"

"Yes, when I see her in the phial I will send her myself as her slave."

The man thrust the silken case into the deep pocket of his flowing vest and went away.

Then began a struggle in Captain Ballaban. Since the capture of the fair girl by the altar of St. Sophia, he had been unable to efface the remembrance of her. She stood before him in his dreams: sometimes just falling beneath the dagger; sometimes in the splendor which he imagined to surround her in the harem; often in mute appeal to him to save her from the nameless horrors which her cry indicated that she dreaded. When waking, his mind was often distracted by thoughts of her. The presence of the Sultan lost its charm, for he had come to look upon him as her owner, and to feel himself in some way despoiled. He was losing his ambition for distant service, and found himself often loitering in the vicinity of the Phranza palace.

This feeling which, perhaps, is experienced by most men, at least once in life, as the spell of a fair face is thrown over them, was associated with a deeper and more serious one in Captain Ballaban.

From the day of her capture until now he had felt almost confident of her identity with his little playmate in the mountain home. She thus linked together his earliest and later life; and, as he thought of her, he thought of the contrast in himself then and now. The things he used to muse about when a child, his feelings then, his purposes, his religious faith, all came back to him, and with a strange strength and fascination. He began to realize that, though he was an enthusiast for both the Moslem belief and the service of the Ottoman, yet he had become such, not in his own free choice, but by the overpowering will of others. At heart he rebelled, while he could not say that he had come to disbelieve a word of the Koran, and was not willing to harbor a purpose against the sovereignty of the Padishah. Still he was compelled to confess to himself that, if the fair woman were indeed his old play-mate, and there was open a way by which he could release her from her captivity, he would risk so much of disloyalty to the Sultan as the attempt should require. Indeed, he argued to himself that, except in the mere form of it, it would not be disloyalty; for what did Mahomet care for one woman more or less in his harem? And was this woman not, after all, more his property than she was that of the Padishah? He had captured her; perhaps twice; and had saved her life in St. Sophia, for only his hand caught her dagger. She was his!

Then he became fond of indulging a day dream. The Sultan sometimes gave the odalisks to his favorite pashas and servants. What if this one should be given to him?

He had gone so far as once to say in response to the Sultan, who twitted him for being in love, that he imagined such to be the case, and only needed the choice of His Majesty to locate the passion. But he did not dare to be more specific, lest he might run across some caprice of the Sultan; for he felt sure that so beautiful an odalisk as his captive would not long be without the royal attention.

Old Kala Hanoum's information regarding the fair odalisk allayed the turmoil in Ballaban's breast, in that it gave certainty to his former suspicions. For her words about the stars above the Balkans, the snows of Slatiza, and Elizabeth Morsiney, were not accidental. He had no doubt that the Albanian odalisk was the little lady to whom he once made love in the bowers of blackberry bushes, and vowed to defend like a true knight, waving his wooden sword over the head of the goat he rode as a steed. In the midst of such thoughts and emotions, Captain Ballaban awoke to full self-consciousness, and said to himself——

"I am in love! But I am a fool! For a man with ambition must never be in love, except with himself. Besides, this woman I love is perhaps half in my imagination; for I never yet caught a full view of her face. As for her being my little Morsinia—Illusion! No! this is no illusion! But what if she be the same! Captain Ballaban, are you going to be a soldier, or a lover? Take your choice; for you can't be both, at least not an Ottoman soldier and a lover of a Christian girl."

Rubbing his hand through his red hair, as if to pull out these fantasies, he strode down to the water's edge, and, tossing a Kaikji a few piasters, was in a moment darting like an arrow across the harbor;—a customary way the captain had of getting rid of any vexation. The cool evening breeze wooed the over-thoughtfulness from his brain, or he spurted it out through his muscles into the oar blades, which dropped it into the water of oblivion.

He was scarcely aware that he was becoming more tranquil, when a quick cry of a boat keeper showed that he had almost run down the old tower of white marble which rises from a rocky islet, just away from the mainland on the Asiatic side of the Bosphorus.

"Kiss-Koulessi, the Maiden's Tower, this," he muttered. "Well, I have fled from the fortress of one maiden to run against that of another. Fate is against me. Perhaps I had better submit. Why not? Wasn't Charis a valiant general of the old Greeks, who sent him here, once on a time, to help the Byzantines? Well! He had a wife, the fair Boiidion, the 'heifer-eyed maiden.' And here she lies beneath this tower. The world would have forgotten General Charis, but for his wife Damalis, whom they have remembered these two thousand years. A wife *may* be the making of a man's fame. If the Sultan would give me my pick of the odalisks I think I would venture."

These thoughts were not interrupted, only supplemented, by the sun's rays, now nearly horizontal, as striking the water far up the harbor of Stamboul, they poured over it and made it seem indeed a Golden Horn, the open end of which extended into the Bosphorus. The ruddy glow tipped the dome of St. Sophia as with fire; transformed the gray walls of the Genoese tower at Galata into a huge porphyry column, sparkling with a million crystals; and made the white marble of the Maiden's Tower blush like the neck of a living maiden, when kissed for the first time by the hot lips of her lover.

So the Captain thought: and was reminded to inspect the silken treasure he had purchased. He would look through the phials, as—who knows—he might see the face of her who sent them. If looking at the red orb of the sun, just for an instant, made his eyes see a hundred sombre suns dancing along the sky, it would not be strange if his long meditation upon a certain radiant maiden should enable him to see her, at least in one shadowy reproduction of his inner vision.

He drew the silken case from his pocket. It was wrought with real skill, and worth the lira, even if it had contained nothing, and meant nothing. The little phials were held up one by one, and divided the sun's beams into prismatic hues as they passed through the twisted glass. In each was a drop or two of sweet essence, like an imprisoned soul, waiting to be released, that it might fly far and wide and distill its perfume as a secret blessing.

"But this one is imperfect," muttered the Captain, as he held up a phial that was nearly opaque. It was larger than the others, and contained a tightly wrapped piece of paper. "The clue!" said he, and, after a moment's hesitation, broke the phial. Unwinding the paper, he read:

"You are Michael, son of Milosch. I am Morsinia, child of Kabilovitsch. For the love of Jesu! save me from this hell. We can communicate by this means."

It was a long row that Captain Ballaban took that night upon the Bosphorus. Yet he went not far, but back and forth around the new seraglio point, scarcely out of sight of the clear-cut outline of the Phranza Palace, as it stood out against the sky above the ordinary dwellings of the city. The dawn began to peer over the hills back of Chalcedon, and to send its scouts of ruddy light down the side of Mt. Olympus, when he landed. But the length of the night to him could not be measured by hours. He had lived over again ten years. He had gone through a battle which tired his soul as it had never been tired under the flashing of steel and the roar of culverin. Only once before, when, as a mere child he was conquered by the terrors of the Janizaries' discipline, had he suffered so intensely. Yet the battle was an undecided one. He staggered up the hill from the landing to the barracks with the cry of conflict ringing through his soul. "What shall I do?" On the one side were the habit of loyalty, his oath of devotion to the Padishah, all his earthly ambition which blazed with splendors just before him—for he was the favorite of both the Sultan and the soldiers—and all that the education of his riper years had led him to hope for in another world. On the other side were this new passion of love which he could no longer laugh down, and the appeal of a helpless fellow creature for rescue from what he knew was injustice, cruelty and degradation;—the first personal appeal a human being had ever made to him, and he the only human being to whom she could appeal. To heed this cry of Morsinia he knew would be treason to his outward and sworn loyalty. To refuse to heed it he felt would be treason to his manhood. What could he do? Neither force was preponderating.

The battle wavered.

What did he do? What most people do in such circumstances—he temporized: said, "I will do nothing to-day." Like a genuine Turk he grunted to himself, "Bacaloum!" "We shall see!"

But though he arranged and ordered an armistice between his contending thoughts, there was no real cessation of hostilities. Arguments battered against arguments. Feelings of the gentler sort mined incessantly beneath those which he would have called the braver and more manly. And the latter counter-mined: loyalty against love: ambition against pity.

But all the time the gentler ones were gaining strength. On their side was the advantage of a definite picture—a lovely face; of an immediate and tangible project—the rescue of an individual. The danger of the enterprise weighed nothing with him, or, at least, it was counter-balanced by the inspiriting anticipation of an adventure, an exploit:—the very hazard rather fascinating than repelling. Yet he had not decided.

CHAPTER XLVII

Captain Ballaban was summoned by the Sultan.

"Well, comrade," said Mahomet, familiarly throwing his arm about his friend, much to the disgust of the Capee Aga, the master of ceremonies, through whom alone it was the custom of the Sultans to be approached.

"Well! comrade, I gave a necklace worth a thousand liras to a girl who pleased me in the harem."

"Happy girl, to have pleased your Majesty. That was better than the necklace," replied Ballaban.

"Think you so? Let me look you through and through. Think you there is nothing better in this world than to please the Padishah? Ah! it is worth a kingdom to hear that from a man like you, Ballaban. Women say it; but they can do nothing for me. They dissipate my thoughts with their pleasuring me. They make me weak. I have a mind to abolish the whole harem. But to have a man, a strong man, a man with a head to plot for empire and to marshal armies, a man with an arm like thine to make love to me! Ah, that is glorious, comrade. But let me make no mistake about it. You love me? Do you really think no gold, no honors, could give you so much pleasure as pleasing me? Swear it! and by the throne of Allah! I will swear that you shall share my empire. But to business!" dropping his voice, and in the instant becoming apparently forgetful of his enthusiasm for his friend.

"We make a campaign against Belgrade. I must go in person. Yet Scanderbeg holds out in Albania. It is useless meeting him in his stronghold. You cannot fight a lion by crawling into his den. He must be trapped. Work out a plan."

"I have one which may be fruitful," instantly replied Captain Ballaban.

"Ah! so quick?" "No, of long hatching, Sire. I made it in my first campaign in Albania with your royal father. The young Voivode Amesa is nephew to Scanderbeg. He is restless under the authority of the great general: has committed some crime which, if known, would bring him to ruin: is popular with the people of the north."

"Capital!" said Mahomet eagerly. "I see it all. Work it out! Work it out! He may have anything, if only Scanderbeg can be put out of the way, and the country be under our suzerainty. Work it out! And the suzerain revenues shall all be yours; for by the bones of Othman! there is not a province too great for you if only you can settle affairs among the Arnaouts.

"And now a gift! I will send you the very queen of the harem."

"My thanks, Padishah, but I——" began Ballaban, when he was cut short by the Sultan.

"Not a word! not a word! I know you decline to practice the softer virtues, and prefer to live like a Greek monk. But you must take her. If you like her not, drown her. But you shall like her. By the dimple in the chin of Ayesha! she is the most perfect woman in the empire."

"But," interposed Ballaban, "I am a Janizary, and it is not permitted a Janizary to marry."

"A fig for what is permitted! When the Padishah gives, he grants permission to enjoy his gifts. Besides, you need not marry. You can own her; sell her if you don't like her. But you must take her." "Of what nation is she? Perhaps I could not understand her tongue," objected Ballaban.

"So much the better," said Mahomet. "Women are not made to talk. But this woman is an Arnaout, from Scanderbeg's country."

Captain Ballaban could scarcely believe his ears.

This then is Morsinia! To have her, to save her without breach of loyalty! This was too much. With strangely fluttering heart he acquiesced, and his thanks were drawn from the bottom of his soul.

The next day he sought Kala Hanoum, and sent by her to Morsinia a gem enclosed in a pretty casket, with which was a note, reading,—

"It shall be so. Patience for a few days, and our hearts shall be made glad."

How strangely Fate had planned for him! It must have been Fate; for only powers supernal could have made the gift of the Padishah so fitting to his heart. No chance this! His secret passion, unbreathed to any ear on earth, had been a prayer heard in heaven!

Ballaban was now an undoubting Moslem that he found Kismet on the side of his inclinations. He belonged to Islâm, the Holy Resignation; resigned to the will of Providence, since Providence seemed just now to have resigned itself to his will. He was surprised at the ecstatic character his piety was taking on. He could have become a dervish: indeed his head was already whirling with the intoxication of his prospects.

Captain Ballaban, like a good Moslem, went to the Mosque. He made his prayer toward the Mihrab; but his eyes and thoughts wandered to the spot at the side of it, where he had saved the life of Morsinia; and he thanked Allah with full soul that he had been allowed to save her for himself.

The Padishah, the following day, bade Ballaban repair to a house in the city, and be in readiness to receive the gift of heaven and of his own imperial grace. On reaching the place an elderly woman—the Koulavous, an inevitable attendant upon marriages—conducted him through the selamlik and mabeyn to the haremlik of the house. The bride or slave, as he pleased to take her, rose from the divan to meet him. Though her thick veil completely enveloped her person, it could not conceal her superb form and marvellous grace. His hand trembled with the agitation of his delight as he exercised the authority of a husband or master, and reverently raised the veil.

He stood as one paralyzed in amazement. She was not Morsinia. She was Elissa!

He dropped the veil.

Strange spirits seemed to breathe themselves in succession through his frame.

First came the demon of disappointment, checking his blood, stifling him. Not that any other mortal knew of his shattered hopes; but it was enough that he knew them. And with the consciousness of defeat, a horrible chagrin bit and tore his heart, as if it had been some dragon with teeth and claws.

Then came the demon of rage; wild rage; wanting to howl out its fury. He might have smitten the veiled form, had not the latter, overcome by her bewilderment and the scorn of him she supposed to have been a lover, already fallen fainting at his feet.

Then rose in Ballaban's breast the demon of vengeance against the Sultan. Had Mahomet been present he surely had felt the steel of the outraged man. Only the habit of self-control and quiet review of his own passions prevented his seeking the Padishah, and taking instant vengeance in his blood.

Then there came into him a great demon of impiety, and breathed a curse against Allah himself through his lips.

But finally a new spirit hissed into his ears. It was Nemesis. He felt that this was the moment when a just retribution had returned upon himself. For he well knew the face that lay weeping beneath the heap of bejewelled lace and silk. It was that of the Dodola, whom he had flung into the arms of the Albanian Voivode Amesa when he was awaiting the embrace of some more princely maiden. And now the sarcasm of fate had thrown her into his arms.

"Allah! Thou wast even with me this time," he confessed back of his clenched teeth.

"But doubtless," he thought, "it was through the information I gave to the Aga that this girl has been stolen away from Amesa."

"Would that heaven rid me of her so easily!" he muttered. "Yet that is easy; thanks to our Moslem law, which says, 'Thou mayest either retain thy wife with humanity or dismiss her with kindness.'[101] Yet I cannot dismiss her with kindness. She can not go back to the royal harem. If I dismiss her I harm her, and Allah's curse will be fatal if I wrong this creature again—to say nothing of the Padishah's if I throw away his gift. I must keep her. Well! Bacaloum! Bacaloum! It is not so bad a thing after all to have a woman like that for one's slave; for a wife without one's heart is but a slave. Well!" He raised the veil again from the now sitting woman.

The mutually stupid gaze carried them both through several years which had passed since they had parted at Amesa's castle.

Elissa was easily induced to tell her story. Assuming that it might be already known to her new lord, she gave it correctly; and therefore it differed substantially from that she had told to Morsinia. She had been but a few days in Amesa's home when he discovered that she was not the person he had presumed her to be. In an outburst of rage he would have taken her life, but was led by an old priest to adopt a more merciful method of ridding himself of her. To have returned her to the village above the Skadar would have filled the country with the scandal, and made Amesa the laughing stock of all. She was therefore sent within the Turkish lines, with the certainty of finding her way to some far-distant country. Her beauty saved her from a common fate, and she was sent as a gift to the young Padishah by an old general, into whose hands she had fallen.

Ballaban assured the woman of his protection, and also that the time would come when he would compensate her for any grief she had endured through his fault. In the meantime she was retained in the luxurious comfort of her new abode.

CHAPTER XLVIII

Captain Ballaban was almost constantly engaged at the new seraglio. It was being constructed not only with an eye to its imposing appearance from without and its beauty within, such as befitted both its splendid site between the waters and the splendor of the monarch whose palace it was to be; but also with a view to its easy defence in case of assault. Upon the young officer devolved the duty of scrutinizing every line and layer that went into the various structures.

He was especially interested in the side entrances, and communications between the various departments of the seraglio. He gave orders for a change to be made in the line of a partition and corridor, and also for a slight variation in the position of a gateway in the walls dividing the mabeyn[102] court from that of the haremlik. Just why these changes were made, perhaps the architects themselves could not have told; nor were they interested to enquire, supposing that they were made at the royal will. Ballaban was disposed to indulge a little his own fancy. If there was to be a broad entrance for public display, and then a narrow passage for the Sultan only, why not have a way through which he could imagine a fair odalisk fleeing from insult and torture into the arms of—himself? But Ballaban's face grew pale as he watched the completion of a sluice way leading from a little chamber, down through the sea wall, to meet the rapid current of the Bosphorus. He remembered the declaration of the Padishah, that, if ever an odalisk were unfaithful to him, she should be sewn into a bag, together with a cat and a snake, and drowned in Marmora.[103]

In the meantime old Kala Hanoum was amazed at the number of articles of Morsinia's handiwork she was able to induce the young captain to purchase. Indeed, he never refused. And quite frequently she was the bearer of gifts, generally confections, sometimes little rolls of silk suitable for embroidery with colored threads or beads, accompanied by the name of some fellow officer of the Janizaries from whom apparently an order for work was given; the Captain acting as an agent in a sort of co-partnership with Kala. Of course this was only secret mail service between Ballaban and the odalisk. If Kala suspected it, her commissions were so largely remunerative that she silenced the thought of any thing but legitimate business.

Ballaban devised plans for her escape which Morsinia found it impracticable to execute from her side of the harem wall; and her shrewdest suggestions were pronounced equally unsafe by the strategist without.

Ballaban had caught glimpses of Morsinia while loitering among the trees at the upper end of the Golden Horn, by the Sweet Waters, where the ladies of the harem were taken by the eunuchs on almost weekly excursions. He had proposed to have in readiness two horses, that, if she should break from the attendants, they might flee together. But before this could be accomplished, the excursions were discontinued, as the attention of all was turned to a new pleasure.

The grand haremlik was at length completed. Perhaps no place on earth was so suggestive of indolent and sensual pleasure as this. There were luxurious divans, multiplying mirrors, baths of tempered water, fountains in which perfumes could be scattered with the spray, broad spaces for the dance, half hidden alcoves for the indulgence in that which shamed the more public eye, and gardens in which Araby competed with Africa in the display of exotic fruits and flowers.

A day was set for the reception of the grand harem from Adrianople—which contained nearly a thousand of the most beautiful women in the world—into this new paradise. The Kislar Aga had arranged a pageant of especial magnificence, which could be witnessed by the people at a distance. Two score barges, elegantly decorated, rowed by eunuchs, their decks covered with divans, were to receive the odalisks from Adrianople at the extreme inner point of the seraglio water front on the Golden Horn. The Validé Sultana's barge was to lead the procession, which should float to the cadences of music far out into the harbor. At the same time, the Sultan in his kaik, and the women of the temporary haremlik, each propelling a light skiff decorated with flags and streamers, were to move from the extreme outer point of the seraglio grounds, until the two fleets should meet, when, amid salvos of artillery from the shores, the odalisks with the Sultan were to turn about and lead their sisters to the water gate of the haremlik. Orders were given forbidding the people to appear upon the water, or upon the shores within distance to see distinctly the faces of the ladies of the harem.

Every evening at sundown a patrol of eunuchs made a cordon of boats a few hundred yards from the shore, within which, screened by distance from the eyes of common men, the odalisks went into training for the great regatta. The Padishah, sitting in his barge, encouraged their rivalry by gifts for dexterity in managing the little boats, for picturesqueness of dress and for grace of movement, as with bared arms and streaming tresses, they propelled the kaiks.

Morsinia found herself one of the most dexterous in handling the oars. The free life of her childhood on the Balkans and among the peasants of upper Albania, had developed muscle which this new exercise soon brought into unusual efficiency. She observed that the attendant eunuchs were deficient in this kind of strength, and had no doubt that, with her own light weight, she could drive the almost imponderable kaik swifter than any of them.

The young Egyptian woman was her only competitor for the honor of leading the fleet on the day of the regatta. To add to the interest of the training, Mahomet ordered that the two should race for the honor of being High Admiral of the harem fleet; and one evening announced that the competitive trial should take place the next afternoon. The course was fixed for a half mile, just inside of Seraglio Point, where the waters of the harbor are still, unvexed by the rapid current which pours along the channel of the Bosphorus. The flag-boat was to be anchored almost at the meeting of the inner and outer waters.

That night Morsinia wrote a note containing these words—

"About dusk just below the Seven Towers watch for kaik. Morsinia."

Kala Hanoum was commissioned early the following morning to deliver a pretty little sash, wrought with stars and crescents, to Captain Ballaban. Morsinia was careful to show Kala the scarf, and dilate upon the peculiar beauty of the work until the woman's curiosity should be fully satisfied; thus making sure that she would not be tempted to inspect it for herself. She then wrapped the note carefully within the scarf, and tied it strongly with a silken cord.

Old Kala had a busy day before her, with a dozen other commissions to discharge. But fortune favored her in the early discovery of the well known shape of the Captain in ordinary citizen's dress, as he was engaged in eager conversation with the Greek monk, Gennadius, whom the Sultan had allowed to superintend the worship of the Christians still resident in the city. Indeed Mahomet was wise enough to even pension some of the Greek clergy to keep up the establishment of their faith; for he feared to antagonize the millions in the provinces of Greece who could not be persuaded to embrace Islam; and was content to exact from them only the recognition of his secular supremacy. Kala Hanoum had too much reverence in her nature to interrupt a couple of such worthies; so she followed a little way behind them. They came to the gate-way—a mere hole in the wall—which led to what was known as the Hermit's Cell, the abode of Gennadius during the siege. The spiritual pride of the monk had prevented his exchanging this for a more commodious residence into which the Sultan would have put him. He said he only wanted a place large enough to weep in, now that the people of the Lord were in captivity.

The monk had entered the little gateway, and his companion was following, when Kala's instinct for business got the better of her reverence; and, darting forward, she thrust the little roll into his hand just as he was stooping to enter the gate, not even glancing at his face. She said in low voice, not caring to be overheard by the monk:

"A part of your purchase yesterday, Sire, which you have forgotten."

She waited for no reply, but trotted off, muttering to herself:

"That's done, now for old Ibrahim the Jew."

The contrast between Morsinia and the Egyptian as they presented themselves for the contest, afforded a capital study in racial physique. The latter was rather under size, with scarcely more of womanly development than a boy. Her face was almost copper colored; her hair jet and short. The former was tall, with femininity stamped upon the contour of bust and limb; her face pale, even beneath the mass of her light locks.

The kaiks were of thinnest wood that could be held together by the web-like cross bracing, and seemed scarcely to break the surface of the water when the odalisks stepped into them. Morsinia had brought a feridjé of common sort; saying to the eunuch, whose attention it attracted, that yesterday she was quite chilled after rowing, and to day had taken this with her by way of precaution. She might have found something more beautiful had she thought in time; but it would be dark when they returned. Besides, it would be a capital brace for her feet; the crossbar arranged for that purpose being rather too far away from the seat. So saying she tossed it into the bottom of the kaik before the officious eunuch could provide a better substitute.

The Padishah's bugle sounded the call. It rang over the waters, evoking echoes from the triple shore of Stamboul, Galata and Skutari, which died away in the distant billows of Marmora. As it was to be the last evening before the pageant of the grand reception, the time was occupied in making final arrangements for the order in which the boats should move; so that it was growing dark when the Padishah reminded the chief marshal that they must have the race for the Admiral's badge. Katub, a fat and indolent eunuch, was ordered to moor his kaik, for the stake boat, as far out toward the swift current as safety would permit.

The two competitors darted to the side of Mahomet's barge. From a long staff, just high enough above the water to be reached by the hand, hung a tiny streamer of silk, the broad field of which was dotted with pearls. This was to be the possession of the fair rower who, rounding the stake boat first, could return and seize it.

The Sultan threw a kiss to the fair nymphs as a signal for the start. Myriads of liquid pearls, surpassing in beauty those upon the streamer, dropped from the oar blades, and strewed the smooth surface; or were transformed into diamonds as they sunk swirling into the broken water. The spray rose from the sharp prows in sheafs, golden as those of grain, in the ruddy reflection of the western sky. Each graceful kaik, and the more graceful form that moved it, almost created the illusion of a single creature; some happy denizen of another world disporting itself for the luring of mortals in this.

The boats kept close company. The Egyptian was expending her full strength, but her companion, with longer and fewer strokes, was apparently reserving hers. They neared the stake. The Egyptian, having the inside, began to round it; but the Albanian kept on, now with rapid and strong strokes. The spectators were amazed at her tactics.

"She is making too wide a sweep," said the Sultan.

"She does not seem inclined to turn at all," observed the Kislar Aga.

"She will strike the current if she turn not soon," rejoined Mahomet excitedly.

The prow of her kaik turned off westward.

"She is in the stream!" cried several. "She will be overturned!" But on sped the kaik, heading full down the current, which, catching it like some friendly sprite from beneath, bore it quickly out of sight around the Seraglio Point; and on—on into a thick mist which was rolling up, as if sent of heaven to meet it, from the broad expanse of the sea.

"An escape!" cried the Sultan. "After her every one of you black devils!"

The eunuchs wasted several precious moments in getting the command through their heads, and, even when they started, it was evident that their muscles were too flaccid, their spines too limp, and their wind not full enough to overhaul the flying skiff of the Albanian.

"To shore! To horse!" cried the raging monarch.

A quarter of an hour later, horsemen were clattering down the stony street along the water front of Marmora, pausing now and then to stare out into the sea mist, dashing on, stopping and staring, and on again. The foremost to reach the Castle of the Seven Towers left orders to scour the shore, and to set patrol to prevent any one landing. Some were ordered to dart across to the islands. Within an hour from the escape every inch of shore, and the great water course opposite the city, were under complete surveillance.

Just before this was accomplished a man arrived at the water's edge, close to the south side of the great wall of which the Castle of Seven Towers was the northern flank. He held two horses, saddled and bagged, as if for a distant journey. A second man appeared a moment later, who came up from a clump of bushes a little way below.

"In good time, Marcus!" said the new comer, who stooped close to the water and listened, putting his hand to his ear so as to exclude all sounds except such as should come from the sea above. "Listen! an oar stroke! Yes! Keep everything tight, Marcus."

Darting into the copse, in a moment more the man was gliding in a kaik, with a noiseless stroke, out in the direction of the oar splash of the approaching boat. Nearer and nearer it came. The night and the mist prevented its being seen. The man moved close to its line. It was a light kaik, he knew from the almost noiseless ripple of the water as the sharp prow cut it. The man gave a slight whistle, when the stroke of the invisible boat ceased, and the ripple at its prow died away.

"Morsinia!"

"Ay, thank heaven!" came the response.

"Speak not now, but follow!" and he led the way cautiously toward the little beach where the horses were heard stamping. They were several rods off, piloting themselves by the sound.

"Hark!" said the man, stopping the boats. Hoofs were heard approaching, and voices—

"She might have put across to the Princess Island," said one.

"Nonsense!" was the reply. "She would only imprison herself by that— more likely she has gone clean across to Chalcedon. But I hold that she has played fox, and turned on her trail. Ten liras to one that she is by this time in Galata with some of the Genoese Giaours. If so, she will try to escape in a galley; but that can be prevented: for the Padishah will overhaul every craft that sails out until he finds her. But hoot, man! what have we here? Two horses! A woman's baggage! She has an accomplice! An elopement! The horses are tied. The runaway couple haven't arrived yet. Dismount, men! we will lie in wait along the shore here. Yes, let their two horses stand there to draw them to the spot by their stamping. Send ours out of hearing. Now every man to his place! Silence!"

"Back! Back! We are pursued on land," said the man in the boat to Morsinia, and both boats pushed noiselessly out again from the shore.

"I had prepared for this, Morsinia. You must come into my boat; we will row below for a mile, where we can arrange it at the shore."

Quietly they shot down in the lessening current, until they turned into a little cove made by a projecting rock. As lightly as a fawn the girl leaped to the beach. Her companion was by her side in an instant. She drew back, and gave no return to his warm embrace, but said heartily:

"Thank Heaven, and you, Michael!"

"Michael?" exclaimed the man. "Indeed I do not wonder that you think me a spirit, and call me by the name of my dead brother. But this shall assure you that I am Constantine, and in the flesh," cried he, as he pressed a kiss upon her lips.

Morsinia was dazed. She tried to scan his face. She fell as one lifeless into his arms.

He seated himself on the rock and held her to his heart. For a while neither could speak.

"Is it real?" said she at length, raising her head and feeling his face with her hand. "But how"——

Voices were heard shouting over the water.

"We must be gone," said Constantine. The excitement of her discovery that her lover was still living, and her bewilderment at his appearance instead of Michael, were too much for Morsinia. Constantine carried the exhausted girl into his boat, which was larger than hers. Towing her little kaik out some distance he tipped it bottom upwards, and let it drift away.

"That will stop the hounds," muttered he. "They will think you have been overturned."

With tremendous, but scarcely audible, strokes he ploughed away westward. It was not until far from all noise of the pursuers that he paused.

CHAPTER XLIX

Imminent as was the danger still, the curiosity of both at the strangeness of the Providence which had brought them back to each other, as from the dead, was such that they must talk; and the freshness of the newly-kindled love stole many a moment for endearing embrace. Indeed an hour passed, and the night might have flown while they loitered, were it not that the rising wind brought a distant sound which awakened them to the remembrance that they were still fugitives.

Constantine at length insisted that his companion should lie upon the bottom of the boat, and take needed rest.

"If I had now my feridjé!" said she. "I have provided for that," replied Constantine. "Yours would be recognized. I have one belonging to the common women, which will be better." In addition to the feridjé, the foresight of Constantine had laid in warm wraps and a store of provisions. These were packed in bundles that they might be carried conveniently on horses, in the hand, or in the boat, as necessity should compel.

"I cannot rest," said Morsinia, "when there is so much to say and hear."

"But you must lie down. I will tell you my story; then you can tell me yours."

"But can we not stop?"

"No. It will not be safe to do so yet."

"I have learned to trust your guidance as well as your love," said she, and reclined in the stern of the boat.

The moon rose near to midnight. The fog illumined by it made them clearly visible to each other, while it shut out the possibility of their being seen by any from a distance.

"It is the blessing of Jesu upon us," said Morsinia. "The same as when He stood upon the little lake in Galilee, like a form of light, and said, 'Be not afraid.'"

Constantine gave his story in hasty sentences and detached portions, breaking it by pauses in which he listened for pursuers, or gave his whole strength to the oars, or, more frequently, did nothing but gaze at his companion: more than once reaching out his hand to touch her, and see if she were not an apparition.

He told of his escape from the Turks, his arrest as a lunatic and the scene before the Sultan, his return to Constantinople after its capture, and the apparent evidence he there had from the old beggar, of Morsinia's death: with all of which the reader is familiar. He also related how he had gone to Albania. The report of Morsinia's death had caused the greatest grief to Kabilovitsch, and thrown General Castriot into such a rage that he found easement for it in a special raid upon the Turkish camp; which raid was remembered, and was still spoken of by the soldiers, as the "Call of the Maiden." For as Castriot returned from fearful slaughter, in which he had completely riddled the enemy's quarters, captured their commander and compelled them to break up the campaign, the general was overheard to say, "The maiden's spirit called us and we have answered." Without knowing the meaning of these words the soldiers probably assumed that they were a reference to the Holy Virgin Mary, whose blessing Castriot had invoked upon the enterprise. After that Sultan Mahomet sent a special embassage and proposal of peace to Albania. In the royal letter he stated,

"She whom the Emperor of the Greeks was unable to keep for Scanderbeg is now in the custody of the royal harem, safe and inviolate; to be delivered into Scanderbeg's hand as a pledge of a treaty by which Scanderbeg shall agree to cease from further depredations and invasion of Macedonia, and to submit to hold his kingdom in fief to the Ottoman throne."

The letter ended with a boastful reference to the Sultan's conquest of Constantinople, Caramania and other countries, and the threat of invading Albania with a host so great as to cover all its territory with the shadow of the camps.

Castriot's reply, when known, filled the Dibrians and Epirots with greatest enthusiasm. It closed with the words,—

"What if you have subjugated Greece, and put into servitude them of Asia! These are no examples for the free hearts of Albania!"[104]

The news contained in Mahomet's missive led Castriot to allow Constantine to go to Constantinople, that he might discover, if possible, whether Morsinia was really living, and was the person referred to by the Sultan. On reaching the city, Constantine had sought out the monk Gennadius, with whom he had been often thrown before and during the siege. From him he learned nothing of Morsinia except the old story of her self-sacrifice by the side of the altar;—which story had become so adorned with many additions in passing from mouth to mouth, that the "Fair Saint of Albania" was likely to be enrolled upon the calendar of the holy martyrs. Constantine was returning with the monk from the church of Baloukli, where they had gone to see the perpetuated miracle of the fishes which leaped from the pan on hearing of the capture of the city, and which are still, with one side black with the frying, swimming in the tank of holy water. He had just reached the little gate of the monk's lodging when Morsinia's message was put into his hand by a little old woman.

"But how did you know of my arrival in Constantinople?" Constantine asked, as he concluded his account.

The question led to Morsinia's story, and the revelation that his brother Michael was still living, an officer of the Sultan, as like to Constantine as one eye to the other; their mistaken identity by Kala Hanoum having led to the present happy denouement. The mutual narratives of the past grew into plans for the future, the chief part of which related to the restoration of Michael from the service of the Moslem.

While they talked, the day broke over the Asiatic coast. The faint glow of light rapidly changed into bars of gold, which were transformed into those of silver, and melted again into a broad sheen of orange and purple tints. But for the shadowed slopes of the eastern shore that lay between the water and the sky, this would have made Marmora like an infinite sea of glory.

But there was a fairer sight before the eyes of Constantine; one more suggestive of the heavenly. It was the face of his beloved, now first clearly seen. It seemed to him that she could not have been more enchanting if he had discovered her by the "River of the Water of Life" in the Golden City, where only he had hoped ever again to gaze upon her.

CHAPTER L

The fugitives landed a good score of miles from Stamboul, on the northern shore of Marmora, and struck the highway which runs westward, following the coast line to Salonika, where it divides, bending south into Greece, and branching north through Macedonia. The fugitives followed the latter highway. The country through which they passed was at the time conquered by the Moslem, but was dotted over with the settlements of the adherents to the old faith, who kept the watchfires of hope still burning in their hearts, though they were extinguished on the mountains. It was by this route that Constantine had gone to Stamboul. He was therefore familiar, not only with the way, but with the people; and easily secured from them concealment when necessary, and help along the journey. His belt had been well filled with gold by Castriot, so that two fleet horses and all provisions were readily supplied.

Their journey was saddened by their solicitude for the fate of Albania. Before Constantine had left that country, Moses Goleme, wearied with the incessant sacrifices he was compelled to make, and discouraged by what he deemed the impossibility of longer holding out against the Turks, had quarreled with Castriot, and thrown off his allegiance. He had even been induced by Mahomet's pledge of liberty to Albania—if only Castriot were overthrown—to enter the service of the enemy. The wily Sultan had placed him in command of an invading army, with which, however, he had returned to his country only to meet an overwhelming defeat at the hands of the great captain, and to flee in disgrace to Constantinople.

This swift vengeance administered by the patriots did not entirely crush the dissatisfaction among the people. Their fields were wasted by the long war; for half a generation had passed since it began. Only the personal magnetism of their chief held the factions to their doubtful loyalty.

After several weeks' journeying, our fugitives reached the camp of Castriot. It little resembled the gorgeous canvas cities of the Turks they had passed. The overspreading trees were, in many instances, the only shelter of voivodes and princely leaders, the story of whose exploits floated as an enchantment to the lovers of the heroic in all lands.

But the simple welcome they received from the true hearts of their countrymen was more to Morsinia and Constantine than any stately reception could have been. Kabilovitsch's joy was boundless. The venerable man had greatly failed, worn by outward toil, and more by his inward grief. Castriot had grown prematurely old. His hair was whitened; his eyes more deeply sunken beneath the massive brows; his shoulders a little bowed. Yet there was no sign of decrepitude in face or limb. His aspect was sterner, and even stronger, as if knit with the iron threads of desperation.

As Kabilovitsch, whom the wanderers had first sought upon their arrival, led them to Castriot, the general gazed upon them silently for a little. Years, with their strange memories, seemed to flit, one after another, across his scarred face. Taking Morsinia's hands in his, he stood looking down into her blue eyes, just as he had done when years ago, he bade her farewell. Then he kissed her forehead as he said:

"Thank heaven! there is not yet a wrinkle on that fair brow. But I wronged you, my child, in sending you among strangers. Can you forgive the blunder of my judgment? It was my heart that led me wrong."

"I have nothing to forgive thee," replied Morsinia. "Though I have suffered, to gaze again into thy face, Sire, takes away even the memory of it all. I shall be fully blessed if now I can remove some of those care marks from thy brow."

"Your return takes away from me twice as many years as those you have been absent, and I shall be young again now—as young almost as Kabilovitsch," added he, with a kindly glance at the old veteran, whose battered dignity had given place to an almost childish delight.

The scene within the tent was interrupted by a noise without. A crowd of soldiers had gathered, and were gazing from a respectful distance at a strange-looking man: "A man of heaviness and eaten up with cares." He was clad in the coarsest garments; his beard untrimmed; hatless; a rope about his neck. As Scanderbeg came out of the tent, the man threw himself at his feet, and cried, as he bowed his head upon the ground:

"Strike, Sire! I have sold my country. I have returned to die under the sword of my true chief, rather than live with the blessing of his enemies. The curse on my soul is greater than I could bear, with all the splendid rewards of my treason. Take out the curse with my blood! Strike, Sire! Strike!"

He was Moses Goleme. Castriot stood with folded arms and looked upon the prostrate man. His lips trembled, and then were swollen, as was noted of them when his soul was fired with the battle rage. Then every muscle of his face quivered as if touched by some sharp pain. Then came a look of sorrow and pity. His broad bosom heaved with the deep-drawn breath as he spoke.

"Moses Goleme, rise! Your place is at no man's feet. For twenty years you watched by Albania, while I forgot my fatherland. Your name has been the rallying cry of the patriot; your words the wisdom of our council; your arm my strength. Brave man! take Castriot's sword, and wear it again until your own heart tells you that your honor has been redeemed. Rise!"

Untying the rope from the miserable man's neck, he flung it far off, and cried,—

"So, away with whatever disgraces the noble Goleme! My curse on him who taunts thee for the past! Let that be as a hideous dream to be forgotten. For well I know, brave comrade, that thy heart slept when thou wast away. But it wakes again. Thou art thy true self once more!"

The broken-hearted man replied, scarcely raising his eyes as he spoke:

"My hands are not worthy to touch the sword of Castriot. Let me cleanse them with patriot service. Tell me, Sire, some desperate adventure, where, since thou wilt not slay me, I may give my wretched life for my country."

"No, Moses, you shall keep your life for Albania. I know well the strength of your temptation. My service is too much for any man. Were it not that I am sustained by some strange invisible spirit, I too would have yielded long ago. But enough! The old command awaits thee, Moses."

The man looked upon Castriot with grateful amazement. But he could not speak, and turned away.

At first he was received sullenly by the soldiers; but when the story of Castriot's magnanimity was repeated, the camps rang with the cry, "Welcome, Goleme!" That his restoration might be honored, a grand raid through the Turkish lines was arranged for the next night. The watch cry was, "By the beard of Moses!" and many a veteran then wielded his sword with a courage and strength he had not felt for years. Even old Kabilovitsch, whose failing vigor had long excused him from such expeditions, insisted upon joining in this. Constantine then rewhetted his steel for valiant deeds to come. And, as the day after the fight dawned, Moses Goleme led back the band of victors, laden with spoil. As he appeared, to make his report to the chief, his face was flushed with the old look; and, grasping the hand of Castriot, he raised it to his lips and simply said:

"I thank thee, Sire!" and retired.

CHAPTER LI

Captain Ballaban was among the first to learn of the personality of the odalisk who had escaped at the time of the race. His first thought was to aid her in eluding pursuit, presuming that she had gone alone and without accomplice. But when the horses were discovered at the Seven Towers, he gave way to a fit of jealousy. In his mind he accused Morsinia of having made him her dupe; for, notwithstanding his assurances of aid, she had evidently made a confidant of another. His better disposition, however, soon led him to believe that she had been spirited away through some plan devised in the brain of Scanderbeg. While he rejoiced for her, he was disconsolate for himself; and determined that, upon his return to the war in Albania, to which field he knew it was the purpose of the Padishah to transfer him, he would discover the truth regarding her. He had learned from her secret missives, which Kala Hanoum had brought him before the flight, of the death of his father Milosch and his mother Helena, and the supposed death of his brother Constantine. There were, then, no ties of kinship, and but this one tie of affection to Morsinia, to divide his allegiance to the Padishah. And Morsinia had faded again from reality, if not into his mere dream, at least into the vaguest hope. His ardent soul found relief only by plunging into the excitement of the military service.

Mahomet had not exhausted his favors to Ballaban by the gift of the Albanian Venus, Elissa. Summoning him one day he repeated his purpose of designating him as the chief Aga of the Janizaries, the old chief having been slain in a recent engagement. Ballaban remonstrated, as once before, against this interference with the order of the corps, in which the choice of chief Aga was left to the vote of the soldiers themselves.

Mahomet replied angrily—"I tell you, Ballaban, my will shall now be supreme over every branch of my service. My fathers felt the independence of the Janizaries to be a menace to their thrones. Their power shall be curbed to my hand, or the whole order shall be abolished."

"Beware!" replied Ballaban. "You know not the alertness of the lion whose lair you would invade. I will serve my Padishah with my life in all other ways, but my vows forbid my treachery to my corps. Strike off my head, if you will, but I cannot be Aga, except by the sovereign consent of my brothers."

"I shall not take off your head, comrade," replied Mahomet. "I need what is in it too much, though it belongs to a young rebel. But begone! I shall work my plans without asking your advice in the matter."

A firman was issued by which the Padishah claimed the supreme power of appointing to command in all grades of the military service. Within an hour after its proclamation, the Janizaries were in open defiance of the sovereign. Before their movements could be anticipated, the great court in front of the selamlik in the seraglio was filled with the enraged soldiery. That sign of terror which had blanched the faces of former Padishahs—the inverted soup-kettle—was planted before the very doors of the palace, and the Sultan was a prisoner within.

"Recall the firman! Long live the Yeni-Tscheri!" rang among the seraglio walls, and was echoed over the city.

The Sultan not appearing, there rose another cry, at first only a murmur, but at length pouring from thousands of hoarse throats,—

"Down with Mahomet! Live the Yeni-Tscheri!"

Still the Sultan made no response. There was a hurried consultation among the leaders of the insurgents. Then a rapid movement throughout the crowd. For a moment it seemed as if they had turned every man against his fellow. But Mahomet's experienced eye, as he watched from the latticed window, saw that the swarm of men was only taking shape. The mob was transformed into companies. Between the ranks passed men, as if they rose out of the ground; some dragging cannon; some bearing scaling ladders.

Mahomet appeared upon the platform, dressed in full armor. He raised his sword, when silence fell upon the multitude.

"I am your Padishah."

"Long live Mahomet!" was the cry.

"Do I not command every faithful Ottoman? Who will follow where Mahomet leads?"

"All! all!" rang the response.

"Then reverse the kettle!" commanded he, his face lit with the assumption of victory.

"Reverse the firman!" was the answer.

"Never!" cried the monarch, infuriated with this unexpected challenge of his authority. The Janizaries retreated a few steps from the platform. The Padishah assumed that they were awed by his determination, and smiled in his triumph. But his face was as quickly shaded with astonishment; for the movement of the insurgents was only to allow the cannon to be advanced.

The sagacity of the monarch never forsook him. Not even the wildness of passion could long lead him beyond the suggestion of policy. Raising his hand for silence, he again spoke.

"We are misunderstanding each other, my brave Yeni-Tscheri. If you have grievance let your Agas present it, for the Padishah shall be the father of his people, and the Yeni-Tscheri are the eldest born of his children."

The Sultan withdrew. Eight Agas held a hurried consultation, and presented themselves to the sovereign to offer him absolute and unquestioning obedience upon the condition of their retaining as absolute and unquestioned self-government within the corps.

While they were in consultation, Captain Ballaban appeared among the troops. He waved his hand to address them.

"He is bought by the Padishah. We must not hear him," cried one and another.

"My brothers!" said the Captain, having after a few moments gained their attention. "I love the Padishah. But I adore that royal hand chiefly because, beyond that of any of the heirs of Othman, it has already bestowed favor upon our corps. But our order is sacred. He may command to the field, and in the field, but it must be from without. We must choose our own Aga as of old."

"Long live Ballaban!" rose from every side.

The speaker broke into a rhapsodic narration of the glories of the corps, interwoven with the recital of the exploits of the Padishah, during which he was interrupted by cheer after cheer, mingled with the cry of "Ballaban! Ballaban forever!"

The Sultan, hearing the shout, shrewdly seized upon the opportunity it suggested, and leaving the Agas, rushed to the platform. He shouted—

"Allah be praised! Allah has given one mind to the Padishah and to his faithful Yeni-Tscheri. Ballaban forever! Yes, take him! Take him for your Aga! The will of the corps and the will of the sovereign are one, for it is the will of Allah that sways us all!"

The soldiers, caught by the enthusiasm of the instant, repeated the shout, drowning the voices of the few who were clear-headed enough to remember that the firman had not been withdrawn.

"Ballaban! Long live Ballaban Aga! Long live Mahomet Padishah!"

The Agas appeared, but were impotent to assert their dissent. As well might they have attempted to howl down a hurricane as to make themselves heard in the confusion. Indeed, their presence upon the platform was regarded by the corps as their endorsement of the Padishah's desire, and served to stimulate the enthusiasm that broke out in redoubled applause.

Mahomet followed up his advantage, and formally confirmed the apparent election by announcing—"A donative! A double pay to every one of the Yeni-Tscheri! and the Padishah's fifth of the spoil shall be divided to the host!"

The multitude were wild with delight. The inverted soup-kettle was turned over, and swung by its handle from the top of the staff; following which, the crowd poured out from the court.[105]

Within a few days Ballaban, as chief Aga, led his corps toward Albania.

CHAPTER LII

After the defeat of Moses as a Turkish leader, and his return to his patriotic allegiance, there was a lull in active hostilities between the two powers. Amesa, like other of the prominent voivodes in Scanderbeg's army, took the occasion offered to look after his own estates. He had added somewhat to his local importance by marrying the daughter of a neighboring land-owner. But neither conjugal delights, nor the additional acres his marriage brought him, covered his ambition. His envy of Castriot had deepened into inveterate hatred.

The Voivode sat alone in the great dining hall of his castle. It was late in the night. As the blazing logs at one end of the room cast alternately their glare and shadows around, the rude furniture seemed to be thrown into a witching dance. Helmets and corselets gleamed bravely from their pegs, suggesting that they were animated by heroic souls. The great bear-skin, with its enormous head, lying at the Voivode's feet, crouched in readiness to receive the lunge of the boar's tusks which threatened it from the corner. Pikes, spears, bows and broad-mouthed arquebuses were ranged about, as if to defend their owner, should any demon inspire these lifeless forms for sudden assault upon him.

Amesa had been sitting upon a low seat between the fire and a half-drained tankard of home-brewed liquor, his brows knit with the concentration of his thoughts.

A slight sound without arrested his attention.

"Drakul is late, but is coming at last. If only he has brought me the red forelock of that fellow who used to be always crossing my track, and has now come back to Albania!" he said, in a tone of musing, but intended to be heard by the delinquent as the great oaken door creaked behind him. Raising his eyes, but not turning his head to look, Amesa changed his soliloquy into a volley of oaths at the comer.

"I thought your name-sake, Drakul, had run off with you, you lazy imp.[106] What kept you?"

"A long journey," was the reply.

Amesa started to his feet, for the voice was not that of Drakul. He faced one whose appearance was not the less startling because it was familiar.

"I have brought the red forelock myself," said the visitor.

Amesa stared stupidly an instant, then reached toward his weapon lying upon the table near.

"Stop!" said the man, laying the flat side of his sword across the Voivode's arm before he could grasp his yataghan.

"How dare you intrude yourself unbidden here!" cried the enraged Amesa.

"It required no daring," was the cool reply, "for I am the stronger."

"Help! Help!" shouted the voivode, as he realized that he would not be permitted to reach his weapon.

The door swung, and a band of strange men stood in the opening.

"I feared, noble Amesa," said the intruder, "that I should not be a welcome guest, and so brought with me a party of friends to help me to good cheer while under your roof. You need not disturb your servants to help you, for, if they should hear, they could not obey, as they are all safely guarded in their quarters. If they should come out they might be harmed. Let them rest. Retire, men! You recognize me, Lord Amesa?"

"Ay. You are Arnaud's whelp," sneered the entrapped man.

"More gentle words would befit the courtesy of my host," was the quiet reply. "But you are as much mistaken as when you took the simple witted Elissa on my commendation. Do not respond, Sire! In your heat you might say that which pride would prevent your recalling. I am a Moslem soldier, and you are my prisoner; as secure as if you were in Constantinople." The visitor threw off the Albanian cape, and revealed the elegantly wrought jacket of the Janizary Aga.

"And what would you have of me? Is there nothing that can satisfy you less than my life?" asked Amesa.

"My noble Amesa," said Ballaban Aga, taking a seat and motioning the Voivode to another. "Years ago I gave you my word in honor that I would serve you against Scanderbeg. I have come to redeem that pledge, and you must help me."

"How can that be, if you are an officer of the Moslems?" asked Amesa, taking the seat, and adopting the low tone of the other; for these words had excited in him all his cupidity, and stirred his natural secretiveness and habit of sinister dealing. His eyes ceased to glare like a tiger's when at bay; they shone now like a snake's.

"Amesa must enter the service of the Padishah."

"Impossible!" cried he; but in a tone that indicated, not indignant rejection of the proposition; rather doubt of its practicability.

"But first you must raise here in Albania the standard of revolt against Scanderbeg, claiming the title of king of Epirus and the Dibrias for yourself. Scanderbeg's sword will, of course, compel the next step—your safety in the Turkish camp. The Padishah will then become your patron, offering to withdraw his armies and restore the ancient liberties of the country, with the solitary limitation that you shall acknowledge the suzerainty of the Sultan. The revenues you may collect shall remain in your possession for the strengthening of your local power. The defection of Moses Goleme well nigh destroyed the leadership of Scanderbeg—yours will complete the work. Yet it will not be defection; rather, as Moses Goleme regarded it, the truest service of your country, because the only service that is practicable."

"But I cannot thus break with the patriot leaders," said Amesa, apparently having felt a real touch of honor.

"It must be," replied the Aga. "You cannot longer remain as you are, even if you would. You, Sire, have been guilty of some great crime. Nay, do not deny it! Nor need you take time to give expression to any wrath you may feel on being plainly accused of it," continued Ballaban, silencing Amesa more effectively by the straight look into his eyes than by his words. "My moments here are too few to talk about the matter, and you should have exhausted any feeling you may have had in private penitence heretofore, rather than reserve it until another person lays it to your charge. But the point is this:—Scanderbeg is aware of your crime, and awaits only the opportune moment to punish you as it deserves."

"How do you know that?" said Amesa, the bright gleam of his eye changing to a stony stare, as the color failed from his face, and he leaned back in ghastly consternation.

"It is enough that I know it. The Janizaries have not roamed these Albanian hills for twelve years without finding out the secrets of the country. The holes in the ground are our ears, and the very owls spy for us through the dark. But enough of words. Sign this, and set to it your seal!" Ballaban presented a parchment, offering formally, in the name of the Sultan, the government of Albania to Amesa, on the condition set forth above.

"I would consider the"—began Amesa; but he was cut short by Ballaban—

"No! sign instantly! I have done for you all the considering that is necessary, and must be gone."

"But," began Amesa again, "so important a matter—"

"Sign instantly!" repeated Ballaban; and, pointing to the door where the soldiers stood waiting their orders—"or neither Amesa nor his castle will exist until the day breaks."

The baffled man took from a niche in the wall a horn of thickened ink, and, with the wooden pen, made his signature, and pressed the ancient seal of the De Streeses against the ball of softened wax attached to it.

"This will serve to keep you true: for if by the next fulness of the moon Amesa's standard be not raised against Scanderbeg's, this, as evidence of your treason, shall be read in all your Albanian camps," said Ballaban, placing the document in his bosom. "And should you need to confer with your new friends, your faithful Drakul may inquire at our lines for Ballaban Badera, Aga of the Janizaries."

With a low salâm he withdrew. A few muffled orders, a shuffling of feet, and the castle was as quiet as the stars that looked down upon it.

CHAPTER LIII

The martial pride of the Ottoman never made a more imposing demonstration than when his armies deployed upon the plain of Pharsalia[107] in Thessaly, and threatened the southern frontier of Albania. Nor had Jove, who, according to the mythologic conception, held his court upon the summit of the not distant Olympus—looked down upon such a display of earthly power since, fifteen centuries before, the armies of Pompey and Cæsar there contended for the domination of the Roman world. For Mahomet II. had sworn his mightiest oath, that, by one blow, he would now sweep all the Arnaout rebels into the sea; and that the waves of the Adriatic over against Italy, and those of the Mediterranean which washed the Greek peninsula, and the Euxine that stayed the steps of the Muscovite, should sing with their confluent waves the glories of the European Empire of the Ottoman which lay between them.

The menace to Scanderbeg's domain was not chiefly in the numbers of men whom the redoubtable Isaac Pasha now commanded in the name of the Sultan; but in the fact that the mighty host was accompanied by Amesa, the new "King of Albania."

The defection of the Voivode had sent consternation through the hearts of the patriots. Their leaders looked with suspicion into one another's faces as they gathered in council; for no one knew but that his comrade was in secret league with the enemy. Wearied with trials, the soldiers whispered in the camps that Amesa was a Castriot as well as Scanderbeg. Italians of rank, who had loaned their swords to the great chieftain, were returning to their homes, saying that it was not worth while to risk their lives and fortunes in defending a people who were no longer agreed in defending themselves. Scanderbeg, apparently unwilling or unable to cope with this double danger,—the power of the Ottoman without, and a civil war within his land—retired to Lyssa,[108] far away to the north.

The Turks determined to inaugurate their final conquest, by the formal coronation of their ally, so that, heralded by King Amesa's proclamations, they might advance more readily to the occupation of the land. The day was set for the ceremony of the royal investiture. As their scouts, ranging far and wide, reported no enemy to be near, the attention of the army was given to preparation for the splendid pageants, the very story of which should awe the simple peasant population into submission, or seduce their hearts with the hope of having so magnificent a patron.

The day before that appointed for this glorious dawn of the new royalty, was one of intense heat, in the middle of July. The snows had melted even from the summit of the Thessalian Olympus, though its bare pinnacle yonder pierced the sky nearly ten thousand feet above the sea. Armor was heaped in the tents. Horses unsaddled were gathered in stockades, or tethered far out on the glassy plain. Soldiers stretched themselves under the shadow of the trees, or wandered in groups through the deserted gardens and orchards of the neighboring country, feasting upon the early ripened fruits. Only the eagles that circled the air high above the vast encampment, or perched upon the crags of distant hills, seemed to have any alarm; for now and then they darted off with a shrill cry.

But an eye, like that of a mysterious retributive Providence, was peering through the thicket that crested a high hill. Scanderbeg, presumed to be far away, had studied the plain long and intently; when, turning to Constantine, who was at his side, he said:

"Now plan me a raid through that flock of silly sheep. Where would you strike, my boy?"

Constantine replied, "There is but one point at which we could enter the plain,—through yonder depression. The hills on either side would conceal the advance until well upon them. Besides, the narrowness of the valley, and the growth of trees would prevent their meeting us with more than man for man."

Scanderbeg shook his head.

"The Turks know that place invites attack as well as we do, and have ranged so as to prevent surprise there. But yonder line of trees and copse leads almost to the centre of their camp."

"But it is exposed to view on either side," replied Constantine.

"So much the better," said Castriot, "and therefore it is not guarded even in Isaac Pasha's thought. It would take longer after the alarm to range against us there than in the ravine. Their cavalry is all on this side the trees. They could not cut through the bushes before we were by the horse-tails yonder, there by the Pasha's tent."

"But is it not too open?" said Constantine, almost incredulous.

"Yes, at any other time than this, when the Turks are not dreaming of our being within a dozen leagues of them. The very boldness of such an attack as this at high noon-tide will be better for us than any scheming. And, if I mistake not, and our beasts are not too jaded by the long march, we shall have the souls out of a thousand or so of the Turks before they can get their bodies into armor. And I give to you, my boy, the care of our nephew, Amesa. Be diverted by no side play, but cut your way straight to him. If possible, spare his life, but he must never get a crown upon his head."

As silently as the summer's fleecy clouds gather into the storm, the band of patriots, summoned from their various quarters, gathered behind the spur of the hill. The Turks were startled as with a sudden rising tempest. Beys and Pashas and Agas had scarcely emerged from their tents, when five thousand Albanian cavalrymen were already turning the line of the woods. On they came with the celerity of a flock of birds just skimming the ground. The sentry flew as the leaves before the wind. The very multitude of the Turks, driven toward the centre, but fed the dripping swords of the assailants. Among the tents wound the compact array of Albanian riders, like a huge serpent. On and on it rolled, scarcely pausing to repel attack. Dividing, one part crushed the headquarters of Isaac, while the other wrapped in its crunching folds the splendid camp of Amesa.

Bravely did this young Absalom defend his unfledged royalty. Surrounded by a group of Albanian renegades like himself, he fought desperately, well knowing the dire vengeance which should follow his capture. But one by one they fell. Amesa remained almost alone, as yet unharmed. The captain of the Albanian troops commanded a halt, and, dismounting, he demanded Amesa's surrender.

"To none but a Castriot will a Castriot surrender!" cried the infuriate man, making a lunge at the challenger. The thrust was avoided.

"You shall surrender to another," cried the Albanian officer. "Stand back, men, he shall yield to me alone."

"Who are you?" growled the challenged man.

"One who has the right to avenge the wrong done to Mara de Streeses," was the reply.

Quick as a panther Amesa leaped upon him. But the tremendous blow he aimed, might as well have been delivered against a rock, as against the sword of Constantine. The effort threw him off his balance; and before he could recover himself, the tremendous slash of his opponent, though warded, brought him to the ground. In an instant Constantine's knee was upon his breast, and his sword at his throat.

"Do you surrender?"

"Yes!" groaned the helpless man.

He was instantly disarmed, and bound by the girth to a horse.

CHAPTER LIV

The corps of Janizaries had been quartered at some distance from the main body of the Turks. Their new Aga comprehended at once the significance of the turmoil in the camp, and hastened to the defence. Though he moved rapidly, and with a well conceived plan of confronting the enemy, yet, most of his troops being foot-soldiers, he was unable to confront the swift-riding squadrons of Scanderbeg. These assailants withdrew from the field, but only to return again and again upon the panic stricken Turks, whose fears had magnified the numbers of their foes into scores of thousands. So rapidly did assault follow assault, and from such diverse quarters, that the Moslem fright imagined one attack was headed by the terrible Ivan Beg with his savage Montenegrins, and another by Hunyades, a report of whose alliance with Scanderbeg had reached the camps before the battle. Indeed the rumble of a coming thunder storm was interpreted into the clamor and tread of unknown myriads ready to burst through the mountains. Never did a more insane panic steal away the courage of soldiers and the judgment of generals. Late in the day the plain of Pharsalia was the scene of one vast wreck. Overturned tents displayed immense stores of burnished arms and vestments, provisions of need and luxury, standards for the field and banners for the pageant; and everywhere strewn amid this debris of pomp and pride the half-armored bodies of the slaughtered Turks. In narrow mountain valleys the freshet following the sudden tempest, never changed the bloom of the summer gardens more completely, than this panic, following Scanderbeg's raid, changed the splendid camp of the morning into the desolation upon which the setting sun cast, as a fitting omen, its red rays. Indeed, we can conceive no similitude by which to express the contrast better than that of Amesa himself, in the morning adorned in the splendor of his royal expectation, and at night lying bound with ropes at the feet of Scanderbeg.

The grand old chieftain looked at the renegade for a moment with pity and scorn; then turned away, saying,—

"Let him lie there until Captain Constantine, to whom he belongs, shall come."

But Constantine came not. Though the main body of the Turks had taken to precipitate flight, the Janizaries had managed, by their unbroken and orderly retreat, to cover the rear, and prevent pursuit by Scanderbeg. Ballaban had reached the group engaged in the capture of Amesa, and almost rescued him. This would have been accomplished had not

Constantine and a handful of his company made a living wall between the Janizaries and those who were leading away the miserable man. Ballaban, feeling the responsibility of saving him whom he had led into this shameful misfortune, pressed to the very front.

"By the sword of the Prophet! the fellow fights bravely," he exclaimed, as he watched Constantine, baffling a half dozen Janizaries who were pressing upon him.

"Back, men! I would measure my arm against his," he cried, as he laid his sword against that of his unknown antagonist.

Both were in complete armor, their faces concealed by the closed helmets. The soldiers stood as eager spectators of the masterly sword play. The two men seemed evenly matched,—the same in stature and build. There was, too, a surprising similarity in movement—the very tactics of the Janizary in thrust and parry being repeated by the Albanian; their swords now flashing like interlacing flames; the sharp ring as the Albanian smote upon the polished metal of his antagonist's armor, answered by the duller thud as the Janizary's blow fell upon the thick leather which encased the panoply of his opponent. Then both stood as if posing for the sculptor; their sword points crossing; their eyes glaring beneath the visors; the slightest movement of a muscle anticipated by either—then again the crash.

But Constantine was exhausted by his previous engagement with Amesa. In an unlucky moment the sword turned in his hand. The steadiness of the grip was lost. He managed to ward the blow which the Aga delivered; but, foreseeing that he could not recover his grasp soon enough to return it, and that his opponent was thrown slightly off his perfect poise by his exertion, he dropped his sword, and closed with him. They fell to the ground; but the Aga, more alert at the instant, was uppermost, and his dagger first in position for the fatal cut. "I can not slay so valiant a man as you," said Ballaban. "You surrender?"

"I must," was the response. As they rose, Ballaban looked a moment upon the vanquished, and said,

"I would know the name of my worthy antagonist, for worthier I never found. Scanderbeg himself could not have done better. But I had the advantage of being in better wind at the start, or, Allah knows, I had fared hard."

"It is enough that I am your prisoner," said Constantine, "and that I have detained my conqueror long enough to prevent the recapture of that Albanian traitor, Amesa. You can have me willingly, now that you cannot have him."

The Albanian threw up his visor. Ballaban stared at the face. It was as familiar as his own which he saw daily in the polished brass mirror. The Janizaries stared with almost equal amazement.

"No wonder he fought so well, Aga!" said one, "for he is thy other self."

"Let him be brought to our headquarters when we halt," said Ballaban, remounting his horse, and dashing away to another part of the field.

CHAPTER LV

Night brought little sleep to the Turkish host. Though danger was past, a sense of humiliation and chagrin was shared by officers and men, as they realized that their defeat was due to their own folly more than to the strength of their foe. In every tentless group the men disturbed the quiet of the night with their ceaseless quarrels. Members of the different commands, hopelessly confused in the general flight, rivalled one another in the rancor and contempt of their mutual recriminations as much as they ever emulated one another in the courage and prowess of a well fought field. Among those of highest rank bitter and insulting words were followed by blows, as if the general disgrace could be washed out by a gratuitous spilling of their own blood.

But a different interest kept Ballaban waking. Beneath the great tree, which had been designated as the headquarters of the Janizaries, and from a limb of which was suspended the symbolic kettle, his prisoner had been awaiting the Chief Aga. The glimpse of his face at the time of the capture had awakened in the Janizary more than a suspicion of the personality of the captive; while the name of Ballaban, which he had heard from the soldiers, revealed to the Albanian that of his captor. With impatience the Aga conversed with the various commanders who thronged him, and as soon as possible dismissed them. When they were alone Constantine rose, and, without completing his salâm, exclaimed, "You play more roughly, Michael, than when last we wrestled together among the rocks of Slatiza."

"Ah, my brother Constantine, I thought of you when you gripped me in the fight to-day; for it was the same old hug with which we rolled together long ago. I would have known you, had you only given me time to think, without your raising the visor."

The brothers stood for a moment in half embrace, scanning each other's face and form. An onlooker would have noted that their mutual resemblance was not in the details of their features, so much as in certain marked peculiarities; such as the red and bristling hair, square face, prominent nose and chin. Constantine's forehead was higher than Michael's, which had more breadth and massiveness across the brows. In speaking, Constantine's eye kindled, and his plastic lips gave expression to every play of sentiment: while Michael's face was as inflexible as a mask; the deep light of his glance as thoroughly under control of his will as if it were the flash of a dark lantern; his appearance revealing not the shadow of a thought, not the flicker of an emotion, beyond that he chose to put into words. This physiognomical difference was doubtless largely due to the training of years. The Janizary's habit of caution and secretiveness evolved, as it were, this invisible, but impenetrable, visor. The custom of unquestioning obedience to another, and that of the remorseless prosecution of whatever he regarded as politic for the service, gave rigidity to the facial muscles; set them with the prevalent purpose; stereotyped in them the expression of determination. A short beard added to the immobile cast of his countenance. Thus, though when separated the two men might readily be taken the one for the other, when together their resemblance served to suggest as wide contrasts.

The entire night was spent by the brothers in mutual narrations of their eventful lives. Though their careers had been so distinct, in different lands, under rival civilizations, in the service of contending nations, and inflamed by the incentives of antagonistic religions, yet their roads had crossed at the most important points in each. They learned to their astonishment that the most significant events, those awakening the deepest experience in the one life, had been due to the presence of the other. As Michael told of his raid upon the Albanian village, Constantine supplied the key to the mystery of the escape of his fair captive, and the arrest of Michael for having at that time deserted his command. Then Michael in turn supplied the key to Constantine's arrest by Colonel Kabilovitsch's men as a Turkish spy. Constantine solved the enigma of Amesa's overtures to Michael in reference to the Dodola Elissa; and Michael solved that of Constantine's rough handling by the garrison of Sfetigrade for having dropped the dog into the well. Constantine unravelled the diabolical plot which had nearly been tragic for Michael in the old reservoir at Constantinople; and Michael as readily unravelled that of the serio-comic drama in the tent of Mahomet, when Constantine's life was saved through the assumption that he was his lunatic brother. Constantine supplied to Michael the missing link in the story of Morsinia's escape from Constantinople; and Michael supplied that which was wanting of Constantine's knowledge of the story of her escape from death in the horrors of the scene in St. Sophia after the capture of the city. They had, under the strange leadings of what both their Christian and Moslem faith recognized as a Divine Providence, been more to each other than they could have been had their lives drifted in the same channel during all these years. In the old boyhood confidence, which their strange meeting had revived, Michael did not withhold the confession of Morsinia's influence upon him, though she had been to him more of an ideal than a real person, a beautiful development to his imagination out of his childhood memory of his little playmate in the Balkans. Nor did Constantine hesitate to declare the love and betrothal by which he held the charming reality as his own. He told, too, of her real personality as the ward of Scanderbeg, and the true heir of the splendid estates until recently held by Amesa.

The dawn brought duties to the Aga which precluded further conference with Constantine.

"We must part, my dear brother," said Michael. "Our armies will probably return through Macedonia, and abandon the campaign: for such is the unwise determination of our commander Isaac. You must escape into your own lines. That can be easily arranged. We may not meet again soon; but I swear to you, by the memory of our childhood, that your personal interest shall be mine. Aside from the necessities of the military service, we can be brothers still. And Morsinia, that angel of our better natures; you must let me share with you, if not her affection, surely her confidence. I could not woo her from you if I would; but assure her that, though wearing the uniform of an enemy, I shall be as true in my thoughts of her as when we played by the old cot on the mountains; and as when I pledged my life to serve her while she was in the harem at Stamboul."

"But why must this war against Castriot continue? I would that our compact were that of the armies to which we belong," said Constantine.

"It is impossible for a Janizary to sheath the sword while Scanderbeg lives," replied the Aga. "Our oath forbids it. He once was held by the vow of the Prophet's service, and deserted it. I know his temptation was strong. In my heart I might find charity for him." The speaker hesitated as if haunted by some troublesome memory, then continued—"But a Janizary may show no charity to a renegade. Besides, he is the curse of Albania. But for his ambition, these twelve years of blood would have been those of peace and happiness through all these valleys, under the sway of our munificent and wise Padishah."

"Your own best thoughts, Michael, should correct you. What are peace and its happy indolence compared with the cause of a holy faith?"

"You speak sublimely, my brother," replied Michael, "but your faith gains nothing by this war. Under our Padishah's beneficence the Giaours are protected. The Greeks hold sufficient churches, even in Stamboul, for the worship of all who remain in that faith. Indeed, I have heard Gennadius the monk of whom you were speaking awhile ago—say that he would trust his flock to the keeping of the Moslem stranger sooner than to the Pope of Rome. I have known our Padishah defend the Greek Giaours from the tyranny of their own bishops. He asks only the loyalty of his people to his throne, and awaits the will of Allah to turn them to his faith; for the Book of the Prophet says truly, Allah will lead into error whom he pleaseth and whom he pleaseth he will put in the right way.[109] Believe me, my brother,

Albania's safety is only in submission. The Fate that directs all affairs has indubitably decreed that all this vast peninsula between Adria and Ægea shall lie beneath the shadow of the Padishah's sceptre; for he is Zil-Ullah, the shadow of God. Who can resist the conqueror of the capital of your Eastern Christian Empire; the conqueror of Athens, and of the islands of the sea?"

"Let us then speak no more of this," said Constantine. "Our training has been so different, that we can not hope to agree. But we can be one in the kindliness of our thoughts, as we are of one blood. Jesu bless you, my brother!"

"Allah bless you, Constantine!" was the hearty response, as the two grasped hands. Eyes which would not have shown bodily pain by so much as the tremor of their lids, were moist with the outflow of those springs in our nature that are deeper than courage—springs of brotherly affection, fed by hallowed memories of the long ago.

Two Janizaries accompanied Constantine beyond the Turkish lines.

"What new scheme has the Aga hatched in his brain now?" said one of them, as they returned.

"He has twisted that fellow's brain so that he will never serve Scanderbeg truly again," was the knowing reply. "The Aga is the very devil to throw a spell over a man. They say that when he captured the fellow yesterday, he had only to squint into his face a moment, when, as quick as a turn of a foil, the man changed his looks, and was as much like the Aga as two thumbs."

CHAPTER LVI

The splendor of the victory, and the inestimable spoil which fell into the hands of the Albanians, elated the patriot braves; and the good news flew as if the eagles that watched the battles from afar were its couriers. Castriot, however, seemed to be oblivious to the general rejoicing. The wrath he had displayed during the time of Amesa's menace from the ranks of the enemy, was displaced by pity as he looked upon the contemptible and impotent man. He touched him with his foot, and said, in half soliloquy—

"And in this body is some of the blood of the Castriots! Humph!"

Turning away he paced the tent—

"And why not Castriot's blood in Amesa! It is not too immaculate to flow in his veins, since it has filled my own. I was a Turk, too, once. But——" looking at the wrinkles upon his hand—"growing old in a better service may atone somewhat for the shame of earlier days. And these hands never murdered a peaceful neighbor and his innocent wife, and robbed a child of her inheritance—though they did murder that poor Reis-Effendi. But God knows it could not be helped. But what is one man that he shall condemn another!" An officer approached for orders.

"What, Sire, shall be done with the prisoner?"

"Let him lie until Constantine comes!" was the response.

Late in the night the general sat gazing upon the miserable heap of humanity that crouched by the tent side. Amesa raised himself as far as his bonds would permit, and began to speak.

"Silence!" demanded Castriot, but without taking his eyes from the prisoner.

A subaltern, anxious to induce the general to take needed rest, again suggested some disposition of the prisoner for the night.

"Let him lie until Constantine comes!"

"Captain Constantine has been captured, Sire," replied the officer; "men who were with him have returned, and so report."

"By whom captured?" asked the general in alarm.

"By Janizaries."

Castriot smiled, and asked, "It is certain he was not slain?"

"Certain, Sire, for Ino saw him being taken away."

"Let the prisoner lie there until Captain Constantine returns." The morning found Amesa still bound. No one had been allowed to speak to him, nor he to utter a word.

During Castriot's absence from the tent not one approached it; only the guard patrolled at the distance of a couple of rods.

"The torture of such a villain's thoughts will be more cruel than our taunts or swords. Let him lie there, and tear himself with his own devil claws!" had been Castriot's order.

Toward noon the camp rang with cheers. Scouts reported that Constantine had escaped, and was returning. Castriot alone seemed unsurprised, though gratified with the news. He went to the edge of the camp to meet him.

"Well, my boy, your brother was not so well pleased with your looks, and let you go sooner than I thought he would. I expected you not until to-night."

"My brother? How knew you, Sire, that I had seen him? for I have told it to none."

"Then tell it to none. To warn you of that I came to meet you, lest your tongue might be unwise. Did you not tell me yourself that Ballaban was the Moslem name of your brother?"

"But how knew you that he was in this service?" asked Constantine.

"As I know every officer in the enemy's service in Albania above an ojak's command. And the Aga of the Janizaries is to my mind as the commander of the expedition. And I will tell you more, my boy;—unless the Padishah has gone daft with his chagrin over this defeat, Ballaban Aga will command the next campaign against us: for none save he kept his wits in the fight yesterday. His plan was masterful, and saved the whole Moslem army. He held his Janizaries so well in hand, and so well placed, that I could not follow up our advantage, nor even strike to rescue you. Ballaban evidently has been much in the Albanian wars, and has learned my methods better than any of our own officers. Should he succeed to the horse-tails, the war hereafter will not be so one-sided as it has been. Mark that, my dear fellow. But we must look to our royal prisoner, after I have heard your story."

Late in the day Castriot summoned Moses Goleme, Kabilovitsch, and Constantine. Amesa was unbound, and was bidden to speak what he could in extenuation of his treason. The Voivode protested his innocence of any designs against the liberties of his country; and declared that he had despaired of obtaining her independence under Castriot's leadership. Better was it to take the virtual freedom of Albania under the Sultan's nominal suzerainty, than to longer wage a hopeless war. In this he was seconded, he said, by the noblest generals and patriots. He was about to mention them; but was forbidden to utter so much as a suspicion against any one.

"I would not know them," said the magnanimous chief. "I will not have a shadow of distrust in my mind toward any who have not drawn sword against us. Let them keep their thoughts in their own breasts. Noble Moses, your lips shall pronounce the sentence due Amesa's treason."

The Dibrian general was silent. "Then, if Moses speaks no condemnation, no other lips shall," said Castriot.

Amesa threw himself at the feet of the chief, and began to pour forth his gratitude.

"The life thou hast spared, Sire, shall ever be thine. My sword shall be given to thee as sovereign of my heart, as well as of my country."

"Hold!" said Castriot. "What says Arnaud, the forester?"

Amesa raised his face, blanched as suddenly with horror as it had been flushed with elation. The venerable Kabilovitsch sat in silence for a time, lost in the vividness of his recollections. At length, with slow speech and tremulous voice, he portrayed the scenes of that terrible night when the castle of the gallant De Streeses was destroyed, its owner slain, the fair Mara driven back into the flames from which she would have fled.

"It is a lie," shouted Amesa. "The deed was wrought by Turks!"——

"Thy words condemn thee!" said Castriot. "The crime was not laid to thy charge, Amesa. But now it shall be. Let Drakul be brought."

Soldiers led in the man. The villain, whose hand had stayed at no deed of daring or cruelty, was now seized with such cowardly fright that he could scarce keep his legs. He was dragged before the extemporized court. In answer to questions, he admitted his part, not only in the original murders, but also in the raid upon the hamlet where Amesa had suspected the heiress of De Streeses to be concealed.

Amesa's rage at this betrayal burst forth in savage oaths, mingled with such contradictory denials of his story as clearly confirmed its truth.

"For his treason against my authority, I refuse to take vengeance," said Castriot. "But Albania, appealing for God's aid in establishing its liberties, must, in God's name, do justice. What says Colonel Kabilovitsch?"

The old man spoke as if the solemnity of the Last Judgment had fallen upon him,—

"As soon I must go before Him whose mercy I shall so sadly need for the sins of my own life, I forgive Amesa the cruelty with which he has followed me. God is my witness, that my personal grievance colors not a thought of my heart. But, as I shall soon stand before the Judge, together with the noble De Streeses, who was robbed of life in its meridian, and that bright spirit whose cry for Amesa's mercy I heard from out the flames, I say, Let justice be done! and let the soul of the murderer be sent to confront his victims there before their God!"

"Amen!" said Constantine. Moses Goleme was silent.

Amesa had lost all his bravado. He trembled as would the meanest of men who should bow his neck to the sword. He confessed his crime, and piteously begged for his life; or, at least, that time should be given him to make preparation for what he dreaded worse than death. A spirit already damned seemed to have taken possession of his quivering frame.

"Your life, Amesa," said the chief, "is forfeit for your crimes. On the citadel walls of Croia, when we shall have returned there, as the sun sets, so shall your life! Jesu grant that, through your repentance and the prayers of Mother Church, your soul may rise again in a better world!"

"Amen!" responded all.

The army returned from the Thessalian border through the country northward, everywhere received with ovations by the people. The fate of Amesa, though commiserated, was as generally commended. No one, however attached by association to the once popular Voivode, raised a voice in dissent from the sentence, or in pity for the culprit.

CHAPTER LVII

The news reached Morsinia at Croia long before the return of the army. She took little joy in the hearty and generous acclaim that welcomed her to her inheritance. She had no vanity to be stimulated by the popular stories which associated her beauty with her wealth. Her thoughts seemed to be palled with heaviness, rather than canopied by the bright prospects which fortune had spread for her.

When Castriot officially announced to her the restoration of the DeStreeses' property, she refused to enter upon her estates, which were to come to her through the ceremony of blood in the execution of her enemy.

"No! Let them be confiscate to the State. I cheerfully surrender their revenues for Albania. I ask nothing more than to be the instrument of so aiding our noble cause and its noble leader," said she.

"Albania will insist that you shall obtain your right. From voivode to lowest peasant, the people will be content only as the daughter of DeStreeses graces his ancient castle."

"But," responded she, "I shall never enter its doors over the body of my enemy. May not some other fate be his?"

"Law should be sacred," said Castriot.

"But is it not a law of Albania that even a murderer need not be executed if all the family of his victim unite in his behalf, and he pay the Krwnina?[110] Am I not all the family of DeStreeses? Let then the estates be the Krwnina."

"That cannot be," replied Castriot. "The law requires the price of blood to be paid by the murderer, and the estates belong not to Amesa. Besides, Albania will be better served by your occupation of the castle, reviving its ancient prestige, and proclaiming thus that the reign of justice has been restored in our land."

"But let justice be mingled with mercy," said Morsinia.

"Nay, the mercy would dilute the quality of the justice."

"Can there be no mitigation of our cousin Amesa's fate, which shall not prejudice the right?" asked the fair intercessor. "If Jesu prayed to his Father that His murderers might be forgiven, may not I plead that my father, the father of his country, shall be gracious to him who has wronged me?"

Castriot was absorbed in deep thought. At length he replied:

"Ah, how little we men, schooled to revenge and bloodshed, know what justice is, and what mercy is, as these sentiments move in the heart of the Eternal! Your pure soul, my child, has closer kinship with heaven than ours. I fear to deny your request, lest I should offend that mysterious Spirit which has seemed to counsel me since, in the land of the Moslems, I swore to return to my Christian faith; and which, in my prayers and dreams, has been strangely associated with you. In all that is right and good your conscience shall still inspire mine: for you are my good angel. Amesa's life shall be spared. But no breath of his must so much as taint the air of Albania. I am summoned by my old ally, Ferdinand of Naples, to assist in driving the French from his domains. Amesa shall go with me, and be kept in custody among strangers. But it must be proclaimed from the citadel of Croia that his life is restored him by the daughter of Musache de Streeses.

"And yet, my dear child," continued he, "in these rude times you cannot dwell alone in the castle. You need a protector who is not only wise and brave, and loyal to Albania, but loyal to you. My duties elsewhere will prevent my rendering that service. Colonel Kabilovitsch's age is stealing the alertness from his energies. Our Constantine—Ah! Does the blush tell that I am right?" He took her hand, as he asked: "May I exercise the father's privilege, according to our Albanian custom, and put this hand into Constantine's, to keep and to defend?"

Morsinia replied frankly. "Since, Sire, I may not give my estates to my country, bestow them upon whom you will; and my hand must go to him, who, since we were children, has held my heart."

The following day, as the sun gilded the walls of Croia with his setting rays, an immense concourse of soldiers and peasants gathered within the citadel court. The executioner led the traitor, followed by a priest, out upon the bastion. A trumpet sounded, and the silence which followed its dying note was broken by the voice of the crier, who announced that, in the name of God and the sovereign people, and by the ordaining of George, Duke of Albania, the decree of justice should be executed upon the Voivode Amesa. Then followed the record of his crimes, together with the declaration that his appearance in arms among the enemy, having been, according to his declaration, not treason against his country, but rebellion against the military chieftaincy of Duke George, was by the grace of that high official forgiven; and further that the sentence of death for his foul murder of Musache De Streeses and his wife Mara Cernoviche, was, through the intercession of Mara, sole survivor of that ancient house, and by the authority of Duke George, commuted to perpetual banishment from the realm, in such place and condition as seemed best to the Duke for the security of the land.

The people stood in amazement as they listened. The relief from the horror of the anticipated spectacle, when the head of the former favorite should be held up by the executioner, led them to accept complacently this turn in affairs, even though their judgment did not commend it. In a few moments the cry rose, "Live Duke George! A Castriot forever!" Soon it changed to wilder enthusiasm, "Long live Mara De Streeses!" This storm of applause could not be stilled until Morsinia permitted herself to be led by Castriot to the edge of the battlement.

As the sun was setting, the huge mass of the citadel rose like a mighty altar from the bosom of the gloom which had already settled about its base. Slowly the shadow had climbed its side, crowding the last bright ray until it vanished from the top of the parapet. It was at this instant that Morsinia appeared. The citadel beneath her was sombre as the coming night which enwrapped it, but her form was radiant in the lingering splendor of the departing day. As she raised her hand in response to the grateful clamor of the people, she seemed the impersonation of a heavenly benediction. The multitude gazed in reverent silence for a moment. Then, as the sun dropped behind the western hill, veiling the glory of this apparition, they made the very sky resound with their shouts; and in the quick gathering darkness went their ways.

A few weeks later, the castle of De Streeses was decked with banners, whose bright colors rivalled the late autumnal hues of the forest from the midst of which it rose. Multitudes of people all day long thronged the paths leading up to it from the valleys around. Gorgeously arrayed voivodes, accompanied by their suites, made the ravines resound with their rattling armor; and bands of peasants, in cheap but gaudy finery, threaded through the by paths. Those who possessed tents brought them. Others, upon their arrival in the proximity of the castle, erected booths and festooned them with vines, which the advancing season had painted fiery red or burst into gray feathery plumes. From cleared places near the castle walls rose huge spirals of smoke, as oxen and sheep, quartered or entire, were being roasted, to feed the multitude of guests; while great casks of foaming beer and ruddy sparkling wine excited and slaked their thirst. The recent defeat of the Turks had led to the withdrawal of their armies, at least until winter should have passed; and the people of the northern country gave themselves up to the double celebration of the well-won peace and the nuptials of Mara De Streeses.

Within the castle the great and the dignified of the land abandoned themselves to equal freedom with the peasants, in the enjoyment of games, and the observance of simple and fantastic national customs. Morsinia and Constantine kissed again through the ivy wreath, as in the days of childhood. The new matron's distaff touched the oaken walls of the great dining hall; and her hand spread the table with bread and wine and water, in formal assumption of her office as housewife. When she undressed and dressed again the babe, borrowed from a neighboring cottage, she received sundry scoldings and many saws of nursery advice from a group of peasant mothers. The happy couple were almost buried beneath the buckets of grain, which some of the guests poured over them, as they wished them all the blessings of the soil. When they approached the fire place they were showered with sparks, as some one struck the huge glowing log and invoked for them the possession of herds and flocks and friends as many as the fireflecks that flew.

Gifts were offered: those of the poor and rich being received with equal grace;—a rare breed of domestic fowls following a case of cutlery from Toledo in Spain; and a necklace of pearls preceding a hound trained by some skillful hunter. On opening the casket which Castriot presented, as he kissed the golden cluster upon the forehead of the bride, there was found within a cap of sparkling gems, such as is worn by oriental brides, a parchment commissioning Constantine as a voivode in the Albanian service, with governor's command of the Skadar country.

The blessing of the priest was supplemented by those of the old men, which were put in form of prophecies. Kabilovitsch inclosed the happy couple in outstretched arms, and gazing long into their faces, said:

"As on that night at the foot of the Balkans I wrapped you, my children, in my blanket, and, in my absence, another greater than we knew, our generous Castriot, took my place to watch over you; so now, as soon I must leave you forever, One greater than man knows, even our Covenant God, shall be your guardian!"

A man, apparently decrepit with the weight of years, assumed the privilege of a venerable stranger upon such occasions, and came to utter his prophecy. His head was covered with a close fitting fur cap, which concealed his brow to the eyes. Straggling gray locks hung partly over his face and down his neck. As he spoke, Constantine started with evident amazement, which was, however, instantly checked. The bride seemed strangely fascinated. Kabilovitsch, who had been too much absorbed with his own thoughts to notice the stranger's approach, lifted his head quickly, and put his hand to his ear, as if catching some faint and distant sound. This was the old prophet's blessing—

"Allah ordains that these walls, consecrated to Justice, and inhabited by Love, shall from this day be guarded by Peace. Even the Moslem's sword shall be stayed from hence!"

He bowed to the floor, touching with his lips the spot where Morsinia had stood. Before the guests could fully comprehend this scene, he was gone. But lying on the floor where he had bowed was a silken case, elegantly wrought. Morsinia uttered a subdued, yet startled, cry as she seized it. The gift seemed to have thrown a spell about her; for, with paled cheeks, she asked that she might retire to rest awhile in her chamber.

"A wjeshtize!" cried several, looking out from the door through which the man had passed.

"Heaven grant he has left no curse!" exclaimed others.

The silken case contained several crystals of atar of roses. In one of these, which was larger than the others, gleamed, instead of the perfumed drop, a splendid diamond. Upon a piece of parchment, as fine as the silk of which the case was made, Morsinia read—

"My pledge to give my life for thine shall be kept when need requires— Meanwhile know that the Padishah, the rightful Lord of Albania, has bestowed this castle upon Ballaban Badera, Aga of the Janizaries, who in turn bestows it upon Mara De Streeses—
"Signed,
"MICHAEL."

Our story has covered a period of thirteen years. For eleven years more the genius of Scanderbeg, which his perhaps too partial countrymen used to compare to that of Alexander and Pyrrhus, withstood the whole power of the Ottoman Empire, directed against him by the most skilful generals of the age. Sinam and Assem, Jusem and Caraza, Seremet and the puissant Sultan Mahomet himself successively appeared in the field; but retreated, leaving their thousands of slain to attest the invincibility of the Albanian chief. Only one Ottoman commander ventured to return for a second campaign. The old Latin chronicles of the monk Marinus Barletius—who records the deeds of Castriot in thirteen volumes—assign this honorable distinction to the Janizary, Ballaban Badera. In six campaigns this redoubtable warrior desolated Albania. From Thessaly, northward over the land, poured the Moslem tide, but it stayed itself at the waters of Skadar; and, as if fate had approved the prophecy of the aged stranger at the nuptials of Constantine and Morsinia, the castle of De Streeses during all these terrible years, looked down upon bloodless fields. Though his lands were ravaged, the courage of Castriot was not wearied, nor was his genius baffled, until, in the year 1467, there came upon him a mightier than

Ballaban, a mightier than Mahomet. In the presence of the last enemy he commended his country to the valor of his voivodes, his family to the protection of friends,[111] and his soul to the grace of Jesu, his Saviour. They buried him in the old church at Lyssa. Years after, no Scanderbeg succeeding Scanderbeg, the Turks possessed the land. They dug up his bones, and, inclosing their fragments in silver and gold, wore them as amulets. Pashas and Viziers esteemed themselves happy, even in subsequent centuries, if they might so much as touch a bone of Scanderbeg; "For perchance," they said, "there may thus be imparted to us some of that valor and skill which in him were invincible by the might of men."

THE END

FOOTNOTES

[1] A title of the Sultan.

[2] Bashaw; an old name for pasha.

[3] Arnaout; Turkish for Albanian, a corruption of the old Byzantine word Arvanitæ.

[4] Koran, Chap. II.

[5] Iscander-Beg; or The Lord Alexander.

[6] Giaours; a term of reproach by which the Turks designate the unbelievers in Mahomet, especially Christians.

[7] 800 of the Hegira; 1422 of the Christian era.

[8] Sanjak; a military and administrative authority giving the possessor command of 5,000 horse.

[9] The Moslems are allowed four wives. Beyond this number their women can be only concubines.

[10] The Moslems call Christians dogs.

[11] These are still Servian customs.

[12] Vide Apochryphal Gospels.

[13] Divan; the Turkish Council of State.

[14] A lake in Albania.

[15] Voivode; a Servian and Albanian term for general.

[16] Gunpowder was at this time coming into general use.

[17] The old chronicles admit, as one weakness of Scanderbeg, a fondness for personal decoration.

[18] The author adds these lines to the meagre details of this battle as known, for the purpose of accounting for its immediate issue, and for the subsequent events.

[19] Some historians represent Scanderbeg as having had Albanian accomplices in this murder.

[20] Spahi: master of cavalry.

[21] Bismallah; "Please God," a Turkish common exclamation.

[22] Lake Scutari.

[23] The Inexpert, or lower grade of Janizaries.

[24] An incident narrated in Turkish history.

[25] Timour-lenk or Timourlane; Timour the Lame.

[26] See old annals.

[27] Vide, the Greek Empress Irene and her son Constantine.

[28] The bridge over hell mentioned above.

[29] Afterward Sultan Mahomet II.

[30] Literally, Man of Blood, a title of the Sultan.

[31] The custom also in other Oriental nations than the Turkish.

[32] Aga; commander.

[33] Kara Khalil Tschendereli, the founder of the Janizaries in the time of Sultan Orchan.

[34] According to a Moslem tradition the beautiful birds of paradise hold in their crops the souls of holy martyrs until the resurrection.

[35] Kaiks or caiques; light row-boats.

[36] Whence the word Ottoman. Also written Osman, whence the Osmanlis.

[37] Yeni Tscheri; new troop; corrupted in Janizary.

[38] *Vide* Koran.

[39] About 1280 A. D.

[40] About the end of the tenth century.

[41] Between 997 and 1030 A. D.

[42] Tribes of Turkius were mentioned by Pliny.

[43] This perversion of the Christian dogma of the Trinity was taught by heretical sects in the time of the Prophet Mahomet, and is embodied in the Koran.

[44] A. D., 1444.

[45] Fiefs or portions of conquered lands given to soldiers.

[46] Sir William Temple.

[47] Still a Servian and Albanian superstition.

[48] Moslems do not remove the hat in making salutation.

[49] Two horse-tails; the symbol of a Beyler Bey, a chief bey of Europe or Asia.

[50] A title of Janizaries given them by the dervish who blessed the order at its institution in the days of Orchan.

[51] According to the Moslems, hell is divided into seven stories or cellars, the lowest being reserved for hypocrites.

[52] Bride of Othman.

[53] Ivo, the Black, or Tsernoi, from whom the mountain country to the north of Albania was called Tsernogorki, or, in its Latinized form, Montenegro.

[54] Lake Scadar or Scutari.

[55] The Tsernoyevitcha, the great river of Montenegro which empties into Lake Scutari.

[56] Still noted by travellers on this river.

[57] An Albanian title of Elijah.

[58] The Albanians regard Mary as the sender of lightning.

[59] Tsigani; a word by which Slavic people designate the gypsies, who are supposed by them to have come from India in the time of Tamerlane.

[60] Help me, Mary!

[61] The death angel.

[62] In Albanian speech the sun is feminine.

[63] Marinus Barletius, a Latin monk of the time, has given us in his chronicles, the most extended account of Scanderbeg.

[64] Filioque; "and the Son." The Latin Church holds that the Holy Spirit proceeds from the Father *and the Son*. The Greeks deny the latter part of the proposition.

[65] A modern Greek talent weighs 125 English pounds.

[66] The present art of "slow approach" was an invention of the Turks.

[67] A face of Christ was wrought in mosaic in the wall above the chancel of St. Sophia. The Turks still have a traditional saying that the Christian shall not again possess Constantinople until the face of Jesus appears visibly in St. Sophia. At the time of its capture by the Moslems this picture of Christ was painted over. It is now again dimly discerned through the fading and scaling paint.

[68] The "Azymites" were those who used unleavened bread in the sacrament, and at the time of which we are writing the word was used among the Greeks as a term of reproach to the Latinizers, that is, those who favored union with the Latin Church.

[69] A suburb of Constantinople, occupied by the Genoese.

[70] Brothers of the infidels.

[71] One of the sultanas of Amurath II. and daughter of George Brankovitch, Despot of Servia.

[72] The type of a beautiful complexion according to the Koran, Chap. XXXVII.

[73] Koran, Chap. XXXIV.

[74] Koran, Chap. IV.

[75] Shadow of God, one of the titles of the Sultan.

[76] The niche in mosques, on the side toward Mecca, in the direction of which the Moslems turn their faces to pray.

[77] The Panurgia, a name given to the Holy Virgin, who at a former siege of Constantinople, in 1422, was imagined to have appeared upon the wall for its defense.

[78] The Ottomans regard the appellation of "King of the TURKS" as an insult, since the Turks are comparatively few of the many subjects of the Sultan in Europe. Some of the most distinguished servants of the empire are of Christian parentage, and either have been conquered or have voluntarily submitted to the domination of the Moslem.

[79] The Moslem superstition led them to believe that witches, by tying knots in a cord and blowing on them, brought evil to the person they had in mind.

[80] Easter.

[81] The Coptic Mary with whom the Prophet was said to have been enamored.

[82] In 1437 the Venetians carried many large ships across the country from the river Adige to the lake of Garda.

[83] At Actium.

[84] Odalisk; the title of a childless inmate of the harem.

[85] Mother of the Sultan.

[86] Hamamjina; bath attendant.

[87] Hanoum; a title given to matrons.

[88] Muderris; professors in the high schools.

[89] Chain of Ulemas; a renowned system of colleges.

[90] Gibbon; Chapter LXVIII.

[91] Porphyry column; now the famous Burnt Column.

[92] Staff of Moses; one of the relics held sacred by the Greeks at the time.

[93] Gibbon's statement of Mahomet II's. opinion.

[94] Punishment of those in hell, according to Koran.

[95] See effigy in the museum of the Elbicei-Atika at Constantinople.

[96] A similar remark was made afterward by Mahomet II. to a chief officer who asked him his plans for a certain campaign.

[97] Koran, Chapter IV. "When you are saluted with a salutation, salute the person with a better salutation, or at least return the same."

[98] According to the Koran the houris perspire musk.

[99] About an English pound sterling.

[100] Kaikji; a common boatman.

[101] Koran, Chap. II.

[102] The mabeyn lies between the selamlik (general reception room for men) and the haremlik; and is the living apartment for men.

[103] The sluice which was supposed to have been used for this purpose is still seen at Old Seraglio Point.

[104] According to Knowles, this was a part of Scanderbeg's reply to Amurath II.

[105] The firman of Sultan Mahomet was never revoked, and from his time until the extinction of the order of Janizaries by Sultan Mahmoud, in 1834, the Padishah always appointed the Chief Aga.

[106] The word Drakul signifies in Servian "the Devil."

[107] Vide Knowles, History of the Turks, and Albanian Chronicles.

[108] Modern Alessio.

[109] Koran, Chapter VI.

[110] The price of blood, generally 1000 piastres among the poorer classes, which was paid by the culprit to the village where the crime was committed, and by it paid to the general government.

[111] Castriot married late in life.

Milton Keynes UK
Ingram Content Group UK Ltd.
UKHW020623050324
438776UK00006B/1034